KENNEDY'S GHOST

GORDON STEVENS

KENNEDY'S GHOST

HarperCollins*Publishers*

HarperCollins*Publishers*
77–85 Fulham Palace Road,
Hammersmith, London W6 8JB

Published by HarperCollins*Publishers* 1994

1 3 5 7 9 8 6 4 2

A catalogue record for this book
is available from the British Library

ISBN 0 00 224591 4

Kennedy's Ghost is a work of fiction.
All of the events, characters, names
and places depicted in this novel
are entirely fictitious or are
used fictitiously.

Photoset in Linotron Aldus and Bodoni open display by
Rowland Phototypesetting Ltd, Bury St Edmunds, Suffolk

Printed in Great Britain by
HarperCollinsManufacturing Glasgow

To Art Kosatka,
for introducing me to Washington DC
through the back door
and without whom this book
would not have been possible

PROLOGUE

It was the sort of day you remembered. Where you were when you heard and what you were doing; who you turned to and who you telephoned.

The assassin was in position at eleven, the cars which would steer the Lincoln into the killing zone at eleven-five. The truck which would break down in the left lane of the traffic lights, ensuring that the Lincoln would move to the right-hand lane, at eleven-six. The yellow sedan which would stall in front of the Lincoln by eleven-seven.

The senator's flight from Boston was on schedule; his Lincoln, plus the man who would accompany him, already waiting. Twenty-five years before, Donaghue and Brettlaw had been undergraduates together at Harvard.

At eleven-fifty Donaghue would join his wife and daughters in his room on the third floor of the Senate Russell Building on Washington's Capitol Hill. At one minute to twelve he would walk with them along the marble corridor to the historic setting of the Caucus Room. And at midday exactly, with his wife at his side and Brettlaw in the wings, Senator Jack Donaghue would formally announce his candidacy for the Democratic nomination for the Presidency of the United States of America.

It was eleven-fifteen. In the Caucus Room the television cameras were in place and the lights ready, the cables running to the scanners outside. The walls of the room were marble, the slim Corinthian-style columns rising to the ceiling, and the ceiling itself was exquisitely decorated with four large chandeliers hanging from it. The windows on the side of the room facing the dome of Capitol Hill were wall-height, arched at the top and draped in purple. On the wall opposite them, on either side of the door leading into the hallway beyond, two plaques listed some of the events to which the Caucus Room had born witness: the 1912 enquiry into the sinking of the *Titanic*, the 1941–42 commission into the World War Two National Defense programme, the 1966 Fulbright hearings on the

Vietnam War, the 1973 Watergate enquiry and the 1987 commission on Iran-Contra.

The platform from which Donaghue would declare was against the right-hand wall, flanked on the right by the Stars and Stripes of the Union and on the left by the flag of his home state of Massachusetts, two massive black and white photographs hanging on the wall behind and dominating the room.

'Why the Kennedy photos as backdrop?' the NBC reporter asked the Donaghue press secretary. 'Why John and Robert?'

'Because they also declared in this room,' she told him.

The floor was packed with supporters, already excited and some singing. Most such crowds were the same, the CBS reporter knew: young and preppy, a blaze of hats and banners. Not this one, though; this one was different. Young and old, a range of ages, creeds and colours. As if they not only stood for what the country had struggled for in the past, but also represented the dream it still clung to for the future. Blue-collar and white-collar, men and women, youthful students and gnarled veterans. Three of them in the second row talking about a Swift boat in 'Nam and laughing about the way The Old Man had bellowed into a bullhorn for the boats they knew didn't exist to follow him in.

The woman in the front row was young, the radiance of youth on her face, her blond hair falling on to her shoulders and her child in her arms. The man next to her was in the dress blues of the Marine Corps, the eagle, globe and anchor on the collar, the sergeant's chevrons on his sleeves, and the medal ribbons across his left breast, the top row the most important and the ribbon on the wearer's right of the top row the most important of all. The ribbon next to it was the Silver Star, after that the Bronze Star, three stars on it indicating it had been won three more times and the 'V' indicating they had been won for heroism in battle. The service ribbons at the bottom, the Vietnam service ribbon in the middle.

'Mind if I take a close-up of the decorations?' one of the cameramen asked.

'No problem,' the marine told him.

'What was that all about?' the reporter asked as he and the cameraman moved on.

'You see what he was wearing?' The response was tight, almost angry. 'Top right, next to the Silver Star. The Congressional Medal of Honor.'

The highest award for valour the nation could bestow.

8

'Mommy,' the reporter heard the voice of the girl in the arms of the young woman next to the marine. 'Why has that man only got one arm?'

It was eleven-twenty, the morning bright and the silver of the 737 gleaming against the faultless blue of the sky. Ten minutes to landing, the pilot informed his passengers. In the second row from the front Donaghue checked the speech for the last time and whispered the words of the first quote. Perhaps to Pearson, perhaps to himself.

Some men see things as they are and say why;
I dream things that never were and say why not.

The boy was ten years old, seated with his mother towards the rear.

'You think he'll mind?'

Of course he'll mind, the woman knew she should say. He's busy, too many things on his mind, especially today. 'Ask him,' she said instead.

'Come with me.'

'Go by yourself.'

The boy gripped the Polaroid camera and made his way down the aisle, the nerves consuming him. Halfway along he hesitated and looked back, saw the way his mother nodded for him to go on.

'Excuse me.' He stopped by the two men seated on the left and realized he had forgotten to say sir. 'Would you mind if I took your photograph?'

Donaghue smiled at the boy and turned to Pearson.

'I think we can go better than that, don't you, Ed?'

'Sure we can.'

Fifteen rows back the woman watched as Pearson stood, took the camera from her son, sat him by Donaghue, and took a photograph of the two of them together. The boy watched as the print rolled out and the image rose on the slippery grey of the plastic.

'What's your name?' Donaghue asked him.

'Dan.'

'Dan who?'

'Dan Zupolski.'

The print was dry. Donaghue took a pen from his pocket and signed it.

To Dan Zupolski, from his friend, Senator Jack Donaghue.

9

It was eleven twenty-five.

In the Caucus Room the doors opened and the supporters turned, suddenly expectant, the television crews cursing that they had not been forewarned. Catherine Donaghue walked in and stood on the platform. Mid-forties and slim; the blond of her hair and the steel and the sun in her eyes.

'Sorry to give you a heart attack, boys.' She knew what the crews had thought and smiled at them, acknowledged the way they laughed back.

He'd seen it all before, the NBC correspondent thought. Except not like this, not like today. He wouldn't admit it, of course, but one hell of a day to be the front man, one hell of a thing to tell the grandkids.

One hell of a smile, the CBS man whispered to no one in particular. One hell of a First Lady.

Cath Donaghue looked round the crowd. 'I thought you'd like to know. We've just heard from the airport. Jack's plane is five minutes out; he'll be landing on time at eleven-thirty, be here at twelve.'

There was a roar. She held up her hands to still it.

If this was the prelim, Christ knows what the main event is going to be like, the CNN reporter thought. Give me some cut-aways now, he told his cameraman. Couple of veterans, couple of kids.

'How's it looking?' He heard the voice of his producer down the line.

'Looking good.'

Looking fantastic, he meant.

'What time's he due?'

'Twelve noon, everything on schedule. Why?'

'We're going live on it.' CNN network, CNN global. 'Coming to you at eleven fifty-five.'

The applause quietened, the supporters waiting. Cath Donaghue looked up and smiled again.

'Before Jack arrives, I just wanted to thank you all for coming today.' As if the honour was hers and Jack's; as if, by being present at that place on that day, it was those in front of her who were doing the Donaghues a favour.

She looked around them again and smiled again. Take care of him, Dave, she prayed; make sure he gets here, please God don't let me down.

'It's a great place to be, a great day to be here. Thank you all.'

Even after she had left, even after she was back in Room 394, the

10

cheers were echoing round the Caucus Room and the applause was ringing down the white marble of the corridors.

It was eleven twenty-eight.

The 737 banked over the Potomac and began its run-in, the wing lights blinking against the silver and the silver brilliant against the morning sky.

Jordan glanced at Donaghue and realized he was looking at the White House.

'Ready, Jack?'

What are you thinking? he almost asked.

I'm thinking about something Haslam said, Donaghue would not have told him. I'm thinking about a conversation Haslam and I agreed never took place.

'As I'll ever be.'

The 737 bumped gently on the runway, the reverse thrust thundering, then taxied to the terminal. The flight-deck door opened and the pilot and copilot stepped out and stood with the cabin crew at the front of the plane. The fuselage door to the terminal opened. In the passenger bridge on the other side Jordan saw the line of officials.

'Okay, Jack. Let's do it.'

Donaghue stood and straightened his suit, Pearson slightly behind him and Jordan at his shoulder. The rest of the passengers were still seated, all watching. He passed along the line of crew members and shook each of their hands.

'Give it to 'em today, Jack.' The voice was from the back of the plane.

'Good luck, Mr President.' Another.

Abruptly the passengers rose and began to clap. Donaghue turned and waved his thanks at them, then left the plane and stepped through the jet bridge and into the terminal, everyone wanting to shake his hand this morning, everyone wanting to wish him luck. Some addressing him as Jack, others as Senator. More than the occasional person calling him Mr President.

The doors of the Lincoln were open. Brettlaw stepped forward and Donaghue shook hands with him, embraced him.

'Good to see you.'

'You too, old friend.'

Eleven thirty-three.

The Lincoln left National.

*

11

Hendricks checked his watch. Not much traffic today, therefore the target on time.

Even though the road out of the underpass was in front of him and the glistening white of Capitol Hill was behind and to his left, he saw it differently, as if he was the driver of the Lincoln, as if he was the man delivering the target to the killing zone.

Right out of National and on to George Washington Parkway – he ran through the route again. Off the Parkway and across 14th Street Bridge. Fork right at the end into the series of underpasses dissecting DC, the cars which would funnel the Lincoln into the correct lane, and into the correct position in the killing zone, already closing. First underpass then second, right at the first exit but still underground, then right again at the second exit, the carriageway of this section single-lane, still climbing and curving left, then straightening into the sunlight. Sixty yards from the underpass to the traffic lights at First. White multistorey housing the National Association of Letter Carriers on the right, and side road joining the underpass road from behind the multistorey, so that at the junction with First the road was two-lane. Six-foot-wide central reservation of grass and trees to the left and wire fence down the middle, and the road on the other side leading only to an underground car park. Grey multistorey of the Federal Home Loan Bank beyond the road. Grass and more traffic lights in front and leading to the Hill.

Everything quiet, little traffic and hardly any pedestrians. Everything perfect.

Eleven thirty-four.

The Lincoln eased on to George Washington Memorial Parkway.

Thirty-five.

The Lincoln pulled right, off the Parkway and across 14th Street Bridge, the grey-blue of the Potomac below them and the white of DC suddenly in front. The white always dazzling, but this morning almost blinding. Fork at end of bridge, Route N1 goes left and Route 395 right.

The Lincoln swung right on to 395.

Eleven thirty-seven.

First exit, to Maine Avenue. First underpass coming up. The dark blue Chevrolet fell in behind them then drew to the outside lane, but not overtaking.

Thirty-eight.

First underpass. Two-lane. Short. Out of the underpass in fifteen seconds.

The pale Chrysler sedan eased in front of them, the Chevrolet behind them still in the outer lane and preventing them from overtaking.

Thirty-nine.

Hendricks saw the truck edge from the feeder road at the side of the Letter Carriers building, the engine clattering and the smoke billowing from its exhaust. The lights at First were on green. The truck crossed to the left lane, jerked apparently haphazardly towards the lights, and shuddered to a halt at them.

Eleven-forty.

Ford replacing the Chrysler and Oldsmobile replacing the Chevrolet. Yellow sedan three hundred yards in front.

Donaghue reached into his jacket pocket and glanced again at the speech, read again the quote he had included at the request of his wife. The quote after which he would pause, after which he would look down reflectively then look up again, after which he would declare he was running for the White House.

> In the long history of the world
> few generations have been granted
> the role of defending freedom
> in its hour of maximum danger.
> I do not shirk from this responsibility
> I welcome it.

Except that in his mind he had rewritten it slightly:

> In the long history of the world
> few generations have been granted
> the role of defending freedom.

> In the hour of maximum danger
> I do not shirk from this responsibility.
> I welcome it.

Two hundred yards in front the yellow sedan drew them in as if they were on a piece of string.

Eleven forty-one.

The Lincoln closed on the second underpass and entered its darkness. The underpass was long and curving, pale in the overhead lights. The underpass was climbing slightly, the first exit – D Street

13

NW and US Capitol – coming up fast. The climb was steeper, they turned right, the yellow sedan in front and the Lincoln behind, the Oldsmobile behind it, the Ford keeping to the main carriageway and accelerating away.

The light of the exit was in front of them, the carriageway still climbing out of the underpass. Second exit, D Street straight on, Capitol right. Yellow sedan going right, the Lincoln following it, Oldsmobile straight on. The underpass still single-lane, still curving and climbing.

Eleven forty-two.

They left the underpass and drove into the brilliant sunlight of the killing zone. The white building of the Letter Carriers Association towering over them to the right and the grey of the Home Loan Bank to the left. The side road joining from the right, so that the single-lane became two lanes and the lights sixty yards in front. The truck broken down in the left lane and the yellow sedan suddenly stalling beside it in the right. The Lincoln immediately behind the sedan, more traffic behind it so it was unable to move, and the man called Hendricks waiting.

Twenty-eight years before, on 22 November 1963, President John F. Kennedy had been assassinated in Dallas, Texas.

Kennedy's Ghost

Four months earlier . . .

1

They should have waited for the back-up, Cipriani knew.

Of course they sometimes got separated, of course they sometimes ran in to problems, but the back-up car should have caught them up by now.

The evening was warm, early June and still two hours of daylight left, the dual carriageway curving slightly in front of them and the pines rising up the mountainside to their left and falling to the valley to their right. Perhaps that was why Moretti hadn't noticed. Because they were from the city and therefore expected trouble in the city; because this was Switzerland and nothing happened in Switzerland except they made cuckoo clocks and lots of money.

South, across the border into Italy, and Cipriani would have begun to worry, would have whispered to Moretti to slow it. Except that Mr Benini liked to be driven fast. If they slowed the banker would glance up from the rear seat and ask what the hell was happening without uttering a single word.

And nobody knew they were here.

He and Benini had flown out of Milan the previous afternoon, stayed last night at London's Grosvenor House Hotel, Mr Benini attending a meeting at the bank's office on Old Broad Street this morning, then the flight back. But not to Italy. To Switzerland. Moretti, Gino and Enzio driving up to meet them. The afternoon in the bank's Zurich office, then the overnight in the slightly old-fashioned hotel in the mountains which Mr Benini preferred to the more modern establishments in the city. More meetings tomorrow, then the flight back to Milan. Depending, of course, on the twists and turns of Mr Benini's timetable.

If it had been Milan – on the way to or from the family villa in Emilia at weekends, from the apartment on Via Ventura in the morning or the office behind La Scala in the evening – they would have been on edge, would have worked one of the dozen variations of route. But this wasn't Italy.

The police car was on the hard shoulder a hundred metres in front of them; as they passed it rocked in their tailstream. Still no back-up Merc – Cipriani adjusted the second of the two rearview mirrors – still no Gino and Enzio sitting like guardian angels behind them. The movement was enough to warn Moretti; the driver glanced up then the rev counter dropped slightly as he eased back. Not enough to disturb the man in the rear seat, but enough to slow them by ten kilometres an hour.

The road was still curving, still climbing gently, no other traffic.

The police car passed them, suddenly and unexpectedly, then slowed in front of them, the observer waving them down.

The layby was gravel, forty metres long and a car's width wide. They pulled in behind the police car and waited. In the back seat the banker glanced up. The police driver left the Audi and walked towards them, the observer remaining seated and facing forward. Cipriani got out and shut the door behind him, heard the dull click as Moretti locked the doors.

Standard procedure. The driver never leaving the car. Doors and windows locked, vehicle in gear and held on the clutch, handbrake off. Enough space to pull away even if it meant driving over whatever or whoever was in front, even a policeman. More correctly, even someone wearing a police uniform. For this reason Cipriani did nothing to obstruct Moretti's get-away route or his line of vision.

The 450 was armour-plated – up to a point. Ten-millimetre glazing on the windows; Spectra plating for doors, sides, roof-liner and floor boards; plus cell fuel tank. Not the protection some of the Saudis carried, but Benini was still Benini.

'One of your tyres is going down.' The policeman spoke with what Cipriani assumed was the regional accent.

'Which one?'

The wheels were reinforced, a steel rim between the hub and tyre, so the car could run even if the tyres had been ripped by bullets. Except that the opposition would know that.

Cipriani confirmed the observer was still seated and his door was still closed, confirmed that the driver's gun was still strapped in its holster.

'Rear left.'

Coincidence that the police car had happened to be parked up on their route out of the city – Cipriani was tight with adrenalin. Coincidence that the tyre was on the driver's side so that he had to walk round the car to see it? Coincidence that if he walked round the front of the car he would obstruct Moretti's vision and exit path, but if he walked round the back he would lose sight of the policeman's hand and gun.

Moretti rolled the Merc back slightly and turned the front wheels so they were pointing out.

Giuseppi Vitali had made the call to the Grosvenor House Hotel shortly after Benini and Cipriani had left. Ask for Benini and he'd never get through; ask for the bodyguard, however, and he'd know everything he needed to about the banker.

'I'm sorry,' he had been told, 'Mr Cipriani checked out fifteen minutes ago.'

Benini running to schedule, probably on his way to BCI's offices on Old Broad Street, then to Heathrow. And from there he would fly either to Milan or Zurich. Except that yesterday afternoon, after they'd dropped Benini and his bodyguard off, his driver and the two gorillas who constituted his back-up protection had left Italy for Switzerland. So after his meeting in London, Benini would fly to Zurich. And that evening Moretti would drive him to the hotel in the mountains which Benini used when his meetings required him to stay in Switzerland. Unless Benini was intending to drive back, which he had never done in the past.

Giuseppi Vitali knew everything about Paolo Benini. His family details, his education and banking career. His business and personal movements, the fact that at that moment in time he did not have a regular mistress. The houses he owned and the hotels and apartments in which he stayed.

The details of his personal protection. The various routes Moretti used to drive him to work and the patterns into which even Cipriani had allowed them to slip when he thought they were safe.

The fact that the bank for which Benini worked carried kidnap insurance.

Cipriani turned slightly and walked behind the Mercedes, eyes flicking between the man in front and the second in the Audi. So where was the back-up, where the hell were Gino and Enzio? The police driver stepped forward, the top of his body above the Merc but the lower half now hidden. Was beside Moretti's window. The door of the police car opened and the second man got out.

Moretti's going, Cipriani sensed; half a second more and Moretti's going to smash his foot on the accelerator and pull Mr Benini out.

His left hand moved inside his coat to the submachine gun hanging on the pull strap from his shoulder.

'Which tyre?' he asked again.

Clear the car then he would have to bend down and look at the tyre, would have to take his eyes off the driver. Then they would take him.

'Left rear.'

He heard the slight rev of the engine. Moretti telling him he had everything under control, that if either of the supposed policemen moved out of turn Moretti would run them down.

The strap was still across the gun in the policeman's holster but the police observer was further out of the door. Cipriani glanced at the tyre. Perhaps it was down slightly, perhaps it wasn't.

'Thanks. I'll take care of it.'

Therefore no need for you to hang around. If you are who you say you are.

And your move if you're not.

There was a burst on the radio of the police car. The observer confirmed their position then called to the driver. 'Accident, let's go.'

'Thanks again,' Cipriani said.

The driver ran to the car and the Audi pulled away.

There was a screech of brakes and the back-up pulled in behind them.

That evening Paolo Benini ate alone, Cipriani three tables away and also alone, and the others only entering the dining-room after Benini had left. Perhaps by instinct, but more probably by habit, Benini avoided giving the impression that he was surrounded by body-guards. When he had finished Cipriani escorted him to the third-floor suite, then returned to the others. Benini poured himself a malt and settled to the paperwork he had brought with him from the Zurich office. Nothing confidential – he was always careful with material he took outside the bank.

Paolo Benini was forty-four years old, six feet tall, with dark, neatly cut hair, and the first signs of good living showing on what had once been an athletic frame. His wife Francesca was six years younger. The couple had two daughters, both in their early teens, a town apartment in Via Ventura, in one of Milan's discreetly fashionable (as opposed to ostentatiously expensive) areas, and a villa in the family village in Emilia.

Paolo Benini also enjoyed a succession of mistresses, a fact which he considered the natural right of someone of his background and profession, but which he also considered he had successfully kept secret from his wife.

Secrets within secrets, he had once thought. It was a principle he also applied to his work, though he would have used a different word. Security. Not merely the separation of one project from another, even the separation of parts of the same project. The creation of a structure in which the beginning could not be traced to the middle, nor the middle to the end. A structure in which key people such as the London manager were all personal appointees, yet in which even those he trusted knew only what he allowed them to know, with no way two of them could fit even a part of the whole together.

Especially the special accounts: the funds originating in what he assumed were front companies in North America and Western Europe, then switched via a system of cut-outs to their target accounts. Not simply because the destinations were tax havens, but because in such places banking regulations were loose and rarely monitored. And because, in routing such transfers through a series of tax regimes, each with its own rules and regulations on secrecy, the job of tracing those funds was rendered virtually impossible.

Every bank had its special account customers, of course, but this normally meant only those clients requiring customized attention. So the handful of executives and board members in BCI who knew he was special accounts assumed his dealings were nothing out of the ordinary.

Black accounts in black boxes, he had once thought. Even he himself in one. Knowing the codes for the accounts and speaking occasionally to the account holders, but knowing nothing more and not wishing to.

The telephone rang shortly before eleven.

'Mr Benini. Reception here. A fax has just come in for you and I thought you'd wish to know immediately.'

Because Mr Benini was a regular, and Mr Benini tipped well.

'The morning will do. But thanks for letting me know.'

He waited ten seconds, then lifted the telephone again and called reception.

Cipriani had drummed the routine into him. If he received a call from someone claiming to be hotel reception, porters' desk, even room service or laundry, he should stall. Then he should phone back unexpectedly on the correct line. If reception or whatever confirmed the call, then everything was fine. If not, he should check the door was locked and hit the panic button.

'This is Paolo Benini. The fax you just phoned about.'

'Yes, Mr Benini.'

Confirmation that it had been reception who had called.

'I just wondered where it was from.'

'One moment while I check.' There was a ten-second pause. 'Milan, sir.'

Confirmation that there was a fax.

'Perhaps you could send it up after all.'

He had barely settled again when he heard the knock on the outer door. He crossed the room and checked through the security hole. The porter was alone in the corridor, his uniform immaculate, his right hand at his side and the envelope containing the fax in his left.

He opened the door.

'Mr Benini?'

'Yes.'

'Reception asked for this to be delivered, sir.'

'Thank you.'

He took the envelope and felt in his pocket for a tip, sensed rather than saw the movement. The porter's right hand coming up for the tip but not stopping, three fingers on one side of Benini's windpipe and thumb the other, cutting off his air. Left hand locked on Benini's right upper arm and steering him to his right.

The shock almost paralysed him, the movement so fast and unexpected. The man was still turning him to his right, his back suddenly against the door and the door serving as a fulcrum, so that he was turning with it into the room. He was fighting for breath, screaming for help but no sound coming. He brought his hands up and tried to prise the grip from his throat, tried to stop the movement backwards and pressed forward, succeeded only in pushing his own body weight against the vice round his windpipe.

Another man was suddenly in the room, picking up the fax from the floor and shutting the door, pulling up Benini's shirtsleeve and inserting the needle into the blue vein running down the centre of his inner arm.

The panic button was on the desk, but the desk was twenty feet away and Benini's mind was already slipping from him, fear taking over everything. He heard the knock on the door. Cipriani, Benini

24

knew. Probably Gino and Enzio as well. The second assailant checked through the security hole, brushed back his hair and opened the door fractionally.

'Mr Benini?'

'Yes.'

'Your fax from reception, sir.'

'Thank you.'

The kidnapper took the envelope, tipped the porter, and closed the door.

Vitali made the call at midnight.

Giuseppi Vitali was from the South. In the kidnap boom beginning in the seventies, three-quarters of which had been controlled directly or indirectly by the Mafia, he had risen in rank from minder to negotiator to controller. Vitali, however, considered himself a businessman. He had therefore bought up an ailing cosmetics machinery factory, turned it into a profitable concern and used it as a front. In the late eighties, when changes in Italian law had made it illegal for a family or firm to deal with kidnappers and had authorized the freezing of funds if they did, profits had dropped and most people had pulled out. Vitali, however, had gone freelance, selecting as his victims those whose families or organizations could pay the money he demanded from outside Italy, and maintaining his association and friendship with his former employers by paying commission on what he termed his transactions.

'This is Toni.' Perhaps it was superstition that he always used the same code name. 'I was checking how our shares went today.'

'We sold.' The code that Benini had been taken.

'Good price?' Any problems, he meant.

'A very good price.' No problems at all.

In Italy people like Benini, as well as those protecting them, were always on guard. Outside the country, however, and especially when they thought no one knew where they were, and most especially when they appeared safe and secure in a hotel, people like Benini relaxed slightly.

Of course the bodyguards would watch over them in the restaurant, or if they took a swim or a sauna. But the moment they were escorted back to their room the balance changed. The moment the bodyguards had made sure someone like Paolo Benini was locked in his suite, the perceived danger evaporated. Then the only problem was getting someone like Benini to open the door.

Phone and say you were room service, or the porters' desk, even reception, and someone like Benini would automatically check, perhaps even call his minders. But send a real fax or telex to the hotel, so that the call from reception was genuine, then you could turn someone's security measures against them. Because someone like Benini would check, but when he checked he would confirm that all was in order, and then his defences would be down.

'What about the paperwork?' Vitali asked.

The transfer to the team who would spirit Benini out of Switzerland and back into Italy.

'Like clockwork.'

The next call was at two. There was no reply. Plenty of time, he told himself, plenty of reasons why the transport team might not have yet made the next checkpoint.

Everything separate – he had always been careful – everything and everyone in their own box. The snatch squad in one box and the transport team to whom they would hand the hostage and who would spirit him across the border into Italy in another. The team who would hold him in the cave way to the south in a third, and the negotiator who would communicate with the family in a fourth; the stake-out who would keep watch on the family home in a fifth. None of the units knowing the details of the others and none of them knowing Vitali.

An hour later he phoned again. The call was answered on the third ring.

'This is Toni. Just wondering how the holiday's going?'

'Fine. Slowed down by an accident. Nothing to do with us. We'll be home on time.'

'Good.'

By this time tomorrow Paolo Benini would be safely locked in a cave in the mountains of Calabria. And because the locals there hated any authority, they would provide the eyes and ears if the police or army started snooping.

Then Vitali would telephone the family. But not immediately. He'd let them sweat a little, turn the screw on them from the beginning. The family and the bank would know already, of course; within thirty seconds of the bodyguards realizing Benini was missing the shock waves would be reverberating down the telephone lines to Milan.

Then the next stage would begin.

Most banks and multinationals had insurance policies covering kidnap. Not that anyone would admit being insured, because the confirmation that an insurance policy existed guaranteed that a ransom would be paid. And most such policies insisted upon the involvement of one of the firms specializing in such situations. Therefore the first thing that agency would do would be to send in a consultant.

Not that this concerned Vitali. A consultant would know the business, so that even though the two of them would play a game it would be according to the rules. Therefore the game would be safe and the ending predictable.

As long as there was nothing about Paolo Benini he didn't know.

2

The photograph was in a silver frame, and the girl in it wore a white confirmation dress. When the photograph was taken she had been six years old, now she was nine. For the past two months of those years she had been missing.

Lima, Peru. Seven in the evening.

The weather outside was hot and humid, the city gasping for breath beneath the cloud which hung over it at this time of year.

Wonder where the next job will be, Haslam thought. South America again, possibly Europe, and Italy was always a favourite. He'd have a break, of course, needed a break after this one. As long as it went down tonight and as long as he got little Rosita home safely.

The room was on the first floor, overlooking the courtyard of the house. The furniture was large and comfortable, the pictures on the walls lost in the half-light. The mother and father sat side by side on the sofa opposite him, one of them occasionally standing, then sitting again, not knowing what to do. Behind them, almost lost in the shadows, the family lawyer sat without speaking.

The mother glanced again at the photograph. You're sure it will work – it was in her eyes as she realized he had seen her looking, in the nervousness on her face as she turned away.

Even now they couldn't be sure – Haslam had been through it with the family the night before, again that morning, yet again that afternoon. But at least they were trying something different, at least they were dictating the rules of the game. Which is what the others hadn't done in the past, which was why their children never came home.

The others hadn't been his cases, thank Christ, but they haunted him nevertheless. In the first the parents had paid the ransom but heard nothing more. In the second they had met the first demand, then a second, yet still heard nothing, received nothing, not even a body to bury. In the third the consultant had insisted upon visual contact with the child before the money was handed over, but then the child had been spirited away in the bustle of the street where the kidnappers had insisted the exchange should take place, the boy's body found three days later.

There were certain similarities, of course – the insistence that a member of the household staff be the courier, for example. And the police had normally been informed. That was one of the things which worried him now: how Ortega would react when he found out what Haslam had done.

Perhaps Ortega had brought some of his techniques with him when he had come over from one of the cocaine units, though more likely they had always been there. Nine months earlier Ortega had agreed with a hostage family not to move on the kidnappers until the victim was safe. Instead he had followed the pick-up to the house where the gang were counting the ransom money prior to releasing the victim. Officially all the gang had been killed; unofficially one had survived, though he had probably wished he had not. It had taken Ortega less than thirty minutes to extract the location at which the kidnap victim was being held and just over two hours to secure the victim's release, though it had been another twenty-four before he had informed the family that their father was safe. After that the kidnappers had switched to children. After that none of the victims came back alive.

It was five minutes past seven.

Ramirez should have received the call by now. Ramirez's instructions were to telephone them to confirm that he had heard. No words though, because the telephone at the house was certainly tapped. Therefore three rings, repeated a second time, if the kidnappers had been in contact. Six rings, also repeated, if they had not and he was returning to the house empty-handed. Ramirez was the girl's uncle, also a lawyer. Good contacts in the presidential palace, though none would do him any good tonight.

It was ten past seven.

Haslam rose and poured himself a mineral water, added a handful of ice and a sliver of lime.

Christ how he hated kidnapping, how he hated Latin America. More specifically, how he hated kidnapping in Latin America. All crimes were against the law, but kidnapping was immoral. Europe, however, was civilized compared to here. In Europe the people holding the victims were still bastards, but both sides played to at least a semblance of rules. In Central and South America you were

29

never sure whose rules you were playing or even whose game. Whether a kidnapping was commercial or political, whether you were being sucked into a feud between political rivals, even between army and police, between the liberals and the death squads.

The mother glanced again at the photograph and he smiled at her, tried to convince her it would work.

Why haven't we heard, why hasn't Ramirez called? It was in the father's eyes now. In the layers of grey the man was seeing the ghosts of the children who had not been returned, was already seeing the ghost of his own daughter.

The phone rang. Instinctively the mother stretched to pick it up then stopped as Haslam's hand fell on her wrist. She looked up at him, eyes haunted, pleading. Counted the rings. Three. Silence. Three again.

Hope came into her eyes for the first time in two months.

Still a long way to go before we get Rosita home, Haslam told her, told them both. Told himself.

Three previous child kidnappings – he was still analysing, trying to see where he had made the right decision and where he might have made the wrong one. Certain threads common to each, plus the policeman called Ortega. He had pored over it every hour of every day since he had been called in, could see there was no way out, no way round the fact that Ortega was the problem. Then he had begun to see: that perhaps Ortega was not a problem, that – conversely – Ortega might be the key. For that reason, seven nights ago, he had made his suggestion to the family.

That for the sake of Ortega and the telephone taps, they continue to negotiate with the kidnappers in the normal way – Rosita's father taking the anonymous calls and the maid acting as courier. But that they also open a separate channel of negotiation with the kidnappers – different phone, different courier, in this case the girl's uncle.

At first the family had been too frightened, then they had agreed. When the kidnappers telephoned the family house the following evening, therefore, Rosita's father had insisted on proof that his daughter was alive. The next evening the maid was directed by the kidnappers from telephone to telephone, to the point where she would pick up the photograph of Rosita holding that day's newspapers. At the second location, however, she had given the caller the number of the public phone where Ramirez was waiting.

When the kidnap negotiator had telephoned that number the uncle had told him that the family had a package for the kidnappers and requested details of where it should be dropped. Inside the briefcase was a letter Haslam had dictated, informing the kidnappers of the police involvement and the taps on the family telephones, and suggesting an alternative system of communication, including the number at which Ramirez would be waiting the following evening. Also in the briefcase were fifty thousand United States dollars, in used notes and a mix of denominations, as a sign of the family's good faith.

The following evening the family had received a call at which the kidnappers threatened the life of Rosita if the family did not pay immediately. Ten minutes earlier the kidnappers had telephoned Ramirez on the second line and agreed to open discussions on a channel concealed from the police in general and Ortega in particular. Then the negotiations had begun.

Three hundred thousand, the kidnappers had demanded. A hundred and fifty, the family had responded. Two-fifty, the kidnappers had come back at them. Two hundred, the family had replied. Two hundred and twenty-five thousand, the two sides had agreed; Ramirez standing by, seven o'clock Thursday evening.

Now it was almost nine; the dusk closing in and Ramirez signalling he was on his way ninety minutes ago. Be careful, Haslam had warned him: they'll build in switches, cut-outs, might go for a double ransom, might seize you as well.

It was gone nine, almost ten; the dusk giving way to the dark and the mother's eyes boring into him. Lose me my daughter and I'll haunt you for ever; bring her back to me and what is mine and my husband's is yours.

She poured herself a whisky and stared at the glass, her strength almost shattering it. Her husband rose, took it from her, and made her sit again.

Ten-thirty, almost ten forty-five.

The headlights swept across the wall and the Lexus turned in to the courtyard. The parents ran to the window, saw the driver alone in the front and Ramirez in the back. Saw the figure clutched to him, clinging to him. For one moment Haslam feared that he had lost, that the figure was too small, too grey, almost too translucent, to be real. That the figure clinging to Ramirez was Rosita's ghost. Then Ramirez stepped from the car and he saw the girl look up and wave.

The mother turned and ran for the stairs, the father close behind

31

her. Haslam crossed the room, poured himself a large scotch, only a dash of soda, and downed it in one.

'So what do we do now?' The family's lawyer spoke from the shadows.

'Square Ortega.'

'How much?'

In the courtyard below the mother was holding her daughter as if she would never let her go, the girl's father embracing Ramirez then looking up at the window to thank Haslam, the tears pouring suddenly and unashamedly down his cheeks.

Haslam poured himself a second drink and offered the lawyer one. In a sense the way they dealt with the policeman was the same as dealing with the kidnappers' offer. Too little and he'd turn it down, too much and he'd want even more.

'Twenty-five thousand should do it. You don't want him on your backs for the rest of your lives.'

The call came twenty-nine hours later, at three in the morning. The settlement with Ortega had been agreed and the money delivered, the family lawyer told Haslam.

'And Ortega's happy?' Haslam asked.

'He appears to be.'

Perhaps it was the lawyer's natural caution, Haslam thought, perhaps it was as close to a warning as he could get. He thanked the man, slept fitfully till the light was streaming through the hotel curtains, then confirmed his flight to Washington via Miami.

Even though he'd been paid off Ortega might not like it, because in his way Ortega had lost. And if he considered he had lost, Ortega would want his revenge. And if he did he would play it dirty, partly because it was his nature and partly to let his own people see he was top dog, partly to let the family know who was really in charge. And if Ortega decided to play it dirty he would go for him on the way out, because that was when Haslam should be relaxed, when Haslam should be thinking he'd got away with it.

He could leave the country illegally, of course; but then it might be difficult to return. He could leave legally, but with some sort of political or diplomatic protection. But that would mean he'd left under Ortega's rules, so that when he returned it would be under Ortega's conditions. Or he could both leave and return under his own terms, his rules of his game.

At seven he took breakfast, at eight he checked out, ignored the

32

cabs waiting outside the hotel, walked to Plaza San Martin, let the first two cabs in the side street behind the Bolivar Hotel go, and took the third.

The city was already hot, and the cardboard slums which covered the foothills outside stretched for miles. No cars following him, he noted, but there wouldn't be. The cab dropped him, he paid the driver and stepped into the terminal building. The departure lounge was cool, the queues already forming at the check-in counters, and the gorillas were waiting for him.

Sometimes you needed to look for them, other times their presence was deliberately obvious and menacing. Today it was somewhere between. Two of them, plus Ortega himself. The boss man wearing a smartly cut suit and seated at a table in the coffee bar. Dark glasses, though everyone wore dark glasses, plus a copy of *La Prensa*.

The business class check-in was clear. He lifted his bag on to the weighing belt and gave his passport and ticket to the woman behind the desk. She smiled at him, then saw the two men, saw the way they were looking at him and knew who and what they were.

'Smoking or non-smoking?' She fought to control the tremor in her voice.

'Non.'

She punched the computer and gave him his seat number.

'Thank you.' He picked up the passport and ticket.

'Have a good flight.' She was mesmerized, like a night animal caught in a beam of light.

His rules, he reminded himself, his game.

The tails were between him and the departure gate, possibly more inside when he was out of view of the most of the public, and Ortega watching, amused. He walked past them, deliberately close, turned into the coffee bar, ignored the other tables and sat at Ortega's.

'Two espressos,' he told the waitress.

Ortega was smiling, arrogant. What are you playing at, mother-fucker, what are you telling me? My country, my patch. So you don't fuck with me. You know the routine, you know what happens to people who fuck with the likes of me.

Haslam sat back slightly, not speaking. Right hand on the table top, the third finger of his right hand tapping only slightly but enough to draw attention to it.

Why so relaxed, Ortega wondered, why so confident? Why the hand on the table? Why only one hand? Why the right? Gold ring on the third finger, symbol on it, but he couldn't see what. So what game are you playing, cock-sucker, what are you trying to tell me?

The waitress placed the coffees nervously on the table. Haslam shifted slightly and picked up the cup with his right hand, fingers round it rather than holding the handle, the gold of the ring sparkling and the image on it clear.

Ortega knew who Haslam was and what he was. Where he had come from and what Haslam was telling him.

Three of you and one of me. The third might be interesting, the second no problem, and you're first. No problems, my friend. I did my job, you did yours, and we both got paid. Next time will be the same. Unless you have problems with that, unless you want to call in your goons. But you're number one, and you're sitting next to me.

'Sorry I missed you at the Abarcas'.' It was Ortega who spoke first. 'I thought I'd come to see you off.'

'It's appreciated. I'd hoped we wouldn't miss each other.'

Ortega snapped his fingers at the waitress. '*Dos cognacs*.' The shake of the head calling off the dogs was barely perceptible, little more than a movement of the eyes. 'A good job, getting the girl back.'

'It wouldn't have been possible without your co-operation.'

*   *   *

The lights of Washington sparkled to the north and the dark of the forests of Virginia spread to the south. The Boeing banked gently and settled on its approach. Fifty minutes later Haslam cleared immigration and customs and took a cab in to DC.

Coming back from a job had always been strange.

The adrenalin that still consumed you mixing with the relief that you were normally in one piece. Depending on the sort of job, of course. Sometimes there were just a couple of you, sometimes a patrol. Sometimes, as in a terrorist scare, there were so many of you trying to get a piece of the action that you wondered if there was anyone else anywhere else. Sometimes you came back fit, other times slightly battered, occasionally torn to hell. It had happened to him twice, the medics waiting but one of his own always there first, staying with him and slipping him a cigarette or a beer when the doctors were looking the other way. A couple of times he himself had waited for an incoming flight, most recently in the Gulf. Inconspicuous, of course, lost in the crowd just as the lads would wait till everyone else had cleared the plane, which was part of what it was all about. Then the telephone call to the family, but that again was different.

Except that was when you were regiment, and now he was by himself.

Because gradually the years sneaked up on you, so that although you did your ten miles a day and worked out whenever you could, you knew the time was coming when you would no longer be running up mountains, when instead of being out there you were the one doing the briefings and sending other guys out. Which was when you sat down with your wife, knowing that when she was alone she would cry with relief. Which was when you emptied your locker, had your last party in the mess, then went off to look for the rest of your life.

Sometimes you did private work, bodyguard stuff, except who in their right minds wanted to stop a bullet or a bomb meant for someone else? Sometimes, and especially if you had Haslam's record and reputation, you joined one of the select companies run by ex-regiment people, even tried to set up your own.

The travel helped, of course; occasionally you were still in the thick of it, even though your presence there was coincidental, like the guys doing the jobs in the former Soviet Union. Sometimes you struck lucky, like the bastard whose people were doing some protection work in a certain African state at the time of an attempted coup, the British ambassador caught in the middle and Whitehall sending in the regiment to get him out. Except they needed someone who knew the ground, so while his wife thought he was supervising a job in Scotland he was really running out the back of a Herc into five thousand feet of velvet African night.

Because none of you could ever quite shake it off, none of you wanted to come off the edge, none of you could resist still looking for that last mountain. Even now he could see the words from James Elroy Flecker's 'Golden Journey to Samarkand' on the clock at Hereford:

> We are the pilgrims, Master, we shall go
> Always a little further; it may be
> Beyond that last blue mountain barred with snow . . .

35

Which was probably slightly literary, and the only words of Flecker's which he hadn't found boring, but it was also probably true. Which was why he'd gone his own way. Why he'd come to DC. Why he'd singled out people like Jordan and Mitchell. Why, in his way, he was still on the edge. Why he had still not given up on his own last mountain.

The condominium was on the eighth floor of one of the modern blocks near George Washington University, looking south-west towards the Potomac River. Most of the other people were university or government, there was a security system on the main entrance, a porter on duty twenty-four hours a day, and laundry facilities plus lock-ups in the basement. The furniture he had installed was comfortable rather than expensive, there was a Persian carpet on the floor, and the desk in the corner of the sitting-room was antique. On the walls were the reminders of his past: a Shepherd print of the battle of Mirbat and a Peter Archer of *The Convoy* in the sitting-room, plus a cut-glass decanter with the regimental badge – what others called incorrectly a winged dagger – the same as on the gold ring which had warned Ortega in Lima. Two photographs of D Squadron next to the basin in the bathroom and the letter from the White House on the back of the door.

It was almost midnight.

He let himself in, skimmed through the mail he had collected from the box in the foyer, laughing at the joint letter the boys had written him and enjoying his wife's, then put the rest aside till morning and went to bed, deliberately not setting the alarm. When he woke it was almost ten, the morning warmth already penetrating the flat. He showered, made breakfast, and began the telephone calls.

The first was to the company for whom he had done the Lima job, the next four were to companies for whom he worked in Washington, informing them that he was in town again, and the sixth was to the office in Bethesda. The call was answered by a receptionist. He introduced himself and asked for Jordan.

'I'm afraid Mr Jordan is at a meeting downtown.'

One of the government bodies for whom the company worked, Haslam supposed.

'Can you tell him I called and ask him to phone back when convenient.'

Jordan telephoned twelve minutes later, told Haslam he had to get back into his meeting, and suggested lunch. When the calls were finished Haslam booked a table at the Market Inn, unpacked his travel bag, and left the flat. The restaurant was fifteen minutes away by metro rail and a little over an hour if he walked. He ignored the station and turned toward the Mall.

The grass was green and freshly cut, and the late morning was hot. The Vietnam Memorial was sunk into the ground to his left and the Potomac was to his right, the Memorial Bridge spanning it and Arlington cemetery rising on the hill on the far side, the Custis-Lee Mansion in the trees at the top, and the memorial to John Kennedy just below it. Even now he remembered the first time he had come to Washington; the night, pitch black and biting cold, when he had stood alone at the Lincoln Memorial and stared across the river at the tiny flicker of light in the blackness. The eternal flame to the assassinated president.

The following morning he had taken the metro rail to Arlington and walked up the slope of the hill round which the cemetery was formed. The ground had been white with frost, and it had been too early at that time of year for the tourist buses, so he had made his solitary way across the polished granite semicircle of terraces, then up the steps and on to the white marble surrounding the flame itself. And after he had stood staring at the flame he had walked back down the steps and stood – again alone – at the sweep of wall which marked the lower limit of the memorial and read the quotations from Kennedy's inauguration speech. Seven quotations in total, three either side and the one he remembered in the middle:

> In the long history of the world
> few generations have been granted
> the role of defending freedom
> in its hour of maximum danger.
> I do not shirk from this responsibility
> I welcome it.

He lay on the grass and imagined Kennedy speaking, the voice fading as the sun relaxed him. Two months on any kidnap took their toll, two months on a kidnap in South America took more than they were entitled to. No more jobs for a while, he thought; he would go home, spend some time with Megan and the boys.

He picked up his jacket and walked on.

The morning was hotter, DC shimmering in the heat and the

humidity already building. The White House was three hundred yards to his left, the needle of the Washington Memorial to his right, and the brilliant gleaming white stonework and exquisite outline of Capitol Hill half a mile in front of him. There *were* other parts of DC, there *were* urban ghettoes and unemployment and homelessness, often violence and murder. But today DC looked good.

By the time he reached the Market Inn it was one o'clock and the restaurant was already filling. The manager escorted him to a table in the room to the left and a waitress poured him iced water.

Most of those present wore suits and almost all were on what Haslam thought of as the computer break. He'd forgotten how many times he'd sat in offices and seen it done: the telephone call, incoming or outgoing, then the swivel of the body to the computer and the telephone hooked on the shoulder, Yeah, let's do lunch . . . The diary called up and the name entered for 1.00 PM. Arrive at five past the hour and leave fifty minutes later, the next computerized appointment at two. Washington Man, in which he also included Washington Woman, at work.

Jordan arrived three minutes later. He was dressed in a suit, the jacket over his arm. The pager was on his belt and the shoes were a give-away to anyone who knew: smart but soft-soled. He dumped his briefcase under the table, hung his jacket on the chair, shook hands, and sat down.

'Good trip?'

'Eventually,' Haslam told him.

'When did you get back?'

'Last night.'

They ordered salad, blue cheese dressing, swordfish steaks and iced tea, and updated each other. At every table in the restaurant the process was being repeated: not the same words or details, but the same thrust. Nothing confidential: even though the voices were low, it was not the place for security. Occasionally someone would glance at another table and nod at a colleague or an acquaintance.

The two men were seated near the front wall. When Haslam had arrived he had nodded to the one he knew; when Jordan had sat down he had acknowledged them both.

'Who's with Mitch?' Haslam asked.

Mitchell was mid-forties, fit-looking, hair thinning and cut short, his body size deceptive and making him appear shorter than his five-nine. The man seated opposite him was a similar age, slim, dark hair neatly combed, an energy about him, and even in the heat of early summer he wore a three-piece suit.

'Ed Pearson.' Jordan did not need to look across.

'Who's Ed Pearson?'

'Donaghue's AA.'

AA, Administrative Assistant; what some called a Chief Executive Officer.

'Jack Donaghue?' Haslam asked.

Donaghue nearing the end of his second term as Senator after two successful terms in the House of Representatives.

Jordan nodded. 'A lot of people in this room would like to be where Ed Pearson is at the moment.'

'Why?'

'Like I said, Ed's Jack Donaghue's AA. November next year the country votes for its next man in the White House. Barring accidents, the president will run again for the Republicans. If he enters, Donaghue will get the Democrat nomination. If he does, he's the next president.'

'How can you be so sure?' Haslam glanced at Pearson.

'You've seen Donaghue, heard him, read about him?' Jordan asked.

'I know about Camelot if that's what you mean.' The words used to describe the thousand days of John Kennedy's presidency before he was gunned down in Dallas. The mantle many had passed to Robert Kennedy until he had been assassinated in Los Angeles five years later.

Jordan nodded again. 'Whichever way, a lot of people think Donaghue's the new Kennedy.'

Funny how even now the name had an aura, Haslam thought. How even now people linked it not just to the past but to the future.

It was as if Jordan understood what he was thinking. 'Donaghue's father grew up with John Kennedy, the families are still part of the Boston mafia. Donaghue's as close as you can get to a Kennedy without actually being one.'

'But he hasn't declared.' Because I've been away, therefore I'm out of touch.

'No, he hasn't declared yet.'

'You'd vote for him?'

'Yes,' Jordan said firmly.

It was fifteen minutes to two, time for the restaurant to start emptying.

'If Donaghue made the White House where would that leave Pearson?' Haslam shook his head at the dessert list and asked the waitress for coffee.

'As I said, Pearson is Donaghue's right-hand man. If Donaghue was elected Pearson would be his chief of staff, the alternative president.'

'So what's Mitch doing with him?'

Jordan laughed. 'Not just having lunch.'

'Who's that?' Pearson asked.

Mitchell did not need to look. 'The one farthest from the door is Quincey Jordan.'

A long journey for the skinny runt who wasn't tall enough to play basketball and who'd got his ass kicked – as Jordan himself would have put it – because he'd therefore had to spend his evenings hunched over his schoolbooks. Because in America in the sixties and seventies, in America today, sports scholarships were the normal way up if you were poor and black.

'I know Quince,' Pearson told him. I know that he used to work the Old Man, as they say in the trade; I know that before he left the Secret Service, Jordan was on the presidential detachment; that now he runs one of the select companies providing specialist services to both government and private organizations, as well as to people like me. 'Who's the other?'

'A Brit. Dave Haslam.'

'Tell me about him.' Who he is and what Jordan's doing with him.

'Haslam's a kidnap consultant. Ex British Special Air Service. Worked with our Special Forces people in the Gulf.'

'What did he do there?'

'He doesn't talk about it much.'

'But?'

'I gather he's got a letter from the president stuck up in his bathroom.'

'Why?' Pearson asked.

'Why what?'

'Why's he got a letter from the president?'

A waitress cleared their plates and brought them coffee.

'One of the great fears during the Gulf War was that Israel would become involved. They didn't because for some reason which no one's ever explained, Saddam didn't launch his full range of Scud missiles against them. Saddam didn't do that because someone took them out. That's why Haslam's got a letter from the president stuck on his bathroom door.'

It was ten minutes to two, the restaurant suddenly emptying. On the other table Haslam paid the bill, then he and Jordan rose to leave.

'Ed, Mitch.' Jordan crossed and shook their hands. 'Good to see you both.'

Haslam greeted Mitchell and waited till Jordan introduced him to Pearson.

'Join us for coffee,' Pearson suggested.

'Thanks, but we've had our fill,' Jordan told him.

'You're from England.' Pearson looked up at Haslam.

'How'd you guess?' It was said jokingly.

'Working or visiting?'

'Working.'

But you know that already, because you've already asked Mitch about me.

'Next time you're on the Hill, drop in.'

It was Washington-style, part of what the politicians called net working.

'Which room?' The reply was casual, no big deal.

'Russell Building 396,' Pearson told him. 'Make it this afternoon if you're passing by.'

He watched as Haslam and Jordan left, then turned back to Mitchell. 'You have much on at the moment?'

The first frost touched Mitchell's spine. 'Nothing I couldn't wrap up quickly.'

'Jack and I would like you on the team.'

'Anything specific?'

'Jack might want to announce a special investigation, but before he does he wants a prelim done to make sure it will stand up.'

'What on?'

'Something the man and woman in the street can identify with and understand. Something like Savings and Loans, perhaps.' The financial scandal in the eighties in which many people had lost their money. 'Banking and the laundering of drug money are also front runners.' But it could be anything Mitchell chose – it was in Pearson's eyes, Pearson's shrug. As long as Mitchell could deliver.

Why? someone else might have asked. 'When exactly would Jack like to announce the results?' Mitchell asked instead.

41

Pearson finished his coffee and reached for his napkin. 'Possibly next March or April,' Pearson told him.

The party would choose its candidate at its convention in the August, but the votes at that convention would be governed by each candidate's share of the vote in the primaries three months before. The right publicity at that time, therefore, and a candidate might leave his rivals standing.

'If not in the primaries, then when?' Mitchell asked.

Because if a candidate's bandwagon was already rolling, his team might hold back certain things till later.

'October of next year,' Pearson said simply.

A month before the people of America voted for their next president.

'When do you want me to start?'

'As soon as you can.'

'And when does Jack want to announce he's setting up an investigation?'

Because then he'd be in the news. Because then he could use it to help launch his campaign. But only if he was guaranteed of delivering.

'A precise date?' Pearson asked.

'Yeah, Ed. A precise date.'

There was an unwritten law among politicians running for their party's nomination: that in order to win the primaries, there was a date by which a candidate must declare. That day was Labour Day, the first Monday of the first week in the preceding September. *This September*. Three months off.

Pearson folded the napkin slowly and deliberately, placed it on the table and looked at Mitchell, the first smile appearing on his face and the first laugh in his eyes.

'Labour Day sounds good.'

The heat of the afternoon was relaxing, which was dangerous, because he might think he had unwound. And if he thought that then he might accept another job before he was ready.

Haslam sat on the steps of Capitol Hill and looked down the Mall.

Thirty-six hours ago he'd been dealing with Ortega, and thirty hours before that he'd been praying to whatever God he believed in for the safe delivery of the little girl called Rosita.

He left the steps and walked to Russell Building.

The buildings housing the offices of members of the US Senate

42

were to the north of Capitol Hill and those housing members of the House of Representatives to the south, the gleaming façades of the US Supreme Court and the Library of Congress between. Two of the Senate offices, Dirksen and Hart, were new and one, Russell, was the original. Five hundred yards to the north stood Union Station.

Haslam entered Russell Building by the entrance on First and Constitution Avenue, passed through the security check, ignored the lifts and walked up the sweep of stairs to the third floor. The corridors were long with high ceilings and the floors were marble, so that his footsteps echoed away from him. He checked the plan of the floor at the top of the stairs and turned right, even numbers on his left, beginning with 398, and odd on his right, a notice on the door of 396 saying that all enquiries should be through 398.

The reception room was pleasantly though functionally furnished, the window at the rear facing on to the courtyard round which Russell was built. There were two secretaries, one female and in her mid-twenties and the other male and younger, probably fresh out of college and working as a volunteer, Haslam thought. He introduced himself, then looked round at the photographs on the walls while the woman telephoned the AA.

Some of the prints were of Donaghue, which he expected, others were of the Senator's home state, which he also expected, and one was of President John F. Kennedy.

Pearson came from the door behind the secretary's desk and held out his hand. He had taken off his jacket, but still wore a waistcoat.

'Glad you could make it. Coffee?'

'Milk, no sugar.' Haslam shook his hand and followed him through. The next room was neat, though not as large as Haslam had expected, with two desks, each with telephones and computers, leather swing chairs facing the desks, and more photographs on the walls. The bookcases were lined with political, constitutional and legal texts.

'So this is where it happens.' Haslam glanced round.

'Sometimes.' The secretary brought them each a mug. 'Let me show you round.' Pearson led him back through the reception offices to the one on the far side, then to those on the opposite side of the corridor, identifying rooms and occasionally introducing people. It was the PR tour, albeit executive class. The sort visiting dignitaries from the Senator's home state might get.

They came to the conference room.

'Rooms are allocated according to seniority and positions held. Senator Donaghue is on three committees and chairs a subcommittee of Banking, hence he gets this.'

If Donaghue's nearing the end of his second term and he's on so many committees, then why doesn't he get a modern suite in one of the two new buildings, Haslam thought.

They were back in Pearson's room. The AA opened the door to the left of his desk and showed him through.

The third door from the corner, Haslam calculated, therefore Room 394.

The room was rectangular, the shortest side to their left as they entered, and the windows in it looked on to the central courtyard. The walls were painted a soothing pastel and hung with paintings and photographs. The Senator's desk was in front of the window, with flags either side. In the centre of the wall opposite the door through which they had just entered, was a large dark green marble fireplace. At the end of the room furthest from the window was a small round conference table, leather chairs round it; in the corner next to it stood a walnut cabinet containing a television set and minibar, a coffee percolator on top.

The desk by the window was antique, the patina of the years giving it a soft appearance. The top was clear except for a telephone and a silver-framed family photograph – Donaghue, a woman presumably his wife, and two girls. On the front of the desk was a length of polished oak, the face angled, on which were carved three lines:

Some men see things as they are and say why;
I dream things that never were and say why not.

ROBERT KENNEDY, 1968

The inner sanctum, Haslam thought. 'May I?' he asked.

'Of course,' Pearson told him.

Haslam walked round the room, looking at the paintings then at the photographs, and stopped at the two above the fireplace.

The first, in black and white and of World War Two vintage, was of two young men in the uniforms of naval lieutenants; in the background was a PT boat.

'I recognize Kennedy. Who's the other man?'

'A friend of the Senator's father,' Pearson explained. 'He was to be the Senator's godfather, but was killed in action before Donaghue was born.'

The second photograph, this time in colour, was of a young Donaghue, also dressed in naval uniform, and the citation beside it was for bravery, the date fixing it in the Vietnam War.

To the right of the fireplace were another set, plain and simple: Donaghue as a small boy, Donaghue at school, Donaghue at Harvard, Donaghue with the woman in the family photograph on his desk.

The print next to them was black and white and had been blown up, so that its images were slightly grainy. The photograph was of mourners at a funeral and there was a tall, good-looking woman in the second row. She seemed deeply distressed. Her head was bent slightly, as if she was listening to someone on her right who was obscured by the mourners in the front row, but her eyes were fixed rigid and staring straight ahead.

They left the room and returned to Pearson's.

'Interesting photos,' Haslam suggested. 'Almost the story of Donaghue's life, except that I don't understand some of them.'

'How'd you mean?'

'Vietnam, for example. I thought he opposed the war.'

Pearson nodded. 'There's something you should understand about Jack Donaghue.' He settled at his desk, swung his feet up and held the coffee mug in his lap, Haslam opposite him. 'Some would say Donaghue is an enigma: of the Establishment but against it. The fact that he's against it makes him a good Senator, the fact that he's from it makes him an effective one.'

'How'd you mean?'

'Jack Donaghue's background is Boston Irish.' It was in line with the PR tour – nothing said that wasn't on a cv or in a file somewhere, nothing controversial or private. 'Privileged upbringing, Harvard of course, which was where his politics began.'

'How?' Haslam asked.

'It was at Harvard that Donaghue first declared his opposition to the Vietnam War.'

'So why the photo of him in uniform? Why the awards for bravery?'

'As some would say, Jack's an enigma.' Pearson switched easily between first and second names. 'He opposed the war yet at the same time felt a duty to his country. Others dodged the draft or used their connections to get safe postings, but when Jack's number came up he did neither. Ended up commanding a Swift boat, doing runs up the deltas. He was awarded a couple of Bronze Stars, plus a Silver Star. Apparently he might have been up for a Navy Medal, even a Medal of Honor, but hinted that he would turn it down. Said he was being considered because of his connections, and that everyone on his boat deserved an award and not just him.'

'What was that for?'

Pearson looked down at the coffee mug. 'He doesn't talk about it much. Seems some recon guys were holed up on a river bank, heavy casualties and surrounded by NVA. The choppers couldn't reach them and they were finished. Donaghue got them out, though he himself was wounded.'

Except if Donaghue got a Silver Star and was up for a Navy Medal or a Medal of Honor, there was more to it than that, Haslam thought. 'After Vietnam?' he asked.

'Law school. Legal practice, then assistant District Attorney. All this time arguing that we should pull out of Vietnam, but at the same time fighting for veterans' rights.'

'Then?'

'Two terms in the House of Representatives.' Which was when Pearson had met him, when Pearson had become his alter ego. 'Now in his second term in the Senate. Outstanding record since his first day in DC.' Pearson smiled. 'Which I'm bound to say, of course. Supports industrial development but not at the expense of the environment. Believes in budget control but not at the expense of things like health care. Sees the need for a strong national economy but not at the expense of the Third World.'

Haslam remembered the photograph on the desk. 'Family?'

'Jack met Cath at Harvard. She's a lawyer, specializes in human rights. They have two girls, both at Sidwell Friends.'

So now you know Jack Donaghue – it was in the way Pearson stopped talking, the way he put the coffee mug on the desk.

'And from here?'

Pearson laughed and stood up, looked out the window. The door from reception opened and Donaghue came in, followed by an aide. He was taller than Haslam had expected, leaner face and steel-grey hair.

'Senator, may I introduce Dave Haslam from England. Dave's a friend of Quince Jordan and Mitch Mitchell.'

'Good to meet you.' The handshake was firm. Behind Donaghue the secretary and aide were reminding both him and Pearson that they were due somewhere else ten minutes ago.

Sorry – Donaghue's shrug said it – have to go. He held out his hand again. 'As I said, good to meet you.' The eyes were unwavering. If Donaghue runs for the Democrat nomination he'll get it, Jordan had said over lunch. And if Donaghue gets the nomination, he's the next president. Donaghue turned and left the room, the aide trying to keep up.

Pearson held out his hand. 'Stay in touch.'

By the time Haslam reached the corridor it was already empty. He walked to the ground floor, found a set of pay phones, called the apartment and activated the answer phone. There were three messages on it, two asking him to call about security consultations and the third from Mitchell inviting him to beer and barbecue at the Gangplank.

Donaghue's last formal meeting on the Hill that evening ended at six. At six-fifteen, and accompanied by an aide, he attended a cocktail party thrown by one of the lobby groups, at seven a second. It was the standard ending to a standard day. At seven-thirty he drove to the University Club on 16th, between L and M. The building was six-storey red brick, with a small drive-in in front. In the daytime the street would have been lined with cars bearing diplomatic plates from the Russian Federation building next door, the parking tickets plastered over their windscreens always ignored. In early evening, however, the only vehicle was a patrol car of the uniformed division of the Secret Service, the White House emblem on the side and the driver slouched in his seat and reading a Tony Hillerman.

Donaghue parked the Lincoln in one of the bays and went inside.

The atmosphere was refined yet relaxed – the University Club had long enjoyed a more liberal reputation than others in town. The main dining-room was on the left, and the library and reading-room on the right, behind the reception desk. On the first floor was another set of rooms, one of which he had hired for his fortieth birthday party, plus a more informal restaurant, and the bedrooms were on the floors above.

He smiled at the receptionist, spent three minutes talking to a group of other members, then went to the fitness rooms in the basement. Even here the upholstery was leather. He collected a towel, stripped, hung his clothes in a locker, took a plunge in the pool, and went into the sauna.

Tom Brettlaw arrived two minutes later.

*

Brettlaw's day had begun at seven. At seven-thirty the inconspicuous Chevrolet had collected him from the family home in South Arlington and driven him the fifteen minutes to Langley. The only clue to its passenger was the greenish tinge of the armoured windows and the slight roll of the chassis. The guard on the main gate was expecting him. The driver turned the car past the front of the greyish-white concrete building, down a drive beneath it, and into the inner carpark. Brettlaw collected his briefcase and took the executive lift to his office on the top floor.

The head of the CIA – the Director of Central Intelligence – is a presidential appointment, as is his deputy, normally a serving military officer. Beneath the deputy are five Deputy Directors, all career intelligence officers. Of these the most powerful is the DDO, the Deputy Director of Operations, the man in effective control of all CIA overt and covert operations throughout the world. For the past four years Tom Brettlaw had been DDO.

His office was spacious: two windows, both curtained, a large desk of his own choosing with a row of telephones to his left and a bank of television screens in front. The leather executive chair behind the desk was flanked by the Stars and Stripes and the Agency flag, and the walls were hung with photographs of Brettlaw meeting prominent politicians, most of them heads of state. The mantelpiece of the marble fireplace was filled with the mementos given by the heads of those foreign intelligence services with whom he had liaised over the years, and the floor was covered by a large and expensive Persian rug. To the left of the main room was a private bathroom. In the area of the room to the right of his desk was a conference table, chairs placed neatly round it, and in the bookcase along on the wall to the left of the door was concealed a minibar. During his street days Brettlaw had done his time in the jewel of the CIA crown, the Soviet division, heading it before his promotion to DDO. It was a background he did not allow to pass unnoticed. Even before the collapse of the Soviet empire, those in the division noted with satisfaction, Brettlaw had always made a point of offering visitors a beer, and suggesting they tried a Bud. Not the Budweiser from the US corporation bearing the name, but a Budvar from the Czech Republic. Failing that a Zhiguli from the Ukraine.

The report from Zev Bartolski had come in overnight, for his eyes only and requiring him to decrypt it personally.

Brettlaw and Bartolski had joined the Outfit at more or less the same time, done their field training together at The Farm, their

48

explosives and detonation training together. Worked together in the Soviet division when the going was rough and the shit was hitting the fan. Shared everything, the risks on the way in and the rewards on the way out. Which was why Zev Bartolski was now Chief of Station in Bonn.

By eight Brettlaw had finished the decrypt and locked the report in the security safe; at eight-fifteen he was briefed on global developments in the past twelve hours. At eight-thirty he held his first meeting with his divisional heads, at nine-thirty his regular conference – when both men were available – with the Director of Central Intelligence, the DCI. From ten to eleven-thirty he conducted a further series of meetings with his divisional heads, plus section heads where appropriate, the topics covering the responsibilities entrusted to his stewardship.

Satellite intelligence; liaison with intelligence bodies in the new republics of what had once been the Soviet empire; economic intelligence and industrial counter-espionage. The significance of the Balkan conflict on Islam fundamentalism, and the march of Islam north and west. The surfeit of weapons on the world market, the possibility and cost of buying up part of the former Soviet stockpile, and the latest reports on the availability of weapons-grade plutonium on the black market.

Brettlaw's personal system of operating reflected the Agency's: each operation, each transaction, was placed in its separate box. Within each box were further boxes, boxes within them. Finance separated from analysis and analysis separated from operations, covert separated from overt. Of course there were overlaps and of course there were areas of shared knowledge, but only where appropriate and only where it would not endanger security. Only the Director of Central Intelligence fully cognisant of all that was happening. And below the DCI only one man knowing and planning where everything came together, where the jigsaw of pieces became one game. The Deputy Director of Operations, the DDO.

The discussions continued: a possible coup in a Central African state, the implications of the success or failure of such a coup and the loyalties of the current head of state and the colonel allegedly seeking to replace him. Developments in Central America, always a delicate issue, and conflict between the former Soviet republics.

All the topics and operations discussed that morning would be reported not only to the White House, but to the politicians on Capitol Hill. Not to all the politicians, of course, but to the

49

select committees on intelligence of the House of Representatives and the Senate, the members of each appointed because of their maturity and sense of responsibility, and their deliberations closed. So that, constitutionally at least, everything the Agency did was accountable.

Except . . .

That sometimes the politicians who held the Agency's purse strings would not understand. That sometimes even experienced men and women like those who sat on the select committees might not like what you were required to do. Because in his world you dealt not just with the present but with the future, therefore some of the sides you were required to support and some of the plans you were required to lay might not necessarily be those which the present politicians would like to be identified with. Because the politicians could never see further ahead than the vote that afternoon and how it would affect their chance of re-election.

It was for this reason that Brettlaw had instigated the black projects, for this reason he had constructed the system of switches and cut-outs by which he could conceal from his political masters those projects of which they would not approve, whose funding was hidden in the labyrinth which constituted the modern banking world.

Of course others had done before what he was doing now, and of course he himself did not always like what he was required to do or the people he was required to do it with. Of course he loathed the right-wing fanatics as much as the left-wing lunatics. Understand such movements, however, get the right people in the right places within them, get his people in the key positions, and in ten, twenty, thirty years' time the US of A would still be safe.

For people like Brettlaw it was not just a dream, not even just a goal. It was the *raison d'être*, the reason for being, the source and the justification and the whole goddamn rationale for everything. That as the world crept sometimes too boldly into the next millennium, the children of his children – the children of everybody's children – would be safe. Even though they did not know of him or the role he played in securing that right for them. Even though it was probably best that they did not know.

Of course some would find it strange: the funds to key figures on all sides of the Balkans conflict, be they Serb or Croat, Christian or Muslim; the politicians, military and intelligence people who would decide the future of the Middle East. The same with the black funds being channelled to those who would be the key people in those countries so recently released from Soviet domination and now facing internal and external crisis, even Moscow itself. Plus the plans for the Pacific Basin, the so-called democracies or the self-confessed dictatorships upon which the economic future of the nation depended.

Even things like economic intelligence.

Industrial counter-espionage, that was the buzz word on the Hill nowadays. Stop the opposition spying on America's industrial secrets. And within the term opposition he included military and political allies. But if even your friends were doing it to you, then what the hell was he doing if he didn't do it back? Industrial counter-espionage was in, however, and industrial espionage was out, so he had to do it through the back door and forget to tell the people on the Hill.

It was eleven-thirty. The man who now sat opposite him, Costaine, was his Deputy Director for Policy, one of the operational people. One of the Inner Circle, therefore part of the black projects. Not the Inner Circle of the Inner Circle, not one of the Wise Men like Zev Bartolski, but there were few men like Zev Bartolski at any time and in any place. Which was why Zev was more than just CoS, Chief of Station in Bonn, why Zev was a cornerstone of Brettlaw's plans for the future. Why his brief lay far wider than the standard operating orders. Why, in the best tradition of the best in the business, Bonn Chief of Station was little more than a cover.

'Everything in order?'

'Yes.'

Costaine was tall, mid-forties, with a crewcut which gave him a fit appearance.

They went into detail. Boxes in boxes, though; Costaine knowing only what he was allowed to know – not even Zev Bartolski was allowed to know everything. And Costaine knowing nothing of the financial arrangements which supported his operational activities.

It was eleven-fifty.

Myerscough was in his early forties and slightly overweight, with light wire-framed spectacles. Myerscough was good, one of the best. It had been Myerscough who had set up the financial network for the black projects, who had chosen the bank through which they would run the funds, then made the contact with the fixer in the bank and got him on side. Established with him the lacework of nominee companies through which the black funds were laundered. But not even Myerscough, especially not Myerscough, knew anything about how the funds were used.

Myerscough was also careful, even had his own little intelligence set-up, people in places like the Federal Bank and Congress who reported on any interest shown in any of his accounts. Not that they realized who they were working for, of course; and not that they looked for specific accounts. More like the old Soviet and East German systems: report on everything. Then Myerscough and his people would pull those in which they were interested. Brettlaw didn't necessarily like it: Myerscough never had been a field man and never would be, therefore didn't have the instinct, didn't know when to shut up shop and get the hell out. But if Myerscough was happy playing in DC then he wasn't looking elsewhere.

'Any problems?' Brettlaw asked.

'Couple of minor things,' Myerscough told him. 'Sorted out within hours.'

'What about Nebulus?'

One of the switch accounts in London.

'Nebulus is fine.'

'Anything else?'

Myerscough shook his head.

Brettlaw concluded the briefing, took his sixth coffee of the morning, lit another Gauloise, and began to prepare for his appearance before the House Permanent Select Committee on Intelligence that afternoon. Two, sometimes three days of every month were taken up with such appointments. For the DCI it was one day a week. When Brettlaw was a politics major at Harvard he would have called it democracy.

It was twelve-thirty; he took a light lunch in the executive dining-room and was driven to the Hill. The committee began at two, jugs of iced water on the tables and the members in a semicircle facing him.

'The payment of $50,000 to a Bolivian government minister was in line with Congressional Order 1765 . . .'

'At present the Agency is running two operations in Angola . . .'

Even though the session was closed there were always too many members wanting to score political points, too many wanting to make names for themselves.

'With respect, Congressman, I have already explained that to the Senate sub-committee on terrorism . . .'

52

You ever been a bag man in Moscow, he had wanted to ask one of them once. Your balls frozen and the KGB hoods sitting on you. Yet still you had to make the contact, still you had to bring it home.

The hearing closed at four-thirty; he made a point of shaking hands with each of its members and was driven back to Langley. At six-thirty he held his penultimate meeting of the day, an hour later he arrived at his last.

The Lincoln town car was parked opposite the University Club and the Secret Service car was half a block down, though he assumed there was another in the alleyway behind. It had been more fun in the old days, before the end of the Cold War, when the building next door had been the Soviet embassy. Now it housed merely the Russian Federation, so that even though the game was still running and the place was still staked out, the edge of driving up 16th had gone for ever.

He walked through the reception area, went to the fitness area in the basement, collected a towel, locked his clothes in a locker, took an ice-cold ten seconds in the plunge bath, and went into the sauna. The wall of heat almost stopped him. He took the towel from his waist, laid it on the wood seat, and sat down.

'How's Mary and the family?' Donaghue asked.

'Fine. Cath and the girls?'

'Doing well.'

It was twenty-five years since they had been room mates together at Harvard, since they had studied together and worked their butts off to make the football squad together. A quarter of a century, give or take, since the long grim afternoon, still remembered, at the Yale Bowl. The annual game between the universities of Harvard and Yale, the Crimsons and the Elis. The last play of the last quarter. Yale leading, Brettlaw quarterback and Donaghue wide receiver, the ball in the air and the world holding its breath.

A little over twenty years since their numbers had come up and they had gone to Vietnam, Brettlaw into Intelligence and Donaghue into the Navy. Fourteen months less than that since Brettlaw had heard about Donaghue and kicked ass – filing clerk up to four-star general – to get him out and on the first flight home, to get him the best doctor in the best hospital in town.

A little less than twenty years since they had been best man at each other's weddings, and, a couple of years after that, godfather to one another's firstborn.

53

'We ought to get together sometime. Have a barbecue.'

'Let's do it.'

The sweat was forming in beads on their foreheads.

'Good session with the committee this afternoon?'

'No problems.'

'But?'

'The enemy's still there, Jack. Others might forget it but we mustn't.'

The sweat was pouring in tiny rivulets down their bodies.

'Hope you're keeping your nose clean, Tom.'

Because if I run for the nomination I'll need all the help I can get. And if I make the White House and if there's nothing you're trying to hide from me, then you're head of it all, you're Top Gun, you're my Director of Central Intelligence.

'You know me, Jack.'

The Potomac was silver in the evening sun. The six of them sat on the upper deck of the houseboat, sipping Rolling Rock and munching through the steaks, plus the crabs and lobsters Mitchell had bought from the fish market at the top end of the marina.

None of the others present that evening were connected with the security industry: two were actors, one was a lawyer and one a landscape architect, though all lived on the boats. Each of them knew of Mitchell's Marine background, of course, each had laughed at the upturned helmet now used as a flower pot and the Marine Corps badge next to the family photographs, but few had noticed the scuba mask and parachute wings above the main emblem, and none had asked. Haslam had, of course, but Haslam knew anyway, because after Vietnam some of the boys from Force Recon had served with the Rhodesian SAS and Haslam had met a couple when, years later, they'd passed through London.

The evening was quiet and relaxing, the others at the front end of the sun deck and Haslam and Mitchell by the barbecue at the rear.

'Make the Hill this afternoon?' Mitchell checked a steak.

'Yeah.' Haslam was tired but relaxed.

'Meet Donaghue?'

'Briefly.'

'What you think of him?'

'Impressive, though all he had time for was a handshake. Quince was suggesting he might run for president.'

'So I hear.'

Mitchell flipped the steak on to a plate and called for someone to collect it.

'How'd you know Donaghue?' Haslam poured them each another beer.

'How do I know Jack Donaghue?' Mitchell threw two more steaks on the grill. 'Long story, Dave, long time ago.' He hesitated, then continued. 'You know what Force Recon was about, behind the lines most of the time, never off the edge. I was lucky, came back in one piece. Thought I'd come home the hero.' He laughed. 'Like the old newsreels of the guys coming back from World War Two, girls and cheer leaders and ticker-tape welcomes. Instead they treated us like shit.'

Criticize the war, Haslam remembered Mitchell had once said, but don't criticize the kids who left home to fight in it.

'No job, no past that anybody wanted to know, so no future.' Mitchell was no longer tending the barbecue, instead he was staring across the river, eyes and face fixed. 'Ended up doing the wilderness thing in upper New York state, a lotta guys up there, then joined the Forestry Service.' He laughed again. 'Finally I ended up on the coast, Martha's Vineyard, picking up any jobs I could. One day I bumped into Jack Donaghue.' When Donaghue and Cath and their first daughter – there was only the one then – were on holiday and he himself was serving take-outs at Pete's Pizzas in Oak Bluffs. 'Jack told me about GI loans.' The following morning, drinking beer in the rocking chairs on the veranda of the wood shingle house on Narangassett Avenue which the Donaghues had rented, the smell of summer round them and the ease of the Vineyard relaxing them. 'He and Cath talked me into taking one, hassled me in to going to law school.' He laughed a third time, but a different, more relaxed laugh this time. 'Didn't even ask for my vote.'

When Haslam left it was gone eleven. He was asleep by twelve. The telephone rang at four.

Could be West Coast, he thought; three hours' time difference so it was only just gone midnight in LA. Unlikely though. Or Far East, where it would be mid-afternoon, though he had few contacts there. Most probably Europe. Nine in the morning in London, ten in the rest of the Continent.

'Yes.'

'Dave. This is Mike.'

London, he confirmed. You know the time? he began to ask.

'The two o'clock flight out of Dulles this afternoon. You're on it. A job in Italy.'

3

The thoughts were like wisps of cloud in the sky. Paolo Benini reached up and tried to pull them down, to bring them into contact with that thing called his brain, his mind, his intellect; so that he would have something to anchor them to, so that his brain would have something to work on.

Something about the fax.

He was not aware of the process of thinking, not even fully aware of the thoughts, was only aware of the images which represented them. He was in his room at the hotel, taking the telephone call about the fax and phoning reception back and checking with them. He was opening the door and feeling in his pocket for a tip, was going backwards into the room, the vice round his throat, the men on top of him and the needle in his arm. Was being bundled along the corridor and down the emergency stairs at the rear of the hotel. Was being pushed into the boot of a car, the lid slamming shut and the car pulling away.

Something about the fax, and if it was about the fax it must be about one of the accounts he'd been working on. His mind still struggled to find a logic in the disorder. If it was about one of the accounts it would almost certainly be one of those he'd just dealt with, probably the last one. And if it was the last one it would be the account codenamed Nebulus.

The car was stopping – ten, fifteen minutes later, perhaps longer – the boot opening, the hands holding him and another needle in his arm. He was being lifted from one car to another. Was coming round, the boot suffocating like an oven and the smoothness of the autostrada beneath him.

The road was rougher, probably a country road, the car climbing. The road was no longer a road, was a track, the car bumping along it and the vibrations shuddering through his body. He was being blindfolded and lifted out, was being half-dragged, half-pulled, half-carried across a patch of ground. Illogical, his mind was telling him, you can't have three halves. He was lying down, the blindfold no longer over his eyes but a pain round his right ankle.

Something more about the fax, something still confusing him. The last account he had checked was Nebulus, but reception had said the fax was from Milan and Nebulus was London. Therefore it wasn't about Nebulus.

He was waking from the nightmare. The pain was still round his ankle and the hotel room was still dark, only the globe of the morning sun through the lines of the curtains. Perhaps not the sun, perhaps the bedside lamp, except that he hadn't switched it on. He reached for it but found it difficult to turn, his hand going through the lamp or the lamp further away than he had thought.

He jerked awake.

The hurricane lamp was on the other side of the iron bars and the bars themselves were set in concrete in the roof and floor of the cave. The cave was small and the floor was sandy. Against the bars – his side of the bars – were two buckets, and the mattress on which he lay was made of straw. He was wearing his shirt, trousers and socks, and the pain was caused by the manacle clamped round his right ankle, the chain some four feet long and ending in a piton driven into the wall.

Paolo Benini curled into a ball and began to cry.

*   *   *

The line of passengers stretched through customs and the ranks of friends and relatives waited outside, the drivers holding the names of their pick-ups on pieces of paper in front of them.

Welcome to Milan, Haslam thought, welcome to any airport in any city in any part of the world. Same noise and bustle inside, same chill of air-conditioning. Different smells once you stepped outside, of course, different degrees of heat or cold, and different levels of affluence or poverty. Different reasons for being there.

Santori was standing by the coffee bar.

Ricardo Santori was the company's man in this part of Italy. Not full-time but paid a retainer, with a successful legal practice outside his kidnap connections. He was in his mid-forties, wearing a business suit and a somewhat colourful tie, and saw Haslam the moment he emerged through the double doors from Customs.

Santori was good: excellent sources and unrivalled access, but because of this he was known not only to those who lived in fear of kidnap, but also to the police units dealing with it. For these reasons, and in case he had been observed, he did not acknowledge Haslam; instead he turned away, paused momentarily for Haslam to spot any tails he might have picked up, then left the terminal. Only in the relative security of the carpark did they shake hands.

'Thanks for getting here so quickly.' Santori's English was good, only a little accented. 'You're booked in at the Marino.' The hotel was in a side street near Central Station and Haslam had stayed there before. Santori gave him a telephone pager and the case file, and swung the Porsche out of the airport and on to the autostrada.

'Any problems?' Haslam asked.

'Not yet.'

'Schedule?'

'You're seeing the family at twelve. I thought you'd like time to change and shower first.'

'Thanks.'

He settled in the passenger seat and skimmed the two closely typed sheets of the briefing document: the victim's name and background, family and friends, approximate details of the kidnapping, going rates and time scales for kidnappings in Italy over the past two years in general and the past six months in particular.

'Have the family heard from the kidnappers yet?'

'Not when I spoke with them this morning.'

'But all telephone calls are being recorded?'

A modified Craig 109 VOX on to the main phone in the wife's flat. VOX – voice activated switch.

'Yes. I set it up myself.'

The traffic was heavy; by the time Haslam checked in at the Marino it was gone eleven, when they turned in to the Via Ventura it was almost twelve.

The street was attractive and expensive, the pavements wide and lined with boutiques and cafés, apartments above them. The block in which the Beninis had their town apartment was modern and, unlike many buildings in the city, it looked out rather than being built round a central courtyard. It was some fifty metres from the shops and set back from the road, with parking space for visitors in front. A striped canopy protected those arriving by car at the front door, and a side road swung round to what Haslam assumed was an underground carpark. Security door on the garage, he also correctly assumed.

There were three cars in the parking area opposite the front door: a top-of-the-range Saab 9000, a dark blue BMW soft-top, and a Mercedes with two men lounging near it, the air of driver and minder stamped upon them.

Haslam pulled his briefcase from the rear seat and followed Santori to the entrance. The front door had a security lock and intercom system. Only after the lawyer had announced them and the porter had confirmed they were expected were they allowed inside. The entrance was marble, lined with busts and statuettes, and the lift which took them smoothly and swiftly to the fifth floor smelt of lavender. There was a moment's delay after Santori had rung the bell on the door to the front right, then it opened and a housekeeper showed them inside.

Even in the hallway, the paintings on the walls – oils, and mainly of flowers – were perfectly positioned and subtly lit. They followed the housekeeper through to the lounge. The room was on a split level and the walls were hung with landscapes, most of them Fattoris or Rosais. The wife, Francesca, was an interior designer, Haslam remembered the brief: if this was their town apartment wonder what the family home in Emilia was like.

The oval mahogany table was in the centre of the lower floor level, three men and one woman seated round it. As Santori and Haslam entered they stood up.

'Signore Benini, Mr Haslam.' Santori began the introductions.

Umberto Benini, the victim's father, Haslam assumed: early sixties, tall and alert, slightly hooked nose and immaculate suit. Businessman with the usual political connections.

The observations were in shorthand, and shorthand inevitably led to value judgements which might or might not be correct, Haslam reminded himself.

Umberto Benini took over from Santori.

'Signore Rossi, who is representing BCI.' Early forties, sharp looker though dressed like a banker, and wearing tinted spectacles.

'Marco, my son.' Mid-thirties and less conservative suit. The victim's brother.

'Signora Benini.' The victim's wife. Late thirties, therefore younger than her husband, five feet four tall and holding her figure, despite the two daughters. Eyes red, had been crying shortly before his arrival but had covered the fact with make-up. Clothes expensive and beautifully cut.

Santori confirmed there was nothing more the family wished to ask him, shook their hands – starting with Umberto Benini – and left.

Interesting order of introductions, Haslam thought: banker, son, and only then the victim's wife. How many times had he sat in this sort of room and looked at these sort of people and these frightened faces?

The positions round the table had already been determined: the father at the head, the banker on his right and the son on his left, the wife two away from him on his left, and the empty chair for Haslam facing him at the other end. Only the father and the banker smoking, and the wife re-positioning the ashtray as if it didn't belong.

The housekeeper poured them coffee, left the cream and sugar on the silver tray in the centre of the table, and closed the door behind her.

'Before we continue, perhaps I should introduce myself more fully and outline what my role is. The first thing to say is that everything said in this room, from you to me or me to you, is confidential.' He waited to confirm they understood. 'As you know, my name is David Haslam, I'm a crisis consultant, in this case the crisis is a kidnapping.'

It was the way he began every first meeting, partly to establish a structure and partly because there were certain things to arrange in case the kidnappers telephoned while they were talking.

'Before you begin, perhaps you would allow me to say a few words.' Umberto Benini made sure his English, and his intonation, were perfect.

Because I'm Paolo's father, but more important than that I'm head of the family and the person in charge. Therefore I say who says what and when.

'Paolo worked for the Banca del Commercio Internazionale. He was based in Milan but travelled extensively. Signore Rossi is a colleague.' The wave of the hand indicated that Rossi should provide the details.

'Paolo was in Zurich. We have a branch there.' The banker looked at him through the cigarette smoke. 'On the day in question he had returned from London, where we also have a branch, with more meetings in Zurich the following morning.'

They were already playing it wrong, Haslam thought. If the kidnappers phoned now they wouldn't be prepared. And once he'd arrived they should be, because his job was to make sure they were.

'After work that afternoon he was driven to the hotel where he normally stays. He arrived at about seven, took dinner at eight-thirty and retired to his room at ten. He was last seen at eleven. When he failed to come down for breakfast the next morning his bodyguards opened his room. The bed had not been slept in and nothing had been touched or taken.'

'How many bodyguards?' Haslam asked.

'One with him all the time, plus his own driver and two more he normally has when he is in Italy.'

Except that Benini wasn't in Italy when he was snatched, but he still had a whole army of minders. 'How did the kidnappers access his room?'

'We're not sure.'

'You said he was last seen at eleven?'

'Apparently a fax was sent to the hotel for his attention. Reception informed him and he asked for it to be sent up. The porter remembered it was eleven o'clock, give or take a couple of minutes, when he delivered it.'

Haslam knew what the kidnappers had done and how they had done it. Months of research and planning behind the snatch itself. Which was bad, because their security would be watertight, but good, because they'd know the rules.

'You've checked the fax?'

'It's being checked now.'

Haslam nodded. 'As I began to say earlier, my name is David Haslam. I work regularly for companies like the one to whom the bank is contracted under the kidnap section of its insurance policy. I'm British but based in Washington. Before that I was in the Special Air Service of the British Army.'

Umberto was about to intervene again, he sensed; therefore he should get the next bit out the way and fast, because that way he was covered, that way even Umberto might begin to understand how they all had to play it.

'Have the kidnappers been in touch yet?'

The father drummed his fingers on the mahogany. 'No.'

'In that case the first thing we do is prepare for when they do.' Why – it was in the way they looked at him. 'Because they might even phone while we're talking.'

His briefcase was on the floor; he opened it and took out an A4 pad.

'Where do we think the call will come?' The question was directed at Umberto Benini.

'I assume it will be to here.'

'So who's most likely to take it?'

'I am.' It was the wife.

Haslam focused on her. 'The man who calls you will be a negotiator. He won't know where Paolo is being held or anything else about him. Nor will he have power to make decisions. He'll report back to a controller. But the negotiator is important, not just because he's the contact point, but because he's the man who'll interpret to the controller how things are going.

'The key thing in the first call is that you don't commit yourself to anything. The negotiator will say certain things. *We have him. If you want him back you'll have to pay.* How you react will govern the rest of the negotiations. So it's imperative, *imperative . . .*' he repeated '. . . that you don't say anything you might regret later. We do this by giving you a script.'

He looked at her. 'May I call you Francesca?'

She nodded, too numb to do otherwise.

He wrote three brief sections on the paper and passed it across the table. The wife read it and passed it in turn to her father-in-law.

CONCERN OVER PAOLO	*Is he alive?*
	Is he being treated well?
MONEY	*Can't even think about money*
	until I know he's alive.
IF PRESSED	*Too much.*
	Don't have that sort of cash.
	Prove he's alive.

Umberto Benini nodded at the wife but kept the paper in front of him.

'Signore Santori gave you the recording device?' Haslam asked.

'Already in position.'

'Good.' He turned again to the wife. 'Tell me about Paolo.'

'We've been married sixteen years; he's away a lot now, so the girls miss him. We have this apartment in town and a home in Emilia.'

'What about you?'

'I run my own interior design company.'

'I can see.' He looked at the paintings on the walls and saw that she'd smiled for the first time. 'Tell me about the girls, where they are now.'

'They're with their grandmother,' Umberto informed him.

'Have you and Paolo ever discussed the possibility of one of you being kidnapped, made any plans for it?' Haslam looked at Francesca. 'Any codes, for example?'

'No.' The wife's face was drawn again, the tension showing through.

'Have the police been informed. And if not, do you wish them to be?'

Most families suffering a kidnapping preferred to keep that fact secret from the police. Partly because Italian law forbad the payment of money to kidnappers; therefore if a kidnap was reported or suspected the first action of the state was to freeze the family's funds to prevent payment. And partly because most families rich enough to attract the attention of kidnappers normally wished to conceal the size of their wealth.

'No to both questions.' Umberto and Rossi answered simultaneously.

'Fine, that's your decision. You should be aware, however, that it's possible they'll find out.' At least they were in Italy, he thought, at least there was no Ortega to worry about.

'That aspect is already covered.'

Because this is Milan and in Milan we pay to make sure that sort of thing doesn't happen. Or if it does somebody sits on it and fast.

Umberto Benini lit another cigarette.

Haslam took them to the next stage.

'In that case the next thing we have to discuss is our own organization, what some people call the CMT, the crisis management team. Who's on it and who fills which roles.'

They went through the positions.

Chairman.

'I would be more than happy to fulfil that role.' Umberto Benini.

Negotiator.

Myself again – it was in the way Umberto sat back, the way he shrugged.

It might be advisable to separate the positions, Haslam told him carefully. The negotiator's job was communication and the chairman's was decision-making, and sometimes the two were incompatible.

'In that case, Signore Rossi,' Umberto suggested.

'In some ways a good choice,' Haslam agreed, 'but in other ways not. In a way it depends whether we wish to reveal the fact that the bank is involved.'

'Why shouldn't we?'

'If the bank is seen to be involved then the ransom the kidnappers will hold out for will be much higher.'

'So Francesca.'

'Yes. But before she decides she should know what it involves.'

Marco, the brother, hadn't spoken at all, and Francesca only occasionally.

'What does it involve?' Umberto gave neither of them the chance to contribute.

The man was on auto-pilot because his son had been kidnapped, Haslam reminded himself. Therefore give him a chance, give them all a chance. Because these people were all in hell, and he was their only way out.

'The kidnapper's negotiator will switch tactics, one moment he'll be reasonable and the next he'll be swearing and screaming. Then he'll be the only friend Francesca has in the world. And all the time she'll not only have to control herself, but try to manipulate the other side.'

'I understand,' the wife said simply.

Courier.

'Tell us what the courier does.' Umberto Benini peered down the hawk nose. To avoid confusion Haslam already mentally referred to the father as Umberto and the kidnap victim as Paolo.

'The courier collects messages and packages the kidnappers leave for us. The courier will also be responsible for dropping the ransom money when that moment comes.'

Therefore Rossi the bank representative or Marco the brother. But Marco was only in the room because he was family, Haslam suspected. Umberto hadn't even decided whether or not Marco should even be involved.

He turned to Rossi. 'It might be that you feel you should play this role. You might also feel, however, that the same problems about the bank's involvement arise.'

'We'll discuss it.' Umberto broke the meeting and called for fresh coffee.

Haslam waited till the housekeeper had served them, then continued.

'In kidnap negotiations there are guidelines, almost procedures.

All the signs are that the kidnappers are professionals, which means they'll know them and stick by them. They'll also try to control the situation through them, but those procedures give us the chance to do the same thing back.'

'For example?' Umberto Benini asked.

'The negotiator will tell you to get a clean phone. That's a number somewhere else in case the police find out about the kidnapping and start tapping this one. We can begin to control the situation by telling the kidnappers we want to use a clean phone before they tell us.'

They went through the alternatives: the properties or offices owned or controlled by Umberto, and the facilities which the bank could provide.

'We have another apartment, an investment.' It was Francesca.

'Whose name is it in, because if it's in your name it's no good.'

'A company name.'

'Empty?'

'At the moment.'

'Fine.'

He wrote the number on the sheet of paper in front of him.

'One more thing our negotiator has to get across.' There were several more things, but at a first meeting he preferred to keep instructions to a minimum. 'The time Francesca, assuming it will be Francesca, will be waiting at the clean phone. The kidnappers will try to leave it open, so that she'd be waiting at the phone twenty-four hours a day. You can imagine the effect that would have. So we specify a time, but that time must be in keeping with Francesca's normal schedule, therefore it should probably be in the evening.'

'Why?' Umberto asked.

'Because however difficult it will be at first, you must continue to lead your normal lives – business appointments, personal matters. One reason, as I've already suggested, is that it maintains a structure to your lives.'

Because otherwise you'll go insane.

But I'm already going insane, he knew the wife was thinking.

So how was she going to stand up to it, he wondered, how was she going to take whatever the kidnappers threw at her. How was she going to take the pressure Umberto would bring to bear on her. Because that was the way it was already going.

'There's another reason for not disrupting your normal schedule.

If you do there's a chance the police might spot it, and if they do it wouldn't be long before they worked out that someone's been kidnapped.'

And the first thing they'd do after that would be to freeze the family funds and even try to intervene in the affairs of the bank.

'Agreed,' Rossi said on behalf of the bank and the family.

Haslam took the holding script and rewrote it.

CONCERN OVER PAOLO	Is he alive?
TELEPHONE NUMBER AND TIME	Keep saying it.
MONEY	Can't even think about money until I know he's alive.
IF PRESSED	Just prove he's alive.

AND CLEAN PHONE AND TIME.

'You'll want some time to yourselves, to talk through what I've told you today. I suggest we arrange a meeting for tomorrow. There are other things to discuss, but I think Francesca has enough to handle until then.'

Why not deal with them now? It was in the way Umberto turned.

'Not today.' Francesca's voice was suddenly tired. I've had enough for one day, more than I can cope with. Just give me twenty-four hours to take on board what he's already told me, then I'll be able to face the rest. She called for the housekeeper to telephone for a cab. 'What time tomorrow?'

'Remember what I told you,' Haslam reminded her. 'That we should build our meetings into your normal routines. Unless, of course, something happens.' He knew she was having difficulty accepting what he was telling them. 'If it's in the evening it shouldn't be over dinner. It should be a business meeting like any other.'

'Six-thirty,' Francesca suggested.

'If the kidnappers make contact what time will you tell them to ring the clean phone?'

'Seven in the evening.'

'Good. I'll be at the hotel. If I leave it for any reason I'll be carrying a pager.' He gave them the details. 'One last thing. In case the kidnappers call, are you happy to be here by yourself or do you want someone with you?'

'The housekeeper will stay when I need her. I'm fine.'

The cab was waiting. He shook each of their hands and left.

The evening was warm and the three cars he had seen when he arrived were still there: the Saab, the BMW and the Mercedes, the driver and minder sitting in it like a calling card. Perhaps he should have said something about it at the meeting, except that then he hadn't been sure that the Mercedes was the banker's.

By the time he reached the Marino it was dusk.

His room was large and well-furnished and faced on to the inner courtyard, so that the sound of the Milan traffic was deadened. The bathroom was well-equipped, the wallpaper was flowered but relaxing, and an ornate fan was suspended from the ceiling, circling slowly. The two armchairs were low but comfortable, and the escritoire set against one of the windows was large enough to work at. The television was in a walnut cabinet in one corner, the minibar beside it.

After the meeting his clothes smelt of cigarette smoke. He stretched the stiffness from his back, unpacked, and took a shower. Then he dressed – casual clothes and shoes – arranged for a dry cleaning service every day, and began the case log. Kidnap and kidnappers; victim and family, in which he included the banker Rossi; security and other problems, plus the bank itself.

KIDNAP   From hotel room. Bodyguards present at all other
           times.
           Switzerland overnight after return from London.
           Police not informed.
           Genuine?

Because sometimes people, even bankers, faked their own disappearances. For money or fear or any number of reasons.

KIDNAPPERS   Professionals.

VICTIM   Bodyguard plus back-up.
             Why? Especially when no specific threat.

Paolo Benini had been carrying three bodyguards and one driver, effectively four minders, but at the time he had been out of Italy.

So either he was special, or whatever he was working on was.

FAMILY   *Father dominant.*
               Wife strong.
               Brother would come through.
               Banker calculating.

So what about them; what about Francesca and Umberto and Marco? What about the banker Rossi?

Francesca was quiet and still in shock, but she already showed signs of strength, which was positive. Francesca was fighting back, trying to get into it. Yet there were also signs of friction in her relationship with her father-in-law, which might prove negative. Plus there was something intangible about her and Paolo.

Which wasn't quite what he meant.

What he really meant was that there had been something about Francesca's description of Paolo that reminded him of himself. *We've been married sixteen years. He's away a lot now, so the girls miss him.* Which was what his own wife would say of him. He brushed the uneasiness aside and continued with the case log.

Francesca would be strong, but Francesca had given him nothing about Paolo. So what about Francesca? Did she have a lover or did Paolo have a mistress? Or was Paolo gay? It had happened before on a kidnap.

Marco would get the courier's job. Umberto would treat him like shit, but Marco would do what was needed.

Which left Umberto and Rossi.

Umberto Benini appeared to be the central figure, yet Umberto wasn't the power-broker. Umberto would puff and blow, but in the end Umberto would snap his fingers for Francesca to pour them each another cognac and then he would do whatever the bank suggested.

SECURITY   *Check cars outside, especially Mercedes.*

PROBLEMS   *Bank involvement might upset negotiations if*
                   kidnappers find out.
                   Family might not accept recommendations.

The bank might be seen to be involved either by the cars outside, or by the way the management team decided to conduct the negotiations. Which led to the second problem, the feeling he'd had the moment he'd introduced himself and Umberto Benini had intervened, the sense, almost a foreboding, that this one was going to be difficult. Of course they were all difficult, of course the families or companies he advised sometimes found it hard to accept what he was telling them. But all through the meeting that afternoon and evening he'd been increasingly aware of the unease growing in him.

It was as if the dawn mist was hanging over them, he had thought at one stage; yet it was late morning, the sun was up, and the mist should have vanished with the day.

It was as if he was dug into an OP, an observation post, he had thought at another point of the meeting; the target in front of him but the eerie feeling that he was facing the wrong way.

He was tired, he told himself now as he had told himself earlier. Kidnap negotiations took it out of you, drained the life and body and soul from you. Because for one or two months, sometimes three, you ate and slept and breathed it; thought of nothing but the kidnapper and his victim and how you could get that victim back safely.

So he was drained, he admitted, especially after the last job. He should have taken that break after Lima, should have gone home and spent time with Meg and the boys. But he hadn't. So he should stop assigning blame, grab a good night's sleep, and get on with it.

He moved to the last item of the case log.

BANK   *Logical they should be represented.*
        Anything else?

Why should there be anything else?

Now that the others had left the apartment seemed empty. Francesca opened the windows to clear the cigarette smoke, then phoned the girls, showered, went to bed, and tried to remember what had been agreed at the meeting with the Englishman and the discussion after he had left.

Some of the things he had said were reasonable, Umberto had conceded, except that they were logical and precisely what they themselves would have done. Then Umberto had downed the cognac and waved to her to pour him and Rossi another.

The family and the bank were behind her, though. She knew she had the full backing of the bank, Rossi had told her as they left. And that was what mattered. Even though she didn't always like the way Umberto tried to dominate his sons, her, her children. Even if she didn't totally trust Rossi.

And what about you Paolo? Why hadn't she told the Englishman the truth? Okay, she hadn't told the Englishman about the other properties they owned and the investments in Italy and overseas, most of them hidden from the authorities. But that wasn't what she meant. Why hadn't she told the Englishman about what her relationship with Paolo was really like? Not in front of the others, perhaps; especially not in front of Umberto.

So what about the Englishman and the things the Englishman had told her? Her mind was too confused and her body too cold to answer. She pulled the bedclothes tight around her and waited for the phone call in the dark. When she checked the time less than an hour had passed; when she checked again only another thirty minutes. The fear engulfed her, gnawed at her, till she was almost physically sick. When first light came she was unsure whether or not she had slept; when the housekeeper brought her coffee she was still shivering.

She wouldn't go to the office today, she decided; today she would sit and wait by the telephone, as she had every day since the first terrible news. She changed her mind. Today she would go to the office, because that was what the man called Haslam had told her to do, and all she wanted, in the grey swirling panic that was her brain, was for someone to tell her what to do and when and where to do it.

Ninety minutes later she drove to the building in one of the streets off Piazza Cadorna. It was good to be out of the house, she thought as she parked the car; good to be in the sun and see people. It was good to have something other than the kidnap to think about, good to check with the secretary and the other designers and artists and craftsmen she employed, good to hear from a client about how pleased they were, even good to sort out a problem.

'How's Paolo?' someone asked, and the clouds gathered again as if they had never cleared.

'Away on business,' she forced herself to say, forced herself to smile, almost decided to return to the apartment. Instead she took a tram to Porta Ticinese and walked along the canal at Alzaia Naviglio Grande. The sky was blue and the sun was hot, but most of the tourists who came to Milan didn't come here. At weekends, when the antique dealers and the bric à brac sellers put up their stalls, the streets along the canal were crowded, but today they were quiet. Halfway along a fashion photographer was taking shots of a male model. The photographer was short and energetic, and the model was tall and beautiful, aquiline features and striking eyes. She sat on the stone wall of the canal and watched.

So what about the Englishman?

May I call you Francesca? he had asked.

Paolo's away a lot now, so the girls miss him, she had said. And for a moment she had sensed that Haslam understood what she meant.

Thank you for allowing me to make decisions for myself, she had thought when Umberto had decreed she should be the negotiator and Haslam had replied that before she decided she should know what the task involved. Thank you for treating me like an individual.

And Haslam had told her what to say on the phone and given her a script to follow, even though Umberto had changed it after the Englishman had left.

So Haslam was her friend. Her guide and her protector. But not always.

Because Haslam had said there was a second reason why she should maintain a normal routine, because if she didn't the police might spot it and freeze the family funds. So Haslam was not only treating it like a business, he had even used the word itself. The meeting this evening should be a business meeting like any other, he had said.

Therefore tonight he would be hard on her, tonight he would tell her she had to treat Paolo like a business item, because that was how the kidnappers would consider him. Tonight he would even say that she shouldn't think of Paolo as her husband but as an item in the profit and loss account.

Rossi's meeting with the chairman was at ten.

'We're sure Paolo Benini's been kidnapped?' Negretti came to the point immediately.

He hasn't done a bunk, hasn't got another woman and run off with some of the bank's funds?

'Positive.'

It was a sign of the future that the chairman had personally chosen him to represent BCI in the Benini kidnapping, Rossi was aware. Yet that future would also be determined by a successful outcome.

72

For that reason his brief to Negretti had been carefully prepared; for that reason he had already decided to emphasize the positive elements of the first meeting with the consultant.

'But the kidnappers haven't yet been in touch?' Negretti had a way of staring at you as he spoke.

'Not yet.' Perhaps Rossi's next statement was factual, perhaps he was already covering himself. 'The consultant says it's normal. He expects them to be in touch soon.'

How much will the ransom be, he assumed the chairman would ask next.

'And once they do, how long will the negotiations take?'

Not long . . . the response was implied in the question, the way it was spoken, the way Negretti rolled the cigar between his fingers. Except that wasn't what Haslam seemed to be suggesting. They hadn't covered it yet, but Haslam seemed to be preparing them for a long and bumpy ride.

'We should be able to wrap it up quickly.'

The chairman stared at him across the desk. 'You're confident about that?'

'Absolutely.'

*   *   *

Francesca was kissing him, running her tongue against him. On the slopes behind the villa where the vines grew he could hear the girls playing, in the swimming pool in front the water shimmered in the mid-morning sun. Paolo laughed as Francesca nibbled him again and thought about the telephone call he had to make and the fax he had to sort out, the check with the bank that everything was in order.

In an hour they'd call the girls and take lunch – bread and wine and cheese. In the winter, when the cold settled and the fire roared in the stone-walled kitchen, it would be a heavier wine, a casserole simmering on the stove.

Francesca's kiss was slightly sharper. He'd make the phone call now, he decided, confirm the details on the fax that had been delivered last night, perhaps contact London and Zurich as well as head office in Milan. He reached for the mobile and felt the bite as he did so. Woke and realized.

The rat was on his leg, eyes staring at him and mouth twitching.

He screamed and tried to pull away. Cursed: cursed the rat, cursed the manacle round his ankle which stopped him moving, cursed Francesca.

The sound came from nowhere.

The routine was always the same: the first shuffle of feet in the darkness beyond the circle of the hurricane lamp, perhaps voices, then a second lamp held high and the two men at the iron bars of his cell.

He looked at them without moving.

The men were roughly dressed and wore hoods, holes cut in them for eyes, nose and mouth. One held the lamp and the other the plate. The man with the lamp unlocked the door of the cell and the second came in, placed the plate on the sand of the floor, took the two buckets from the corner, and stepped out. The first locked the door again, then the two disappeared in to the darkness.

Paolo Benini waited. His back was against the wall and his legs and body were pulled into a bundle, his legs up and his arms wrapped round himself. His shirt was stained with food and drink, and his trousers smelt of urine.

The sounds of feet came again from the darkness, the second lamp appeared again and the two men stood outside the bars of the cell. Not once had they spoken to him, or to each other in his immediate presence. The man with the lamp unlocked the door and the second placed the two buckets of fresh water on the floor.

It was the moment Paolo Benini already feared the most.

The doors of the cell clanged shut, the key rasped in the lock, the footsteps faded in the black, and he was alone again.

*   *   *

The weather had changed slightly, was more humid, more oppressive. Haslam felt the change as he left the hotel.

Maintain a timetable independent of the kidnapping, he had told Francesca, build a routine that will keep you sane. The same for himself. That morning, therefore, he had begun his own schedule: an hour's run, breakfast, examination of the options, then the first of the museums – one in the morning and another that afternoon. Except he'd been there before, done it before: the last time he'd had a job in Milan and the time before that.

At three he took a cab to Via Ventura, even though the meeting was not till six-thirty.

Via Ventura sloped slightly east to west, the apartment block towards the lower end and set back on the left. At the top of the street, on the right, was a café, the Figaro; the waiters were smartly dressed and there was an awning over the tables and chairs on the pavement. Below it was a line of shops and boutiques, all expensive yet all busy, and all with apartments above them. The pavement was wide and lined with lime trees, an occasional bench beneath them. Down the right side of the road, though not the left, were parking spaces, cut into the pavement rather than on the road itself.

Sixteen bays – he divided the area into units and counted them. The apartment block and the parking area at its front visible from bays eight to thirteen, counting from the top; the line of vision from numbers one to eight obstructed by trees on the left side of the road, and from numbers fourteen to sixteen by trees on the right.

From just below the parking area a side road cut right, again lined with shops and apartments. On the opposite side of the road was a small garden, a fountain in the middle and an apartment block behind. Most of the accommodation seemed private, except for a small hotel overlooking the fountain and a block of service flats near the Beninis' apartment, both expensive.

The Saab and BMW were parked in front of the apartment, and the same two men were sitting in the Mercedes. He gave his name at the security grille and took the lift to the fifth floor. The family, plus the banker, were already at their places round the table. He shook hands with each of them and accepted a coffee.

'No contact from the kidnappers?' he asked.

'No.'

'What about the crisis management team?'

'We've agreed.' Umberto Benini told him. 'Myself as chairman and Francesca as negotiator. I would have liked Signore Rossi to play a more prominent role, but the bank really should keep a low profile, so Marco's the courier.'

Haslam nodded and took the meeting on.

'There are certain things to discuss: how we ask the kidnappers to prove that Paolo is alive, the details of the ransom, and the ways of communicating with the kidnappers. Plus something else, something basic.'

It was better to confront them with it and make them confront it now.

'Kidnapping is a business. They have something you want – Paolo. And you have something they want – money. You have to think of it like that, nothing more. It sounds harsh, but it's the best way, perhaps the only way, of getting Paolo back.'

She knew what Haslam would tell her, Francesca thought, and now he had.

'Their first demand will be a starting point; what they expect will be substantially below that. The amount they accept depends on a number of factors, things like how much the research and preparation has already cost, plus their other expenses, past and present. The longer the kidnap lasts the more the man controlling it is paying out. What the kidnappers ask, and what they will accept, also depends on the going rates.'

Francesca could not believe what he was telling her, how he was telling her.

'The major kidnappings in Italy at the moment are breaking down into two distinct groups, depending on the size of the first demand. Where the first demand is ten miliardi, the amount agreed is averaging 500 million lire.'

Which, at an exchange rate of £400 to a million lire, was a start price of £4 million and a settlement of £200,000.

'Where the first demand is in the region of five miliardi, the average final payment is 450 million.'

Thus a starting price of £2 million and a final figure of £180,000.

How can you put a price on my husband's life? Francesca's eyes bored into him. How can you say on average this, on average that?

'When the starting demand is ten miliardi, the victim is being released after an average of one hundred days; when it's five miliardi the victim is released after an average of sixty-six.'

Christ, thought Rossi. The chairman would kill him if it took half, even a quarter, that time.

'The obvious temptation is to pay as much as you can as quickly as you can. This is wrong. The kidnapper starts high and we start low, so that we encourage him to lower his expectations. When we raise our offer we don't add too much too quickly.'

'Why not?' Francesca heard her own voice.

Because the bank was insured, she thought; therefore the company paying the ransom would want to keep it to a minimum, therefore Haslam was on a bonus if he came in with a low settlement.

'If we pay too much we run the risk of the kidnappers thinking there might be a lot more. If we pay too quickly he might say thanks for the deposit, now for the real money. He might even demand a second or even a third ransom.'

How do you know? She was still staring at him. How can you say such things?

Because I've been here before – he stared back at her. Because long after Paolo's home I'll be in a room like this with someone like you staring at me and accusing me the way you are now.

'I'm not saying it will come to this,' he told them. 'All I'm doing is telling you the structure. Which is why I'm here.'

'What else?' The question was from both Umberto and Francesca, the disgust in his voice and the fear and the hate in hers.

'We have to decide the proof question Francesca asks to make sure that Paolo is alive.'

'Something to do with the bank.' Rossi's intervention was short and sharp. 'That way I can verify it.'

That way I not only control the situation, but prove to the chairman that I do.

'It's normally personal.' Haslam looked at the banker then at the others in turn. 'Something only Paolo would know, nothing the kidnappers could find out from their research.'

'We'll think on it.' Umberto again.

Haslam focused on Marco. 'The last point is communication. After the first calls they might tell you to collect a letter or package, and specify the place. It'll be close to the clean phone, probably two or three minutes away. That gives them time to place it after they've given Francesca the message, but it gives you time to get there in case the police are tapping the phone and try to get there before you. It will also be a place where they can keep you under observation.'

The younger son began to speak but Haslam stopped him.

'There's something else you should keep in mind. Just as they'll try to put pressure on Francesca in the phone calls, so they'll use the dead letter drops to apply a similar pressure on all of you.'

How . . . no one asked.

'If it's a letter, it might simply contain instructions, or it might contain a note from Paolo. What you have to remember is that whatever he writes will have been dictated to him.'

And if it's a package . . . Francesca had heard the stories and read the newspaper articles.

'If it's a package it might contain an audio or video tape of Paolo. Either way he'll probably sound or look bad. You don't worry about that. They'll have made him sound or look that way.'

'What about other packages?' Francesca allowed the fear to grow.

'The key thing to remember is that packages are also part of the bargaining process,' Haslam told them all, but talked to her in particular. 'Packages are one of the ways the kidnappers will put pressure on you. Therefore they might contain something which is blood-stained, they might even contain a part of a body. In ninety-nine per cent of cases the blood is fake and the body part didn't come from the victim.'

How can you tell me this? Francesca stared at him. How can you do this to me? Yesterday you helped me, protected me, gave me strength. But today you're taking it all from me, today you're treating me worse than Umberto treats me.

'The other part of the communication is you to them.' Haslam took them to the next stage. 'You obviously can't phone them, so you tell them you want to speak with them by placing adverts in newspapers. You put a specified advert in and they then know you're waiting at the telephone at the appointed time. It's also a way of you telling them to get in touch with you after a prolonged period of silence from them.'

'Why silence?' Umberto.

'Because silence is another weapon; sometimes kidnaps go for weeks without contact.'

This wasn't what the chairman would want to hear – Rossi glanced at Umberto then back at Haslam. So begin thinking it through now, begin to plan what he could use and how he could use it. Work out how he could hide behind Haslam and how he could use Haslam when the crunch came with the chairman.

'Anything else?' Umberto again.

'The first is your personal security. Double or triple kidnappings are not common, but not unknown. Marco is an obvious target when he makes the pick-ups, but he also has a certain inbuilt protection as he's part of their communication system with you.'

'The next?' Umberto stared at him, elbows on the table, chin resting on his hands and eyes unblinking.

'We've said that the bank will keep as low a public profile as possible.'

'So?'

'If the Mercedes driver and bodyguard outside belong to BCI, it might not be the sort of profile the bank wants.'

'We'll sort it out.' And meeting over. It was in the way Umberto Benini snapped shut the file. 'If you would leave us so that we might consider what you have just told us.'

The family meeting which followed lasted little more than thirty minutes. As he and the Beninis left, Rossi took Francesca's hand.

'I know what Haslam said about not offering too much too quickly, but if it means getting Paolo out, the bank will pay whatever it takes.'

A good man to have by your side, Umberto Benini knew, the right man to rely on.

'Thank you.' Francesca tried to smile and went to the window, watched as the cars pulled away.

She had been right about Haslam. The bastard *had* told them to put a price on Paolo's life, had almost gone further. Had only just stopped short of telling her to think about how much she was prepared to pay and of suggesting that there might be a moment when she should abandon Paolo to the vultures. At least Umberto was adamant that they wouldn't give in, at least Rossi had said the bank would pay whatever it took.

The telephone rang.

Oh God no, she thought; please God no, she prayed. She turned and began to call for the housekeeper then remembered she hadn't asked the woman to stay. Why hadn't she listened to Haslam when he'd asked if she'd be all right by herself ? Why hadn't he asked her again tonight?

She made herself pick up the phone.

'Hello, Mama, it's me.'

She sank into the chair and fought back the tears as her younger daughter asked after her father, heard herself lying.

'And where's Gisella?'

'Riding. Do you want her to phone you when she gets in?'

'That would be nice.'

The evening was slipping away. She stared out of the window and told herself it was time for bed.

The telephone rang again. Francesca smiled and picked it up. 'Gisella,' she began to say. 'Good to hear you. How was the ride . . . ?'

*   *   *

The Benini kidnap was going well, Vitali decided: the banker was safely concealed in the fortress which was Calabria, and the family had been waiting long enough to be feeling the strain.

It was eleven in the morning, the light playing through the window on to the large wooden desk in the centre of his office; the telephones on the left, fax and computer on the right, and the recording equipment and mobile phone in the drawer. The mobile rented and paid for through a false name and bank account to which he could not be linked, in case the carabinieri broke the organization's security and tried to trace him. Plus the scrambler which he would use because mobiles were notoriously insecure.

He was alone, as he always was at this time of day. He opened the drawer, clipped on the scrambler and dialled the first number.

'Angelo. This is Toni.'

Angelo Pascale was in his mid-thirties, thinly built so that his suits hung slightly off his shoulders, and lived in a two-room flat up a spiral staircase off a courtyard close to Piazza Napoli, in the west of the city. He had never met the man he knew as Toni, but Toni paid well and on time, and as long as Toni was in the kidnap business then there was always work for people like himself.

He clipped on the scrambler and keyed in the code Toni told him.

'Tonight, nine o'clock.' Vitali gave him the address. 'I'll phone again at ten.' He ended the call and sat back in the chair.

So how much?

The going rate was between 450 and 500 million lire and the first demand was around either five or ten miliardi, so that was what they would be expecting. Nobody would pay that much, of course, but after deducting his expenses even 450 million would still show a good profit.

He leaned forward again and dialled the number of the negotiator, again using the scrambler. In the old days it had been anonymous calls to faceless people waiting at public telephones. Some organizations still used the old techniques, he supposed, but a man had to move with the times.

'Musso, it's Toni.' Mussolini was good, not as good as Vitali himself had been, but still one of the best. Mussolini was not his real name, but it was what the man called Toni called him, and what the negotiator called himself when he spoke to the families of Toni's victims. 'Tonight, nine o'clock.' He gave him the telephone number.

So how much? He was still rolling the figures in his head. The fact that the bank carried a kidnap insurance meant that a consultant would already be involved. And if a consultant was involved he would already have told the family about the going rates and the opening demands, so that was what the family would be expecting, would have forgotten that the consultant would have told them the figures were only guidelines.

'Open at seven.'

Miliardi, Mussolini understood. Interesting figure.

'The victim is called Paolo Benini, the number is his town apartment. Wife Francesca, who'll probably take the call. Otherwise father Umberto or younger brother Marco. I'll call again at nine-thirty.'

Angelo Pascale left the flat at one, collected the Alfa, checked the *tuttocittà*, the city map which came with the telephone directory, and drove to Via Ventura.

The street was busy and the shops and pavements crowded, mostly with young people and all of them apparently with money. The address was towards the bottom on the left, a number of parking places just visible when he stood outside the address. He drove up and down the street for twenty minutes till one of those he required came vacant, and went for a cappuccino in the Figaro. At five he noted the cars parked outside the block, again an hour later. From six he logged the movements of every car leaving or arriving at the address, paying special attention to those left at the front.

Mussolini was in position by eight-thirty. He would use a public telephone, because if the carabinieri were trying to trace the call it would get them nowhere. And he would switch locations: Central Station tonight, perhaps the airport the night after. Places a businessman would pass unnoticed.

The recording equipment was in his briefcase. At eight fifty-five he went to one of the kiosks in the marble mausoleum which was the ground floor of Central Station, confirmed that the phone was working, placed the suction cup of the cassette recorder on to the mouthpiece, and checked the time. Punctuality was not only a virtue, he had long understood, it was also a tool.

It was nine o'clock.

He inserted the phone card and punched the number.

'Gisella. Good to hear you.' It was as if the woman had been expecting someone else, as if she was talking to a child. 'How was the ride?'

'Signora Benini.'

Francesca almost froze. 'Yes.'

'We have him. If you want to see him again we want seven miliardi.'

81

Her mind was numb, refusing to function, the thoughts suddenly spinning and the brain struggling to navigate through the shock. Oh Christ what should she say, dear God what should she do? The script – it was as if she could hear Haslam's voice – just read the script. We'll re-write the script slightly, Umberto was telling her, just to make it right, just to make it proper; don't tell Haslam though, just keep it to ourselves. We'll pay anything to get Paolo home with you and the girls, the banker Rossi was telling her, let's just make sure we get him back.

'Seven miliardi, Francesca,' Mussolini told her again. 'Otherwise you never get him back.'

Don't even think, Haslam's voice was telling her, calming her, just read the script. A clean phone – it was as if she could hear him – make sure you get across the number and the time. She was shouting the number, almost screaming the number. Seven-thirty in the evening, she was telling him. 'Is Paolo alive, tell me how he is. Let me speak to him.' She was scrabbling for the script, still saying the number and the time.

'Seven miliardi, Francesca.' Mussolini's voice was calm but assertive. 'That's what you pay if you want to see him again.'

Now that she had started saying the number she couldn't stop. How much, her mind was still asking. Seven miliardi. Oh my God. Not even the bank could pay that, she began to say. She was still saying the number, telling the man on the phone that she'd try but the bank wouldn't go that high. Realized that the kidnapper had put the phone down.

Her entire body was shaking. She stood for two full minutes, the telephone in her right hand, the fingers of her left holding the cradle down, and her entire body convulsed. Then she told herself to breathe deeply and keyed the number of her father-in-law.

'They've called,' was all she managed to say.

Haslam was crossing the Piazza Duomo when the pager sounded. He used the telephones on the edge of the square and called the control, then Umberto Benini.

'Meeting in an hour at Signora Benini's apartment,' Benini told him, and rang off.

No explanation, Haslam thought; there was only one reason for Umberto to call him mid-evening, though. Not *Francesca's apartment*, not even *my son's* or *my daughter-in-law's apartment*. The man's son has been kidnapped, he reminded himself; therefore give him time to come to terms with that fact and with what he has to do. At least Umberto hadn't given anything away on an open phone.

When he arrived the cars were parked outside and the others were seated round the table. Francesca white-faced and fingers wrapped tight round a cognac; Umberto Benini at the head of the table, Marco saying nothing; Rossi apparently summoned from a function and wearing an immaculate evening suit, the white silk scarf still round his neck.

The cassette recorder was in the centre of the table, and the script which he had written for Francesca was in front of Umberto Benini. He took his place opposite the father.

'Signora Benini received the call at nine o'clock.' Benini led the discussion. 'The kidnappers want seven miliardi.' Not the five or ten you said – the stare conveyed the message. 'The signora managed to pass on the number of the clean phone, plus the time.'

'Good.' Haslam nodded then looked at Francesca. 'The first call is always the worst. You were here by yourself?'

She nodded.

'Then you've done better than anyone could expect.'

He turned back to Umberto.

'You've listened to the tape?'

Of course you've listened to it, the tape was the first thing you checked after you'd talked to Francesca, though you might not have told me because you've rewound it. Because you called the others before you called me, made sure they got here first.

The father pressed the play button.

'Gisella. Good to hear you. How was the ride?'

'Signora Benini.'

Haslam heard the change in Francesca's voice as she realized and saw the tightening of her face as she listened now, saw her age Christ knew how many hundreds of years.

'Yes.'

They listened in silence. When the conversation was finished they listened again, then Haslam turned to her. 'You really did do well, much better than we could have expected.'

You really didn't do that badly, he wanted to tell, but you'd have done better if you hadn't received conflicting instructions.

'Francesca managed to get over the number of the clean phone, and the time she'll be there. The first thing we have to decide now is who goes with her. Marco is the courier, therefore if anything is to be collected at any time it makes sense that he's there to take the message.'

And . . .

'If the kidnappers have done their research properly, which they seem to have, they'll already know that he's Paolo's brother and might even have chosen him to be the go-between.'

Marco, they agreed.

'When they phone tomorrow, the key thing is that Francesca insists on proof that Paolo is alive. We want this anyway, but it also gives her a way of not replying to the kidnapper's ransom demand. We'll work on the script later. In the meantime Francesca needs the question that the kidnappers will put to Paolo.'

'Anything else?' Umberto Benini asked.

'Only one. The cars. I appreciate that tonight was an emergency, but the Mercedes is outside again.'

Vitali's call to Mussolini was at nine-thirty precisely, the call scrambled and Vitali recording it.

'How'd it go?'

'Well. She was expecting another call, possibly from one of her daughters, and was therefore disoriented. You want to hear it?'

Of course he wanted to hear, Vitali thought. 'Why not.'

The woman was frightened and confused, which was normal, yet she had been controlled enough to pass on the number of a clean phone and the time she would be there. Which suggested that a consultant was already involved.

'Sounds good. Make the call tomorrow. I'll phone at eight.'

Thirty minutes later he placed the call to Angelo Pascale, noting the car models and numbers the stake-out read to him.

The Saab belonged to Benini's father and the BMW to his brother – the details had been part of his research. The Mercedes hadn't been seen before, but the fact that there was a bodyguard in it, and that the man it had taken away had left the flat with Umberto Benini, suggested that it was someone from BCI. It was interesting that the bank was so open about its involvement.

The dark wrapped round her, suffocating her. Francesca lay still with fear and tried to see the light, saw only the tallow yellow of the lamp and the shadows flickering against the wall of a cave. Thank God I didn't panic on the phone, she thought; thank God Haslam told me I did all right; thank God I didn't let Paolo down. Paolo's face was looking at her, his eyes searching for her and his voice calling out her name. Hold on, she tried to tell him, we haven't forgotten you, soon you'll be free again. The cave was cool but the night was hot and oppressive around her. She tried to fight it off, to pull the layer of fear from her face. It was two in the morning, the clock ticking by the bedside. She sat up and reached for a glass of water, sipped it slowly, then lay down again.

The sounds came from the darkness, the glow of the lamp, then the silence of the warders bringing him his food. Paolo Benini waited till they had gone then began to eat, not minding if the liquid of the soup splashed down the front of his shirt or if the remnants of the bread fell on to the floor. When he had finished eating he sniffed at the buckets, tried to remember which he had urinated in, then drank from what he hoped was the other.

Some time it would come to an end, of course. The bank carried kidnap insurance, and the bank would have paid anyway.

Every client wanted an efficient service, every client wished to avoid the red tape which might hinder their activities, and everyone bent over backwards to satisfy them. That was what banking was all about. Arab money, Jewish money, it made no difference. Money from the Middle or Far East, from Russia or America, it didn't matter. Except sometimes someone wanted a little more, which brought the bank an extra commission. But to get that commission the bank needed someone like Paolo Benini to set everything up, someone like Paolo Benini to make sure it was all in order and to sort out any problems which might arise. And the more clients who were happy the more custom came to the bank and the happier the bank was. Especially with the extras they were able to charge and the clients were prepared to pay.

You're clutching at clouds in the sky, the voice tried to tell him. You're thinking of things you did in the past, rather than what you have to do to survive the present.

Part of the groundwork had already been done before, of course, but it had been he, Paolo Benini, who had structured and developed it. Especially in the United States. He who had suggested they look for one of the small regional banks in danger of collapse in the eighties, buy it up but conceal the ownership, then make it profitable and use it as a front for BCI's black operations. He who had faced up to the conventional thinkers on the board and rejected the various banks which they had suggested, especially those with connections in Florida because those were the sort of places investigators from organizations like the US Federal Bank and the Justice Department and the Drug Enforcement Administration automatically looked to, because those were the sort of places already being used to launder money. He who had suggested they go west, look for a nice little bank in a nice little town where no one would suspect. A bank which no one knew was in trouble and with a president who could be persuaded to bend the rules to maintain the financial standing of the bank in general and himself in particular. He, Paolo Benini, who had personally chosen First Commercial of Santa Fe, and he, Paolo Benini, who had made the arrangements.

Forget all that, the voice told him, forget what's gone before. Just work out where you are and who you are. What you should be thinking about are Francesca and the girls, because they are the ones who will save you, who will provide the anchor which will moor your mind to some kind of sanity.

And just after he had arranged the takeover of First Commercial of Santa Fe, he and Myerscough had met – it was as if his brain was flicking between television channels.

Why was he thinking of Myerscough, the voice asked him.

Because Myerscough ran Nebulus, because Nebulus was the last account he had checked in London, and because he had therefore thought that Nebulus might be the subject of the fax he had received at the hotel. Except, of course, that the fax hadn't been genuine.

If any of his clients found out, however . . . If ever it became public knowledge, even within the limited public of that corner of the banking world, even within BCI itself, that he had been kidnapped . . . Therefore the bank would do everything in its power not just to secure his release, but to achieve it quickly.

You're still deluding yourself – the voice was fainter now, almost gone. Look at yourself, at the mess you're in. Food spilled on the floor and down your clothes and urine on your trousers. You don't even know which bucket you're urinating and defecating in and which you're drinking from. No wonder the rat came feeding.

The feet shuffled from the black, the lamp appeared, the guards removed the remnants of his food, and he was alone again.

4

Cath was curled beside him.

It was a long time since they'd met at Harvard, since they'd got to know each other in their final year. Then they'd gone their separate ways, she to law school and he, when his number had been drawn, to Vietnam. And that would have been the end of it. Except that once, during R and R, he'd written her; when he finally came home he'd found her number and called, and she'd visited him in hospital. Halfway through his own spell at law school they'd married; the night he'd got his first job she'd cooked him a candlelit dinner. Two years later she'd stood at his side when he'd run for his first public office.

Donaghue swung out of the bed, switched off the alarm before it woke her, and went to the bathroom. When he returned the bed was empty and the smell of breakfast was drifting up from the kitchen.

It was five-thirty. He started the Lincoln, waved back as she watched him from the front door, and drove to National airport. Twenty minutes later he was on the shuttle to La Guardia.

Pearson woke at six-thirty, showered, shaved and dressed. Evie was still asleep, her legs sticking out from under the duvet and her hair across the pillow.

The house was on 6th SE, half a block from Independence Avenue and ten minutes' walk from the Hill. They'd bought it for a knock-down price, then sweated God knows how many weekends and holidays to get it as they wanted, had somehow squeezed the renovation between her professorship at Georgetown and his job on the Hill.

When he went upstairs she was still half asleep.

'See you tonight.'

She rolled over so he could kiss her.

'Be good.'

The morning was already warm; he left the house, crossed

Independence, and turned left on East Capitol Street. In front of him the white dome of the Hill glistened in the early light. By seven thirty-five he had collected a coffee and doughnut from the basement canteen and was at his desk checking his electronic mail. At eight-thirty he briefed the morning meeting.

'Senator Donaghue's in New York for a fund-raising breakfast. He'll be back at ten. Terry to collect him from National. Ten-thirty he meets a business delegation, Jonathan has the details. At eleven he's in the Senate; Barbara in charge of TV and radio interviews after. Eleven forty-five he's at the Vietnam Veterans Memorial; family paying their respects.'

For years now the families of the MIAs, the servicemen missing in action in Vietnam, had been campaigning in the hope that some of them might still be alive. Donaghue had championed their rights for greater information on reported sightings whilst cautioning against excessive hope. Six months earlier photographic evidence had been produced supposedly showing MIAs in a village in North Vietnam. One week ago they had been proven to be forgeries. Now the family of one of the men was coming to pay their respects at the polished black granite memorial in Constitution Gardens, and had asked Donaghue to join them, even though they were not from Donaghue's state.

One of the lawyers raised his hand. 'What chance of some coverage?'

'ABC, CBS and NBC feeding to local affiliates,' the press secretary told them. 'CNN there as well unless something else breaks, plus radio and newspapers.'

Pearson nodded, then continued.

'Twelve-thirty, Senate vote, Maureen accompanying him. One o'clock lunch at the National Democratic Club.'

There was a similar list of engagements for the afternoon and early evening, the final one at seven and lasting half an hour. And after that the meeting that wasn't on any schedule. The one they called the war council.

Mitchell woke at seven, the sun streaming through the windows of the houseboat and the sound of a helicopter beating up the Potomac. It was a Gangplank joke that you could always tell when something was up and running by the number of choppers coming up the river and banking left for the Pentagon and right for the White House. Just as you could tell how much communication traffic was going out of the Pentagon – and therefore whether something was going down – by the television interference, and whether the White House was working overtime by the number of late-night pizza deliveries.

The photographs were by the upturned steel helmet next to the Marine Corps badge, more by the television.

Don't forget, he told himself.

He showered, dressed, had breakfast on the sun deck, then took the metro rail to Union Station and walked to Dirksen Building.

The staff rooms of the Senate Banking Committee were on the fifth floor: three secretaries and a cluster of offices, some staffers having their own rooms and others sharing, computers and telephones on the desks, and the computers linked to the various databases to which the committee had access.

The desk he had been assigned was in a corner of one of the open plan areas, beneath a window. It was slightly cramped, but that was standard on the Hill, despite what people thought, and at least he could look out of the window. It was a pity he didn't have more privacy, but everyone in the office was on the same side, and if he needed to make any really secure calls he could do them from somewhere else.

He fetched himself a coffee from the cafeteria and settled down.

Money laundering or banking, Pearson had said, as long as it was something with which the ordinary man or woman in the street would identify. And nothing too official yet, by which Pearson had meant nothing too obvious. Just a trawl, see what there was around. More than just a trawl, though; make sure he had enough evidence so that when Donaghue officially launched the enquiry he already knew it would produce results. The announcement of the enquiry timed to give Donaghue extra publicity once he'd thrown his hat into the presidential ring, and the results ready for when he and his advisers decided to use them. Everything planned, nothing left to chance.

Mitchell sat forward in the chair and began the calls.

'Dick, this is Mitch Mitchell. Doing a job for the Senate Banking Committee and wondered if we should get together . . .'

To a lawyer at the Fed.

'Angelina, this is Mitch Mitchell. Assigned to Senate Banking for a while and thought I should give you a call . . .'

A banker in Detroit.

'Jay, this is Mitch Mitchell. Yeah, good to talk with you. How're you doing . . . ?'

To a journalist on Wall Street.

Look for his own investigation, try to find something that nobody else had, and he'd spend light years on it and get nowhere. Pick up on something somebody else was already working, though, take it beyond where their expertise or resources could go but offer to cut them in on the final play, and he might make it.

'Andie.' Drug Enforcement Administration in Tampa, Florida. 'Mitch Mitchell, long time no see. How'd you mean, you knew I was going to call. Why, what you got going?'

It would have to be good, though, have to be right. And he wouldn't mention Donaghue unless someone asked, because Donaghue was money in the bank and only to be used when necessary.

By lunchtime he had spoken to ten contacts, by mid-afternoon another three, two more phoning him back. Tomorrow it would be the same, the day after the same again. And after he'd talked to them he'd hit the road, get hunched up over a beer with those who might have a runner. Sometimes it would be coffee, sometimes dinner, sometimes twenty minutes behind closed doors. And not all the contacts male, some of the best would be female.

'Jim Anderton, please.' Anderton was an Assistant District Attorney in Manhattan, smart waistcoats and friendly manner. When it suited. Political ambitions and on the make.

'I'm sorry, Mr Anderton's in court. Can he call you back?'

Mitchell gave the receptionist his name and new office number. Anderton would call back even if he didn't have anything, because assistant DAs with political ambitions always did.

Tampa and Detroit seemed front runners at the moment, he decided, plenty of other options already emerging, though. He switched on the computer, built in a personal security code, and opened the first file of the investigation.

The armoured Chevrolet collected Brettlaw at seven. The family were seated round the breakfast table. Great house, great wife, great kids – he always appreciated being told. Great barbecues in the summer, great hiking trips in the fall, great skiing in the winter. When he'd had the time.

Fifteen minutes later the driver swung through the gates at Langley and turned under the main building. Brettlaw collected his briefcase and took the executive lift to the seventh floor. By nine, shortly before his meeting with the DCI, he was on his third coffee and his fourth Gauloise.

Costaine telephoned at eleven, via Brettlaw's secretary, asking if the DDO had ten minutes. If Costaine, as his Deputy Director for Policy, asked for ten minutes, it was Costaine's code for saying something was wrong. Not necessarily something that would change the world, just something which the DDO should know about, perhaps something which it would take the DDO to sort out. Besides, Costaine was Inner Circle; not Inner Circle of Inner Circle, but still part of the black projects.

Brettlaw told him to come up, and asked Maggie to put the remainder of his morning's engagements back ten minutes.

Costaine arrived three minutes later.

'There's a slight problem with Red River.'

He was seated in the leather armchair in front of Brettlaw's desk.

'What exactly?'

Red River was a worn-out mining town turned ski resort eight thousand feet up in the Southern Rockies. Apparently run down, apparently redneck. Great people and great snow. Red River was also the code for one of the black projects.

'Certain funds which should have been in place two days haven't arrived.'

'Important?'

Costaine ran his fingers through his crewcut. 'Delicate rather than important, but we should get it sorted out.' But he couldn't, because he was operations, not finance.

'Leave it with me. If it's not sorted by tomorrow let me know.'

He waited till Costaine left then telephoned for Myerscough to come up.

'The Nebulus accounts. Apparently some of the funds which were scheduled for transfer two days ago haven't made it.'

'No problem.'

Almost certainly it would be something as obvious as a bank clerk transposing two digits, Myerscough thought. It had happened before and would happen again. It was probably better to start in the middle rather than at the beginning or end of the chain — that way he'd reduce the work. Therefore he'd contact the fixer and get him to check that the funds had passed through the switch account in London. That way they could narrow down the problem area. And if the funds hadn't reached London he'd go back to First Commercial and ask why the money hadn't exited the US.

It was eleven Eastern Time, therefore he might just catch Europe before it closed down for the night. He left the seventh floor and returned to his own department on the fourth.

His office was in one corner, the rest of the section open plan, desks and computers, the technological whizz kids bent over them, sometimes fetching a coffee or iced water and leaning over someone else's shoulder, cross-fertilizing ideas and statistics or just talking. It was a good department with good people. He closed the door, called the first number before he'd even sat down, and looked through the glass.

Bekki Lansbridge was in her late twenties, an economist by training, and had been with the Agency five years and his department for the past eight months. She was five-seven, he guessed, almost five-eight, blond hair and long face. And there his description of her slipped in to the vernacular. Great ass, great chassis, great mover. Probably moving it for someone, except that it wasn't him. Perhaps one day she would.

The ringing stopped and he heard the voice of the personal assistant. Swiss and efficient.

'Is he there?' he asked.

'I'm afraid not.'

No enquiring who was calling and no suggestion he might like to leave a message. If he wished either then he would say so.

'When will he be back?'

'Probably tomorrow.'

He called Milan.

'Good afternoon. Is he there?'

'I'm afraid not.'

'When could I speak to him?'

'Possibly tomorrow.'

There was the slightest hesitation, he thought. Certainly the day after . . . it was implied, but without conviction, as if the secretary was unsure herself.

It was unlike the fixer. The contact was often away setting things up and meeting people like Myerscough. The two of them tried to meet at least twice a year and to talk at least once a month, even when there was nothing much to discuss, because the two of them had set up the system, and set it up good. So it wasn't unusual for the Italian to be out and about – that was his job. What was unusual was for him to be out of touch – not phoning his office at least twice a day, even if he couldn't tell his people where he was and who he was with.

'Thank you.'

There was no problem, though. All he had to do was check with the bank which would have made the wire transfer to BCI in London, and if the problem had come up before London there'd be no reason to worry about Europe. He glanced at Bekki Lansbridge again and punched the number.

'Good morning,' the switchboard operator answered immediately. 'First Commercial Bank of Santa Fe.'

'Good morning, may I speak to the president?'

The lawyers were waiting. For forty minutes Brettlaw checked with them the testimony he would deliver to the Senate Select Committee on Intelligence that afternoon, then took a working lunch of coffee and Gauloises. The committee was at two. At one-thirty the Chevrolet pulled out the main gate and turned on to Route 123.

At any other time, perhaps, on any other day, he might have sat back and allowed himself thirty seconds to think about Nebulus, about the money going into and through it. Perhaps he was about to. Perhaps he would have told himself there was no need, that it was Myerscough's job.

The secure telephone rang. The sky above was crystal blue, he would remember later, and the trees were a peaceful green.

'Red Man.' The code – even on the encryptor – for Operations. 'Bonn's hit the panic button. Nothing more yet. Will keep you informed.'

Nobody hit the panic button for nothing; Ops didn't inform the DDO unless it was five-star. His mind was calm and ordered. There were two things he could do: order his driver back to Langley, or tell Ops to keep him informed and continue with his schedule. He had been in crises before, that was his job. Had worked out – in the dark of the night, when a man was alone with himself or his Maker – what he would do in certain scenarios. It was how he had survived Moscow, how he had made himself the man he was.

'Keep me informed.'

The Chevrolet crossed Theodore Roosevelt Bridge and headed east up Constitution Avenue, the crowds in the parks and the bands playing. So why had Bonn hit the panic button, what was happening?

The secure phone rang again.

'Bonn Chief of Station down. Repeat. Bonn CoS down. No more details.'

Oh Christ, he thought.

Zev Bartolski was Chief of Station in Bonn, and Zev Bartolski was his friend. More than that. Zev Bartolski was his point man in the black projects. Zev Bartolski was Inner Circle of Inner Circle, Zev Bartolski was Wise Man of Wise Men.

'The DCI knows?' He sliced through the disbelief and the shock.

'Yes.'

'Keep me informed.'

He raised the partition between himself and the driver, and considered what might be happening. Shut his eyes and tried to work out the connections. Sealed off the image of the man, wiped out every trace of Zev's wife and children, and focused on what the hell might be going down.

Who? Why? How? What was Bonn working on that connected to anything else? At least the CoS hadn't been kidnapped, at least they wouldn't have to worry as they had worried over poor Bill Buckley in Beirut. At least Zev wasn't going to be tortured for what he knew.

The logic divided, separated Zev Bartolski as Bonn CoS from Zev Bartolski in his role in the black projects. The position of Chief of Station almost a cover. For the other side, even for his own people.

A problem with Red River, Costaine had said that morning, certain monies not through on time. Now Zev taken out. The link screamed at him. Except that the two were separate – in personnel and region, in objectives and functions. No connection at all, different and distinct parts. Except they were both black ops.

He keyed in the DCI's number and activated the Gold Code.

'This is Tom. I've just heard. I'm on my way to the Hill but will return if necessary.'

There was no panic in his voice, not even an edge of excitement or adrenalin.

'What do you think?' The DCI had a Texan drawl.

'No need at the moment. Perhaps the best thing is an even keel, show everyone we're not panicking.'

'Agreed.'

The Chevrolet passed by the Washington Memorial. The phone rang again. In Europe it was early evening.

'Red Man. Bonn CoS was killed when the car in which he was travelling was blown up.'

'His car?' Brettlaw asked. 'How was it blown up? Where was he going and what was he doing?'

94

Zev's car was armoured, but even the best armoured cars were vulnerable to a bomb or land mine exploding beneath them.

'Unclear. The First Secretary has also been killed.'

Brettlaw was still calm, still almost cold. He could speak to Bonn direct, but everyone would be speaking to Bonn. Bonn would be so jammed with communications that they'd be snowed under. Even so he was tempted to call off the session that afternoon and return to Langley.

'Check on the vehicle the CoS was travelling in,' he issued the orders. 'Check whether the First Secretary was killed in the same incident or a separate one. Find out what they were doing and why. Get some indication why the CoS might have been targeted.'

The Chevrolet passed Senate Russell Building and approached Senate Hart. He keyed his secretary's number and activated the encryptor. Maggie Dubovski was mid-forties, career Agency like himself. One of the warhorses, one of the reliables. When he made DCI Maggie would go with him, would consider it the pinnacle of her career as he would consider it the pinnacle of his.

'You've heard?' he asked her.

'Yes.'

He named those officers to be placed on standby. 'Meeting in my office at five, unless you hear from me before.'

There was one other thing.

'Find out where Martha Bartolski and the kids are. Make sure they're okay.'

The driver showed his pass to the policeman on duty at the entrance to the parking area below Senate Hart and drove down into the half-light. The Director of Security for the Intelligence Committee was already waiting. Brettlaw shook his hand and was escorted to the set of rooms known simply as SH 219.

SH 219 housed the most secure room on Capitol Hill. The lift from the parking area was connected to it by series of other internal lifts, therefore no member of the public was able to see who was entering or leaving. The room itself was on the second floor of Hart Building, the hallway outside overlooking the courtyard round which Hart was built. The reception desk was opposite a set of double doors, but the doors themselves were opaque so that no one could see inside, and there were imitation doors along the rest of the wall on to the walkway. The committee room proper was entered through steel doors, the walls of the isolation area in which the committee held its deliberations were lead-lined, and further protection against electronic surveillance was provided by white noise.

Brettlaw smiled at the receptionist, signed the register, including the time he was entering the isolation area, and went inside.

The members were already waiting in the semicircle of seats on the platform in front of him. Today was the bad one, today the bastards would be after his blood. He took his place, and the doors were closed and locked, sealing off the committee. Then, and only then, did the chairman call the meeting to order and ask Brettlaw for his opening remarks.

'Before I begin, I have an announcement to make.' It would soon be public anyway, but there were certain members who would remember that the DDO had seen fit to brief them first. 'I have just been informed that the CoS Bonn has been assassinated.' He waited for the room to settle. 'This information was passed to me on my way here, as yet no other details are available. If any do become available during this session I will, of course, inform you immediately.'

The senior Republican rose. 'Mr Chairman, may I put on record the committee's horror at the news, and its appreciation of the Deputy Director's decision to attend despite it.'

'Noted.'

Even the liberals were shocked, Brettlaw thought wryly. Zev serving the Agency in death as in life.

The questioning began, slightly less ferocious than on previous occasions, but barbed anyway.

There were tricks, of course, almost tradecraft. Never tell a lie, because one day they might come back at you on it. But never tell the truth. Unless, of course, it suited you. Make what the politicians call lawyer's answers, play one committee against another, the Senate against the House of Representatives. And if they had you, if you were really up against it, run a dangle, either to them or the press, lay a bait that would make them think they were on to something but which would take them so far off course they were the other side of the globe from what you wanted to protect. But never make enemies, because one day you might be sitting in front of them at a confirmation hearing for the job at the top.

'Item 12d in budget document 4.' The committee man was like a buzzard, Brettlaw thought, hungry eyes and hooked nose.

So what the hell was running in Bonn? Why in Christ's name

did Zev have to die? How was it connected to the black projects? Was it connected to them? What about the financial discrepancy on the Red River project?

'Perhaps we could look at paragraph 10 . . .'

Don't patronize me, you bastard. Don't try your smooth *perhaps we could look at* . . . Don't try to sucker me. Today of all days. With Zev Bartolski splattered across some fucking street in some foreign fucking country.

'Yes, Senator.' His voice was calm and controlled.

'This is a major item of expenditure.'

He checked the relevant document. 'Yes.'

'Then could you explain how it relates to item 3, sub-item 9, on document 8 . . .'

The ass-hole was off course and out of sight. If he was anyway near the truth he'd be so far off the wall he'd be in the next room.

'If you insist, Senator . . .'

At three-thirty, and at Brettlaw's request, the committee broke early. By ten minutes past four he was receiving an overview briefing on Bonn in his office at Langley. At four twenty-five he met with the DCI, at five o'clock, according to the log which was kept, he received a fuller briefing on Bonn station, the men he had summoned seated round the conference table of his office.

'Zev and the First Secretary were travelling together.' Costaine led the briefing. 'They were killed when a bomb exploded near or below the car. They were on their way to an aeronautical exhibition. The explosion took place as they were nearing the location. The car was the First Secretary's, not Zev's. Detonation of the charge was probably by remote control.'

It was logical that Zev should be with the First Secretary and that he should be doing something public, Brettlaw was aware. Everyone knew who was Station Chief. In places like Bonn it was almost a public appointment.

'What was Zev doing there?' he asked.

'How'd you mean?'

'Was it in his diary for the day?'

'I'll get it checked.'

Brettlaw nodded and allowed him to continue.

'A team is already airborne in case Bonn needs extra cover. All operations from Bonn have been iced. The analysts are backtracking to see if they can pick up anything.'

'Any idea yet who's responsible?' He chainlit another Gauloise.

'No.'

'Where's Cranlow?'

Cranlow was Zev's number two.

'On his way back from Hamburg.'

'Effective as of now he's Chief of Station.' Brettlaw had already cleared it with the DCI; there was no point in showing indecision, every point in acting quickly and decisively, and being seen to do so. 'Samuelson transfers from Berlin as his point man. Don . . .' He turned to the man on his left. 'You fly to Bonn tonight, oversee things till the shit stops flying.' Not to get in the new CoS's way, just to be on hand to cover everyone's back. Good decision, they knew, the DDO reacting the way they knew he would. 'Sep, you're in charge of family arrangements. Fly out with Don; make sure Martha and the boys are properly taken care of.' Because Zev was family, and family takes care of its own. Thank Christ Brettlaw was the man in the big office, the feeling was already permeating round the table, would seep its inextricable way through the rest of the building. Thank Christ it was Brettlaw who was DDO.

The meeting broke shortly after six Washington time, midnight in Bonn. Brettlaw closed the door, told Maggie he was not to be disturbed, and made two telephone calls. The first was to a house on the outskirts of Bonn. He identified himself and was put through.

'Martha, it's Tom. I'm phoning from my office but I don't know what to say. Sep's on his way to take care of things, you and the boys, that sort of thing.' He allowed her to talk: about the barbecues the families had shared, the morning Brettlaw and Bartolski had rolled home drunk and she'd locked them out; about the boys. Sometimes he simply listened to her silence.

The second call, twenty minutes later, was to Milton Cranlow in the secure room at the embassy. For three minutes Cranlow briefed Brettlaw with his account of events, plus the possibilities which spun from them, then waited for the DDO's reaction.

'It's your show now, Milt.' Brettlaw was hard, factual. 'You're Chief of Station. I want the fuckers. I want their balls.'

No matter how long it takes and no matter where you have to go or what you have to do to find them.

He ended the call, tilted back in his chair, swivelled round and peered at the tree tops outside through the slatted blind. It would be another late night; he could sleep in the bedroom attached to his office, or make the usual arrangements for his stays at the University

Club. Not tonight, he almost decided, knew what Zev would have said. Big boys' games, big boys' rules. So what the fuck, Tom, have one on me.

He swung back to his desk and telephoned home.

'Mary, it's me. There's some bad news.' He gave her time to prepare herself. 'Zev's dead.' He imagined the images flashing through her mind: the trips, so long ago now, when they had all been young and new to the Agency; the family holidays together; the photographs of the kids growing up together.

'How?'

'He was blown up in Bonn this afternoon.'

Therefore we've hit the panic button, therefore I have to stay on.

'What about Martha and the boys?'

'I've spoken to them, they're being taken care of.'

'Should I phone?'

'It would be better in the morning. She'll appreciate it.'

'Thanks for letting me know.' Because I know that tonight you won't be home.

Costaine called just before eleven. 'You want some good news?'

'I could do with some,' Brettlaw told him.

'The missing Red River payment.'

Their conversation that morning was already a lifetime ago.

'Yeah.'

'It's turned up. Someone transposed a couple of digits in the account number.'

Therefore no connection with Zev's death, Brettlaw thought; thank Christ for small mercies. 'Thanks for letting me know.' Myerscough would already have begun checking, he remembered. Myerscough would be in early to catch Europe as soon as it opened. Time to tell him tomorrow. He checked his watch and saw that tomorrow had begun more than an hour ago.

When his driver dropped him at the club it was fifteen minutes past midnight.

'What time in the morning?'

In little more than four hours the night would be getting lighter and the first grey would be rising above the city. Perhaps it was then that Brettlaw decided, perhaps he had already done so. What he would do and why. In a way, he reflected, he had already set it in motion.

'Five-thirty.'

*

Donaghue's last formal meeting of the day began at seven in the evening and ended at seven-thirty; at seven forty-five he joined the men and women waiting in his office. Officially it was simply the Senator's closest staff gathering for an end-of-day drink. In twelve months' time, the three men and two women knew, they might be gathering for the final onslaught on the Democratic convention. And five months after that they might be meeting in the Oval Office of the White House.

Donaghue hung his coat on the back of the chair, helped himself to a beer from the fridge, checked that everyone else had one, sat behind his desk, and rolled up his sleeves.

'Timetable.' The question was directed at Pearson, no preamble.

'As we've discussed before, if you decide to run you should declare on or before Labour Day. The run-in to September fits that. Congress breaks in five weeks; at present there are three major votes outstanding in which you can expect to play a leading role. During the recess there are two major party functions we can also use, plus a meeting of the Democratic leadership conference. We'll probably know about Mitch's progress by the end of July, mid-August at the latest. If he thinks it's on, we can then work out when you announce an enquiry, and how that would tie in with your declaration.'

'Plus Angel Fire weekend after next.' It was the press secretary.

Angel Fire was the Disabled Veterans Vietnam Memorial on a hillside in the Sangre de Cristo section of the Rockies, in New Mexico.

'Yes.'

'And Arlington the last week in August.' The press secretary again.

Every year Donaghue made the pilgrimage. Even now he remembered the first time he had gone there, even before he had entered politics. Then as a young man, alone and slightly frightened. The day he had stood by his father's grave and told him he had volunteered for Vietnam. The afternoon after he had come back from the war, hardened, more committed to what he believed in. Not quite the day he had come home, of course. Rather, the day after he had been released from hospital. The day he had come as a Congressman, then the day he had bowed his head as a US Senator.

'Yes.'

'Other runners?'

They went through the list.

'Who's ahead at the moment?'

They went into the details.

'Anything on me?'

Any skeletons in the cupboard I don't know about? Anyone come up with something that the opposition will be looking for? Anyone done anything which might come back at me? Anyone made any political agreements I might regret, put my name on a piece of legislation which might rebound on me?

Politics was always dirty, but presidential politics was the dirtiest of all.

'Not so far.'

Donaghue looked round the room. 'Check on it. Make sure.' He swung his feet on to the desk. 'Funds and key support staff?'

'Nobody's signed up yet. The funds are there for whoever wants them.'

'Key decision-makers?'

The businessmen and politicians, even the entertainment moguls, who would throw their weight and money behind whoever emerged as the front runner.

'Still undeclared.'

He turned to the press secretary. 'Ideas for now?'

'Op eds are set up, plus selected pieces on you and Cath. We're ready to float a few balloons, opinion pollsters standing by to test the water.'

Without Donaghue announcing he was preparing to run, of course. Just the occasional article or poll by a strategic newspaper in a strategic state at a strategic time, getting people to think of Donaghue as a potential runner.

It was wide open, the feeling hung in the room. For Donaghue. For them. Donaghue was good, Pearson was good, they were good. All believing in what they stood for, believing in Donaghue. Believing in the words of Robert Kennedy which Donaghue had on the oak strip on his desk, the words he quoted at them when their spirits were down or their visions blurred.

> Some men see things as they are and say why.
> I dream things that never were and say why not.

The primaries, still nine months off, were theirs if they wanted them. The nomination in August of next year was theirs for the

101

taking. The walk down Pennsylvania Avenue the January after, the oath of office on the steps of the Hill, were theirs if they really believed.

'Thanks for waiting round. Same time next week.'

It was already nine-thirty, the light fading. The others filed from the room, leaving only Donaghue and Pearson.

'Can I ask you something, Jack?'

'Sure.' Donaghue was almost lost in the half-light, the corners darkening and the shadows deepening.

Sometimes he thought he knew everything about Jack Donaghue, Pearson was aware he was thinking; yet sometimes he thought he knew almost nothing. 'What does Cath think?'

Because if you decide to run you're going to need her. If you decide to run we'll put the team around you – the people here tonight plus others. But at the end of each day, each week, each month, when you're feeling battered and bruised and the bastards are throwing everything they can at you, you're going to need someone you can turn to and to whom you can say what you're really thinking. And you've got to trust that person enough to know that they'll tell you the truth. Tell you to quit or tell you to go out fighting. You're going to need your wife more than you need any of us.

Donaghue was quiet, looking at the room.

'If I go for it, Cath will be beside me.'

The shadows in the corners were deeper, playing against the dark green marble of the fireplace.

'See you in the morning.'

'Yeah.'

Pearson picked up his coat and left.

Donaghue collected the cans and threw them in the trash bin in the outer office, came back in and tidied the papers on his desk, then sat back in his chair and looked round the room. The light was fading fast. He rose, walked to the fireplace and looked at the photograph above it, remembered the inauguration words of the other Kennedy, the president shot dead in Dallas. Then he collected his coat and briefcase, and left the ghosts to themselves.

The evening was still warm, the sound of a party from somewhere on 4th. Eva was waiting in the side bar of the Hawk 'n Dove, a glass of draught Rolling Rock and a steak sandwich in front of her. At this time of evening most of the people in the Hawk 'n Dove were from the Hill, some talking politics but most discussing the game on the TV set above the bar. She saw Pearson as he came in and turned to kiss him. He dropped his briefcase on the floor, said hello to the barman and ordered a beer. When they left thirty minutes later the light was gone.

'He's going to do it, isn't he?' Eva asked.

'Yes,' Pearson said. 'I think Jack's going to run.'

Capitol Hill was behind him. Donaghue headed west on Constitution, rounded the Lincoln Memorial, and turned on to Memorial Bridge. Directly in front of him, just visible through the foliage of the trees, the eternal flame flickered in the dark.

Perhaps you never leave the ghosts, he thought.

He swung off the bridge and picked up Route 66.

The house in McLean stood in a quarter-acre plot, the houses round it similar though not identical. Donaghue parked the car in the garage, then went through the connecting door into the side hallway, and into the kitchen. Cath was watching television in the sitting area beyond, a pile of legal briefs on the coffee table, and the girls were asleep upstairs. He took off his coat, kicked off his shoes, poured them each a drink and sat beside her.

'Good interview about the MIAs.' She sensed he wanted to talk and huddled slightly closer to him. 'All the networks carried it.'

'Anything else?'

'Two American diplomats were killed in Bonn today. One of them might have been CIA Chief of Station.'

Oh Christ, he thought, and sat back in the sofa.

She knew the signs, had lived with him too long not to, and waited.

'Ed came up with something today,' he told her. 'Something he said I should ask you about.'

She switched off the television.

'If I ran, you know how it would affect us all.' How it would affect her and the girls, he meant.

'We've already discussed this.' So what is it, Jack? What's on your mind?

'I looked up at Arlington on the way back.'

'And you thought about Kennedy being assassinated, you thought about Lincoln. About somebody going for Reagan.'

'What I actually thought was what would happen if you and the girls were there.'

'If I was beside you like Jackie Kennedy was beside her husband in Dallas, you mean.'

'Yes.'

'The hour of maximum danger.' She threw the Kennedy quote at him, even though it was out of context, even though it was part of the speech Kennedy had made when he had been sworn in as president, even though – at that time – it was nothing to do with the November morning in Dallas. 'And you'd be all right, because you met yours in Vietnam.'

The day you won the Silver Star – she looked at him. The day you were wounded. The day you don't talk about even now, even though I've asked you enough times.

'Something like that, I guess.'

She slid her hand round his arm and kissed him.

'I think the girls and I are prepared to take that on board.'

When Myerscough reached Langley the moon was lost in the clouds and the night was not half over. The check with First Commercial of Santa Fe the previous day had been useful, at least the missing money had not only reached there but had been wired to London.

It was opening time in Europe: early enough for the fixer to have had his first cappuccino but not late enough for him to be embroiled in his first meeting. He collected a coffee from the cafeteria on the first floor, went to his office, and called Zurich. Sorry, he was told, he's not with us today. He called Milan. Sorry, the PA told him, he's overseas and can't be contacted.

So where are you, Paolo, what the hell are you playing at? You haven't done a bunk, have you? Haven't gone AWOL with the missing Nebulus money?

Brettlaw's Chevrolet collected him a minute early. At fifteen minutes to six it turned through the front gates at Langley, the barrier rising and the guards waving it through. The driver slid through the snake of roads inside the grounds, down the ramp into the underground parking area and stopped at the DDO's space. Held Brettlaw's door open for him and waited for Brettlaw to step out, reach back for his briefcase, straighten his jacket, and take the executive lift to the seventh floor.

Brettlaw got out of the car, took off his jacket, rolled his shirt sleeves to just below the elbow, folded the jacket and placed it across his left arm. Then he reached for his briefcase and took the lift to the first.

The cafeteria was quiet, some of the night shift grabbing coffee before they went home, some of the day shift getting the first caffeine they needed for the new day. Only when he stopped behind the two men and one woman at the counter did anyone realize and offer him their place in the queue. Brettlaw shook his head and waited his turn.

The DDO in early – everyone suddenly saw him and checked the time, stopped talking about the death of Zev Bartolski in Bonn the day before.

Brettlaw placed his briefcase, lid up, on the rail at the front of the counter, helped himself to coffee and a sesame bagel, then placed both on the top of the briefcase and slid it along the rail to the till.

'Dollar twenty, Mr Brettlaw.'

Brettlaw held the briefcase in place with his left hand and fished for change with his right.

'Thanks, Mack.'

Shirtsleeves, they all noted, jacket over left arm, briefcase carried square in front of him like a tray, coffee and plate with bagel balanced on it. So why was the DDO in so early, why had he come to the canteen?

The briefing on the shooting of Zev Bartolski began at nine, the relevant divisional and departmental heads in Brettlaw's seventh-floor office, Cranlow on conference from Bonn and leading the discussion.

'Indications at the moment are that the First Secretary, rather than Zev, was the target. Neither Bonn station in general, nor Zev in particular, was running anything which might have led to such an attack. At the present time, that is.' Terrorists had long memories, it was implied, Langley would know whether there was anything from Zev's past which might invalidate the hypothesis. 'The First Secretary, however, had just been transferred from the Middle East.' Cranlow went into the details. 'There are suggestions that whilst at his previous posting he might have attracted the attention of certain factions.' And those factions might have been responsible for the attack.

'Specifically?'

Cranlow listed them. The usual range, they all knew, and even if the Germans had something substantial the suspects would be out of the country by now. Yet even if they weren't, even if the Germans had something on them, they would be reluctant to move against them. Bonn, in particular, had learned from bitter experience. Arrest someone, put them inside, and you became a target. For hijackings, hostages, ransoms. There had been too many examples.

'Russian involvement?' It was the Director, Soviet division.

'No suggestion so far.'

'Forensics? Anything on the bomb?'

'Not yet. The German authorities are working on it.'

'Witnesses?'

'Several, but nothing has come from their statements.'

'Suspicions?' The tiniest tremors on the intelligence grapevine?

'Nothing substantial.'

But . . . Brettlaw detected it. Perhaps because he was looking for it, perhaps because it was he who had promoted Cranlow.

'Funeral arrangements?'

They went in to the details.

'What about the family?'

'Cold storage so the press can't get at them.'

'Good. How's Martha shaping up?'

'As you'd expect. A pillar of strength.' But it will hit her later, it was implied. 'The boys minding her said she appreciated your wife's call.'

The meeting ended at nine-forty. At nine forty-five Brettlaw spoke again to Cranlow.

'Thanks for the update earlier. I got the impression there was something you might know but didn't want to say.'

'Only a whisper. Give me another half-day.'

'You got it.'

He sat back in the chair.

Two Americans dead in Bonn and those responsible still free to boast about it – it wouldn't look too good at his confirmation hearings if Donaghue did make the White House and he himself was nominated DCI.

And he owed.

Because Zev Bartolski was a friend, Zev and he went back years. And Zev was Inner Circle of Inner Circle, one of the Trusted Few. He still remembered the night they had discussed it, the night he had told Zev what he wanted of him. Just like rewriting history, Zev had joked. Except that it wasn't history, it was the future.

So what was he going to do about Zev? The Germans would investigate, the Germans would have their suspicions. But in the end nothing would happen. Except there was another way, of course. He poured himself a Black Label and lit a Gauloise. Rules were rules, but rules were made to be broken. Sometimes, in the world in which he lived and breathed, you yourself made the rules so you yourself could break them. Therefore what he was about to do was irregular, but only to those who didn't understand.

He told Maggie he did not wish to be disturbed, downed the Jack Daniels, and punched the direct line in to the room on the third floor of the building next to the University Club on 16th.

Of course anything was possible, but even then things had a certain logic. Zev's death – at least the manner of it – didn't have a logic. Wouldn't have had a logic even in the arctic conditions of the Cold War. Even then the Soviets would have been more subtle, wouldn't have made it so obvious. Unless they wanted to, in which case the Soviets were capable of anything. But even then there had been the rules of the game. Even then there had been a logic.

'This is Universal Exports. We have a delivery for you.'

It wouldn't have been the Soviets – the Russians as he now had to call them – but it might have been someone financed by them, either at the present time or somewhere in the past. And if it was, and if they'd stepped out of line, then it was in Moscow's interest just as much as Washington's to sort it out.

'What time?'

'Nine o'clock.'

Kirolev wasn't just old KGB, Kirolev was higher-placed in the new order than anyone dared imagine. Kirolev was an old confidante of Malenko, and over the last years of turmoil and change Malenko had played his hand quite beautifully, had shown the acumen and timing which had marked his career in the past. But Kirolev was more. Kirolev was not only Malenko's eyes and ears in DC, Kirolev was the conduit between old enemies and new friends. Not friends, perhaps, not even allies. There was probably a word for it, but Brettlaw couldn't think of it.

'Nine sounds fine,' he agreed.

One other thing, he decided. He booked a room at the University Club that night, then telephoned Mary and told her he probably wouldn't be home again.

Cranlow's last call of the day came through at eight that evening – two in the morning in Bonn.

'There may be a development.' The new CoS was calm, assured. 'This morning I said that Zev might not have been the target, that the indications were it was the First Secretary.'

'Yes.'

'It may be that neither of them were.'

'Tell me.'

'The First Secretary's attendance wasn't guaranteed, it certainly wasn't circulated to the press, and neither he nor Zev were on the official guest lists.'

'So?'

'A number of West German politicians and industrialists were known to be attending. One of them drives the same model car as the First Secretary, same colour. Apparently the Germans had intelligence four weeks ago that he was being targeted. They think whoever was responsible got the wrong car.'

Christ – Brettlaw felt the anger. Thank God – he also felt the relief. The Zev box not sprung open after all and the Red River payments in order.

He hadn't told Myerscough about the Red River money, he remembered; time to do it in the morning, he decided. Zev was still dead, of course, and he would still make whoever was responsible pay, but at least everything was watertight again, everything was in order.

He left Langley and was driven to the University Club. In a briefcase he carried a mobile phone and encryptor in case anyone needed to call him that night. No calls would be made to him via the switchboard at the club: both his office and his family were familiar with the routine. Pick-up five-thirty, same as this morning, he told his driver. He checked in, went to the room on the fourth floor, showered and changed, then took the lift to the basement.

The door to the leisure centre was in front; he turned right, along the corridor, then right again and through the first set of swing doors. The dark green metal service doors were in front of him and the back-up Chevy was outside, the keys beneath the brick two feet from the rear nearside wheel.

He started the car, drove on to 15th via the parking lot at the rear of the *Washington Post* building, took Key Bridge over the river, and turned on to the Parkway, the road climbing and the Potomac below and to his right. The light was fading fast and there was little traffic. He passed the first pull-in, what locals called an over-look because of the views from it across the valley of the Potomac, checked the time, and came to the second. The Chrysler was already parked, its lights off. He stopped behind it, left the Chevy, and climbed over the wall and down the other side. The other man was already waiting. The land in front of them was dark, only the occasional lights, the river below. Two decades before the bagman for the Watergate burglars had used the same location.

'I need to meet with Malenko.'

Brettlaw spoke facing forward, looking across the river to the other side. He selected a Gauloise for himself and offered the packet to Kirolev.

Kirolev took one and pulled out a lighter. Kirolev was good, Kirolev was also a charmer. Kirolev was reputed to possess a sexual stamina matched only by his imagination. Spanish Fly, the surveillance boys had nicknamed him. Some ways of access never changed.

Perhaps he ought to check on who Kirolev was screwing at the moment and what they had access to. Not yet, though, not while he wanted Kirolev for something else.

'When?' the Russian asked.

'As soon as reasonably possible.'

'He'll probably suggest a neutral ground.'

Even though you and Malenko know each other, Kirolev thought. Even though you and he helped set up the 1982 agreement between the KGB and the CIA governing rules of interrogation for captured agents. You and Malenko probably go back longer than that. And now you're DDO and he's the equivalent in the new set-up in Dzerzhinsky Square.

'Where do you suggest?' Brettlaw asked.

'Probably Berlin.' Kirolev drew on the Gauloise.

'Berlin would be fine.'

The cigarettes glowed in the dusk and the smell of tobacco drifted in the air.

'Sorry to hear about Bartolski.'

Perhaps it was genuine, perhaps it was Kirolev's way of saying that he knew why Brettlaw wanted the meeting, perhaps both.

'Thanks.'

Myerscough was at his desk by three – nine in the morning in Europe – the night still dark outside but the summer warmth hanging in the trees. Thank Christ the DDO had been wrapped up with other things, thank Christ Brettlaw hadn't had the time to ask him about the missing money on the Nebulus account. He telephoned

Zurich and received the same reply as the previous afternoon, then called Milan.

'I'm sorry.' The PA was suddenly too nice, too friendly. 'Yesterday I made a mistake. Mr Benini isn't overseas, he's on vacation.'

5

Francesca's mind was locked in fear and her fingers were welded together.

'Don't worry.' Marco patted her hand. 'They'll make the phone call, you'll answer, and you'll do as Haslam says. Then it'll be okay.'

The flat with the clean phone was empty of furniture, the telephone was on the floor of the sitting-room, and the recording device had been fitted that morning.

'It won't happen yet,' Marco told her. 'They'll phone at seven precisely, not before or after.'

They stood near the window and watched the storm clouds rolling on to the city from the north. All day the oppression and humidity had mixed with the fumes of the traffic, now the threat of thunder hung like electricity in the air and the sky was a translucent grey.

Perhaps they needed the storm, Haslam thought, perhaps they needed to clear the air. It was seven o'clock – for the past three minutes he had checked the time every thirty seconds. The negotiator would be dialling the number now, planning how to put the fear of God into Francesca. The script, he told her, just read the words on the script.

The telephone rang.

'Yes.' Francesca spoke automatically, did not even hear the click as the recorder automatically switched on.

'We want seven miliardi. If you want to see him again you'd better pay.'

The fear and panic seized her. The script, she heard Haslam's voice.

'Seven miliardi, Francesca, or you don't see him again.'

Just read the words on the script, Haslam's voice was still telling her.

'Before I do anything I need to know Paolo's alive. You understand that . . .' The fear threatened to take over again. '. . . I need to know he's okay.'

'What do you want me to ask Paolo?' The edge in Mussolini's voice was deliberate and threatening. The call had lasted twenty seconds, plenty of time before they could trace it – if the police were involved – but time to get off anyway, time to screw the pressure on her.

'Ask Paolo the name of his grandmother's first dog.'

The line went dead.

It was thirty seconds past seven. The storm broke, the lightning sheeting across the sky and the rain falling in large drops, at first a few then suddenly a torrent. How had Francesca managed, Haslam wondered, how had she stood up to the kidnappers? Ten minutes later the BMW screeched into the parking area at the front of the block, and the figures ran inside. The door opened and he looked for her face.

I've done it, it was in her eyes and body movements. I was terrified but I remembered the script and I did it.

'Francesca was terrific.' It was Marco who was in charge, Marco who was helping Francesca take off her coat. 'They phoned on time. Francesca told them that she needed to know that Paolo was alive.' He went to the table and slipped the cassette into the player. 'They tried to put her off, to talk about the ransom, but Francesca insisted on getting the question to Paolo over to them.'

They sat and listened, Francesca suddenly in shock again, as if the sound of her own voice had torn her back into the fear.

'You were good. You did exactly as we wanted.' Haslam played the cassette again. 'Tomorrow night they'll phone with the answer. Once you've got that they'll start pressuring you again for money. Our job now is to prepare you for that.'

'They'll still ask for seven miliardi?' It was Umberto.

'Yes.'

'So tomorrow we give them our response.'

'No.'

Why the hell not? It was in the wave of the hands and the violence in the eyes.

'Tomorrow the negotiator will re-state the asking price, but both sides know that's just a starting position. The negotiator and his controller have played this game before so they'll allow Francesca time to decide. Plus they'll give her instructions about what she has to do when she wants to notify them that she's come to a decision.'

'They won't phone again?' Rossi asked.

'Not until we tell them to,' Haslam told him.

Oh God, Rossi thought.

'So what will they do?' It was Umberto.

'Probably give the wording of an advert to place in the *Corriere della Sera*.' The newspaper was one of Milan's leading dailies. 'When you put it in, that means you've made a decision and want them to call.'

'What about the amount we offer?'

They weren't listening to him, Haslam thought; they weren't taking on board a single thing he was telling them. Give them time, part of him said, because in the end they will understand. But even at the end they would still be ignoring him, he almost admitted.

'The key thing tomorrow is that Francesca gets the proof that Paolo's alive. They'll repeat their demand but she'll stall, say it's too much, that she can't raise that sort of money. Then they'll give her the newspaper instructions.'

They listened to the tape one more time and moved to the wording of the script.

Vitali's call to the negotiator was at eight; outside the evening was fresh after the cleansing of the storm.

'How was she?'

'She started badly, then pulled herself together.'

Mussolini played the cassette.

'Same time tomorrow,' Vitali told him, 'same demand. Then give her the newspaper details.'

An hour later he telephoned the stake-out.

A good thing he'd parked the Alfa in Via Ventura that afternoon, Pascale thought, a good thing he'd had the car to sit in during the deluge. The Saab and BMW had parked outside again, he told the controller, the Merc had dropped off a passenger then disappeared. The BMW had left at fifteen minutes to seven, a man and woman in it, and returned half an hour later. The Saab and BMW left for good at about nine, and the Merc had made a pick-up at the same time.

The Mercedes was registered under the ownership of BCI, the Banca del Commercio Internazionale – Vitali had checked that morning.

'Anything else?'

Because there should be.

'A cab arrived just after six, dropped someone off, a man. Another cab picked someone up, possibly the same man, at about eight-thirty.'

113

The consultant, Vitali supposed. Interesting that he was leaving before the rest, though. Might be significant, might not be.

'Well done. Same plan for tomorrow.'

The night was dark, the images circling like vultures above her. It was as if she was almost a skeleton. As if she was weak and tired and thin, the flesh tight on her bones and her breasts useless and empty and folded like leather purses against her ribs. Umberto and the banker Rossi were somewhere in the void above her – she could hear their voices, hollow and echoing – then descending and picking at her flesh.

She felt alone and frightened. Christ, how she needed someone to talk to, needed someone to tell her how to bring Paolo home, someone to tell her that everything would be all right. Christ, how she needed to tell someone how afraid and lost and alone she felt. How she simply needed someone.

Phone the girls, she thought.

Phone Umberto.

Phone Marco.

Phone Haslam, because despite everything Haslam was the only one who understood.

Don't call Haslam, she decided, because if she did Haslam would think she was weak. And Haslam was the bastard who'd told her to treat it all as a business.

The next morning she rose at six-thirty and was at work by eight. That afternoon she made herself remain in the office till later than usual. When she and Marco arrived at the clean phone in the evening there was a rug on the floor of the sitting-room, table and chairs in the centre, and armchairs to the side. In the kitchen was a coffee percolator. The telephone and its attachments were on the table.

'Thanks, Marco.' She sat down and placed the script in front of her.

'Haslam told me to do it.' Marco went to the kitchen and made coffee, and put a cup in front of her.

She smiled her thanks and tried to study the script which Haslam had written.

ANSWER   *Prove Paolo is alive.*
              Give me answer to my question.

114

IF IN DOUBT	*Ask question again.* *Name of grandmother's first dog.*
MONEY	*Too much.*
IF PRESSED	*More than I can get.*

Except that Umberto had changed it, so that the last two sections now read *It's too much, but I'll try.*

Marco was to her right, close enough to support her but far enough away not to distract her. Even so the ring of the telephone shocked them both.

'Francesca, this is Mussolini.'

She looked at the script and couldn't remember whether or not he had used her name before, whether he had given himself a name.

'Have you spoken to Paolo?' she asked. 'Have you got the answer to my question?'

'If you want him back the price is seven miliardi. You hear that, Francesca. Seven miliardi.'

She knew she was about to panic and looked at the script again. Thank Christ for it, for the guidance and structure it gave her.

'Prove Paolo is alive. Give me the answer.'

'The dog was called Tiberius,' Mussolini told her.

Marco was on earphones. She glanced at him and saw the sign he made, saw that it was all right, that Paolo was alive. Thank you, she almost said. To Marco, to Mussolini.

'Seven miliardi, Francesca.'

She looked again at the script and read the words.

'It's too much but I'll try.'

'When you decide, place an advert in the motor column of the *Corriere della Sera*: 1947 Maserati wanted, good condition. Use a box number but don't give your correct address with it. I'll telephone the evening the advert appears.'

Paolo's alive, the relief pounded through her. She turned to Marco and began to say something, then broke down. He helped her up and led her to the bathroom, then he returned to the sitting-room, took out the cassette and replaced it with a new one. From the bathroom came the sound of retching.

Twenty minutes later, according to the log kept by the stake-out Pascale, they arrived back at Via Ventura. The BMW travelling faster than before, the man and woman jumping from it and almost running into the building.

'Tiberius,' Francesca panted before she even sat down. 'They gave the right answer. Paolo's okay.'

Umberto snapped his fingers for Marco to give him the cassette, then inserted it in the player and switched it on.

She was going to collapse, Francesca suddenly knew; she'd had all she could take and now her body and her soul were going to give in. 'Please, could I have a drink?' Her voice was a whisper, almost inaudible.

Umberto turned sharply and glared at her, waved at her to be quiet.

'I'm sorry, I think I'm going to faint.'

'Quiet,' Umberto snapped back at her and concentrated on the tape.

Haslam rose, crossed two paces round the table, leant over Umberto's shoulder, and pressed the stop button of the cassette player.

'Where's the drinks cabinet?' His voice was low and totally controlled.

Christ, Marco thought, he makes the negotiator Mussolini sound like the Virgin Mary. 'I'll get it,' he said. He left the table and poured a cognac, glanced at Haslam once, saw the way he moved his head, poured some more and gave Francesca the glass.

'Thanks, Marco.' Francesca downed the drink and put the glass on the table.

Haslam nodded and Umberto began the tape again.

Francesca had done well, Haslam thought: Francesca had remembered the script and stuck to it. Except . . .

Umberto switched off the player and sat back. 'Congratulations, Francesca. She did brilliantly. Didn't she, Haslam? So what do you suggest we do now?' He realized he had gone too far, that even he should not have addressed the consultant merely as Haslam, not used the tone he had used.

'Francesca did do well.' Haslam's voice was still quiet. 'So first we examine the conversation, then we decide how we respond to certain aspects of it.' He rewound the tape and played it again. 'At first Francesca was shocked, which was to be expected. The key thing, however, was that she recovered and stuck to the script.'

Except that she hadn't, of course, or the script had been re-written.

'So let's break down the conversation. One: the answer to the question was correct, which means that Paolo is alive. Two: the demand is the same, but as we've already discussed it's only their starting-point. Three: and as we also expected, they've given us the way of communicating with them. The question now is at what level do we make our first offer.'

'And what do you suggest?'

What I've already suggested, Haslam thought. 'The average settlement at the moment is between 450 and 500 million lire.' Between £180,000 and £200,000. 'The kidnapper will know that as clearly as we do. He'll try for more, but this is the sort of figure he'll be ready to settle for. Our first offer therefore has to be reasonable, not too low or too high. It must also begin to give the impression that Francesca has to find the money, or most of it, herself.'

'So how much?' Umberto was insistent.

'As I said at our first meeting, the decision is yours. What I suggest, however, is that we place our first offer between a hundred and fifty and two hundred million.' Between £60,000 and £80,000. 'That's just below half the going final settlement, so it gives you a good platform to build from.'

'Two hundred and seventy-five.' Benini turned to the others for their approval.

Umberto had already discussed it with Rossi, Haslam thought; Umberto had already decided a figure. A hundred and ten thousand pounds, he also thought.

'Two hundred and seventy-five is too much. If you offer that much now you push up the kidnapper's level of expectation. The kidnapper knows that what you finally pay will be at least double, even treble, what you first offer. If your first offer now is two hundred and seventy-five million, your final offer will be between six and nine hundred million, perhaps one miliardo.' One miliardo was £400,000. 'And this will have major repercussions on the way the kidnapper plays it from here in.'

'It's too late for tomorrow's paper.' Umberto closed the discussion. 'We'll run the advert the day after.'

Vitali's conversations with Mussolini and Pascale were finished by eight-thirty. When they were over he poured himself a Prosecco, listened to the tape of the evening's conversation, then analysed the notes he had made over the past days, including the car lists supplied by the stake-out.

Every indication was that the family or the bank had brought in a consultant, yet every indication was that they weren't listening to what he would be telling them. The first thing he would be telling them would be to camouflage the role of the bank in the discussions. If they didn't it would indicate to the kidnappers that the bank was prepared to contribute to the ransom amount, and this would force up the final settlement. Yet for at least one of the visits to what he supposed were meetings of the family's management team, someone from BCI had not only turned up in an official Merc, but had left his driver and bodyguard outside. And even after the consultant had presumably cautioned him, all the banker had done was have his car drop him then wait three blocks away.

Plus something else.

He poured himself another Prosecco and listened again to the recording of that evening's conversation.

The wife had been good, had followed the script the consultant had written for her until the end. And then she had blown it.

He rewound the last part of the tape and listened again to her final words.

It's too much but I'll try.

The consultant wouldn't have written that. The consultant would have told her merely to say it was too much. Either she'd forgotten the script at that point, or someone had re-written it. And the consultant would have picked it up the moment the family had played their recording of the conversation.

The courtyard in the centre of the hotel was quiet; Haslam opened the window, poured himself a whisky and updated his case log.

The way Benini was going, his second offer would be in excess of five hundred million, and with that sort of money there would be no way they could pretend that the burden of payment lay with Francesca. Plus there was Rossi. At least the banker's car wasn't parked outside, but all that had probably happened was that it dropped him off and waited a couple of blocks away. Which, assuming the kidnappers had the apartment under surveillance, would be just as bad.

He was going to lose this one, he thought; either that or it was going to lose him. And he didn't need it: didn't need Umberto, didn't need the flak he was having to take, didn't need Rossi either. Because in the end either Umberto or Rossi or both of them was going to drop him in it.

118

He poured himself another whisky, turned to the CNN channel on the television, watched it for ten minutes, then picked up the *Herald Tribune*. The photograph of the wrecked car was across the top of the front page, and the lead item was on the killing of two American diplomats in Bonn. Nothing changes, he thought, and turned to one of the inside pages.

The article was from the *Washington Post*, and was a profile of the leading candidates for the Democratic Party's nomination for the US presidency. The writer detailed the four men who had already declared, but the paragraphs which caught Haslam's attention were those towards the end, apparently tucked in as an afterthought. Independent polls conducted by newspapers in a range of states across the country in the past days had suggested the name of another candidate, not yet declared.

So Donaghue had started. Not just started. Donaghue was already dictating the agenda, because the photograph at the top of the article was not of any of the politicians who had already declared, but of the man who had not.

Met him, he smiled to himself, and thought back to his few days in DC, his lunch with Quincey Jordan and his meeting, albeit brief, with Ed Pearson. At least Mitch Mitchell had got it right.

He flicked through the case notes again, then went to bed.

He was going to lose this one, he thought again; either that or it was going to lose him. So perhaps he should pull out now, allow another consultant to take his place. But perhaps it wasn't just Umberto and Rossi, perhaps it was the kidnap business. Perhaps he should pull out of everything and look for another mountain.

Except what about Paolo Benini? What about Paolo Benini's wife?

Thanks Dave, Francesca thought.

For organizing the coffee and the table and the chairs at the clean phone. For stopping the meeting and allowing Marco to get me a drink. For not rebuking me even though you knew I'd blown it with Mussolini. Sorry I let you down over the script, sorry I allowed Umberto to change it, sorry I read his version and not yours.

You're still a bastard, though. First you look after me in a way I have no right to expect, then you destroy me by telling me Paolo isn't worth more than a hundred and fifty million lire.

So what about Paolo? She lay in bed and stared at the ceiling. Paolo was her husband, the father of her children. But in many ways Paolo was the image of Umberto. Concerned with money and consumed by his job; believing he was a good husband and father, in his terms probably being a flawless husband and father. In a way treating her like shit just as Umberto and Rossi treated her like shit. But Paolo was still her husband.

Perhaps Haslam was right: offer too much too soon and the kidnappers would want more, might keep Paolo longer to get more. But Umberto and Rossi had been insistent. And in the end, as they pointed out after Haslam had left that evening, the decision was theirs, not his. He had said so himself.

She was lost again, frightened again. Wanted and needed to talk to someone. Not the girls, because with them she had to be their mother figure, strong and calm, and never showing any sign of anger or weakness. Not Umberto or Rossi or Marco. The fears circled like vultures above her: she could see them in the black and hear them in the silence. It was as if she was waiting by the clean phone, the nerves eating away at her body and her soul. Tonight she wouldn't last the night; and if she didn't make it through tonight then she wouldn't make it through tomorrow. And if she didn't make it through tomorrow Paolo was finished. She lifted the telephone and called the number, heard Haslam answer on the third ring and almost put the phone down.

'Yes.'

His voice was alert, as if he hadn't just woken up, as if he expected there to be a problem.

'It's Francesca.'

'What's wrong?'

'Nothing,' she said. 'Sorry. Nothing at all.' It's two in the morning, she expected him to say. 'I was just suddenly frightened . . .' she heard her own voice. 'Just needed someone to talk to. I'm sorry to have woken you.' She began to put the phone down.

'Don't hang up.' She heard his voice again. 'If you were afraid you were quite right to phone.' So what do you want to talk about, she expected him to ask, how could he help. She didn't know what she wanted to say, so said nothing.

How were her daughters, he asked her, had they phoned? When were their birthdays, what did they enjoy doing? The girls were good, she told him, the girls were fine; they'd talked that evening, about summer holidays.

Five minutes passed, almost ten.

'Thanks.'

'You okay now?' he asked her.

'Yes, I'm okay now.'

Haslam woke at seven, breakfasted at seven-thirty, and checked the motor columns of the *Corriere della Sera*, even though he knew the Benini advert wasn't due till the next day. Motoring sections had always been favourite places for kidnap communications, there was even a sub-species of criminal who specialized in spotting adverts placed by families then working out their phone numbers and contacting them, pretending to be the kidnappers and receiving the ransom money without being able to deliver the victim. The kidnappers themselves had a name for them – they called them jackals.

When he had finished checking he read the *International Herald Tribune*. The Bonn killings still held a place on the front page. One of those killed had been confirmed as the First Secretary at the US embassy, the paper said, and the other was reported to be one of the CIA's top men in Europe.

That morning he spent three hours in the Biblioteca Ambrosiana, that afternoon another three in the south of the city. That evening a fruitless hour at the flat on Via Ventura.

Next morning he rose at six, bought a copy of the *Corriere della Sera*, and read it over his first coffee of the day. The Benini entry was in the second column of the motoring adverts; he confirmed the wording, then turned to the *Herald Tribune*.

The authorities in Germany now believed that the killing of the two Americans in Bonn was a mistake, the paper said. According to intelligence sources the target was an industrialist and the Americans had been blown up because the car in which they were travelling resembled his.

The poor bastards were still dead though.

Francesca Benini read the newspaper before breakfast. Even though she had dreamed about it all night it still shocked her. She tried to calm herself and knew it was impossible. Cancel work today, she thought, stay at home and wait. Do as Haslam told her, she decided instead; because if she didn't she would be insane by the time she and Marco went to the clean phone.

The day was endless, somehow she muddled through it. She'd handled the last two calls well, she reminded herself constantly; tonight would be easier, tonight she'd simply have to tell them the price. The word repulsed her, nauseated her. She made herself stop thinking about it and concentrated on the conversation with one client and the designs for another. Even so she left early, telling herself she wanted to do some shopping, but driving straight to the flat.

Haslam watched as she arrived.

Do nothing to jeopardize the negotiations, he had decided, nothing that the kidnapper's stake-outs on the apartment would spot. Just get a feel for the other side, a nose for what might be going on. See who they were. Assuming they were there.

Via Ventura sloping down slightly – the first time the observations had been general, now they were specific. Pavements wide and lined with trees, expensive shops and boutiques. Benches where a tail might sit if he or she was bored, and enough parking places for sixteen cars. He confirmed that the apartment could only be observed from what would have been bays eight to thirteen, then noted the vehicles parked in those numbers, remembering the details three at a time, then turning the corner halfway down and entering them in the notebook he carried.

Red Porsche.
Blue Audi 80.
Yellow Ferrari, vintage model.
Red Alfa.
Black VW Golf, slightly dilapidated and therefore slightly out of place.
Blue Fiat 127, also out of place.

At fifteen minutes to six Marco's BMW stopped outside the flats, two minutes later Umberto's Saab. At ten to six the Mercedes stopped, Rossi got out, and the car pulled away. Haslam left Via Ventura, skirted round the side streets, and approached the apartment block from the opposite direction.

Remember the script, he told Francesca as she and Marco left at six-thirty. Tonight there was no problem, Francesca told herself as she waited at the clean phone; tonight all she had to do was read the size of the offer. She picked up the telephone on the second ring.

'Good evening.' Mussolini's voice was firm and slightly harsh. 'You have something for me.'

'Two hundred and seventy-five millions.' She almost said miliardi.

Mussolini knew precisely how he would react to whatever she said: the slightest menace in the voice and the hint of threat never manifested yet always so close to the surface.

'Same time tomorrow.' He kept his response to a minimum.

Is that all, Francesca wanted to scream at him, aren't you going to say anything else. Aren't you going to say it's enough, or laugh and say it's too little? Control it, she told herself, control herself. Not too bad, she said to Marco, and looked away before her willpower dissolved.

It was going well, Umberto announced at the management meeting fifteen minutes later. Please no ghosts, tonight, Francesca prayed, please may I be able to sleep. It had already taken too long, Rossi knew, had all the signs of going on even longer. Okay, he agreed with Haslam, perhaps it had been a mistake to have the Mercedes drop him off, but how else was he supposed to get here?

Each move the family made now would be a mistake, Haslam confirmed later as he updated the case log in the sanctity of his hotel. Yet the more he advised against it the more fixed they would become in their decisions. It was a business, he told himself, just as he had told them, which was the reason he always insisted on payment in ten-day blocks.

The following day he was in position in Via Ventura by five. All the parking places were taken; the blue Audi and the dilapidated Golf parked again, though the Golf might not have moved from the day before, plus the Alfa. So how was it going to go from here, he thought as he waited for Francesca and Marco to return from the clean phone, what was he himself going to do?

'He's come down.' Francesca spoke even before Marco closed the door behind them. 'Three miliardi.' Even though her hands were shaking, Francesca's eyes were bright. 'They're phoning again tomorrow.'

Thank Christ, thought Rossi. Now I've got something to tell the chairman.

We told you so – the triumph was in Umberto's eyes. 'They've come down by over half, therefore I suggest we go up to five hundred million.' He was assertive, almost aggressive.

To his right Rossi nodded.

Five hundred million lire was £200,000, Haslam thought. 'You're going up too much too quickly,' he broke the fragile euphoria. 'I know the kidnapper's come down a lot, but he's nowhere near the level to which he's prepared to drop, and you're getting close to where you can go.' He knew what Benini was going to reply and corrected himself. 'By that I mean that you're already over the

123

average for ransoms beginning with a five miliardi demand, and close to the average final settlement for those starting at ten miliardi. It could be that you do finally settle at this amount, but it could also be that you have to go up a lot more.'

Don't say this, Francesca wanted to tell him, this isn't what I want to hear. Listen to him, she wanted to tell the others, because he's telling the truth, except that we've already gone too far the other way.

'The way you're playing it you're also laying yourselves open,' Haslam also warned them.

'To what?'

'To anything the kidnapper wants to do to you.'

Rossi leant to his left and whispered in Umberto Benini's ear.

Tomorrow night you'll offer five hundred million, Benini told Francesca. And the night after they'll phone back – it was on his face and in his mannerisms. And when they did they'd drop another miliardi as a ploy. Then he, Umberto Benini, would bring his offer up to 750 millions and Paolo would be home.

The night seemed unending, the images coming at her, dismembered and disjointed but none of them with an ending. Francesca tried to fight them off, tried to work out what they meant and how she could resolve them. Twice she woke and checked the clock. The first time was just after one, and she was bathed in sweat. The second it was almost four-thirty and she was shivering with cold.

The day was long, partly because she was afraid and partly because part of her thought that tonight the issue might be settled. We've got them on the run, she sensed Umberto's mood at the management meeting that evening; we've spelled out the rules of the game and told them that's what they've got to play to.

Good luck, Haslam told her as she left. Don't worry, Marco's with you, and whatever happens Marco will look after you.

When they returned the panic was frozen on her face.

'You offered the five hundred million.' Umberto was framed in the doorway.

Francesca saying nothing, Haslam noted, Marco replying, Marco protecting her.

'Yes.'

I asked Francesca – it was in Umberto's tone, in his mannerisms. Why the hell can't she answer for herself? 'And what did they say?' he asked.

'They didn't,' Marco told him.
'They didn't what?'
'They didn't say anything. They just hung up.'

6

Tampa was hot, but Tampa looked promising.

Mitchell had spent the day with the Drug Enforcement Administration, a formal briefing in the morning and a less formal exchange of information over lunch: the seizure of a cocaine assignment leading to the identification of one of the financiers in the case, and the first details of the money man's bank arrangements. Except that the DEA team were field agents, thus not equipped to deal with the intricacies of banking above a certain level, and the investigation had ground to what seemed its inevitable stalemate. And the frustration had showed. Christ how it had showed. In the eyes of the men who'd made the bust and in the way they told what it was like banging their heads against a brick wall.

So Tampa looked promising, as did Detroit, plus a couple of others. Different cases, different angles. But that was all. Anyone on the inside, Mitchell had asked each time, anyone who would prise it open for him, give him the way in. Even though he knew that if there had been they would have already been snapped up and hidden away.

He said he'd be in touch and caught the late afternoon flight back to DC.

The message from Anderton was one of five on his desk the following morning. Anderton was the assistant District Attorney from Manhattan. Anderton with the flash waistcoats and the political gleam in his eye. Anderton who had been in court when Mitchell phoned but who'd returned his call because assistant DAs with ambition always did.

He checked the number and called New York.

'Jim, Mitch Mitchell. Thanks for getting back.'

'Sorry I wasn't round before. Big case going down.' It wouldn't have been anything else, Mitchell thought. 'So how can I help?' Which is really to say, what can I do for you so that you can do something for me some day?

'I'm doing a stint with the Senate Banking Committee and wondered whether we should be talking about anything.' Mitchell leaned back in his chair and looked out the window.

'Congressional investigation?' Anderton asked.

That is to say: how much mileage is in it, what sort of weight do you have?

'Not yet.'

In other words I'm trawling, but you and I both know that.

'Senate Banking, you said.'

Anderton was a shit, but Anderton was also smart.

'Yeah.'

'Anyone in particular?' Anderton asked.

Which was why Mitchell had kept Donaghue's name back, why he'd held it for when it was necessary.

'Donaghue,' Mitchell told him.

'Jack Donaghue?'

Because I hear stories that Jack's about to throw his hat into the ring. Go for the Big One.

'Yeah,' Mitchell said. 'Jack Donaghue.'

There was a pause while Anderton appeared to consult his diary.

'Let's do tomorrow. Ten o'clock.'

Perhaps Anderton had something, perhaps he didn't.

'Sure, let's do tomorrow.'

Mitchell switched on the computer, typed in his security code, and logged the appointment in his diary.

'Coffee?'

The secretary was standing behind him.

'Please.'

Brettlaw was collected at five-thirty; fifteen minutes later his driver stopped in the underground carpark below the Langley complex; at ten minutes to six Brettlaw entered the cafeteria and stood in line at the counter. The DDO in early again, it was noticed; the DDO collecting his coffee and bagel with the rest of them, shirt sleeves turned up, jacket over his arm, and plastic cup and plate balanced on his briefcase. Perhaps some understood, but if so they did not say.

'Dollar twenty, Mr Brettlaw.'

'Thanks, Mack.'

By the time he reached his room it was six o'clock, twelve noon in Bonn. He hung up his coat, put the briefcase to the side of his

127

desk, placed the bagel and coffee on the blotting pad, lit a cigarette and called Cranlow.

'Update me.' He pulled the top off the cup and swung the chair sideways.

'Forensics may have come up with something. The bomb which killed Zev was a platter charge using a manhole cover, detonation by remote control. A number of similar charges have been used in Europe recently.'

'For example?'

'The Renault boss in France.'

'Any connections between the Bonn device and the others?'

'The Germans are looking.'

'But no one's claimed responsibility?'

'No.'

Which was unusual. Except that in this case they'd got the wrong people, which would make them appear less than efficient.

'Zev's body?' Brettlaw asked.

It's on its way, he knew Cranlow was going to say.

'Zev's on his way home,' Cranlow told him.

'Thanks, Milt.'

For taking care of him. For not calling the remnant they were sending back *it*. For still calling him Zev.

'Speak to you later.'

'Yeah, speak to you later.'

There were sounds in the outer office. Maggie wasn't due in till eight, Maggie Dubovski always showed at five minutes to eight precisely, no matter what was happening, no matter what the weather. Maggie would have arrived at five to eight even if it was Armageddon Day or if she'd had to persuade Noah to give her a lift in the ark.

It was twenty-five minutes past six. Margaret Dubovski took off her coat, switched on the percolator, and knocked on the door.

'Thought you'd need some fresh coffee.'

'Fresh coffee would be good.'

The meeting on the funeral arrangements for Zev Bartolski began at eight and ended fifty minutes later. The fact that Zev was Agency was no longer a secret; it hadn't been from Day One, but now it was different. Now the fact that he was coming home for the last time and they were going to lay him to rest meant that both the arrival at Andrews and part of the funeral service would be public, and because it would be public it would be televised. Therefore the

Agency would have to contend with the politicians who would wish to be present. The DCI's problem, Brettlaw decided, not his.

Myerscough made the first call at eight-thirty. Just to check, just to make sure before he took it to the DDO. In the main office Bekki Lansbridge was already at her desk. She was looking good this morning, Myerscough decided, looking even better than usual. Almost a glow about her. Great ass, he thought, moving it for someone. Christ, Bekki Lansbridge wasn't just looking good this morning, Bekki Lansbridge was looking great. He ended the first call and made the second, then telephoned Maggie Dubovski.

'Myerscough. I wonder if I could see him this morning.'

'How urgent? His schedule's pretty full.'

'It's urgent.'

'I'll get back to you.'

Which meant he would have his meeting. He left his desk and crossed the main office to Bekki Lansbridge's desk. 'I'm seeing the DDO later. Better have the Mentor and Centurion files ready in case he wants to see them.'

Aides loved being summoned to the seventh floor, aides got off on bosses who had access to the executive level.

'Myerscough phoned asking for a meeting,' Maggie Dubovski informed Brettlaw when he returned from the session about the Bartolski funeral.

'How urgent?'

'Urgent.'

Christ, he remembered: he hadn't told Myerscough that the Red River money had turned up. 'Anything else?'

'Senator Donaghue called, asked you to call back.'

'Myerscough in ten minutes and the senator now.'

The call was connected forty seconds later.

'Tried to get you at home,' Donaghue told him. 'Mary said you're something of a night bird nowadays.'

'You know how it is,' Brettlaw laughed. 'Good to speak to you.'

'I was just phoning to say that I won't be at Zev's funeral.' Even though he knew Bartolski, even though they had met more than once over barbecues at Brettlaw's house. 'I think you'll have enough people from the Hill there anyway.' Not just from the Hill: every politician in town would be there, trying to get his place at the ringside and his face on network TV. 'I'd appreciate it, however, if you could pass my condolences to the family.' Plus . . . 'I know you'll have it covered, but if there's anything I can do.'

At any time, now or in the future, Brettlaw understood. Especially as regards the children. Places at the right universities and good jobs after.

'Like you said, we've got it covered, but it's appreciated.'

'Mary was saying we ought to get together again soon,' Donaghue suggested.

'We ought. Why don't you, Cath and the girls come over for a barbecue?'

'Let's get the girls to arrange it.'

Three minutes later Maggie showed Myerscough in. Meeting with the DCI in fifteen minutes, she reminded Brettlaw.

'You ordered a check on the Nebulus accounts.' Myerscough settled in the chair in front of Brettlaw's desk. 'Everything's in order. I checked with First Commercial in Santa Fe, apparently a clerk made a mistake but they'd already spotted it. By the time I got there the correct amounts had been wired to Nebulus in London and everything was okay.'

Sorry, Brettlaw thought: meant to tell you yesterday but things got a bit hectic with Bonn and all that. Except that wasn't why Myerscough had asked to see him.

'Something's up with Benini.' Myerscough tried to cover his nervousness.

'How'd you mean?' It was eight minutes to his briefing with the DCI.

'He's not there. I've phoned his offices in Zurich and Milan and spoken to his personal assistants. Each time they said he wasn't there, but each time they gave a different reason.'

'Even when you told them you were a client?'

'No need. I phoned on the private line.'

'So where do you think he is?'

'I don't know. The problem is that the bank doesn't know either and is covering that fact.'

Zev down and the Red River money going missing, Brettlaw thought. Zev's death accounted for and the Red River money reappears. The world in order again and everything fine. Now Benini going missing.

'So what do you suggest we do?' he asked.

'Let it run for a couple more days. I'll keep trying to reach him. Plan to switch the accounts elsewhere if there's something wrong.'

'Stay in touch on it. Anything else?'

'A couple of things.' Myerscough leant forward and used one of

130

Brettlaw's internal phones to call Lansbridge. Ninety seconds later Maggie Dubovski showed her in. Two minutes to the briefing with the DCI, she reminded Brettlaw.

Myerscough took the files. 'Bekki Lansbridge, Tom Brettlaw.' Bekki Lansbridge was impressed, he could see: the faint flush in the face and the slight tightening of the back. Bekki Lansbridge loved it.

'I think we met once.' Brettlaw smiled politely.

'I think we did. Good to see you again.' She turned and left the room.

Brettlaw glanced at his watch. 'Thanks for the files, I'll look at them later. Keep in touch on Benini.'

He confirmed his room at the Club that night and went to his meeting with the DCI. Two hours and twenty minutes later he was driven to Andrews.

The day had contrived to be grey: grey buildings, grey runways, grey sky. Grey plane dropping out of it. He stood in the background and watched as the C130 landed, then turned back along the runway to the point where the marine guard of honour was standing at attention.

Zev down, he thought again, but then Zev's death had been explained. The Red River transfer going missing, then the money reappears. No links and no lapses of security. Except that Red River was run through Nebulus, Nebulus had been set up by Benini, and now Benini had disappeared off the face of the earth.

The Vice President waited at attention, the DCI representing the Agency on his right and the Secretary of State representing the Defense Department on his left, the television crews hovering. The coffins appeared and were brought carefully down the steps till the pall-bearers carrying them came to a halt side by side. There was barely enough wind to flutter the corners of each of the flags with which the coffins were draped. The muffled roll of the anthem drifted across the grey, then the last note faded and the command broke the silence which had taken its place. The guards carrying the coffins moved forward, the timing and movements precise and co-ordinated, and laid the coffins in the rear of the hearses.

Only after the vehicles and their escorts pulled away and the television crews had been cleared did Brettlaw move forward and join the official party. Then he returned to Langley.

So what to do about Benini? Assuming Myerscough was right and Benini really was missing.

The telephone rang thirty minutes after he had returned: one of the direct lines, and the call on a pay phone. Kirolev, he assumed, Malenko's man in Washington. Probably from one of the booths at the rear of the Capitol Hilton foyer, less than a block from the embassy.

'I'm phoning about the delivery you're expecting.'

'I was hoping to hear about it.'

Kirolev, the former KGB man at the Russian Federation coming back with Malenko's reply from Moscow. And if Malenko was replying it meant he was prepared to go along with what he must know Brettlaw would propose.

'Ten-thirty tonight.'

'Fine.'

So what about Benini?

Let it run for a couple of days, Myerscough had said. Which was logical in some ways, but Myerscough wasn't DDO, Myerscough didn't know the half of what was happening.

Therefore he himself should find out, but to do that he would need to be on the inside. Therefore he should send someone. But Benini was separate, just as everything was separate from everything else. Boxes within boxes. And by sending someone he risked establishing a connection, however tenuous.

Only if he sent someone from within the Agency, however. Send someone from outside, someone he trusted, someone who had worked for him without knowing who he was actually working for, and he would be covered. Boxes within boxes.

But that person would have to be good, that person would have to be the best.

Therefore if he sent someone he would send Hendricks.

Don't forget, Mitchell reminded himself.

The morning was hot and the Donaghue investigation was going predictably: some doors opening and others closing. It was the way the game went. He left the houseboat, drove to National, dropped the car in the satellite area where parking was cheaper, and caught the shuttle to New York. At ten he was taking coffee with the assistant District Attorney called Anderton.

Don't forget, he told himself again.

'So how can I help?'

Anderton was as confident and abrasive as always, but abrasive because he wanted something. It was in his eyes, in the way he tried to appear relaxed.

'As I said, I'm doing an investigation for the Senate Banking Committee and wondered whether you had anything we should be talking about.'

Not because we work for the same people, because we don't. But because I work for Donaghue and Donaghue might be your way to the future.

'How's Jack?' Anderton asked, as if he and Donaghue were acquainted.

'Jack's fine. What have you got?' Sometimes you played round the edge, other times you went straight to the point.

'It's a little awkward, Mitch.' Which he had to say, they both understood. 'Rules of confidentiality and all that.' Which he had to say as well. 'What I mean is, it's my jurisdiction and I don't want the gorillas from Justice or the apes from the Fed stamping over my patch.'

'What are you really saying, Jim?'

'What I'm saying is: what's in it for me?'

Mitchell helped himself to more coffee. 'I'm seeing Ed Pearson this afternoon.' You know Ed Pearson of course. Know of him at least, because once you knew I was working for Donaghue that's the sort of thing you'd check. Therefore you know that Pearson is Donaghue's AA, his Chief of Staff at the White House if Donaghue makes it. 'The first thing I tell Ed Pearson is your name.' And Ed won't forget, because Ed isn't in the business of forgetting who helped him and who didn't.

Anderton appeared to hesitate, appeared to work out what he would say next even though he had already done so.

'As you know, the Federal Bank's rules on the recording of money transfers overseas are stringent. Designed mainly to prevent the laundering of drug money. Which I'm sure is of interest to Jack.'

He couldn't resist any attempt to get on board, Mitchell thought.

'Recently, however, we've picked up a whisper that as long as you're prepared to pay over the odds in terms of commission, there's a bank which might help you out.'

Which bank, he expected Mitchell to say.

'How reliable's the source?' Mitchell asked instead.

Which he didn't want to hear, Anderton thought. 'As I said, it's just a whisper.'

'Anyone on the inside?'

Because that's what I need, that's what I don't have on the other cases.

'Not yet.'

As if there would be, Mitchell thought. But Anderton was smart, and even though he didn't have the evidence he must be sure it was a goer, because Anderton was looking to the future.

Don't forget, he reminded himself. He should have made a note of it, stuck it on his wallet or inside his briefcase, somewhere he was bound to see it.

'As I said, Ed Pearson gets your name this afternoon.'

Anderton handed him the file. 'What's the name of the bank?' Mitchell asked at last.

'First Commercial of Santa Fe.'

He told Anderton he would be in touch, took a cab to Macey's, and spent half an hour getting the right present giftwrapped in the right way. Just don't forget to post it, he told himself.

His meeting with Pearson was at four, in Pearson's office in Russell Building.

'The groundwork's done,' Mitchell told the AA. 'There are half a dozen investigations which we can access at the moment, it's just a matter of deciding which we go for.'

'When will we know whether you have enough for Jack to announce an enquiry?'

Because unless you can deliver there's no enquiry, and unless there's an enquiry we go into the campaign with one shot less in the locker.

'Give me a couple more weeks.'

'Anything else?' Pearson was already running behind time.

'One other possibility came up this morning. A contact in the Manhattan DA's office. Might make it, might not. I told him I'd give you his name.'

Pearson understood why. 'Who is he?'

'Jim Anderton, Assistant DA.'

'Any good?'

'So-so.'

'I'll give him a call.'

When Mitchell returned to the committee offices in Dirksen the last secretary was just leaving.

'No home to go to?' he joked.

'You wouldn't think so,' she joked back.

He watched as she left, added the First Commercial reference to the computer list, and checked the number of the next contact. The number he dialled was a direct line in to the Internal Revenue Service.

'Jed, it's Mitch Mitchell. Long time since we had a beer.'

'I'm just leaving. How about one on the way home?'

Because things sometimes get tight. Because the people upstairs don't like IRS men like me helping investigators like you.

'See you at six.'

The bar was just south of what the locals called the 14th Street Bridge, looking across the river.

'So what do you want this time?' The IRS man settled in the seat and ran his finger up the beads on the side of the glass.

'A list of employees and social security deductions at the First Commercial Bank of Santa Fe for the last four years,' Mitchell told him.

The employees list would give him the names of people who had left the bank, and if someone had left the bank he or she might have a reason for talking to someone like Mitchell. The higher the salary, the more important the person and the greater their access into the bank's secrets.

But the details of the salaries would be held by the bank and not in a block by the Revenue Service, therefore to trace each one individually would be impossible. By using the federal tax ID number of the bank, however, the IRS contact could access the social security numbers and names of the bank's employees, plus the amount of money withheld for each employee's social security contribution. And because the amount withheld was a standard 15 per cent of gross, the salaries of all employees at the bank could be worked out from it.

As long as Anderton was right and First Commercial was the one he was looking for.

God knew what they were going to do about Benini, Myerscough thought, but at least the Nebulus money hadn't gone missing and he'd covered himself with the DDO. It was seven in the evening; he locked the security safe and prepared to leave.

Perhaps he ought to get update reports from the department's sources on the Hill and in the defence industries spread round DC, though. Check out what was happening. Not because anything was happening. Except Benini of course. And not because anything connected. But just to cover his back because of Benini.

Three of the department were still at their computers. One of them was Bekki Lansbridge. Good move this morning, he told himself, good idea to ask her to join him in Brettlaw's office. Somebody else was making it with her and some day it might be his turn. He smiled at her and called the lift. Someone was making it with her tonight, he suddenly thought; it was in the way she was moving, the way she was looking, and the electricity around her.

Twenty minutes later Lansbridge cleared and locked her desk, took the lift to the ground floor, collected her car, and drove in to DC. Her first stop was at the flat off Washington Circle. She changed, took a cab to 15th, and checked in at the Madison.

He'd be good tonight, he always was good. All day the excitement had been growing in her, beginning the moment she had woken and mounting throughout the morning, increasing as she became aware of it. She placed the case on the bed and opened it. Perhaps it was the risk, perhaps because he was always on the edge, and that gave him a rawness, a naked energy. Perhaps it was a combination of both. She could always tell how close to the edge he was, almost understand what was happening by what he wanted done and what he wanted to do to her.

The bottle of Jack Daniels was in the corner of the case, the two crystal glasses carefully wrapped. She undressed, slowly and carefully, enjoying it and occasionally glancing at herself in the mirror. Pity he wasn't here now, pity she couldn't have him now. She half-filled one of the glasses with ice from the minibar, broke the seal of the bottle, and poured herself a whisky, watching the clear brown liquor trickle between the cubes. Then she drank it in one, poured herself another, and took it to the shower.

The over-look was empty, the last of the evening light faded and the occasional light blinking in the woodlands on the far side of the river. Brettlaw locked the Chevy, climbed the wall, dropped down the three feet on the other side, lit a cigarette and stood looking across the river.

Red River in one box, Zev Bartolski in a second and Benini in a third, he thought. And if Benini was a problem then Hendricks was the right person to sort it out.

Send Hendricks and nobody could make connections. Send Hendricks, build in the cut-outs that would separate Hendricks from Langley in general and himself in particular, and it would give him the one thing by which he judged all his actions: a plausible deniability. He would think about it some more, of course, but probably he would contact Hendricks.

Behind him he heard the car engine, then saw the sweep of headlights across the gossamer black of the summer night. The engine was cut, the silence fell on the woodlands, then Kirolev climbed the wall and joined him.

'Ten o'clock, two days' time,' the Russian told him.

The day after Bartolski's funeral.

'Morning or evening?'

Kirolev was on edge, Brettlaw sensed. Probably because of the meeting and the message he was passing on.

'Morning.'

'Where?'

'The bar on the corner of Heidelberger Strasse.'

'Give him my thanks.'

Kirolev wasn't on edge because of the meeting, Brettlaw realized, Kirolev was on edge because he was on his way to meet a woman. He remembered the file details about the Russian, about his proclivities and his stamina. Wonder where he's going and who he's going with, he thought, whether it was business or pleasure. Whether Kirolev was on his way to screw someone Malenko had targeted, or simply someone who attracted him.

'I will.'

The knock on the door was distinctive. Three knocks, silence, then one. Bekki Lansbridge slid off the safety chain and let him in.

The lights were out, the candles flickering in the dark, and the smell of incense filled the room. The Jack Daniels was on the bedside table, the two glasses beside it, and the silk dressing-gown he had bought her on his last trip to Thailand was tied loosely at the waist.

'You're late.'

She lifted her arms round his neck, head tilted back and lips soft and open. He tasted the Jack Daniels in her mouth and slid his arms round her waist, inside the dressing-gown, the half-knot breaking and the silk falling loosely round her. Perhaps he'd had the erection at the meeting at the over-look on Parkway; perhaps as he'd pressed the button of the lift. Perhaps he'd had it all day.

She brushed her right hand down and felt him, unzipped his trousers and held him. Christ how strong he was already, the energy pumping through him. How he was already moving, even before she had touched him, how he was gasping as she ran her fingers lightly over him and stroked him, then grasped him hard.

'You want a shower?'

'As long as you join me.'

He slipped his hands behind her back and round her buttocks, and pulled her tight into him. She was undressing him and guiding him into the shower, the water cascading round them. She was reaching down and holding him again, not waiting, lifting herself up and guiding him into her.

'Myerscough thinks you've got the best ass in town.'

Even now he could remember the way Myerscough's eyes had followed her that morning, the way he had turned back, the smile on his face and the images in his mind.

'Screw Myerscough.'

'I think that's what he had in mind,' Brettlaw said.

7

Rossi's meeting with the chairman was at ten. Negretti was in his usual position behind the antique mahogany desk. We have fifteen minutes – it was in the way he glanced at his watch – so make it fast.

If he told the chairman the truth then he was making problems for himself now, and if he didn't he was merely storing up bigger problems for the future. But unless he told Negretti what he wanted to hear there might not be a future. Therefore stall, Rossi had decided, begin to slide the blame elsewhere. Except how and to whom?

'It's going as the consultant predicted.' Rossi made sure his delivery was firm, not understated but not over-confident. 'The kidnappers have provided proof that Paolo is alive, they've made their first demand and we've countered with our first offers. The next stage is to inform them we wish to talk, via a series of newspaper adverts.' Then they'll establish contact again, he almost said, except that implied there was no contact at the moment. Which was true, but not what the chairman wanted to hear. 'At that point, according to the consultant, negotiations will resume.'

'But it's on course?' Negretti asked.

'Yes,' Rossi told him.

The café on the corner was crowded and the afternoon was hot, couples sitting beneath the sunshades at the tables on the pavement, and the boutiques busy. No Alfa in the parking bays, Haslam noted, therefore no stake-out, but there wouldn't be until the negotiations began again. As long as there was a stake-out, and as long as the Alfa was connected with it. But the Alfa had been the only car regularly in place when there was reason for a stake-out.

It was a week since the last contact with the kidnappers. Each evening since then the management team had met, each time Umberto Benini had suggested it was time to place the advertisement in the newspaper, and each time Haslam had argued against it. Tonight Umberto would override him, he sensed. If he hadn't done so already, if he hadn't gone behind everyone's back and already put the advert in. In which case it would be time to stand back, take a serious look at the situation, and ask whether it was time to pull out and for another consultant to be sent in.

He left the street and went to the apartment.

'Developments?' Umberto brought the meeting to order.

There were none.

'In that case the time has come to place an advertisement asking the kidnappers to contact us.'

'It may still be too early,' Haslam warned them again. 'You think that by sitting here you're doing nothing to help Paolo, but this isn't true. Silence is a weapon they're using against you but which you can also use against them. It sounds harsh, but you have to call their bluff. Each day they hold Paolo costs them money. By not asking them to make contact you begin to put pressure on them, but by asking them to make contact so soon takes that pressure off and gives them the advantage.'

Haslam was right, of course – Rossi sat back slightly. Haslam was always right, but Haslam was dropping him in it. Haslam would get Benini out, but too late. And unless there was a development soon the chairman would have his balls.

'Our decision is to ask them to make contact.' Benini sat slightly straighter in his chair. 'The notice will appear tomorrow and will run for a week.'

'Which means you've already put it in?'

'Yes.'

In that case I leave now, they all knew Haslam was going to say. Because even though his presence was a requirement of the kidnap clause of the bank's insurance policy there was no point in staying if they continually overruled him.

'In that case you should bear in mind how the kidnappers might react and prepare for it.'

'Perhaps you might give us the benefit of your experience.' Umberto folded his hands in front of him and looked down the table.

'There are a number of alternatives. The first is that they might not reply. The second is that they do and you increase your offer. The third is that they do something totally different.'

'What will they do?' It was Francesca.

'We can't be sure.'

140

That's the difference between us – Umberto almost snorted his irritation and contempt. You waste time telling me the alternatives and I make decisions.

'But what would you do if you were them?' It was still Francesca.

'I'd see your ad in the paper, assume that you were running it for a week, and let you sweat for the first two or three days. Then I'd change the game. I'd phone on, say, the third evening, tell you there was a package and that I'd phone again the following night with details of the pick-up.'

And that way I'd scare you so much you'd do almost anything. Which I've already done just by telling you.

'What would you say would be in it?' Francesca's voice was lower.

'I wouldn't, I'd let you worry about it.'

Why are you treating me this way? she almost asked him. Why are you putting me through it? 'What would be in it?' She changed the question slightly.

'A note, perhaps a Polaroid or a video.'

'But whatever it is will be bad?'

'Whatever it is will appear bad. But it won't be. Whatever it is will be carefully set up. If it's a tape recording it will probably end with a scream; if it's a photo Paolo will look as if he's been beaten up. If it's a handkerchief it will be soaked in blood.'

She almost vomited.

'The advertisement.' Umberto brought them back to his agenda. 'To run for one week, starting tomorrow.'

The bastard, Haslam thought. Umberto knew they were only part through the conversation yet had cut it off when Francesca was at her lowest and before he'd had a chance to bring her up again.

Umberto Benini tidied his papers and began to bring the meeting to a close.

'Whatever the kidnappers do, it won't be as it seems.' Haslam made them sit down, made Francesca listen to him. 'If it's a message from Paolo they'll have written it for him, even edited the tape. If it's a photo they'll have made him up to look bad. If there's blood involved it probably won't be his.'

Only probably, she almost screamed at him.

'If it's his they'll have nicked his finger, nothing more.'

The advertisement was on the eighteenth page, the fifth item in the second column. Francesca had been awake since four, had slept only fitfully before. At six she rose; at seven she left the apartment, walked up Via Ventura, and bought a copy of that day's *Corriere della Sera*. Today was the first day of the new life, she tried to convince herself, today they would begin the process of bringing Paolo home.

Haslam was in position at two. It was still too early for the stake-out to be in position personally, but not too early for the car to be in place. He went to the café on the corner, sat at an outside table, and waited. Today was no man's land; today the family's advert would appear, today Francesca would wait at the clean phone, and today the bastards would tear her heart out. When he arrived at the apartment Francesca and Marco were preparing to leave.

'You have the script?' He walked with her to the lift and held her arm as they waited.

'Yes.' She could barely speak.

'If they phone just read it. But if they don't, everything's still all right.'

They crossed the reception area, Marco going ahead to the car.

'It'll be all right,' Haslam told her. 'You'll be all right.'

The apartment was quiet, Umberto in an armchair in one corner, Haslam in another on the other side of the room, and Rossi by himself.

Tomorrow he would have to inform the chairman that the first of the new adverts had appeared, Rossi thought. Then Negretti would ask about the solution and he, Rossi, would say that it was confidently expected that the issue would be resolved quickly. Except that it wasn't. And there was the catch. If he pressed for the quick release the chairman wanted it might actually lengthen the time Benini was held, in which case he would screw himself. But if he waited for the long option he would screw himself anyway.

So work it out, he told himself. Now that he'd identified the problem, work out how he could turn it to his advantage.

Quick release or long option? Go for either and the chances were that he would lose. Go for both, however, and he might win. Except that to do that he would have to cover himself, which, in a way, he had already begun to do.

Paul on the road to Damascus, he thought, the proverbial flash of lightning. Haslam was the key, because they needed him but at the same time weren't acting on the advice he was giving. So turn it, use it to his advantage. Christ, why the hell hadn't he seen it before?

Arrange Haslam's removal, so that if the quick release plan succeeded he rather than Haslam would get the credit, but if it didn't work he could blame it on Haslam's absence. But arrange that absence in such a way that if the short release idea didn't work he could still bring Haslam back to go for the longer solution. The only question was how.

It was seven o'clock. Haslam stared at the window. Francesca would be reaching for the phone now, might even be picking it up; would be looking at Marco and realizing that it hadn't rung. It was ten past seven; Marco would be suggesting they leave, Francesca insisting they wait another couple of minutes. Quarter past: even Francesca would be shaking her head and admitting the kidnappers weren't going to call that evening.

It was seven-thirty. He stood at the window and saw the BMW drive into the area in front of the apartment. No figures running from it, no one even moving. He went downstairs and stood by the car, helped her out.

'Don't worry,' he told her. 'They will phone and you'll be okay when they do.'

At least the kidnappers were giving him time, Rossi thought. Plus he knew what he would do. Once he'd thought about it, it had almost been too simple.

The call to a lawyer friend, then the lawyer's call to a high-ranking contact in the carabinieri. The policeman's call to a colleague in the kidnap division, and the call from the kidnap division to Villa, the head of security at BCI. Followed by the appropriate fee.

He'd have to cover his tracks, make sure the lawyer was not only someone he could trust but someone who would have the contact in the kidnap squad. And it would cost, of course, but everything did in Milan.

The devil looks after his own, he remembered, therefore he would start the arrangements tonight. And hope to hell they were in place before the kidnappers got round to making contact.

The room was dark and the dream filtered through the layers of sleep.

The sand was golden and the sun was hot. Francesca was twenty metres from the beach, her feet barely touching the bottom. She waved at Paolo, then turned and swam out into the surf. Don't swim into the break, she reminded herself; dive under it, wait till it had gone over her, then surface. And if the break was big, then dive

143

deeper, even if she had to hit the bottom; even if she had to wait till the bubbles rose before she went back up.

She swam on, the waves bigger and more powerful, tumbling at her in sets of threes. The third wave of each set the biggest, she remembered the rule, the third set biggest of all. The white was coming at her again; she held her breath and dived beneath it, waited till it had passed then kicked up and swam on, the second wave coming at her. She dived beneath it then surfaced, went below the next and came up again. The sky was all she could see now; only when she'd swum beyond the break would she be able to rise with the lift of the unbroken wave and look back at the beach.

The third wave hit her, bigger than she'd thought and stronger than she'd experienced. She looked up and saw the sky again then the first wave of the second set, the wall of white suddenly towering above. She took a breath and dived deep but not deep enough, found herself in the turmoil, her body tossed about as if it was a rag doll or a piece of seaweed. No problem, she told herself, she had plenty of air in her lungs, would have plenty of time before the next wave. She kicked up and broke the surface, began to breathe and glanced up, saw the next wave crashing down already, jack-knifed her body and dived beneath it. Not so much air in her lungs now, she was aware, dived deep anyway, tried to get away from the force of the wave, tried to escape the turmoil of water. She swam up, broke surface, saw the next wave crashing down and dived again, held her breath except there was no breath left to hold, swam up again even though it was probably too early, even though she'd probably be caught in the maelstrom of white water, lungs bursting and brain panicking.

She woke up.

It was two in the morning, the room was dark and her hands were shaking. Francesca turned on the bedside lamp and made herself sit up, tried to remember how the nightmare ended and whether she'd made it. It was like sitting at the phone that evening, the fear clamped round her and the cold settling on her. She was back in the dream and screaming for help, aware that in doing so she was throwing away what remained of her precious air but screaming anyway. She was shaking even more, the fear and panic wrapping in layers round her, each layer making her colder, making her panic more. She looked back and couldn't see the beach, knew therefore that nobody could see her, that nobody could help her.

*

144

At nine the following morning Rossi telephoned the chairman's secretary and asked for a meeting. All he needed was ten minutes, he explained. It was a pity he hadn't seen the way out a week ago, because then the chairman would have had time to absorb the preamble before he got the call from the bank's head of security, but at least everything was set up and running.

The chairman could see him at eleven-forty, the secretary told him. He made sure he was early and was shown in immediately.

'The Benini negotiations.'

Of course – it was in the way Negretti sat forward. No other reason you'd be here.

'I share your concern that Paolo should be released as quickly as possible.' There were dangers whichever way he played it. Play it wrong and the chairman might blame him and he might lose, but not play it and he certainly would. 'As you are aware, the bank is being advised by a consultant. Originally the consultant seemed to suggest that Paolo's release could be secured quickly.' And therefore, Mr Chairman, I reported back to you accordingly. 'Now it seems that may no longer be the case.' The groundwork was set and the blame attributed. Indirectly, of course, but that was always the best way. 'We are still trying to secure a quick solution, but I felt it only right to warn you.'

The chairman nodded. 'The consultant . . .' He searched for the name.

'Haslam.'

'Yes. How good is he?' Because kidnap insurance doesn't come cheap, and unless something moves quickly I have a lot of thinking to do.

The question was expected and the answer carefully worked out and perfectly delivered, the correct degree of doubt sown in the correct way.

'He's probably very experienced.'

Haslam was in position on the Ventura at four-thirty. There was no Alfa, therefore there would be no contact tonight. Francesca was going through it, he thought at the meeting with the family two hours later; she hadn't slept for days and looked and sounded like hell. 'You all right?' he asked her. No, she wanted to say. Of course she was all right, Umberto told him.

There was no contact again and she was disintegrating. Francesca made herself get out of Marco's car and walk inside before her resolve collapsed totally.

No kidnappers, therefore there was a chance the message would get to the chairman in time. Rossi saw her face as she entered the apartment and offered her a drink, told her everything would be okay.

The night was dark and the waves were coming over her again. Tonight she wasn't going to make it, Francesca knew, tonight she wasn't going to pull through. It was two in the morning, the cold and dark around her and the waves towering round her, the last breath in her body. She wrapped a dressing-gown round her, went to the kitchen and made coffee, her feet cold on the marble floor. Sat in the lounge and stared at the wall, even colder, her hands and her feet and her entire body.

'Sorry, Dave . . .' She hadn't realized that she'd picked up the phone and dialled the number.

The cab dropped him off in front of the block. He tapped the code Francesca had told him into the security combination, went inside, and took the lift to the fifth floor. Against the rules, he knew; he shouldn't be doing this, shouldn't be going to Francesca's flat at two in the morning even though she was in a bad way. He should be phoning Marco, getting him to help; shouldn't be coming here himself, shouldn't be coming here alone.

The door of the flat was unlocked. Something wrong – it was as if he flicked to auto-pilot; no reason for there to be anything wrong, but the door shouldn't be open. He was already inside the apartment, moving silently. The door to the lounge was slightly ajar in front of him. He turned right, through the kitchen and into the lounge from the side. Francesca was sitting on the sofa, rocking just perceptibly, no one else in the room. He moved past her, quickly now, and checked the bathrooms and bedrooms, Francesca staring after him as if she did not understand who he was or what he was doing.

He returned and knelt in front of her. 'The door was open.' It was part explanation and part question.

'I opened it for you.' She looked at him. Her fingers were wrapped round a mug and there was a cigarette in her hand. You don't smoke, he almost said.

'I was drowning,' she tried to explain. 'Couldn't get to the surface . . .'

'It's all right,' he told her. The coffee in the mug was cold, he took it from her and put it on the floor. Her fingers and hands were also cold. He knelt by her and felt her feet – cold as well. Felt her face – like ice. The housekeeper's night off, he assumed; then remembered that the woman only came in during the day unless specially asked. The dressing-gown was silk and tied at the waist, but the knot had loosened and the gown had slipped. He pulled the silk high round her neck and tightened the knot, then fetched a blanket from one of the bedrooms and wrapped it round her body and her feet.

She was still shivering, though not simply from the cold.

'It's all right,' he told her. 'Everything's okay.' He brought her a glass of cognac, helped her raise it to her lips. When he was sure she would not drop it he went to the bathroom, ran a bath, then went back to her.

'Come on.'

He lifted her up and walked her to the bathroom, arm round her and supporting her. She was still shivering, as if the cold went to the bone. He took the blanket from her shoulders.

'Warm you up, you'll feel better then. I'll be outside.'

She tried to smile and he began to leave, saw that she was stepping into the bath without taking off the dressing-gown. He turned back and stopped her, slid the dressing-gown off and helped her into the bath, holding her arms as she settled back.

When he returned fifteen minutes later she was half asleep. He helped her out, laid a towel over her shoulders and handed her another, then left. When she came into the lounge she was wearing the dressing-gown and brushing her hair.

'You don't wear anything in bed?'

'No.'

'Perhaps you ought tonight. You've got something warm?'

'Yes.'

'Where?'

'In my bedroom.'

He walked her to the bedroom, his arm round her and her body fitting beside him, then left her and tidied the bathroom. When he returned, knocking before he went in, Francesca was curled in bed.

'You've got something warm on?'

She held her arm above the bedclothes so he could see.

'Good girl. You okay now?'

'Okay now.'

'I'll see you tomorrow.'

'Yes, see you tomorrow.'

He began to leave.

'Dave . . .'
'Yes.'
'Thanks.'

It was time to make contact, the kidnapper Vitali decided, time to really turn the screw on the family. Especially on the wife. He telephoned the stake-out Pascale and the negotiator Mussolini in that order, and gave them their instructions for that evening. Then he telephoned the house in Calabria and spoke to the head of the unit holding Paolo Benini.

The parking spaces Pascale needed were full. He parked at the end furthest from the apartment, and waited till one became free, cursed when he was beaten to it and got the next.

Alfa in place, Haslam noted, therefore the stake-out on standby. Therefore the stake-out was the thinly-built man, mid-thirties, dark hair and loose-fitting charcoal-grey suit. If the car stayed in position till later and the man used it as a base. If Mussolini phoned tonight.

At five Pascale returned briefly to the car. BMW arriving, the Saab five minutes later. No Merc, but the man the Merc had dropped off last time now arriving by cab and hurrying inside.

The Alfa – Haslam was confident. He cleared Via Ventura and approached the apartment block from the other direction. The others were already seated round the table.

'You know what you're going to say if they telephone?' He ignored everyone else and focused on Francesca. 'You have the script?' Though Christ knew how much Umberto and Rossi had altered it.

'Yes.' Her throat was dry and the word barely audible. 'Yes,' she said again, stronger this time. 'You think they'll phone tonight?'

'Yes.'

He walked to the lift with her, almost as if Marco didn't exist, walked to the car with her. 'If they phone just read the script, don't do anything else.' He put his arm round her. 'And if they phone just remember that tonight they're going to ring the changes, so be ready for it.'

The apartment with the clean phone was quiet, the sunlight playing through the window on to the table. Marco poured them each a cold mineral water while Francesca settled at the table and placed the script in front of her. How's Paolo, she rehearsed the structure. Is he still alive? Why didn't you reply to our last offer? How much

148

do you want? We can raise our offer by another two hundred and fifty million.

She smiled her thanks at Marco and began to drink. The telephone rang. She was confused, mesmerized by the fact that she would normally pick it up with her right hand but couldn't because she was holding the glass. No panic, it was as if Haslam was telling her, no problem; they want to speak to you as much as you want to speak to them.

'Yes.'

'Francesca?'

'Yes.'

'Another phone call tomorrow. Same time. Make sure Marco's with you. Tell him he'll be collecting something.'

8

The war council met at six-thirty.

'Update.' Donaghue hung his coat on the back of his chair and looked round the room.

'No one has declared since our last meeting, which means that at present there are five runners for the nomination.' Pearson led the discussion. 'Two of these are already faltering, mainly due to lack of funding, and are expected to pull out soon. Three others are expected to at least wave the flag in the fall.' He detailed the names and backgrounds, even though each person in the room was fully aware of them. 'The prediction at present is that four runners will be contesting the first primaries next spring.'

He looked at Donaghue. Five if you run.

'The front runners are the same as before?' Donaghue ignored the look.

'Yes.'

'Anything on them?'

Anything that would wreck their presidential ambitions? Any financial scandals or unpaid taxes, any showgirls about to say they've shared the marital bed?

'Not yet.'

'What about anything on me?'

'We're still looking.'

Because the opposition would be.

'What about your side?' He turned to the press secretary.

'Three newspaper polls have been run since we last met. In two of them you had a good show, especially as you haven't declared. In the third you came top.'

'Sounds good.' Donaghue went to the fridge and threw them each another beer. 'What about key staff and backers?'

'Still no one moving. The big backers haven't signed up with anyone yet and nobody's committing themselves on the staff level until they know where the money's going.'

'But . . .' Donaghue looked at one of the two lawyers on the war council.

'I had a call from an old Penn classmate yesterday; he suggested we got together for lunch some time.'

'So?'

'He works for Lavalle.'

Lavalle was one of the party faithfuls, one of the few industrialists who didn't back both sides. Lavalle was the one they all wanted. Nobody who was a lawyer with Lavalle would phone one of the inner team of a senator named as a potential presidential runner simply because they'd been at college together. Even if the college was Ivy League like Penn.

'When are you seeing him?'

'Friday next week.'

'Make it somewhere quiet.'

'Already done.'

They passed to the next point.

'O'Grady.'

Donaghue had been one of Senator John O'Grady's main supporters when he had been elected chairman of the party. O'Grady wouldn't show his hand openly, but he would be important in the back-room deals that would have to be struck if Donaghue was to win.

'Who's seen him? Who's trying to muscle in on him?'

Because he owes and we mustn't let him forget it.

'Everyone.'

'Any feedback?'

'Not yet.'

The early evening sun was shining through the windows on to the yard in the centre of Russell Building.

'What about Pamela Harriman?' It was one of the lawyers. 'Who's she inviting to dinner?'

Harriman had long been the king-maker of the Democratic Party. The daughter of a British earl, she had been married three times, on the last occasion to the statesman Averell Harriman. On their marriage she had taken out American citizenship, and on his death had inherited $150 million. Invitations to her Georgetown dinners were considered an indicator of position, both present and future. If a Democrat won the next election, it was rumoured, she would get one of the big ambassadorships, probably Paris.

'Nobody we need worry about.'

It was the sort of detail Pearson checked as a matter of routine. Donaghue was a regular guest, of course; Donaghue had even been invited before he was elected to the Senate. The Boston Mafia, he himself joked.

'What else?'

'Angel Fire this weekend.' The press secretary took over. Angel Fire was the Disabled Veterans Vietnam Memorial in New Mexico; Donaghue had been there before, she reminded the meeting, but not with his wife. 'Jack and Cath fly to Albuquerque Friday afternoon, early evening meeting with the Governor and state Democrats, then private plane to the hills. The service is the next morning, you're not scheduled to give any speeches unless you choose to do so.'

'No speeches?' It was the same lawyer. 'How many people will be there?'

'A lot. Mainly veterans and their families, obviously.'

'Television and press?'

'Local confirmed, networked if it's worthwhile.'

'And Jack isn't speaking?'

'No.'

'Why not?' Because unless Donaghue made a speech he wouldn't get coverage, and at this stage Angel Fire was the sort of coverage every candidate was screaming for.

'Any speech Jack makes is bound to be seen as electioneering. We both feel, however, that this weekend is a memorial service, and that if Jack was on the platform and made a speech, it would be inappropriate.'

Which is very fine and noble, the lawyer thought, but Jack's not a virgin, Jack's an experienced politician about to run for the White House.

'The people at Angel Fire appreciate this,' the press secretary continued. 'They also appreciate, however, that Jack shouldn't forgo the PR opportunity Angel Fire offers. What we'll get this weekend is worth a hundred speeches.'

'What are we going to get?'

'Pictures.'

If you say so – the lawyer shrugged. Only hope you know what you're doing. 'Jack and Cath fly to Albuquerque then on to Angel Fire the same evening?' he asked.

'Yes.'

'So where are they staying at Angel Fire?'

Because a United States senator, especially one tipped as a presidential runner, doesn't just fly in without a reception committee waiting for him, hands to shake and functions to attend.

'An RV's been arranged for them.' RV – recreational vehicle.

'What else?' Because some one like Jack Donaghue doesn't overnight in a camper van.

'Nothing else. That's what it's all about.'

The meeting broke up, Donaghue leaving immediately for another engagement. Pearson tidied his desk then left. Eva was waiting for him at the Hawk 'n Dove. When they left the evening was warm and the dome of the Capitol was glinting in the last sun.

'How'd it go?'

'Well,' Pearson told her. 'Jack got a good showing in a couple of trial polls. One of Lavalle's lawyers just happened to phone yesterday to speak to one of the guys he'd been at college with.'

'Lavalle's mega money.'

'I know.'

They turned down 6th.

'So the first of the big boys is declaring for Jack.'

'Not declaring. Just a lunch between old buddies.'

Except someone like Lavalle wouldn't just be checking the temperature.

They had slowed, slightly, almost imperceptibly.

'What's wrong, Ed?'

I don't know. It wasn't spoken; was in the way Pearson hunched his shoulders and dug his hands in his pockets.

'Jack's a great senator, Jack would make a great president. Not just because he's my man, not just because he and I have fought our way up together since he first made the House.' He stopped walking and faced her. 'It's what he's dreamed of, planned for.' What they'd both dreamed of and striven for, Eva knew he meant. Pearson was looking at the sky, fists clenched and the muscles of his face tight. Then suddenly he relaxed. Not relaxed, just became quieter, almost subdued. 'But sometimes I wonder. Not whether Jack wants it, because he does. But sometimes I wonder whether he really is going for it.'

'Why not? Why shouldn't he?'

They began to walk again.

'I don't know.'

*

153

The Chevrolet collected Brettlaw at five-thirty.

The DDO in early again, it was noticed; collecting his coffee with the rest of them, shirt sleeves turned up, jacket over his arm, and plastic cup and plate balanced on his briefcase. The DDO not pulling rank, but sharing a joke with the guy in front of him. In a way it was already more than a routine; in a way it was almost a ritual, an act of faith. The DDO telling them he was going after the bastards who'd taken out the CoS in Bonn.

I want them, Milt.

Brettlaw's words to Cranlow in Bonn had seeped back, had done the rounds in the offices and cafeterias at Langley, been whispered about in the deli in McLean where the old hands gathered.

I want their balls.

Not literally, of course.

Except . . .

The Middle East in the early eighties: US personnel in constant danger of assassination or, more probably, kidnapping or hostage-taking. So why were the Soviets getting away scot-free, they had all asked; why, when Agency people walked such a tight rope, did the Soviets not suffer from the same problem? And then the story had seeped out: that a KGB officer had been kidnapped, but the next day those considered responsible had disappeared, and when they were returned the day after, their genitals were stuffed in their mouths. And the following day the KGB man had been returned – no ransom, no protracted negotiations – and after that no KGB man or Soviet official had been threatened again. Even the name of the senior KGB officer who had sanctioned the move had been allowed to slip out. Malenko.

'Dollar twenty, Mr Brettlaw.'

'Thanks, Mack.'

He balanced the cup and plate on his briefcase and took the lift to the seventh floor.

Normal briefings until eleven – he put the briefcase down, hung up his coat, opened the coffee and checked his schedule. Special briefing with Cranlow, who was coming in from Bonn, at eleven-fifteen, lunch with the DCI and visiting dignitaries at twelve, and Zev Bartolski's funeral at three. Then the drive to Andrews and the overnight flight to Berlin, a briefing in the city as cover, and the arrangements for the meet with Malenko as secret as the request he would make at it.

The bagel was fresh and reminded him of breakfast with the kids

154

in the old days. He took a bite, turned on the computer, checked his electronic mail, then loaded Procomm Plus and dialled up the Zeus bulletin board.

If there was a problem about Benini it was better to deal with it now rather than wait for any developments Myerscough might report. And if it was better to deal with it now then it made sense to put Hendricks in and pull him out if Myerscough reported that Benini had reappeared and everything was in order again. Boxes within boxes: he using Hendricks but preferring not to know all of Hendricks's details, and Hendricks himself not knowing who was employing him or who was his controller.

He typed in his password, went into the Zeus electronic mail door, and left the message on Hendricks's e-mail. Nothing obvious, not even encrypted, just asking Hendricks to leave a number and time at which he could be contacted. And only Hendricks able to access his e-mail by using his own password and code.

In the old days it would have been a message at a dead drop or a telephone call to an unlisted number. Today it was a message left on one of the electronic bulletin boards run by a myriad small companies springing up everywhere; in DC alone there were over three hundred. Hendricks wouldn't even need to be at home to read it: he could use any computer in any part of the world, connect the modem and access the system. And once he had read the message Hendricks would delete it then leave the reply – again apparently innocent – giving the contact number at which he could be reached. In Hendricks's case it would be a public telephone, either at a railway station or in a hotel foyer, the telephones checked to confirm they would accept incoming calls. Plus the times he would be waiting.

In the old days there would also have been cut-outs – officers between Brettlaw and Hendricks whose function was to remove the DDO from direct contact with the case and therefore absolve him from responsibility if anything went wrong. But in a way the e-mail supplied the cut-out.

Boxes within boxes.

Brettlaw logged off and enjoyed the coffee while it was still hot.

Myerscough's meeting with Bekki Lansbridge was at nine. The session was routine, the type he had with each of his aides. She was looking good, he thought, this morning she was looking tremendous. When she left he telephoned Milan for the second time that day, then turned his attention to the reports she had collated from the various individuals whose positions in the defence industries in DC or the political offices in places like Capitol Hill might occasionally allow them access to material which could be of interest to the Agency. None of the contacts aware to whom they were reporting, of course, and none of the aides who ran the contacts knowing details of who the others were running, the nature of the material being supplied, or the position or identity of the suppliers.

The reports that morning ran to fifteen pages. Three of the reports contained nothing of interest, two referred to evidence about to be presented to Congressional investigations already under way, and another two indicated possible areas of such investigations in the future.

His request for a meeting with the DDO was made at quarter past eleven.

'Where's Cranlow?' Brettlaw asked Maggie Dubovski.

'Message just come through. His flight's delayed and he can't make it till two.'

'In that case tell Myerscough I'll see him in ten minutes.'

Six minutes later he was informed that Myerscough was waiting. Myerscough was like that, Brettlaw almost laughed: early and getting earlier. One day Myerscough would be so early he'd arrive before he left from the time before.

'Benini's still missing. His office is still being vague about his whereabouts and there's no response at the emergency contact numbers.'

Which is important, Brettlaw thought, but not why Myerscough had asked for a special meeting. 'Still no idea what might have happened to him?' he asked.

'No.'

'Are the accounts okay?'

'Yes.'

'In that case let's hope they stay that way and he turns up soon. Anything else?'

'Nothing at the moment.'

Myerscough had changed his mind. Myerscough had come to his office with two things to tell him. Had needed to tell him about Benini, but had decided against telling him whatever else it was, probably decided at the last moment to check it out before he passed it on. Therefore it wasn't important enough for Myerscough to stick his neck out, because when it was Myerscough would tell him, if only to pass the buck.

'Thanks for updating me.'

He was right in not telling Brettlaw, Myerscough tried to convince himself. The fact that one of the Senate banking sub-committees was investigating money laundering didn't mean it would necessarily touch upon any of their operations. It was still a long way from the Agency, still too far to suggest to Brettlaw that he was worried about it, even though one of the banks under scrutiny was First Commercial of Santa Fe. He'd keep an eye on it, though, keep in touch with where the investigator called Mitchell went next.

Thirty-five minutes after the Myerscough meeting Brettlaw left his office and walked to the DCI's dining-room. The Director's guests had already arrived: someone from the White House, half a dozen members of Congress, key chairpersons of key committees whom the DCI would wish to lobby and who saw political mileage in attending the funeral of Zev Bartolski. Plus some of the bastards who'd tried to grill him on the Hill. He put on his Harvard smile, stepped into the room, and forced the small talk.

If some of those present ever knew, he found himself thinking – about the details of the black accounts and the projects they were funding. Yet somewhere out there were men and women – brave men and women – who were risking everything for what they believed in. Some of whom would die, just as Zev Bartolski had died. Yet most of these smooth-suited bastards on the committees, even some of those here today, would have him by the balls if they so much as suspected what he was up to.

He smiled at them and wondered.

How far he would go to protect the men and women out there in the field.

More than that.

How far he would really go, who and what he would be prepared to sacrifice, to protect what he believed in.

On the far side of the room one of the DCI's staff motioned that he was wanted on the telephone. He crossed the room and picked up the set.

'Yes.'

'Maggie here. Cranlow's just arrived. He's grabbing a sandwich.'

'Tell him I'm coming down.'

Five minutes later the Bonn Chief of Station was seated in his office, a sandwich on a plastic plate. Just what he himself would have done, Brettlaw thought.

'Bud?' Brettlaw offered.

'If it's cold.'

Brettlaw opened the fridge and pulled out two Budvars.

Heard about these, Cranlow thought, heard the DDO had his supply even before the Berlin Wall came down.

'So tell me.' Brettlaw snapped the cap off the bottle and settled behind his desk.

'As you know, the device which killed Zev was a platter bomb. As you also know, a number of others have been used in Europe over the past months. The Germans are still trying to establish links, but we've come up with a list of three front runners.'

'Who?'

'The Armed Crescent, the 3rd October, and the Revolutionary Movement of the Martyr Mahmoud.'

All Middle East, which was as Brettlaw had expected. The first was a generic name, the second named after the date of a previous incident, and the third after a member arrested and allegedly tortured to death by one of the Middle East states supported by the West. The main groups probably sponsored by Moscow, he also assumed, at least in the old days, and the bomb-maker also Moscow-trained. Old friends new enemies, he thought, old enemies new friends. Christ knew who would be on which side in five years' time.

'Any chance they're still in Europe?'

'Possibly.'

'Keep on it.'

He concluded the briefing, sat back in his chair, wondered whether he should return to the official lunch, and asked Maggie to arrange some sandwiches. Two hours later he said farewell to Zev Bartolski.

The coffin was draped in the Stars and Stripes, and the sound of the anthem was low and haunting. The Battle Hymn of the Republic. The Cold War had ended and the enemy had changed, but the enemy was still there. Today, this afternoon, Brettlaw believed it more than at any other time.

It was the wrong time of the year to bury someone like Zev, he suddenly thought; spooks should be buried in winter, the ground hard, the faces of the mourners muffled but still slightly pinched, and the breath hanging in the air. Instead the sun was beating down and the sweat was drenching his back.

The last note of the band hung on the hillside and the last words of the anthem lingered in the still.

As he died to make men holy,
Let us live to make men free.
His truth is marching on.

The politicians were in the front of the mourners, making sure the TV crews got good shots of them. At least Jack Donaghue had the decency not to come, he thought.

Martha Bartolski stepped forward and cast the first handful of soil on the coffin, the earth rattling like gravel on the oak lid. At her side the younger son saluted. Brettlaw remembered the photograph of another son saluting his father. The young Kennedy saying goodbye to the president. Zev's widow turned away and began to walk unsteadily toward the waiting cars. The television crews began to leave, the politicians with them, one or two pausing to give interviews. Brettlaw left the graveside and touched her arm.

'Don't leave yet.'

She nodded without understanding and clutched the hand of her eldest son.

'Journos and politicos out of here.' Brettlaw was suddenly angry. 'Make sure they don't come back.'

The crew cars of the journalists and the town cars of the politicians wound their way through the gates and back towards Washington. The graveyard was empty, except for the widow, the two sons, and the closest of colleagues and friends. Brettlaw at the head of the grave, Martha to his right and the two boys to his left.

'Be proud of your father,' he told them. 'Be proud of what you are about to see.'

It was five minutes since the last car had left. He checked his watch and waited. The second column of cars drove in.

The men and women left the cars and took their places round the gaping hole. Not the Director of Central Intelligence nor the political appointees, not the names and faces known to the public. The analysts Bartolski had worked with as a desk man and the agents he had worked with in the field. Some were stationed at Langley, but others had flown in that morning.

The procession began, each man and woman stooping for a handful of earth then casting it upon the coffin, some pausing, some even smiling as they remembered something, nodding their heads at the exploits of Zev Bartolski in some God-forsaken corner of the world, then shaking hands with his widow and sons.

The last filed past, then they left the grave and allowed Martha

Bartolski her final moments with her husband. When she caught up with Brettlaw she was fighting to control the tears.

'Thank you.' She tried to smile but couldn't. 'Will you be joining us later?'

That evening, and in the Polish tradition of his forefathers, there was to be a wake.

'I'm sorry, but I have to go somewhere.'

She looked at him, sadly and thinly, then her face changed. You're going after Zev's killers, aren't you? . . . It was in her eyes and on her face . . . That's why you can't come tonight.

You know better than to ask me that . . . Brettlaw took her arm and led her to the family car.

The Internal Revenue Service list of employees at the First Commercial Bank of Santa Fe over the past four years ran to twenty-seven computerized sheets. Mitchell began examining the list at eight in the morning; by eleven he had drawn up a list of those employees who had left in the preceding year, by early afternoon those who had left in the previous two, and by mid-afternoon those who had left in the previous three.

The Tampa investigation was folding. Tampa had been a good drugs case but didn't give him access to the money laundering involved. Detroit might be beginning to come together; a couple of insiders possibly prepared to talk, though neither of them was high enough up the organization to know what was really going on.

He spread the lists of former First Commercial employees on the desk and compared the salaries he had computed. Four interested him: two slightly above average, one marginally higher, and one almost at the top of the bank's scale.

Latino first name, good Scottish last name, he thought, but New Mexico always was a mixing bowl. So who was Carlos Menzies? What had he done in First Commercial and why had he left?

It was five in the evening, three in the afternoon in Santa Fe. He checked on the computer file and called the number, tried to imagine what the bank looked like, inside and out, and where the telephonist was sitting. It all helped.

'Hi. Carlos Menzies, please.'

Not *Hello* or *Good afternoon.*

Hi. Relaxed and informal.

Not *Mr Menzies.*

160

Carlos Menzies. As if he knew what he was talking about.

'I'm sorry, Mr Menzies left us a couple of years back.'

'Really.' Doesn't time fly. Can't be that long since we last saw each other. It was in his voice, in his surprise.

'You want to speak to Mr Richards?' Because he's taken over.

'Sure.' He waited to be connected.

'This is Mr Richards' office. How may I help you?'

'Mr Richards?' Sorry, whose office am I speaking to? The questioning was in his tone, as if he might have been put through to the wrong number.

'Buck Richards.'

Everyone had a nickname, he supposed. 'Sorry, I think I've got the wrong person. What does Mr Richards do?'

'VP MIS.'

Christ, Mitchell thought.

'Sorry. I do have the wrong person.'

VP. Vice President.

MIS. Management Information Systems. Essentially the bank's computers.

'Thanks for the help.'

He checked the Santa Fe telephone directory and confirmed that a Carlos Menzies was still listed. It was five-thirty. Haven't forgotten, he almost laughed at himself. He dialled the other number and waited for it to be answered.

'Hi, Matti. This is Mitch. Talk to you in a minute, but I guess I ought to speak to the little lady first.'

It had been great when Belinda had been born – they had called her after her maternal grandmother. Not so great when the marriage had soured and he and Matti had decided to divorce. Bad for a while after that, then gradually better, so that when Matti had written him that there was someone else he'd meant it when he'd wished them good luck.

He heard the phone changing hands.

'Hello, Daddy. Thanks for the present.'

'Hi, sweetie. Happy birthday.'

Next morning he caught the first flight to Albuquerque. At the airport he had a coffee, then rented a hire car, drove the fifty minutes to Santa Fe, checked in at the Travel Lodge in case he had to overnight, and bought a map of the town.

Menzies' address was in one of the developments creeping into the hills. Mitchell showered, put on a fresh shirt, and drove through

161

the plaza and up the road towards the pines of the mountains over-looking the town.

Some people might have telephoned beforehand, confirmed Menzies was in. Some people would have been wrong. First contact, Mitchell knew, first impressions. Him of Menzies and Menzies of him. If Menzies was his man. People talked for different reasons: revenge or guilt, greed or immunity. Sometimes a combination. Sometimes they didn't talk at all.

He dropped off the road and into the development, and checked the map again. The house was two-storey adobe-style, the garden was large and well-kept, and the car in the driveway to the right was a Lincoln. He parked and walked up the garden and across the patio. The door was Spanish-style, a bell rope on the right. He pulled on it and stood back, heard the slight shuffling inside and the slightest squeak of the door opening.

The man who faced him was late forties, perhaps early fifties, but aged beyond his years. His hair was thinning, his eyes were sunken, and his body was beginning to stoop. Christ, Mitchell thought, he looked like death.

'Carlos Menzies?'

'Yes.'

'Good morning. My name's Mitchell. I'm a special investigator for the Banking Committee of the United States Senate.'

He held his identity forward for Menzies to inspect.

'I think you'd better come inside.'

He's been expecting me, Mitchell suddenly thought, me or some-one like me. And now I've come it's almost as if he's relieved.

'Thank you.'

He stepped through the door and into the cool of the house. Most times you searched for years and got nowhere, occasionally you struck lucky.

The sun was a brilliant gold to their left, to the west as they flew north, the desert stretching to the horizon on both sides and the pine-covered fingers of the Sangre de Cristo and the Jemez ranges creeping toward them.

Cath Donaghue knew the story of the DAV, the Disabled Vet-erans, monument at Angel Fire, even though she had never been there . . . How the memorial had been started by one man after his son had been killed in Vietnam.

She knew the stories of how Angel Fire had been given its name

162

. . . How, long before the white eyes, there had been a terrible fire, and the Indians who lived there had prayed to the Rain Angel for help; how, that night, the Rain Angel answered their prayers and put out the fires. And the second story of how, when the clouds were right and because of the sun shining on the red soil of Taos to the west, the sky itself caught fire.

And she had heard the other story . . . Of how, one night, the father of the dead soldier had inadvertently locked the door of the chapel; how, when he had arrived the next morning, he had found a message scrawled in crayon on a piece of plyboard: *Why did you lock me out when I needed to come in?*

The Cessna cleared the mountains and dropped into the long, lush valley between the mountains on each side, the lake to the north, the road running along the valley itself and the tall gentle sweep of the chapel on the rise above it, its twin white walls almost like wings, and the sky behind it a fiery brilliant red.

The pick-up was waiting; she and Jack climbed in and were driven to the memorial. The exterior walls of the chapel were whitewashed. In front of the exhibition halls, from flagpoles sunk into the grass of the knoll on which the memorial stood, four flags flew stiffly in the breeze: the Stars and Stripes, the state flag of New Mexico, the flag of the state whose veterans were being remembered that month, and the black and white banner of the MIAs, those missing in action, whose families prayed they might still be alive.

On the ground behind, and stretching to the trees which ringed the foot of the hills, the camp had begun: pick-ups, RVs and saloons; some people in tents and others under makeshift canopies, more unrolling sleeping bags in the open. Hundreds of people, she thought, more than hundreds, maybe two or three thousand. Already the light was fading and the dusk was closing in, already the cooking fires were sparkling.

The pick-up dropped them and they walked to the exhibition hall and offices, shook hands with the staff, then went into the chapel.

The interior was simple: a stained glass window at the front; a plain wooden cross with a pair of infantry boots at its base; half a dozen rows of seats, then the photographs and personal stories of the veterans being remembered that month on the wall at the rear.

'Give me a minute, Jack.'

He left her and she stood alone, looked at the cross and the pair of boots, looked at the stained glass window and the photographs of the young men – the boys – at the rear, then at the cross again and the infantry boots at the foot of the cross. She was still alone. I'm proud of you, Jack, she almost said: proud that you supported this place even when its construction was not receiving official approval, even when it might have cost you votes. She felt in her pocket, took out a fresh white handkerchief, knelt in front of the cross and dusted the boots. Then she went outside, rejoined her husband and walked with him up the slope to the campsite.

The evening was drawing in. She walked with him through the camp and sat at his side as he stopped by the fires, ate with him as he ate with those there and listened to those who talked to him. Mostly men and mostly veterans, some able-bodied but many – too many – disabled. Occasionally their families with them, their wives and their sons and their daughters.

'Good to see you again, Jack.'

The man was tall, black, his face scarred and the right arm of the combat jacket was pinned at the elbow.

'Preacher, my wife, Cath. Cath, this is Preacher.'

She began to offer her right hand, then remembered and shook his left hand hard and firm.

'Good to meet you, Preacher.'

'You too, Mrs Donaghue.'

'Cath,' she told him.

'You too, Cath.'

They left the group they were with and walked with him to the fire he had built for himself near the top of the camp, drank a beer with him and shared a plate of ribs and potatoes, the two men talking and Cath listening. It was late evening, the sky clear and the stars shining, others joining them and Donaghue drifting off with them. Cath walked through the camp by herself, stopping and talking, listening, sitting by another fire and accepting another beer. Moving on till she stood alone at the memorial, listening to the flags in the night breeze.

'Amazing place.'

She turned and saw the man called Preacher.

In the shadows and around them the veterans moved like ghosts.

'I heard a story once,' she said. 'About the flags in the wind.' Perhaps it had been that evening, perhaps another time. 'Somebody said they sounded like the rotor blades of helicopters.'

'Nothing sounds like the choppers coming in for you.'

She stared at him. 'You were there, weren't you? You were there the day Jack won his Silver Cross.'

164

'Yeah, I was there.'

So tell me, she allowed the silence to say. Because Jack never has and I need to know.

'We were a recon unit.' Preacher stared across the valley and into the dark. 'Standard op, insert overnight, hole up, look round for a couple of days then call the big boys in.' The air strikes and the napalm. 'Extraction by chopper when it was done.'

Behind the lines, she knew. Of course behind the lines.

'Except this time something went wrong.' Preacher laughed. 'In 'Nam things were always going wrong, but this time it was kinda serious. Ran into some NVA and the slicks couldn't get in to us.'

Slicks . . . she almost asked. Helicopters, she understood.

'Anyhow, we came to a river bank, slicks still couldn't get in to us and NVA were getting close. Looked like we were finished, then this little Swift comes up the delta, guns blazing and mad bastard of a commander shouting through a bullhorn for the rest of his boats to follow him in. No more boats, of course, but he got us off.'

The valley in front of them was dark, just a handful of lights.

'That's how Jack got his Silver Cross,' Preacher shrugged. 'That's how he should have got more but he turned it down, said it would have been political and that all the guys there deserved it and not just him.'

So now you've told me, Cath Donaghue thought; except that you haven't told me. Just as Jack has told me but never really told me.

'And that was it?' she asked.

'Yeah, guess that was it.'

They left the memorial and walked back up the slope to the camp, found Jack and sat with him for a while, then Preacher went to his own place at the edge of the trees.

'Preacher was telling me about the day you got the Silver Cross.' Cath sat closer to Donaghue, took the beer he was drinking and shared it with him. Was not sure what he would say.

Donaghue smiled and put his arm round her, stared at the camp fire. 'Preacher tell you about what *he* did that day?' he asked at last.

'How'd you mean?'

He's going to tell me, she thought. After all these years he's going to tell me the truth of what *really* happened that day.

'Did he tell you that he got the Medal of Honor?'

'Preacher won the Congressional Medal of Honor that day?'

The highest award for gallantry the nation could bestow.

'Yeah,' Donaghue said simply.

165

They left the fire and walked past others, the people huddled round them, past the tents and the bivouacs, nobody sleeping in them yet.

'There was this recon unit,' Donaghue began to tell her.

Insert overnight, she knew: look round for a couple of days then call in the big boys.

'Second afternoon they're going through a sort of valley, NVA patrol coming the other way. Except the NVA aren't a patrol, they're point for a battalion. The recon boys start running. Standard procedure, give yourself time and space for the slicks to get you out.'

They stopped by a fire and accepted a beer, then carried on walking, Jack talking quietly now, so that she had to concentrate to hear him.

'C130 up above providing the radio net and air strikes sowing death and destruction round them to give the slicks a chance, what they called hot extraction. NVA down to a hundred metres away, sometimes fifty even. Recon boys still running and the slicks still coming in though.'

She made him stop walking, made him stop to tell her, even though he was still looking into the night.

'Then the first slick goes down, closer to the NVA than the unit. One of the recon guys goes back, gets the crew out, covers them while they pull their own wounded clear, even though he himself is getting shot. Gets them back to the rest of the boys.'

Preacher, she began to understand.

'Everyone still running, trees ahead. Air crew hauling their wounded and the recon guys covering them. Air strikes still making hell round them, trying to give them a chance, then a second slick goes down.'

She couldn't believe it, couldn't even visualize it.

'The recon guys keep shooting while one of them goes back to get the crew out.' Preacher again, she knew. 'The fit, or the less injured, dragging and carrying their own wounded. One recon man on each side of the square covering them. Carnage.

'They're in the trees, still running, then they come to this river. Nowhere left to run and air cover out now 'cause they don't know where their own people are. Slicks can't get in because of the foliage, can't even drop lines. No point anyway, 'cause there are too many wounded.'

Then this little Swift boat comes up the delta, Cath Donaghue remembered Preacher's words. Guns blazing and mad bastard of a commander shouting through a bullhorn for the rest of his boats to follow him in. No more boats, of course, but he got the guys off.

'Preacher was the last man out.' Donaghue was still staring into the dark, staring into the abyss called Vietnam. 'Covered his men till the end, even though he himself was badly wounded, and he had to fire with his left hand because his right arm was a mess. NVA sometimes as close as five metres from him, some of them between him and the boat and cutting him off, and the rest pouring in the fire at him. Almost didn't make it.' Donaghue came back to the present, back to the place called Angel Fire. Turned to his wife and smiled at her. 'That's why Preacher got the Medal of Honor.'

So now you know . . .

But I don't, she thought; because even now neither of you have told me the truth. Part of the truth, yes. More than you've told me before. But not the whole truth.

They stopped by another fire and sat down. Someone gave them a rug. Jack wrapped it round them and they lay down. It was one, perhaps two in the morning. Cath curled into him and tried to sleep, stared instead at the stars. It was gone two, almost three. She left the warmth and walked up the hill to the fire on the edge. Preacher was awake, as if he had been waiting for her, the poncho loose round his shoulders. She sat down and shared it with him.

'Jack told me about you,' she said. 'About how you won the Medal of Honor.'

'Guess he didn't tell you why he should have won one as well then.'

I thought you already told, Cath didn't say, I thought that was what you'd talked about earlier. Except that it wasn't, except that was why Preacher had been waiting for her.

'There's this little Swift boat, you see. Recon unit insertion down-river and on the way out.'

I know this, she thought.

'Had a few problems and ran in to a firefight of its own.'

Which she didn't know, at least not in detail.

'Actually it was more than a firefight. Shot to hell, basically. One, two of the crew wounded, including the Old Man. Then they started picking up messages from these other recon guys about how they're in trouble. But the guys in the Swift boat are clear and on their way out and going home. No guarantee they'd reach the recon guys upriver even if they wanted, because even to reach them they've got to go back through the fire zone they'd just come out of. Then run whatever the recon guys were facing, and that clearly wasn't good. Then back through their own fire zone again on the way out. If they ever got that far.'

He leaned forward and threw more wood on the fire.

'Anyway, like I said, dusk coming down. NVA licking their lips and tasting blood. Recon guys almost out of ammunition, air crews and wounded between them, last message to the C130 suggesting they ask the Pentagon permission to swim for it. No more tomorrows. No more anything.'

'Then this little Swift boat comes up the delta,' Cath said.

'Yeah, then this little Swift boat comes up the delta. Gets us off.'

'But that wasn't all, was it, Preacher?'

'How'd you mean?'

'Because even though you were wounded you covered the others while they got out. You almost didn't make it, did you? You were the last one to leave.'

In the east the dark of the night was giving way to the first grey of dawn.

'Jack told you that?'

'Yes.'

'But did Jack tell you how I left?'

'No.'

In the sky to the east the grey was streaking pink.

'He carried me.'

'Who? Jack? My Jack?'

'Yeah, Jack, your Jack. Came in for me and carried me out. That was why he should've got the Medal of Honor.'

The day was coming on them, the fires rekindled and the smell of fresh coffee in the air. At eight they broke camp, at ten they stood in a vast semicircle in front of the flags for the memorial service. Behind them the New Mexico sun was rising, warming their backs. The speeches ended and there was a moment's silence, then a voice lifted from the platform and the anthem rang across the valley.

Who, she had asked. Jack? My Jack?

Yeah, Jack, your Jack.

She was in another time and another place. Was lost in the sounds of a firefight which had taken place twenty-odd years before. The anthem was ending, the words lingering on the knoll and across the valley to the mountains on the other side.

'Can I ask you one thing, Cath?'

'What's that, Preacher?'

'When Jack takes the oath of office for the presidency I want to be there.'

9

He should stay in place till the next stage was over, till they received whatever the kidnappers were going to deliver, Haslam decided; he should be there to guide the family through the trauma of the next days, then he would pull out. Perhaps he should contact London, though; brief them on what was happening and tell them to have someone else on standby, even suggest someone should come in now so the transfer would be smooth.

The night was warm and pleasant; by the time he returned to the hotel it was eleven o'clock. He checked there were no messages for him, switched the television to CNN, and began updating his case log, only looking at the screen when something which interested him came up.

The programme changed to a report on the front runners for the Democrat nomination for the US presidency. He glanced up, then sat back and watched. The item detailed those politicians who had already declared, including a profile of each plus their most recent speeches, then moved on to those who had not yet declared but who might be expected to. Each of those featured had made speeches over the past weekend, each had been interviewed afterwards about their presidential ambitions, and each had made the predictable responses. No Donaghue, he noted.

The image changed. Incredible shot, he thought, incredible place, but what did it have to do with the US election? The other pictures in the report had been the grey of the cities; this, by contrast, was the side of a mountain. On a small knoll in the foreground was what seemed to be a chapel, its walls rising like wings into the sky. Behind it there seemed to be a camp site, the fires sparkling in the dusk, the trees dark beyond it, but the sky a brilliant blazing red.

There was one other potential candidate, the report was saying: Senator Jack Donaghue. Last weekend he and his wife had attended a service at the Disabled Veterans Vietnam Memorial at Angel Fire, in New Mexico.

The shot changed again: now it was night, the camp fires blazing and the faces flickering in the light from the flames. Jack Donaghue walking – T-shirt, windcheater and jeans; Donaghue sitting by a fire and sharing a beer, Donaghue talking with men in wheelchairs. Cath Donaghue wearing sweatshirt and jeans, sometimes with him, sometimes not, sometimes hands in pockets listening to someone, sometimes visibly moved by what she was hearing, then nodding and opening a beer which someone passed her. Most of the others at the camp were men, though some were with wives and families. The report was giving Donaghue's record: how he had opposed the Vietnam War, but still fought in it and been wounded in it; how he had returned highly decorated, then argued against it. The shot changed again, to the chapel and the flags, the report telling the story of Angel Fire. Changed again, Jack and Cath Donaghue walking together, arms round each other, then stopping by another group, sometimes laughing, sometimes serious. Americans didn't refer simply to the role of the President, Haslam reflected, they also thought of it as the Commander-in-Chief. The shot changed for the last time; it was morning now, the chapel brilliant white against the sky, the four flags stiff in the breeze and the handful of speakers on the platform at the base, the several thousand who had come to pay homage gathered in a semicircle. Yet Donaghue not on the platform, Donaghue not among the dignitaries. The speeches and prayers ended and the strains of the anthem lifted past the chapel, past the flags and into the sky, the camera dwelling on the faces of the men and women in the crowd. Donaghue standing to attention among them, Cath Donaghue at his side and the other man beside her tall, only one arm.

Jack Donaghue just made president, Haslam thought, Cath Donaghue just made First Lady. He switched off the television, picked up the telephone, dialled Mitch Mitchell in DC, and heard the answer phone inviting him to leave a message.

'Mitch, this is Dave Haslam phoning from Milan. Just saw the CNN report on Donaghue. Calling to wish you good luck.'

The sand was golden, the waves were a glistening white, and she was beginning to drown, already beginning to shiver with the cold and the fear of the waves, of what would happen tomorrow when the kidnappers phoned and asked to speak to Marco.

'Talk to me, Dave . . .' Francesca was sitting by the phone, a rug wrapped round her. 'Tell me everything's going to be okay.'

'You want me to come round?'

'If you want to.'

'Fifteen minutes, but don't unlock the door till I get there.'

'Have you eaten tonight?' he asked when he arrived. 'When did you last eat? Have a shower, get dressed, and I'll make you something.'

She went to the bathroom, took off the dressing-gown and stepped into the shower, was unsure whether or not she'd locked or even shut the door. What she wanted was someone to talk to, she had told him, told herself. But what she really wanted was not to be alone, what she really needed was someone to hold her and tell her it was all right, who would take the cold not just from her body but also from her soul, someone she could curl up with and go to sleep against knowing she was safe and that when she woke in the morning everything would be well.

Against the rules, Dave, he reminded himself, but rules were made to be broken. He found some eggs and mushrooms, and made a pot of tea, poured two mugs and took one of them to the bathroom.

'Okay to come in?'

Francesca tightened the cord of her dressing-gown.

'Yes.'

Put on something else, he suggested, it would make her feel better. She went to the bedroom and took off the dressing-gown, heard him in the kitchen. For the first time since she could remember she was relaxed and warm. If he came in now she was naked; if he came in now and took her to bed she would open up for him and take him into her, let him fill her. She chose jeans and a sweater, then sat down and put on some make-up.

'Feeling better?' he asked when she joined him.

'Much better.'

'Certainly looking good.' He smiled at her and put the omelette and bread in front of her.

'Whisky?' she suggested when she had finished, and poured them each a large malt.

'Tell me about Paolo,' Haslam said. 'Tell me about you and him.' It was the question he had asked at the first meeting.

Paolo was a good husband, she repeated, good father to the girls, Paolo cared about them all a great deal. Paolo took care of them all, paid for whatever they wanted. Paolo was very successful, of course, Paolo had always been very successful, very busy.

'What about you?' she changed the subject. 'Are you married, do you have children? Tell me about them, tell me about what you did before you came into this sort of job.'

He was married, he told her, his wife was called Megan and they had two boys; before he had become a kidnap consultant he had been in the army.

'The SAS.' She'd heard about it, about what it did.

Yes, he told her; the SAS. Which was what he'd said at the first meeting with the family.

'You've killed people?' she asked.

Haslam shrugged.

'What did you think when you killed someone?' she pressed him. 'What did you say when you went home after?'

Not on, he told her; this is something Meg and he had agreed they would never talk about. It wasn't as straightforward as that, he began to say: normally, if he was operational, he would be away from home. But what did he do, she pushed him, how did he bring himself to do it? It's not as you think, he told her; sometimes you're by yourself, but most often with a team. And that's what you've been trained to do.

What would have happened if he'd been killed, she asked, did he ever think about it?

He told her about the clock at Hereford and how the names of men killed were recorded on it; about the expression they had picked up from a TV game show: 'Tick tock, beat the clock'; about how it was sometimes in the back of his mind when he went on a job, so that his name wouldn't be on the clock.

So what happened when a friend didn't beat the clock, she asked; what happened when a friend was killed at his side?

He'd made sure his friend was dead then taken what he needed from the body, he said simply; ammunition plus the coat the friend was wearing because it was warmer than his. And when he and the others had got back they'd auctioned the friend's possessions and given the proceeds to his family, because that was what they always did.

'And his name would go on the clock?' she asked.

'Yes,' he told her. 'Then his name went on the clock.'

'What about you and Paolo?' he asked again.

Because this conversation is getting too close to home. This is the sort of conversation I never have or had with my wife, yet I'm talking to you freely and easily. Telling you about the regiment and how you only really live when you're on the edge. How, even when you've finished, you're still looking for the edge, still taking it when you can. Quoting the lines from the poem at you and telling you how it's also on the clock at Hereford. Flecker, 'The Golden Journey to Samarkand':

> We are the pilgrims, Master, we shall go
> Always a little further. It may be
> Beyond that last blue mountain barred with snow . . .

Telling you how people like me go through life looking for the last mountain, telling you how people like Mitch Mitchell are lucky because they might have found a mountain worth climbing, but I'm still looking.

'What about you?' he asked for the third time. 'What about you and Paolo?'

She was sitting opposite, looking at him.

'You want to know about me and Paolo? You want to know the truth?'

She leaned forward.

'When did you last see your wife?' she asked.

'Six months,' he told her. 'What has this to do with you and Paolo?'

'So you haven't had your wife for six months?'

He understood what she meant.

'No, I haven't made love with my wife for six months.'

'I haven't had Paolo for a year.' She was surprised that she had said it, almost relieved that she had told someone. 'More than a year, if you count having him properly.'

He was always away, she was saying, always concerned with the bank, always thinking about business, even when he came home.

Sounds familiar, Haslam was thinking, sounds like someone I know.

'What else is it?' he asked.

She looked at him and told him. 'Sometimes I think I don't want him back. It's terrible, I know, but it's true.'

At least she was honest, Haslam told her, at least she admitted it. And the most difficult person to admit something to was yourself.

So what about tonight, she was thinking. Because we both know what we want, but we both also know that we're the only people who can save Paolo, and that's the only thing that matters. Shame

174

that you're not going to try to stay, shame that I would have said no if you'd tried.

He leaned forward and kissed her on the cheek, then sat back. How was the nightmare, he asked her, got past the break of the waves yet? Safe where she wanted to go?

'Yes, Dave, safe where I want to go.'

'Sleep well, Francesca; see you tomorrow.'

The request that Rossi attend an immediate meeting with the chairman was made at ten-forty. When he arrived Negretti was in conference with two board members; Rossi waited three minutes, then was shown in. The chairman left his desk, crossed the room, took one of the large armchairs by the window and indicated that Rossi should take the other.

'The consultant Haslam.'

'Yes.'

'Where's he staying?'

'The Marino.'

'*Cazzo*,' Negretti swore.

'Why?' Rossi asked.

The call to the lawyer colleague, then the lawyer's call to a high-ranking contact in the carabinieri. The policeman's call to a colleague in the kidnap division, and the call from the kidnap division to Villa, the head of security at BCI.

'We have a problem.' Negretti formed an arch with his fingers and looked over it.

'What?'

'Villa's just had a tip-off from one of his carabinieri contacts. Apparently the kidnap squad have discovered that a consultant is staying at the Marino.'

'It might not be Haslam,' Rossi suggested carefully. Except it would be a hell of a coincidence if it wasn't. It was in his manner. So how the hell do they know, what in God's name did Haslam do that told them? 'Why did they phone Villa? Do they know Haslam's connected with us?'

Because if they do they'll work out about Paolo. And once they do that they'll freeze the family's money. Even the bank's.

'No. It was someone warning Villa just in case.'

'And we can trust him?' Which is to say Villa's paid him off.

'Yes.' The chairman was grey-faced. 'So what do you suggest?' How do we handle it from here and what do we do about Paolo?

175

'The first thing we do is to distance ourselves from Haslam.' Rossi spoke with authority. 'Or rather, we distance Haslam from us. From this moment he's off the case. London can tell him. We shouldn't even have that degree of contact with him.'

'What about the family?'

'I think you should phone Umberto yourself.'

The chairman nodded. Then he stood and took Rossi's hand.

'Thank you.'

It was two hours before he would recce Via Ventura for the Alfa. Haslam was crossing the Piazza Repubblica when his pager sounded. He called the control from a telephone on the corner, then London from the pay cabins at Central Station.

'Where are you phoning from?'

Because if it had been the hotel the line might have been bugged.

'The station.'

Even so London would be careful, wouldn't use the client's name or give any clue to his or her identity.

'There's a problem. The client has just been on. They've just had a tip-off from the carabinieri kidnap unit that you're at the Marino and are on a case.'

'What else does the client say?'

'They want you off the case. No contact with them or the family.'

Which was logical.

'Who're you sending instead? You want me to brief them?'

'No one at the moment.'

Which was not logical.

'Who's decision was that?'

'The bank's.'

There was no more to be said till he was back in London. He ended the call, went to the coffee bar at the end of the concourse, and ordered a cappuccino.

So what was going down? Was the call to the bank genuine, or were Umberto and Rossi playing their games again? One hell of a day to be pulled off, though. And what about Francesca? He returned to the post office and telephoned Marco Benini.

'It's Dave. I won't be at the meeting tonight. Umberto will explain, but don't say I called. Whatever you do make sure that Francesca understands that anything that happens tonight is just a trick. You understand that. Whatever happens, whatever they do.'

'Why?' Marco asked.

'Just look after Francesca. Tell her she'll make it.'

It was just gone six. Haslam left the café on the corner and walked down Via Ventura. The Alfa was in place, the stake-out – dark hair and charcoal grey suit – not quite lost in the crowd. Briefcase in hand, therefore probably doubling as courier. If he was still on the case he'd phone the company's lawyer and get the stake-out's name and address by running a check on the Alfa's ownership. Umberto Benini's Saab pulled in to the parking area in front of the apartment block, Marco's BMW two minutes later. It was ten past six. The Mercedes stopped beneath the canopy and he saw Rossi hurry inside. The man in the charcoal suit returned to the Alfa and the car pulled out of the parking space and headed down the road.

Francesca was tight-faced, the skin drawn round her eyes. Where are you, Dave, what are you playing at? Tonight of all nights.

'Before you leave there's something you should know.' Umberto Benini looked down the table. 'This morning BCI received information that the carabinieri were aware of Haslam's presence in Milan, as well as his occupation, though there was nothing linking him with ourselves or the bank. It has been decided, however, that he should no longer be associated with either.'

Francesca felt the shock. Umberto shouldn't have come out with it now, Marco thought, Umberto should have waited. He took Francesca's arm and guided her out.

Marco's BMW leaving, Haslam noted; funny to be watching everything from the outside. Pity he couldn't have talked to Francesca, perhaps he should have done. Perhaps he should do now.

Francesca was still shocked, trying to work out what had happened and why. I relied on you, Dave, and you let me down. You were the one person I trusted. More than that. I was the only person you trusted. And now you've run out on me.

'Haslam phoned this afternoon.' Marco spoke quietly, almost casually.

She looked at him. 'What do you mean? What did he say?'

'He said to give you a message. He said he was off the case, that Umberto would explain this evening. He said to tell you that whatever happens tonight is a trick. That you'll make it in the end.'

*

The music spilled from the café and the Alfa was parked a block and a half away. It was fifteen minutes to seven. Pascale sat at an inside table facing the door. The timing would have to be precise: if he left the package in the toilet too early someone else might pick it up, too late and the toilet might be occupied, and the brother might arrive before he'd made the drop. He sipped the beer and scoured the pavement and street for the slightest sign of police surveillance.

Francesca settled at the table, the telephone a little to her right, and the script in front of her. Marco straightened the pad of paper and two pens and checked his watch.

In the apartment on Via Ventura, Umberto Benini rose from the table and walked to the window. Bloody Haslam. Lucky Paolo had someone like him as a father, though, lucky he himself had someone like Rossi to rely on.

Almost time to move, Pascale thought. The plastic bag was by his feet. He finished the beer, slipped some notes on to the table and looked round him. No one in the toilet and no signs of surveillance in the street, but someone rising from one of the tables outside and coming in. Possibly coming to use the toilet. It was still too early, probably just half a minute, but no time to wait. He pushed his chair back and walked towards the door to the toilets.

The telephone rang.

'Francesca?'

'Yes.'

'Give me Marco.'

Marco took the phone from her, held it in his left hand and adjusted the writing pad with his right, fingers suddenly slippery round the pen.

'This is Marco.'

'Go out of the block. Turn left. One block down turn left again. The Inter Café is one and a half blocks up, on the left. It has an awning and tables on the pavement. The toilet is in the wall to the right, as you go in. The package is in the litter bin under the hand basin. You've got three minutes.'

The line went dead. Marco checked that Francesca shut the door behind him and ran for the lift. Out of the apartment building and turn left. It was suddenly hot, his head was thumping and his throat was dry. He turned left, walking quickly, almost running. Across the next junction, traffic and people round him. Awning ahead, Inter Milan colours; thank God he could see it. Calm it, he told himself, slow down. He was almost at the bar. Nobody goes into a bar without asking for a drink, so if you have to, order a beer. The waiter was serving a table outside. Marco passed him and stepped into the bar. Sit down and order something, he told himself. Door to toilets in wall on right as Mussolini had instructed. Oh Christ, what if they were waiting for him in the toilets, if there was a back door out. If they were going to kidnap him as well.

He opened the door and went through, saw the two other doors and the signs painted on them. For God's sake may the gents be vacant, may no one be in it. He opened the furthest door and stepped inside. Saw the hand basin on the wall, the closet next to it and the automatic hand drier plus paper towels. Saw the litter bin beneath the basin. Nothing, no package. He knelt down and tore away the used towels, saw the faded red of the plastic bag. Pulled the bag out, spilling the paper on to the floor, and felt inside. Not a letter. Oh Christ. A package. It's okay, he told himself, you've done it, got it, whatever it is. He turned on the cold tap, and splashed some water over his face and through his hair.

The stake-out's Alfa back in Via Ventura, Marco's BMW returning and Marco and Francesca running inside, Francesca carrying a red plastic shopping bag, therefore the pick-up had been made. Haslam walked to the café on the corner, chose an outside table and ordered a Prosecco.

It was strange, suddenly being off the job, suddenly being isolated, but perhaps he always had been on this one. Of course he felt angry about what had happened, plus a fear for the poor sod still manacled to a cave wall in Calabria. Not just that. A fear for Francesca as well.

The tiredness swept over him. Perhaps he really had been wrong to take the Benini case so soon after the job in Peru; perhaps he'd only paid lip service to the pressures of working in a city like Lima; perhaps he should have insisted on a break. Perhaps it really was time to give up the kidnapping business, to cut free and find himself another mountain.

The tiredness was seeping into relaxation. Tonight he'd phone Megan, say he was coming home and ask her to pick him up from Heathrow. Pity he couldn't phone Francesca, though, pity she couldn't phone him.

Umberto was framed against the window, hands behind his back. The key turned in the door and he spun round. Francesca was in front of Marco, the red plastic bag clutched in her hand. Umberto wanted the package, she knew, wanted to seize it from her, to demonstrate to her that Paolo was his son first and her husband second.

179

She turned the package in her hand and tried to undo the tape round the brown paper wrapping. Marco handed her a knife. She sliced through the tape and peeled off the paper. Inside was a box, bound by more tape.

'Give it to me.'

Umberto snatched the package and knife, slit through the tape and opened the box. Inside was another package. He cut through the tape and ripped off the paper. Inside was a video cassette box. He shook it on the table, expecting a cassette, and the third package fell out.

This is bizarre, Francesca thought, this is awful, this is like pass-the-parcel at Christmas. Remember what Haslam told you, she struggled to tell herself, struggled to believe it: that whatever happens tonight isn't really happening, that whatever the kidnappers do tonight is a trick.

Umberto tore open the fourth package and exposed a fifth. The shape and size were vaguely familiar, even through the tight brown wrapping. Audio cassette, he muttered, right size and feel for the plastic container, therefore a message from Paolo, despite what Haslam said. He slipped the blade of the knife across the tape, then through the wrapping, took out the cassette box and opened it.

The blood on the cotton wool had coagulated and the ear had been severed at the stem.

10

The sky to the west was inky black, to the east a violent layer of blue and orange. Brettlaw remembered another morning, colder than today, the wind biting and the red rising behind the Kremlin. The blood pulsing in him and the meet half an hour off, the KGB hounds sniffing the streets for him and Malenko baying for his blood.

It was four in the morning, the patchwork of Germany below, the details sharpening as they dropped in altitude, and the meet with Malenko five hours off. The Boeing banked over Berlin and he looked down as he always did. There was no Wall now, no patrol vehicles or guards, but the distinct line of the former death strip still wound its way like a ribbon through the trees and the houses. The Boeing bounced on the roughness of Tempelhof and the unmarked black car pulled across the grey of the tarmac. Even though the Cold War was over there was still something about flying into Berlin.

Fifteen minutes later he was in the safe house in Charlottenburg.

At eight he left, only one shadow with him. The security section going ape-shit, but he *was* DDO.

The city was coming to life. He walked quickly, remembering the old days and glancing round him without appearing to do so, the tradecraft instilled in him. The S-bahn station at Zoologischer Garten: he looked for the signal from the newspaper vendor and almost laughed at himself. Another time another place, Tom old friend. Kottbusser Tor: change lines, sit still until the doors began to close then dart out, check down the platform to see if anyone had followed, body tensed to jump back on if they had. Hermannplatz: last change. A long way from the Ku'damm and the city centre and the carriage almost empty. Rathaus Neukölln: he left the station and crossed Sonnen Allee.

The hotel was two blocks off Weser Strasse. The varnish on the double doors was beginning to peel and the curtains of the café on the ground floor had shrunk with the years and faded with the sun.

The meet's upstairs, Brettlaw told the shadow, you stay in the café, you can still keep your eye on the hallway and stairs.

'Which room?' It was against all the rules, but Brettlaw was the DDO. Plus he was carrying a panic button in case anything went wrong.

'Twenty-three, two floors up.'

They crossed the road and went inside. The reception desk opposite the doors was empty and the carpet was thin and worn. The shadow watched uneasily as Brettlaw went left up the stairs, then turned right himself. The café was busy and the air was thick with cigarette smoke; he chose a stool from which he could see through the glass of the swing door to the hallway and asked for coffee.

The landing on the first floor was at the front, the light piercing the dust on the windows. Brettlaw checked that he was alone, turned left along the corridor to the bedrooms at the back, through the broom cupboard and down the emergency stairs which spidered from it. At the bottom one door led right, to the kitchen, and one left, locked by a safety bar. He pushed the bar, opened the door, stepped into the alleyway behind, crossed the canal and walked quickly up Bouche Strasse. The road was cobbled and lined with trees, shops on either side and flats above them. In his mind he saw the concrete of the Wall across the top of the street, the tram lines cut off and the watchtower behind it, the guards already picking him up and swinging their binoculars on him. Even today this wasn't the fashionable area of Berlin, wasn't the place where the tourists came. The tram trundled past him into what had once been East Berlin.

The bar was on the corner, grey apartment blocks stretching away from it, four metres of cobbles in front of them then the ragged wasteland which had once been the Berlin Wall, the grass crumpled on the death strip and the weeds poking through what had once been the tarmac run for the Grenztrabants of the frontier troops.

Heidelberger Strasse hadn't changed, he thought: the same drab fronts of the same old blocks; the same washing hung from the same windows and the same smell of the same cooking hanging in the same air. In a way the Wall had given the street a dignity, now the wasteland which had once been the Wall merely emphasized its poverty.

Even the bar on the corner looked different. With the Wall it had had a location, something which established its geography. And the watchtower looming over it, plus the fact that the Wall dog-legged at that point so that the flats in the East had only been thirty yards away, had given it an unmistakable character. Then it had been the front line, now he hardly recognized it. The lamp over the door, of course, and the curtains halfway up the windows, but not a lot else.

Hendricks en route for Milan and the Benini affair about to be sorted out, the thought drifted across his mind, now it was time to settle Zev Bartolski's death. He opened the door and went inside.

The bar was on the right, most of the shelves behind filled with miniatures with labels showing couples copulating; the half-dozen tables had plastic tops and rickety legs, and the green cloth on the pool table was already shiny, the yellow wallpaper heavily embossed and discoloured by cigarette smoke. The only customer sat at the third table from the left, his back against the wall and facing the door. He was casually dressed: medium-priced suit, shirt open at the neck, no tie. His hair was grey, brushed back and slightly thinning, and the cup and glass on the table in front of him were both empty.

Same smell of the same beer, Brettlaw thought, same shadows. 'Two coffees, black; two cognacs, large.' He banged on the counter for the barman.

The man at the table looked up at him. The face was fuller – the new capitalism, Brettlaw supposed – but there was the same hardness beneath it, the same eyes.

'Sergevitch.'

'Tom.'

They shook hands.

'Not like the old days.'

The barman shuffled from the rooms at the back. His slippers were loose and worn, his trousers fitted badly, kept up with belt and braces, and his cardigan was baggy and patched at the elbows. He poured two brandies, then edged sideways across the floor like a crab, placed the glasses on the table and removed the old glass and cup.

They raised the glasses and downed the cognac in one. 'Same again.' The barman brought them another and disappeared into the tangle of rooms behind the bar.

'You've been downstairs, of course,' Brettlaw suggested.

Behind the bar, half along the corridor then through the trap door and down the wooden stairs to the cellar, the ceiling low so you had to duck. The metal shutter in the wall to the east, beneath the cobbled street, and the hole behind it four feet wide and four feet deep, stretching probably six feet under the street before it was sealed by a brick wall.

'I was never sure whether or not it was genuine.'

'Neither was I.'

They emptied the glasses a second time.

'Christ, this is shit.' Malenko rose, walked behind the bar, surveyed the shelves, took down another bottle plus two fresh glasses, and returned to the table.

'So?' He filled their glasses.

The Russian knew why he had asked for the meet, Brettlaw understood; probably already had the answer, part of it at least.

'Zev Bartolski.' Brettlaw raised his glass.

'Zev Bartolski.' Malenko raised his. 'My people send their condolences.'

Strange world, really. Brettlaw nodded his thanks. But only if you weren't part of it. Enemies, of course, fight against each other. But look after each other as well, protect the game. 'A mistake, of course.'

'Of course.' It was Malenko's turn to nod. 'Any indication who's responsible?'

'Bonn thinks one of three groups: the Armed Crescent, the 3rd October, or the Martyr Mahmoud.' All of which are or have been financed by Moscow, them or the parent organizations that spawned them. So in a way Zev's death isn't just my problem, because in a way you killed him as much as the bastard who pressed the button.

'The 3rd October.' Malenko downed the cognac in one, flicked the top off the bottle and refilled their glasses. 'Three-man squad. They were after Krenz, the industrialist, which even the BND have worked out. Somebody got their intelligence wrong.'

'Names?' Brettlaw asked. 'Current whereabouts?'

'Not yet.' But give me time.

They each put a handful of notes on the table and went outside. The morning was warming, two women talking, both with headscarves and one with a pram, cars rattling past and a three-legged dog leaning against the wall and trying to scratch itself.

They shook hands.

Thanks . . . Again unsaid but again understood.

You can do the same for me one day. Also unsaid.

Brettlaw turned west and Malenko east. Old habits die hard.

11

Lufthansa flight LH419 landed in Frankfurt at seven-thirty in the morning; by eight Hendricks had cleared customs and immigration, then made his way to the shop tucked discreetly in the terminal building itself. With him he carried a light travelling bag containing the few clothes he would need, a briefcase containing a Zenith laptop computer, and an empty Zero aluminium case. Most people made their airport purchases on the way out; at Frankfurt, Hendricks always made his on the way in. When he left the shop thirty minutes later, it was with two surveillance devices – one operating on radio frequency and the other on infra-red – plus an ICOM R1 pocket receiver and an earpiece for the RF.

At nine-thirty he checked in to the InterContinental, hired a day room, confirmed his reservation for a first class sleeper on that evening's night train to Milan, and went for breakfast. At eleven he took a cab to a hotel near the airport, carrying with him the Zero case. When he left twenty-five minutes later it was with a Heckler and Koch MP5K sub-machine gun, an MP7 automatic pistol, and what he considered an adequate supply of 9mm and Glazier rounds.

The first set of purchases had been necessary, the second a precaution, and both had been paid for in cash. It was the way Hendricks organized his world: a job in one and himself in another, and no links between the two. So the items were bought in Germany, the job would be done in Italy, and the fact that he was travelling to Milan by train rather than plane removed the problem of airport security. Even the receptionist who had checked him in to the InterConti that morning would not have remembered him. Tall, she might have told the police if they had come asking. Thin, though she would not have been sure. Dark hair, but only probably. Might have been European or possibly American.

At ten forty-two that evening he took the Frankfurt–Ventimiglia overnight express to Milan's Central Station, sleeping well so that when the train arrived two minutes early at seven forty-three the next morning he had virtually shaken off his jet lag. By eight-fifteen he was in his room at the Romanov Hotel, off the Piazza Repubblica.

The room was large: double bed; desk, chairs and telephone in one corner and minibar and television in another.

He showered, then unpacked.

The Zenith laptop was in the briefcase. He placed it on the desk, disconnected the telephone lead from the jack in the wall, replaced it with the lead of the computer modem, and inserted the telephone lead into the second jack on the Zenith so that both computer and telephone could work without disconnecting either. He turned on the laptop, loaded Procomm, dialled up Zeus, left a message on The Man's electronic mail that he was in place, then showered and went for breakfast.

The instructions had been as clear and precise as ever. Paolo Benini, banker, missing for approximately one week, perhaps kidnapped, perhaps absconded. Two addresses: town apartment and country villa. Surveillance requested to confirm Benini's disappearance and, if confirmed, to establish reason.

Forty minutes later he left the hotel and bought a roll of plastic sheeting, a detailed street map of the city and one of the area to the north, plus a general motorway map. Then he rented a car, collected the Zero case from his room, and left the city on the Bergamo road.

The traffic was even heavier than he anticipated, so that it was almost ninety minutes before he left the autostrada and turned east. The sun was beating down and the land was dry and climbing. He checked the map, drove another two miles, then turned off left on to a narrower road, the surface twisted with the sun and the road itself winding beneath the trees. Four hundred yards along it he stopped the car and switched off the engine. The only sounds were the songs of the birds and the hum of the cicadas. He spread the map across the bonnet, checked the details of the countryside around him, and drove on. Five minutes later he turned right, up a track, the trees thinner and the suspension of the car just high enough to clear the ruts.

The land in front and on either side of him was uncultivated and there was no indication that the track was in use, even though it had once been cobbled. He pulled off, parked under a tree and checked the map again. The thread of road he had left ran along the floor of a shallow valley, the track he was now on beginning to climb up the eastern side, and the ridge of the valley above him. On the other side of the ridge, according to the map, was a valley and a road similar to the one he had just left behind.

One way in, another way out.

The outcrop of stones was just off the track. Hendricks checked that he wasn't being observed, shifted the smaller of the stones, made a cache beneath them, wrapped the case containing the weapons and ammunition in the polythene sheeting, and buried it. The sun was directly above him and the sweat was pouring off his face, his shirt clinging to his body. He replaced the stones and swept the ground to remove any trace that he had disturbed anything.

The sun was hotter. Check the ridge, he knew, check the valley on the other side, check the back door. He left the cache and walked up the track.

The farmhouse was almost lost among the trees, the plaster on the walls had begun to crumble and the first holes had appeared among the red tiles of the roof, yet even now he could imagine it: the courtyard in front, cobbled like the track which had once led to it; the wall and the outbuildings for the animals. He left the farm, climbed to the top of the ridge, and scanned the valley below. The track ran along it, the slope down to it covered with trees and shrubs. Half a mile to his right, according to the map, the track joined a tarmac road, the road itself linking to another which led to the autostrada. He left the ridge, dropped to the farmhouse and went inside.

The house was on two floors and built into the slope, so that at the lower end there was a room below. Even now it smelt of olive oil and garlic. He walked along the wooden floors, leaving his footsteps in the dust, past the stairs leading to the bedrooms, then through what had once been a family room to the kitchen. In the corner of the floor was a trapdoor to what he assumed was the store-room below.

He left the house, walked back down the track, collected the car and drove back to Milan.

By the time he returned to the Romanov it was four o'clock. He went to his room, showered, helped himself to a cold Pepsi from the minibar, switched on the Zenith and checked there were no messages on his e-mail.

The room was hot; he adjusted the air-conditioning and read through his instructions again. The town and country addresses and telephone numbers of the missing banker were in the fourth paragraph. He telephoned the first number – the country house in

Emilia – and allowed it to ring for a minute before replacing the phone. Benini and his family not in the country, at least not answering the phone. He left the hotel, returned the hire car, and took a cab to Via Ventura.

The target apartment block was set slightly back, a canopy over the main door, a combination security lock on the door itself and, he assumed, a porter inside. The entrance to the residents' underground parking was at the rear and opened by a security code, and the emergency exit was close to it. Therefore there were several points of access, depending on which he chose. Which in turn depended on when the apartment was empty.

The block had a flat roof, he also noted. He left the block and walked the streets in front, at the side and behind it.

Within the hundred-metre radius he needed there was one hotel – discreet and expensive, and tucked at the side of the fountain opposite the shops – and a block of service flats slightly below the Benini's apartment. A flat was preferable – in a hotel there would be no way he could prevent people like the cleaners entering the room – but the line of vision between the service block and the flat roof of the Benini block seemed to be obstructed, at least on the lower floors.

He left the area and began the arrangements by which The Man would contact him.

Ideally Hendricks would have used public telephones, preferably in the foyers of the big international hotels and switching between them. When he checked, however, he discovered that the public phones did not have numbers, so could not take incoming calls. That evening, therefore, he spent an hour in the bar of the Leonardo, a large modern hotel near Central Station. At the side of the reception area was a set of booths where guests could take incoming calls. When he left, shortly after eleven, it was with an arrangement that he could use them to take calls, even though he was not a resident. Then he returned to his room, switched on the Zenith, and left a message on The Man's e-mail giving the telephone number at which he could be contacted, omitting the Italian and Milan codes, plus the times at which he would be waiting.

The dark was on her, the cold gripping her and the fear wrapping round her. Remember what Haslam would have said, Francesca told herself. She went to the bathroom, showered, put on a warm woollen dressing-gown, and made herself an omelette. The ear needn't be

188

Paolo's, Haslam would also have told her, and the blood could be from an animal. And even if it was human it wouldn't necessarily be Paolo's. She made herself eat, then went back to bed. When she woke it was seven in the morning and she had managed to sleep at least fitfully. At seven-thirty the housekeeper arrived, at eight Francesca left for work, even though all she wanted to do was to sit by the clean phone for the moment Mussolini would ring.

At ten Umberto phoned to confirm that he had sent the cotton wool in which Paolo's ear had been wrapped to a forensic laboratory for analysis. It had been Francesca who had said they should not send the ear. Sending the cloth and asking for the blood on it to be typed was dangerous enough, despite the confidentiality of the arrangement. Send the ear and it could mean only one thing. And the news would seep out within hours.

At four Umberto phoned again.

'The lab has just come through with the preliminary results. I've asked for confirmation, of course.'

I don't care whether the results are preliminary, the voice shrieked through her. I don't care that you've asked for confirmation or whatever the hell you've done. Just tell me.

'What sort of blood is it?' She managed to control herself.

'Human.'

She felt the resolve begin to drip away.

'What type?'

Things had been bad when Haslam had been here, she thought, but now he'd gone everything suddenly seemed so fragile, so unstructured.

'Paolo's,' Umberto told her.

The devastation engulfed her. 'So what do we do?' She wiped her face and tried to speak clearly.

'Meet as planned. I'll talk to Rossi now.'

'Thank you.'

She regretted it the moment she said it: not the thanks, which she meant, but the way she had said it.

'It's all right.'

The wife's Lancia arriving home early – Pascale was positioned under the trees near the parking bays. The Saab and BMW arriving just before six, the Mercedes no longer dropping off its passenger and disappearing but parking outside with them.

The meeting that evening was short and to the point, Umberto Benini covering the items he wished to discuss quickly and succinctly, based on his conversations with Enrico Rossi and the decisions they had jointly taken, and not allowing discussion on anything else. When it was time for her and Marco to go, Francesca stood and tried to pull the strength back into her body.

'Not tonight, my child.' Umberto straightened the cuffs of his shirt. 'Tonight I'll talk to them.' Because I'm Paolo's father, therefore the responsibility is mine. Because this is for men, not for women.

For one moment even Rossi saw the fear leave Francesca's face and the anger flash in its place. Thank you, Umberto, for all you're doing for Paolo, but don't call me *my child* like that. I'm a grown woman, a mother. Don't treat me like shit just because you've got a *cazzo* between your legs and I've got a *figa*.

The brother leaving to go to the clean phone, so where was the wife? Pascale watched as the two men slipped into the Saab, not the BMW, and the car pulled away. Pity there wasn't time to tell Toni, but the controller's security dictated that Pascale didn't know his number. Pity there wasn't time for Toni to alert the negotiator.

The telephone was on the table, the Craig connected to it and the notepad and pens beside it. Benini moved the pens and replaced them with his own. Coffee, he ordered Marco. He sat forward slightly and stretched his arms in front of him. When the telephone rang he allowed it to ring for five seconds before answering.

'Umberto Benini.'

'Where's Francesca?'

Got the bastard going already, Benini knew. 'She's not here. I'm doing the talking now.'

'Three miliardi, or you get another bit.'

Not the other ear, not even another part of the body. Another bit, as if Paolo was cattle meat.

'Seven hundred and fifty million.' Benini was abrasive and businesslike. Listen, you little *stronzo*, I'm Umberto Benini. I have more political and banking connections than you've had whores. I'm Umberto Benini and you're just a stinking rotting little piece of filth from the South.

'I'll phone tomorrow with the arrangements.' Perhaps the other ear — it was in the way Mussolini said it — perhaps something else. 'Make sure Marco's with you.'

'Eight hundred million.'

'Same time, Umberto. You or Francesca, it doesn't matter. Just make sure Marco's there.'

You don't call me Umberto, you bastard. You use my surname, you call me signore. 'Eight-fifty.'

After last night they might go for it, Toni had said; after the game with the ear they might go up to seven-fifty, even eight. And if they did, tonight was the time to hit them.

'Stay by the phone,' Mussolini told him. 'I'll call you again at nine.'

Keep the initiative, Umberto knew, don't let them dictate to him like they'd dictated to Francesca. 'The family and I need to talk. I'll need to leave for thirty minutes.' Even the idiot on the phone would understand this, would realize that it needed to be done in person.

'No tricks.'

The *cazzo* must think he was born yesterday, Umberto thought. 'No tricks,' he agreed. He pushed the phone away, snapped out the cassette, and replaced it with another, and rose to leave. What's happening, Marco began to ask.

'They've agreed to release Paolo. They're phoning back to confirm.'

Francesca knew something had happened the moment Umberto burst into the apartment: the way he ignored both herself and Marco, the way he swept everything before them.

'They want to settle,' he told Rossi. 'They started again at three miliardi, threatened to cut off his other ear if I didn't pay up. I knocked them down, not sure how much yet. Had to go up to eight-fifty and might have to go higher, but there's no chance they'll get their three bloody miliardi.'

Speak to *me*, she wanted to shout; tell *me*. I'm Paolo's wife. So stop ignoring me as if I don't exist.

Eight hundred and fifty million lire, Rossi was calculating: three hundred and forty thousand pounds. Umberto was already offering way over the average, but Paolo Benini had already been out of circulation too long. 'They'll agree tonight?'

'Yes.'

'The bank will need confirmation that he's still alive.'

'Of course. What?'

'I don't know yet. When they phone back agree the price with them, then tell them you'll give them the question tomorrow.'

Vitali's call to Mussolini was on time. The family was going for it, the negotiator told him. Umberto had taken the call, not Francesca, and was making offers like money was going out of fashion. Had come in at seven-fifty million, then gone up to eight then eight-fifty as if it was peanuts.

So where was the consultant, Vitali wondered: no consultant would allow the family to behave like this. Get a coffee, he told Mussolini, he'd phone him again at eight-thirty, before the next conversation with Umberto.

Pascale answered his call on the second ring. Something had happened, the stake-out told him: this evening the father had gone to the clean phone with the brother. Anything else, Vitali asked him. Yes, Pascale reported: this evening the Merc stayed outside the apartment again. Not if the consultant was there, Vitali thought. So where was the consultant? Unless it was a scam, unless the bastard was trying to pull a fast one.

He told Pascale he'd done a good job and phoned Mussolini. Make Umberto go up one more time, then accept, he told him. Umberto would probably say he needed time to get it together, so tell him you'll phone with the drop instructions the evening after tomorrow.

The call came at nine precisely.

'Benini.' The exclusion of his first name was deliberate.

'Hello, Umberto. What have you decided?'

Don't call me Umberto, you little prick. 'I said eight-fifty.'

'That's eight hundred and fifty million lire.' Mussolini was deliberately pedantic.

Of course eight hundred and fifty million, you illiterate bloody peasant. 'Yes.'

'Two miliardi,' Mussolini came back at him.

Umberto always knew the bastard would try to bargain. 'Nine hundred million.' Christ, why hadn't he been the front man from the beginning, why had he allowed the bloody consultant to put his spoke in? Why had he allowed Francesca to fuck it up?

'One miliardo five hundred million.'

'Nine-five.'

'One-one.'

'Even it up,' Umberto suggested. 'One miliardi.'

Toni wouldn't believe it, Mussolini thought. Not even Toni could have played it better.

'Agreed.'

Got him, Umberto Benini glanced at Marco in triumph.

'We want the money in hundred thousand lira notes, delivered in two pilot's briefcases.' Because pilot's briefcases were easy to handle and the money would just about fit into two.

'And I'll need confirmation that Paolo is still alive.'

'Give me something to ask him.'

'Phone tomorrow. I'll give you a question then.'

'Tomorrow evening, normal time, for the question,' Mussolini confirmed. 'Then I'll call the following evening with the answer. You have the money ready. Make sure Marco's with you and that he has a mobile phone.'

The Saab screeched into the parking area and the two men hurried into the apartment block. The negotiator had pulled it off – Pascale almost laughed. The boss had done the deal.

Done it – the triumph was on Umberto's face as he entered the apartment, in the way he held out his hands for Rossi to congratulate him.

Speak to *me*, Francesca wanted to scream at him, tell *me*. I know Paolo hasn't screwed me for months, I know he thinks about the bank more than about me, probably has a mistress or two on the side like his bloody father, but I'm still his wife, I'm still the mother of his children.

Umberto brushed past her, went to the fridge, and pulled out a bottle of champagne.

'To a good deal well struck.'

Via Ventura was quiet, the shops and café not yet open. Seven in the morning and the heat already rising from the pavements. Hendricks was dressed smartly and carried a briefcase; no one would suspect a businessman, but no one would have suspected him anyway. The Fiat Uno turned off the street and disappeared round the back of the block housing the Benini apartment.

The emergency exit was at the rear of the apartment block, close to the entrance to the underground garage, and took him ten seconds to open. He stepped out of the sun into the cool inside, and dropped down the eight steps to the carpark.

The spaces were allocated to apartments, the numbers of the apartments in white on the concrete floor. There were two cars in the area allotted to 5A: a Lancia Delta, the latest model, and the Fiat Uno he had just seen arrive. Probably the housekeeper, he thought, and looked in the back. The shopping bag was plastic: definitely the housekeeper. He noted the registration number and left the building.

Ninety minutes later he called at the block of service flats he had noted the night before. The manager was already in her office. He told her he was enquiring about renting an apartment and accepted her offer of coffee. Ten minutes later she escorted him upstairs. The first floor was too low and he couldn't see the flat roof of the Benini block, the second was better, and the third was what he wanted. He agreed a month's rental, payable in advance, suggesting he might want to extend the period depending on how business went, but saying that he did not require the flat to be serviced. The manager took the details he gave her and asked how would he like to pay. Cheque and he would need an Italian bank, cash and it might seem suspicious. Money order, he told her – cash into a bank and an order issued immediately – delivered to her office or wired into her account.

Francesca left the apartment block at nine, a figure waving to her from the window. Wife leaving – Hendricks recognized the Lancia – therefore it was probably the housekeeper in the window. The telephone kiosk was under the trees opposite the apartment. He called the number, heard the ringing, and saw the woman in the window turn back. The housekeeper, he confirmed.

Forty minutes later the Fiat Uno pulled out of the underground garage. He telephoned the apartment again, allowing the number to ring for a full minute before he was satisfied the flat was empty. The housekeeper was probably shopping, but if she was taking the car it wouldn't be local, therefore the apartment would probably be clear for at least an hour. He crossed to the rear of the apartment, and let himself in through the emergency door.

The building was quiet; he walked to the first floor, then took the lift. It was helpful that the apartment was on the top floor, though he could have managed even if it hadn't been. He walked to the rear of the building and found the door to the roof.

The roof itself was unused, the surface gravelled, with a parapet round the edge and the ventilation shafts sticking up from below, the Benini's apartment immediately below him, therefore serviced by the ventilation shaft closest to the front rather than the two at the back. Thank God no one had considered a roof garden, he thought. He went to the southern edge and confirmed that the line of vision from the parapet to the flat he had rented that morning was uninterrupted.

The two devices he would use operated in different ways. The infra-red would be his main source, but the radio frequency system was quicker to install, even though its duration was limited by the size of the batteries needed to operate it and despite the fact that it was more easily detectable. Therefore he would drop the RF device in place, so that if he had to leave in a hurry he would at least have something in the apartment, and hope he could install the IR later.

He unlocked the briefcase, connected the batteries of the IR device, set the transmitter on the parapet, pointed it at the flat, and taped it in place. Then he took the wire from the briefcase, connected one end to the device, taped the wire down to the bottom of the parapet then across the roof, and dropped the end with the microphone connector down the shaft. The morning was getting warmer. He checked the position of the transmitter, scuffed some gravel over the wire, and returned to the floor below. Fifty-three seconds later he was inside the apartment. He shut the door, laid the briefcase on the floor and opened it.

The sofa was close to the window in the lounge. He undid the stitching at the back, slipped in the RF aerial, then the device and batteries, and finally the microphone, making sure it was at the top of the sofa and pointing up. There was sufficient space inside the sofa to place enough batteries for a month – if they discovered one they would have discovered everything anyway. Then he sewed up the stitches, made sure he hadn't moved the sofa from its original position, and searched the flat for the air vent.

There were three: one in the bathroom, a second in the kitchen, and a third at the bottom of the lounge wall, behind the television.

He unscrewed the plate in front of the third and felt inside for the connector wire he had dropped, then replaced the plate and moved on. The wire was hanging in the vent in the kitchen. Not bad, he told himself: the door between the kitchen and the lounge was open, so that anything said in the lounge would be picked up easily. He plugged the microphone on to the wire, pushed the wire as far back up the vent as he could reach, so that the microphone was an arm-length above the vent hole and therefore not easily detectable, replaced the plate, checked there was no sign of his entry, and left.

Four hours later he installed the receivers in the service flat, making sure that the IR receiver was in a direct line with the transmitter on the Beninis' roof, then attached the two voice-activated Craig cassette recorders.

He wouldn't use the flat to sleep in, would only visit it when he needed to copy or change the cassettes, and then only when he was sure it was not under observation. When he left, therefore, it was with the other device he had purchased from the shop at Frankfurt airport – an ICOM R1 pocket receiver, tuned to the frequency of the RF device, plus earpiece, so that as long as he was within range he could listen in to the conversations in the Benini apartment without needing to confine himself to the surveillance flat.

Rossi's meeting with the chairman was at eleven-thirty. The agreed price was slightly over the odds, he conceded, but with Haslam's departure it was a matter of picking up the pieces.

'How will we know that the person we're getting is Paolo, even that Paolo is still alive?' Negretti stared at him.

'This evening the father will pass a question to the kidnappers, to be put to Paolo before we move to the next stage. In case the kidnappers might know the answer to a personal question from their research into Paolo's background, I have insisted that the question be related to the bank.' He waited till the chairman nodded. 'To do this, however, I might need access to a limited range of Paolo's files.' He stressed the *limited*. 'Preferably with yourself available to confirm your authorization should it be necessary.'

Negretti was still staring at him. For one long terrible moment Rossi thought that the chairman knew what he was doing, the game he was playing.

'Agreed,' Negretti said.

Rossi thanked him, returned to his own office, ordered coffee, and asked his secretary to inform Paolo Benini's PA that Signore Rossi would be with her in fifteen minutes. When he arrived the woman was waiting for him. She was in her mid-thirties and dressed like the career woman she was. Signore Benini's diary, Rossi asked, knowing she had checked who he was and where he stood in the company.

'I appreciate your concern about the confidentiality of Signore Benini's business matters,' he told her. 'Please feel free to confirm my position with Signore Negretti.'

She handed him the diary. Rossi waited till she had left, then settled in Benini's chair. If Benini didn't return, this office might be his: the expensive antique desk, the bookshelves on the right wall and the cabinet to the left; the private bar discreetly concealed, the occasional clues to wealth and position. Except that to guarantee Benini's job he would have to secure Benini's release, in which case Benini's job wouldn't be available. He pushed the thought aside and focused on the question Umberto would put to the kidnappers.

The problem was simple: given the fact that he didn't know Paolo Benini's physical or mental condition, how could he guarantee that

Benini would know the answer to the question Umberto would ask him?

The solution was equally simple, he told himself: by making it something Benini had dealt with just before his kidnap. And by making it something where there had been a problem. That way Benini would remember it.

The diary was bound in leather and the edges of the pages were gilded. He moved the coffee to one side, placed the diary in front of him, and opened it to the day before Benini had been kidnapped. Milan, then the evening flight to London. Meeting in the morning with Manzoni, the BCI manager in London, then flight back to Zurich.

Not Milan, he decided: too many things had happened after Benini was last in Milan. And not Zurich, Zurich was too close to the event. Therefore London. He confirmed the name of the manager in Old Broad Street and telephoned his direct number.

'Signore Manzoni, this is Enrico Rossi, from head office. I need a couple of details of accounts Paolo Benini checked when he was with you on the sixteenth.'

Trouble, Manzoni knew immediately. 'Why?' he asked.

'A technical matter that's been thrown up and we need an answer to it right away.'

'Why can't Signore Benini help you?'

Rossi was one of the bank's trouble-shooters – Manzoni knew him by reputation though they had never met. But the accounts which Benini handled were confidential, even within the bank, even to people like Rossi.

'As I said, it's urgent. I don't need any details from the accounts, just a couple of file names.'

'As I said, why isn't Signore Benini dealing with the matter?'

Benini was in trouble, Manzoni suddenly thought, Benini had been caught fiddling the accounts. Except that Benini had no need to make money that way, and if he had he was too smart to be caught. And if that had been the case Rossi would have been in London, going through the files personally rather than simply asking for a couple of names. So something else had happened.

'Unfortunately Paolo's not available at the moment.'

Christ, Manzoni realized: Paolo Benini's been kidnapped. Rossi's handling the negotiations and wants a question he can put to the bastards to make sure Benini was still alive.

'I need to check that you are who you say you are, and that you're acting with the bank's authorization,' he told Rossi.

'Telephone the chairman's office in five minutes. Speak to him personally. He'll give you the confirmation, plus the number of a direct line to phone me on.'

Six minutes later the formalities were complete. Paolo Benini had been kidnapped, Manzoni was sure, and the bank was covering it up so that key clients wouldn't pull their accounts.

'What do you want?'

'The name of an account which Signore Benini would have dealt with on his last visit and which he would remember.'

'You're sure?'

Because the accounts he deals with are the special accounts. Not just the special accounts. What he sometimes refers to as the black accounts. Blacker than black. The ones we keep separate from the others and which no one is supposed to know about.

'Yes. Was there any account he would definitely remember?'

Because if he's being held hostage there's no guarantee of his physical or mental condition. And if there's no such guarantee then the question will have to be one he can recognize and to which he will have the answer.

'Yes, there is such an account.'

Because there had been a problem with it. He himself had sorted it out immediately, but Benini had insisted on checking it when he had flown in.

'Which account?'

Oh Christ . . . For one moment Manzoni almost changed his mind; almost decided to put Rossi on hold and phone the chairman back and ask Negretti if the bank really knew what it was doing in ordering him to reveal details of the black accounts. 'The Nebulus account.'

'I need a direct question to ask him about it.'

The panic had evaporated but the cold of the sweat still settled on Manzoni like a shroud. 'Ask him what came before and after Nebulus last time.'

What came before . . . the account from which the last electronic transfer had originated.

What came after . . . the next link en route to the target account.

Last time . . . because Nebulus was a switch account, different funds from different sources going through it to different destinations on a regular basis. Therefore *last time* would signify which transaction.

'What did come before and after?'

'Romulus and Excalibur.'

Romulus Investments, the name of one of the front companies through which funds were wired from the First Commercial Bank of Santa Fe. Excalibur Home Funds, the offshore account through which such funds began the next stage of their journey.

And for Christ's sake don't ask me for any other details.

The family meeting that evening was at six, Umberto arriving first and Rossi shortly after him, Marco two minutes after that. Francesca had returned home at four – Hendricks had heard her arrive from his position at the side of the fountain eighty metres away. The Merc parked outside again, as Pascale would report later.

Benini called for coffee, straightened the pad in front of him, and brought the meeting to order. 'I think you have a question you wish me to put.'

Pompous shit, Rossi thought. 'Tell the kidnapper to ask him about the last Nebulus. What's either side of it.'

'I don't understand.'

'It doesn't matter.' For the first time Rossi dropped his veneer. 'Just get them to ask him what came before and after the last Nebulus.'

So Paolo Benini had been kidnapped – Hendricks moved position slightly and watched the two men leaving. Thirty minutes later they returned. He waited another forty minutes, till the people he assumed were Umberto, Marco and Rossi had left, went to the surveillance flat and copied the relevant sections of the day's tapes. Then he returned to the Romanov, switched on the computer, and left a message on The Man's e-mail asking him to make contact.

Even though the Chevrolet was early, Brettlaw was waiting for it. By ten minutes to six he had collected his coffee and bagel from the canteen and was in his office. Each morning now there were more people in the canteen when he arrived, more men and women in the queue. He checked his schedule for the day then telephoned Bonn.

The Chief of Station was out, Cranlow's secretary told him.

'What time will he be back?'

'Around four, sir.' Ten, Washington time. 'You want him to phone?'

'No, I'll call him.'

He cleared the plate and cup from the desk, switched on the computer, and logged into Zeus.

Hendricks in Milan – the message two nights ago. Hendricks ready to put the surveillance in – yesterday. Hendricks waiting every twelve hours: midnight and midday Milan time, six in the morning and evening in DC.

He accessed his e-mail, saw the new message, and checked the time. It was almost ten past six. He swivelled slightly and dialled the number in Milan.

Hendricks was just leaving when the porter told him there was a call for him. He went to the booth and closed the door.

'Good day. How can I help you?'

The code was prearranged.

'Can I speak to the duty manager?' Brettlaw replied.

'Speaking.'

Brettlaw told him the code; Hendricks clipped on the encryptor and keyed in the correct number.

'You left a message asking for contact,' Brettlaw came straight to the point.

'Benini's been kidnapped.'

Christ, Brettlaw thought. 'Tell me.'

Hendricks briefed him, based on the family's discussions that evening.

'But they're about to settle,' Brettlaw confirmed.

'Yes.'

Boxes within boxes, Brettlaw thought: one bursting open occasionally, of course, but then all you did was nail it down again. Except that once one popped open others tended to follow. The British had an expression for it: Sod's Law; and Sod's Law dictated that boxes became connected. Everything was still contained, though, still containable. At least the kidnap was almost over.

'What are the arrangements?'

'The family have asked for proof that Benini's alive. They'll talk to the kidnappers again tomorrow. If they're satisfied, the exchange takes place then.'

And when Benini was out Brettlaw would give him time – not too much, not too little – then confirm that he was all right, confirm that the experience had not made Benini a security risk.

'The key things are on tape.' Hendricks had the edited cassette in his pocket. 'You want to hear it?'

Say yes and he had information, Brettlaw thought; say no and he disguised the importance of Benini. 'Not if he's being released. I'll call tomorrow.' Thank Christ he'd sent Hendricks to Milan, though. Thank Christ he'd taken precautions. The first rule of the first game: know what the hell was going on.

The call from Bonn was patched through three hours later, an hour before Cranlow was supposed to return to his office. It was what Brettlaw had assumed.

'Thanks for getting back. What developments on the Bartolski affair?'

'The indications are that we can eliminate Martyr Mahmoud,' Cranlow told him. 'We're therefore concentrating on Armed Crescent and 3rd October.'

Perhaps the meeting with Malenko had been a risk, Brettlaw thought, but perhaps it might pay off. 'The feeling is that it's 3rd October. As you said originally, they'll be out of Germany but they might still be in Europe. In case we receive any more detailed intelligence you should be thinking about a team now.'

If Brettlaw said there was a feeling then Brettlaw had a source, Cranlow understood. And if the DDO was ordering him to organize a wet job then the source was reliable.

'I'll get it together.'

'Just make sure it's far enough from us to be deniable.'

*   *   *

The light from the kerosene lamp was flickering and the walls of the cave were dark. The first sounds came down the tunnel and the first yellow of the guards' lamp swung in the black. Two men as always, hooded. The first unlocked the cell door and the second placed the metal plate with the cheese and bread on the floor, collected the two buckets, then retreated to the other side of the bars. The first man locked the gate then the two disappeared. Five minutes later they returned, opened the cell again, and placed the buckets inside. Paolo Benini edged forward and began to eat.

The sound of shuffling came back down the cave, the first yellow shaft of light. Not time for another meal, he knew, and the only times they came were what he assumed were the morning and evening, to give him his food and clean the buckets. Except when they'd asked him about his grandmother's dog, of course; and except for the terrible day when he'd seen the knife, when one of them

201

had held him down and the other had sliced his finger and let the blood drip on to the wad of cotton wool.

They stopped in front of the gate.

'There's another question for you to answer.'

He could barely understand the accent. He began to ask the guard to repeat what he had said, then saw the piece of paper the man was carrying. It was small, little more than a scrap torn from an exercise book. The man held the lamp over it and squinted at the words.

'Give it to me.' Benini stretched out his hand.

The first guard unlocked the gate and the second stepped in to the cell and gave him the paper. It was too dark to read anything. He held up his hand again and the man passed him the lamp. The flame was dull and smelled of kerosene, the heat suddenly close to his face. Paolo Benini held it close to the paper and squinted at the words.

What came before and after the last Nebulus?

He almost laughed, almost cried.

The guard stepped out of the cell and the other locked the gate behind him and left Paolo Benini to himself.

He sat staring at the paper, as if he could still read the words on it. How did anyone know about Nebulus – it was a wisp of apprehension in the dark. More specifically: how did anyone involved in the kidnap negotiations know about Nebulus, or how had anyone who knew about Nebulus become involved with the negotiations?

It wouldn't be Francesca: Francesca was probably behind the first question, the one about the name of his grandmother's first dog, but that had come to nothing. In a way it was no more than he expected, especially in retrospect. Francesca wouldn't have handled it well, Francesca should have called in Umberto and let him run things. Umberto or someone from the bank.

But why Nebulus, why something important, why not the name of an account that didn't matter? Because whoever had asked the question was unsure about his physical and mental state, and therefore had to risk asking about something he was bound to remember.

Not even the bank would ask him about Nebulus, though, because it was the policy of the bank not to involve itself in such detail. Especially with the black accounts, especially with accounts like Nebulus. And Nebulus was supposed to be secret, was supposed to remain hidden, so how was someone asking him about it?

Because it was someone from Nebulus, he realized. Because it was the man with whom he had set up Nebulus. Because it was the American called Myerscough, even though he didn't know who Myerscough was or the identity of the company or organization he represented. Myerscough had tried to contact him about something and been unable to reach him; the bank had tried to put him off but Myerscough had insisted. And eventually the bank had told Myerscough the truth; probably made him swear not to tell anyone else, not that Myerscough talked to anyone anyway. And now Myerscough was working with the bank to secure his release.

Thank God for the bank, he thought; thank God for Myerscough and whoever Myerscough represented.

What came before and after Nebulus? Christ, it could be anything. Except he hadn't remembered the question correctly. What came before and after the last Nebulus: he tried to work out what the question meant and what Myerscough wanted in reply. Nebulus was a switch account, therefore what accounts came before and after it? Lots of accounts, he thought, that was why Nebulus was in place. The last Nebulus: that was the clue; that was Myerscough telling him what he wanted. Thank God there had been a slight problem, something for him to sort out: something which gave him a reason for remembering.

The sounds came down the tunnel again, then the yellow beam of the guards' lamp. The guards wouldn't understand, Benini knew, the guards were just thick peasants who didn't know what a bank was, let alone the sort of accounts he dealt with. The men were staring at him, indicating they wanted his answer. Okay to tell them the name of a dog and expect them to get the spelling right, he thought. Not okay to trust them now Myerscough was involved. Pencil, he said. The guards left him, returned ten minutes later and handed him the stub through the bars. Bring the light, he told them. One opened the gate and the other stepped inside and held the lamp close to him. Paolo Benini turned the food plate upside down, rested the scrap of paper on it, wrote the two words, and handed the paper to the guard. The man nodded, then he and his companion disappeared again.

So Myerscough and the bank were involved – Benini looked through the bars to the lamp beyond. Okay, so the bank would have been involved with Francesca; but now Francesca was out and the Big Boys were running the show. And if they were getting things sorted so should he. He sat up and looked round the cell, looked at himself. Christ what a mess. But now there are negotiations – real negotiations. So get things running properly: get the cave clean, sweep the crumbs from the floor and work out a system for the buckets: wash once a day, then use that bucket for his personal waste and keep the other for drinking; move one to one end of the bars and the other to the other end. Clean himself up and work out a routine, do some exercises.

Thank Christ for the bank, he thought again. Thank God for Myerscough and whoever Myerscough worked for.

*   *   *

Francesca's Lancia returning early – Pascale had been in position since three. Umberto Benini arriving at five-thirty. Marco, the courier, at five forty-five and the Merc ten minutes later, the man leaving it carrying two pilot's briefcases. The stake-out left Via Ventura and drove to the first location.

The conversation in the apartment was terse, the little there was between Umberto Benini and Enrico Rossi, Marco and Francesca barely contributing.

Umberto and Marco leaving at six-thirty – Hendricks stood beneath the trees by the parking bays fronting the boutiques. The two of them using the Saab again, and the younger man carrying the briefcases the banker had carried in earlier. Christ what a giveaway if the police had staked the place out.

Mussolini's call was five seconds early.

'Umberto.'

'Yes.'

'You have the money?'

'Yes.'

'Let me speak to Marco.'

Not so fast, you bastard. Don't think you can take me for a ride. This is Umberto Benini you're dealing with now, not some bloody woman. 'What about the answer to my question?'

'What was the question?' It was as if Mussolini had forgotten.

'What comes before and after Nebulus?'

'Romulus comes before, Excalibur after. Now give me Marco. Marco, you have a mobile phone as I instructed?' Marco gave him the number. 'Now listen carefully. You drive to Central Station. You park on the side between the station and the Anderson Hotel, close to the petrol pumps. Then you go into the station and wait by the fountain overlooking the platforms in the middle of the main concourse. Always have the money with you. Be there at seven-thirty. Don't be late.'

'I understand.'

Umberto snatched the phone from his son. 'What about Paolo?' Mussolini had already hung up.

The streets round Central Station were busy; Marco locked Umberto's Saab and hurried inside, the briefcases suddenly heavy. Someone was bound to stop him, uniformed or plain clothes police; someone from the authorities was bound to guess what he was doing. It was almost seven-thirty. He had only just stopped at the fountain when the mobile rang.

'Marco.' It was a different voice, not Mussolini.

'Yes.'

'Take the metro to Piazza Duomo.' Pascale was at the line of telephones thirty metres away. 'Be on the front steps at eight o'clock.' He watched as Marco put the phone in his pocket and picked up the briefcases. There were no tails as far as he could tell, but that was what any tails would be trying to make him think.

Where are they, Francesca thought. What's happening?

It was eight o'clock. The mobile rang.

'Frankie?'

Yes, Marco almost said. 'No.' Wrong number, for Chrissake get off the line.

'Who is it?' Pascale asked.

Marco recognized the voice; bastard, he thought. 'This is Marco.'

'Okay, Marco, listen carefully. Leave the mobile in the litter bin on the left side as you go into the Galleria Vittorio Emanuele, then go back to the car. We'll use the mobile to call you on the other one.'

Okay, Marco began to say. What other one? he almost screamed, he only had one. Please God may they still be there, please God may they not have hung up.

What the hell did he mean, Pascale asked; Mussolini had told him to bring two, so what the hell was he playing at?

Mussolini hadn't, Marco tried to say, couldn't get the words out.

Okay, Pascale told him, change of plan. Keep the phone but be at the Orchid Bar on Garibaldi in fifteen minutes and for Chrissake don't get it wrong again.

Not enough time and the Saab still at Central, Marco thought. He ran to the cab rank on the corner of the piazza and heaved the briefcases into the front car.

The bar was quieter than he had anticipated. His head was thumping and he barely heard the telephone on the corner of the bar ringing, barely registered the fact that the barman picked it up.

'Anyone here called Marco?' The barman cupped his hand over the mouthpiece and shouted to be heard.

Christ, Marco thought. 'Yes. That's me.' He dragged the brief-cases to the telephone.

'Yes?'

'Return to your car.'

The night was blacker than he'd remembered and the envelope was pushed under the windscreen wiper. He opened the car, sat inside, tore open the envelope and read the instructions in the quarter light.

Leave the mobile phone on the pavement. Leave the briefcases in the waste bin at the side of the petrol pumps then take the Autostrada del Sole south. Be at the Agip motel at the service station at ten.

Bastards, he thought: the whole bloody thing about a second phone had simply been to test whether he was carrying another one. Because if he had been then he could tell the family or carabinieri what was happening and where he'd been instructed to drop the money.

Don't worry about the phone, he told himself, don't waste time thinking about it. He'd only just make it to the service station, but he couldn't be late because Paolo would be waiting there and Paolo was relying on him.

He put the phone on the ground, started the engine, and drove the thirty metres to the petrol pumps. The pumps were under the trees, so there was little light, the cabin was locked, and the waste bin was at the side. He checked he was alone, took off the top, put the briefcases inside, and put the top back on, checked again that he was not being observed.

Almost there Paolo, he told his brother, almost got you home.

It was four and a half hours since they had left, almost five. For the last two hours Francesca had stood in the window and watched the road below. The lights picked their way down Via Ventura and the Saab turned in to the parking lot in front of the apartment block. She ran to the hallway and waited for the lift. Please God may everything have gone smoothly, please God may they have Paolo. That was why they had been so long, probably going from place to place till the kidnap gang considered it was safe to meet them and do the swap. The lights above the lift blinked then stopped. The door opened and Umberto brushed past her into the flat.

'Where's Paolo?' It was between a scream and sob.

'I don't know.' Umberto poured himself a large cognac. 'He followed their instructions.' The glance was toward Marco. 'He dropped the money as they told us and went to the last point.' Benini downed the drink in one and poured himself another. Therefore his responsibility, he did not need to say.

'But what about Paolo?'

'I don't know.' He turned on her, snapped at her. 'Ask him.'

Marco was in shock. Ask Haslam, she thought; except that Haslam was no longer in Milan.

'It's obvious.' Umberto recovered his composure. 'They'll release him tomorrow.' He poured himself another cognac. 'Tomorrow we'll hear from them about where to pick him up.'

It was logical, Francesca tried to convince herself; because the kidnappers needed to count the money. And when they'd counted it they'd phone with the details of Paolo's release, or Paolo himself would phone to say he'd been dropped at a telephone kiosk somewhere and could Francesca come and pick him up.

The following evening, and for the two after, Umberto and Marco Benini waited at the clean phone; for each of those days Francesca waited by the telephone at home. On the fourth day Umberto placed an advertisement in the motor section of the *Corriere della Sera*, to run for three days. On the evening of the first appearance he and Marco were at the clean phone by six-thirty and stayed until eight. On the evening of the second Francesca watched them leave and watched them return, stood at the doorway to the apartment and waited for the lift to bring them up. Watched the doors of the lift and waited for them to bring Paolo home.

The doors opened and she saw Umberto's face. The resolution in it had disintegrated and he was suddenly an old man, irrevocably aged and withered.

'What's happened?'

She followed them into the apartment and watched as Marco placed the cassette in the player. Listened to the words.

'Umberto?'

'Yes.'

'That was the deposit. Next time we'll talk about the real money.'

207

12

The meadow was an English green and the brick of the mill to their left was faded and red, the dragonflies hovering over the water and the ducks paddling against the white of the weir. They sat beside the river and looked at the spire of the cathedral rising between the trees on the other bank.

'Penny for them?' His wife's hair was loose over her shoulders and her face was slightly tanned.

'Not worth it,' Haslam told her.

'What about Italy?'

'Ten per cent,' he admitted.

He had been back a week, perhaps ten days. It was funny how time slipped by when you were beginning to relax, when things were as they should be. Him and Megan and the boys. Then London had phoned. An apparently straightforward kidnap in Mexico City, what the trade called a weekend job, but the company were worried about complications and wanted him on standby in Washington in case they needed help in a hurry. Had asked for him specifically.

'Sure you won't change your mind about a few days in DC?'

'Not won't, can't,' she told him. 'Next time give me more warning and I'll arrange it at work.'

It was almost time for the concert: they walked across the footbridge, through the meadow, then along the cobbles of the street and under the arch of the gateway to the cathedral.

That night the images came at him: the terrified stares of the hijack hostages and the eyes of the gunmen as they glanced across at him from the car in Belfast; the binoculars scanning for him in the scrublands round the Argentinian airports in the Falklands War, different eyes looking for him through different binoculars but the same reason in the cold and the sand of the Gulf. Plus the other faces. Rosita's mother in Peru: pleading with him, accusing him. Francesca's in Italy. He rolled over and saw that his wife was awake, her face turned to him and her eyes staring at him. Why me, he knew she was thinking. Why am I the one who cannot rely on you?

The next morning she drove him to Heathrow.

United Airways flight UA919 landed at Washington's Dulles airport at two-ten. He cleared immigration and customs, collected his bags, checked on one of the pay phones that the Mexico job was proceeding according to plan but they still wanted him on standby, then took a cab to the apartment.

Coming back from a job was always unreal; coming back the way he'd come back from Milan even more so.

At six-thirty he left the apartment and took a cab to the Gangplank. The river was glistening, the wash of a cruiser churning white. Quincey Jordan's Buick was parked near the gates, Mitchell and Jordan sitting on the sun deck, and the coals of the barbecue smouldering.

'When did you get back?' Mitchell gave him a beer.

'This afternoon.'

'How was Italy?'

'Up and down, mostly down. Had a few days in England, could have done with a lot more.'

'You should have brought Meg with you.'

'I tried, but she couldn't get away from work.'

Good to see him back but he had to go – Jordan rose to leave. Work to do and mouths to feed. Might have to go to Mexico for a couple of days, Haslam told him, but how about lunch tomorrow if he didn't. Lunch tomorrow, Jordan agreed, unless Haslam was in Mexico. He pronounced it Mejico.

They watched him leave then stretched out in the chairs and enjoyed the sun.

'Thanks for the message about Donaghue.' Mitchell glanced at the couple on the next boat.

'I saw the report of him and his wife at Angel Fire. Good coverage, impressive couple. Donaghue declared yet?'

'Not yet.'

'But he will?'

Mitchell laughed. 'If he didn't declare after Angel Fire he should be shot.'

'How's Ed Pearson?'

'Still working more hours per day than most people work per week.'

'You as well, I guess.'

Mitchell laughed again. 'Yeah, me as well.'

'Connected to Donaghue?'

Mitchell checked the barbecue. 'Banking enquiry, see if there's enough evidence for an official Congressional investigation.'

'How's it going?' Haslam asked.

'Probably okay. You know how it happens. Start with a couple of leads and build up. In this case a small bank running two sets of accounts to cover up money transfers overseas. Probably via an international bank which bought them up a few years back.'

The early evening joggers straggled along Hains Point, on the other side of the river.

'Which bank?' In case I know them and can help you on them. Unlikely, but you never know.

'First Commercial Bank of Santa Fe.'

Haslam shook his head. 'Sorry, never heard of it. What about the bank that bought it out?'

'Italian number,' Mitchell threw on two steaks.

'What name?'

'BCI, the Banca del Commercio Internazionale.'

Of Milan, Haslam thought. 'I've come across it. Nothing that might help, though.' I've come across it because the kidnapping I was working on in Italy was connected with BCI. But because of client confidentiality I can't say anything.

The call from London came at seven the next morning. Haslam had been up half an hour.

'The Milan job. They want you back.'

'Why?'

He could have done without Umberto and Rossi before, he thought, and he certainly didn't need their hassle now.

'Something went wrong.'

Of course something went wrong, because Umberto and Rossi had ignored everything he'd told them.

'What about the reason I had to leave?'

'Apparently that's no longer a problem.'

Remember what it was like, he told himself; remember how it even made you consider quitting the kidnap business.

'I'm locked into a standby here.'

'How big?'

Remember how it made you tell Francesca about going off and finding another mountain. Remember Francesca.

'Probably not very.'

'What if we can arrange temporary cover?'

What are you doing, Dave; why the hell are you allowing yourself to be drawn in again?

'Check with the clients. Offer them alternative cover for thirty-six hours. I could catch the afternoon flight to Milan, meet the family tomorrow morning and be back in DC by tomorrow afternoon.'

'Sounds tight.'

'It will be. If they agree, arrange the meeting in a hotel near the airport so I don't waste time getting into and out of the city.'

The confirmation came through an hour later. He phoned Jordan's home, then his office, and left a message cancelling lunch. Jordan phoned back thirty minutes later. Mexico? he asked. Back to Milan, Haslam told him. Thought you said it was up and down but mostly down, Jordan reminded him.

At two Haslam left Washington Dulles, flying business class, eating little and declining alcohol, and arriving at Milan's Malpensa airport at seven the following morning local time. The lawyer Santori was waiting by the bookstall. Standard situation, Haslam thought, standard routine: he confirmed there was no tail and followed the lawyer to the carpark.

'What's happened?'

'I'm not sure.'

'They know I have to leave again this morning?'

'They're already waiting at the hotel; I've also booked another room so you can shower and change.'

The Saab and BMW were parked outside the hotel and the driver and bodyguard were sitting in the Mercedes. Some things never changed, Haslam thought. He followed as the lawyer escorted him to the room on the sixth floor. Fifteen minutes later he entered the suite where the family was waiting.

The positions at the table were the same but the faces were different. Umberto a shell, face thin and body suddenly shrunken, shoulders sagged and eyes deep in their sockets. Rossi more tense and eyes darting slightly. Francesca had lost weight, both on her body and her face, and Marco had the look of a man who had faced his Maker.

He shook hands with each of them, helped himself to coffee and scrambled egg from the hotplate on the side table, and sat down.

'What happened?'

The answer took a long time. At last Francesca spoke. 'We paid.'

Another eternity. 'Then nothing. After that we put adverts in the paper. Finally they phoned again.'

'What did they say?'

'They said that what we'd paid was the deposit and that next time it would be for the real money.'

Which was what you warned us might happen, but we ignored you. More specifically, Umberto ignored you, but now isn't the time for recriminations.

Good to have you back, Dave. I'm falling to pieces, we're all falling to pieces; but I can't show it because I'm the only one holding it together.

Good to be back, Francesca, good to see you again. So what about it, was he staying or was he recommending that another consultant came in?

'You made notes, like I told you? You've kept the tapes?'

'Yes.' It was still Francesca.

'And you have them here?'

'Of course.'

'So tell me exactly what happened.'

Francesca told him, occasionally suggesting that someone else describe their part of the story in detail, though excusing Umberto.

'How much did you pay?' he asked at last.

'One miliardo,' she told him.

Four hundred thousand pounds, he thought. 'But you got proof that Paolo is still alive?'

'Yes.' Francesca again, as if it was entirely between the two of them. 'So where do we go from here?'

Decision time, he told himself.

'It depends on whether you want to hire me. If you don't, then fine. I'll give you some guidance on what to do now, of course, then we'll bring in another consultant. If you do, we begin again.'

So . . . he left it to them. Unfair, he knew, because he was putting the pressure on Francesca and he should be making the decision.

'If you wanted to hire my services I'd be happy to come back,' he told her.

'Of course we do.' Francesca's voice was a little stronger. 'So what do you suggest?'

'You have a holding script in case they phone?' It was still between the two of them.

'Sort of.'

She gave him the paper.

Good girl, he smiled. You're doing well, doing fine. You're much stronger than you realize.

'What about the question?'

She already had one, she told him. So when would he be back, she asked.

'The case I'm working on in Washington should be over soon. I'll be back as soon as it is.' He understood what she was thinking. 'I can't. I have to be as committed to them as I am to you.'

But you're not as committed to us, because you're leaving us. You're not committed to me because you're leaving me.

'Things are happening in the other case,' he told her. 'They aren't with Paolo's. Therefore we – you and I and Paolo – have a few days' grace.'

'Okay.' Francesca's smile was slightly firmer.

It was time for him to leave.

'You said you have the notes you made, plus the cassette tapes?'

'Yes.'

'In that case I'll study them on the way back.'

He took them, stood up and shook hands with each of them.

The return flight from Malpensa was delayed an hour because of air traffic control problems; by the time he landed at Dulles and took a cab to George Washington it was late afternoon and his body clock was in turmoil.

So what about Milan, what about Paolo Benini and his kidnappers? What about Francesca?

He checked the answer phone, made a quick telephone enquiry about Mexico City, left a message that he was on call again, and went to bed. He slept well till four in the morning, then fitfully till seven. At seven-thirty he made his first call of the day about the Mexican job and was informed that it looked as though his services would not be needed. By eight he had been to the delicatessen two blocks away and was sitting on the balcony having breakfast. Then he went inside and concentrated on the notes he had made in Milan and the tapes of Umberto's conversations with the kidnappers.

Mussolini and the man controlling him were good. God, how they must have been laughing, especially with the certain knowledge that the bank was involved.

The question the family had requested be put to Paolo was connected with the bank, which was predictable. Presumably accounts Paolo

Benini had been working on and which he would remember and possibly a London connection, because that was where Benini had flown in from the afternoon of his kidnap.

There were two obvious dangers from here in: the possibility of the kidnapper trying the same trick a second time and the kidnap going to a third ransom; plus the chance that, having made his profit, the kidnapper might simply sell Paolo on to another kidnapper and the entire process would begin again. And there were equally obvious ways he could play it, plus the less obvious.

The jet lag was creeping up on him; he strung a hammock on the balcony and drifted into some form of sleep. The call cancelling the Mexico City job came at four. He checked the time and dialled the lawyer in Milan.

'Ricardo, it's Dave. I'm back in. I'll be arriving tomorrow. Perhaps you could tell the family.'

'Of course. Anything you want?'

'A vehicle check.' He gave the lawyer the registration number of the Alfa. 'Can you get the details of the owner?' On the quiet, of course.

He made fresh coffee, left a message on Mitchell's answer phone that he'd be dropping by that evening, then returned to the tapes and the notes. When he reached the Gangplank, Mitch was on the sun deck and the barbecue was glowing.

'Life's hell,' Haslam told him.

The decks of the other boats were similarly occupied, the beer was ice cold and a CD of Marcus Roberts on piano drifted up from below.

'If you can't beat them join them.'

Haslam laughed. 'You mentioned BCI.'

He couldn't disclose any details of the Benini case, but an exchange of information which might at some stage be in the interest of the client was totally ethical.

'Yeah.'

'Probably nothing, but some names came up the other day. No idea what they are, but they could be accounts.'

Mitchell sat up slightly.

'The middle name is Nebulus,' Haslam told him. 'Romulus before it, Excalibur after. There might be a London connection.'

*   *   *

214

Overnight it had rained; when Brettlaw was driven to Langley the water was still dripping from the trees and the first steam was rising from the tarmac. The DDO in even earlier than usual, those with a mind to such matters noted. By five forty-five he had collected his now customary coffee and bagel from the canteen and was at his desk.

The world was still quiet. He took a sheet of paper from the top right drawer and wrote down the two agendas which would dictate his life that day.

The first was formal: the regular meetings with the DCI and other Deputy Directors; the routine briefings with departmental chiefs; the open meetings on finance – open being a relative term – and the closed nature of those dealing with covert matters.

The second was less formal: the death of Zev Bartolski and Cranlow's preparations for the moment Malenko delivered; plus the meeting Myerscough had requested late the previous afternoon, presumably concerned with the Nebulus account and Paolo Benini, and whatever it was that Myerscough had decided not to tell last time.

It was six o'clock. He finished the coffee and dialled Milan on the encryptor.

'The kidnappers have been in touch.' Hendricks informed him.

'What did they say?'

'That the first payment was a deposit and that the real money would be next time.'

Plan for the worse and anything better was a bonus, Brettlaw supposed. Which was why he had sent Hendricks. 'You have the cassette?' he asked.

'Yes. You want to listen to it?'

'Yes.'

'What about the rest? I've edited the key conversations down in case you want to record them.'

Brettlaw clipped on the Craig and told Hendricks he was ready. The transfer took eight minutes; when it was finished he told Hendricks he would speak to him in twelve hours, fetched a cold mineral water from the fridge and lit a cigarette.

It was fifteen minutes to seven, time for Maggie to be in – his secretary was always early nowadays – and an hour to his first appointment. He rewound the tape, started it from the beginning, and skimmed through the paperwork for the first meeting. The information on the tape was interesting but no more than that, nothing to turn the world upside down.

'Hello, Umberto. Do you have anything for me?'
'Paolo is still all right?'
'Of course.'
'I have a question for him.'

The report in front of him was the same: material he had to know about but nothing he really wished to know. The voices on the tape were running together, the Italian confusing him and the statistics in the report threatening to flood his mind

'Umberto.'
'Yes.'
'You have the money?'
'Yes.'
'Let me speak to Marco.'
'What about the answer to my question?'
'What was the question?'

Maggie checked in and asked if he wanted coffee, put the mug on his desk and told him it was time for his first meeting. He switched off the tape and locked the cassette in his desk. The meeting itself overran, so that the one with Myerscough began ten minutes late, the briefing with the DCI already looming.

'Benini's still missing,' Myerscough told him.
'But we're covered?'
'Yes.'

Perhaps he'd been wrong not to tell the DDO about the Mitchell enquiry, Myerscough thought, perhaps he'd been right.

'What else?' There was enough hint in Brettlaw's voice, enough of a suggestion that it was time for Myerscough to tell him.

'Probably nothing.'

But . . . Brettlaw lit another Gauloise.

'One of the Senate sub-committees is looking into banking.'

'That's what they're paid for.'

'One of the banks they've begun to look at is First Commercial of Santa Fe.'

Oh shit, Brettlaw thought. First Zev, then Benini, now this. Boxes in boxes, he told himself, the security watertight. Even so he knew he was shaken, had to fight not to show it.

'How'd you know?'

'A source on the secretarial side.'

'You're covered?'

'She passes everything, so this time she isn't even aware of what she's passed me.'

'What about in-house?'

'My people are covering every committee and sub-committee, so no one knows which I'm interested in.'

'Who's running the investigation for the sub-committee?'

'A lawyer, name of Mitchell.'

'How close is he to us?'

'He's not, he's just trawling.'

It was time for the DCI meeting. 'Stay with it.' He stood up. 'A banking sub-committee you said.'

'Yes.'

'Who's the chairman?'

'Senator Donaghue.'

The meeting with the Director of Central Intelligence began in the normal manner: a private session, then the larger briefing with the DCI's number two and the other four Deputy Directors, the cream thick on the coffee and the smoke thick over the table. The second part was fifteen minutes old when Brettlaw was asked to take the telephone call.

'Could you come down?'

Maggie Dubovski always said down, even though the offices were on the same floor. Other Deputy Directors might have asked why, might have reminded their secretary that they were with the DCI.

'On my way.'

He excused himself and returned to his office.

'Just came through. I took the call myself.' She gave him the sheet of paper.

'No identification?'

'No.'

The message was six words long. He read them standing at her desk and understood why she had summoned him.

Not the location: *Zanzibar drop.*

Or the sign-off: *Petuchkin.*

But the time: *Nine P.M., local.*

He was back in his early days with the Agency, the Zanzibar dead drop in a wall in the south of the city and Petuchkin the code for the asset. The name had later appeared on a report, which was how Maggie Dubovski knew it was Moscow and why she had summoned him. Local meaning Moscow time, and Moscow nine hours ahead, therefore the pick-up from the dead drop in three hours.

He thanked her, went to his office, and shut the door.

Only a limited number knew the Petuchkin code, only a handful knew of the Zanzibar drop, and only an inner circle knew its location. Only three people, however, knew all three: himself, Malenko, and Petuchkin. The asset coded Petuchkin wouldn't have sent the message, though: Petuchkin was long dead, Petuchkin had met his Maker in a dingy basement in the Lubianka. Therefore Malenko was keeping his promise but covering himself and keeping it personal, the deal between the two of them and no one else. Unless it was a scam, unless Malenko was setting him up into handing him an Agency man on a plate, but that was a risk he'd run from the beginning.

Not much more than two hours to get someone there, though, and Malenko wouldn't take any risks. In the old days, perhaps, but not now, not when his own neck was in the noose of the new Russia, just like everybody else's. He lifted the phone and asked for Moscow. The instructions he gave three minutes later were precise and succinct, the last as important as the details of the pick-up. The material at the drop for his eyes only, whatever it was.

Something he had missed, he thought, something he had overlooked.

The morning was dragging. At twelve he left Langley for lunch at the British embassy – an old colleague returning to London to be put out to grass. The table conversation was exclusively shop and mainly small talk: anecdotes about the old days, both sides taking care not to wake old ghosts. Something he had missed – the feeling was there again; something he should have picked up. He glanced at the clock: one-fifteen, ten-fifteen in the evening in Moscow. Too late to call off the pick-up now. A Third Secretary coughed politely behind him and informed him there was a telephone call for him. He thanked the man and followed a porter to the office.

'Yes.' The line was secure for the Brits but not for him; even Queen Elizabeth stared down at him from the wall.

'Maggie here. Your wife just phoned. She's done the shopping.'

Moscow okay and the pick-up fine.

'Thanks for letting me know.'

By the time he had returned to Langley it was two-thirty. 'The courier will be airborne in ninety minutes.' Maggie Dubovski told him. 'Transfer to military aircraft in Berlin. ETA Andrews zero three hundred tomorrow, our time. Transport already arranged.'

'What would I do without you?' he asked and meant it.

Moscow was okay. So why was the feeling still there?

The afternoon was long, his attention on the package en route from Moscow. At six, midnight in Europe, he called Milan. The family had re-employed a consultant, Hendricks told him; the man was due back that day, then he and the family would try to contact the kidnappers and resurrect the negotiations.

Something still wrong, and if it was nothing to do with Moscow then it might be to do with Milan. Brettlaw put the phone down and asked Maggie for fresh coffee, then he shut the door, unlocked the desk, and took out the Benini cassette.

'Umberto Benini.'

'Where's Francesca?'

'She's not here. I'm doing the talking now.'

The tape poured out details he didn't need to know. Brettlaw lit another Gauloise and admitted that perhaps there really was nothing.

'Umberto.'

'Yes.'

'You have the money?'

'Yes.'

'Let me speak to Marco.'

His attention was beginning to waver. Perhaps because his Italian wasn't fluent enough, perhaps because Umberto was such an arrogant son-of-a-bitch. Perhaps because he was thinking about what was incoming from Moscow.

'What about the answer to my question?'

'What was the question?'

It was mid-evening, the sun sinking fast and the purple of dusk sweeping the sky. He crossed the room, poured himself a large Jack Daniels and tried to listen again to the tapes, then locked them in the desk and pulled out a file. At midnight he went to the room off the main office and lay on the bed. The phone rang at three thirty-five.

'Message from Andrews. Package on its way.'

In an hour, not much more, it would be getting light. He showered, then started the coffee machine in Maggie's office. At this time of the morning the roads would be clear and the car carrying the courier, plus the escorts, would be moving fast. He stood at the window, pulled back the blinds slightly, and looked at the last grey of night outside; imagined the lights of the cars coming through the night, the courier coming home.

The telephone rang again. Package on its way up, the security executive told him. The courier was shown in forty seconds later. He was young – late twenties, casual suit, no signs of tiredness.

Brettlaw nodded to the escort to leave and shut the door behind him.

'You have something for me?'

I know who you are – he read it in the man's hesitation. I know where I am, and whose office I'm in. But my orders were specific. No one gets what I'm carrying except the DDO. And not even he gets it till he's proved he's DDO.

'You want to see my ID?'

'Yes, sir.'

Brettlaw pulled his wallet from his jacket, took out the security pass and handed it across the desk.

'Thank you, sir.' The courier gave him the envelope – plain white, no markings on it, nothing to distinguish it.

'Excuse me.' Brettlaw walked to the far corner of the room, sat at the conference table, facing away from the courier, and opened it. The envelope inside was also plain white, no markings, and the flap was double-sealed. He opened the envelope and took out the single sheet folded inside. The paper was plain, a slightly grey-white, again with no markings, and the words on it could have been typed on any machine in any office. He read the names, plus the address, then he placed the sheet back in the envelope, returned to his desk, placed the envelope in the top right drawer, telephoned for a security escort, and held out his hand to the courier.

'You did a good job.' Asking for an ID, they both understood.

'Orders.'

'Some people would have been too shit-scared.'

The escort arrived and the courier left the room. It was four-thirty, mid-morning in Europe; he took the envelope from the drawer and called Bonn on the scrambler.

'Milt, this is Tom Brettlaw. I have something for you.'

He read the names, then the address.

'Keep me informed, no go till I say so. Just make sure it's totally deniable.'

The dawn was coming up, the first warmth of the new day. The DDO was in early, those arriving for the morning shift suggested. The light in the DDO's office had been on all night, those leaving corrected them.

It was five minutes to six. He went to the cafeteria, stood in line, and collected his coffee and bagel.

'Dollar twenty, Mr Brettlaw.'

'Thanks, Mack.'

He went back upstairs, sat behind his desk, and opened the coffee. Christ. It hit him.

He unlocked the desk, inserted the cassette in the player, and chainlit the Gauloises.

'What about the answer to my question?'

'What was your question?'

'What comes before and after the last Nebulus?'

'Romulus comes before, Excalibur after.'

How the hell had the banker Rossi known about Nebulus? Why the hell had he asked a question about it? More to the point, why in God's name had Paolo Benini answered, because he must have known that to do so would undermine the security of that part of the banking operation which he controlled.

He heard Maggie outside, making fresh coffee.

But Paolo Benini had to answer, because that was the only way of securing his freedom. So whatever Benini decided was wrong.

Maggie Dubovski knocked on the door, brought him a mug, and put the file for his first meeting on the desk.

So what about Paolo Benini?

Paolo Benini had been a problem, but now Paolo Benini was more than that, now Paolo Benini was a threat. Benini should have been contained in a box, but now Benini himself had opened that box. Not only that, Benini had opened the possibility of others being opened. Therefore he, Brettlaw, had to close them down; therefore he had to close Paolo Benini as priority.

He checked his diary for the day, called Maggie and asked her to rearrange his late afternoon schedule. At six that evening he called Hendricks in Milan and gave him his new orders.

The street was a blaze of colour and people. Haslam left the bar on the corner and walked to the point where he could observe the apartment block. Umberto arriving first and parking the Saab in its usual place, but needing a walking-stick to cross to the front door, his back bent and his frame thin. Marco arriving as his father was entering the building and Rossi two minutes later, unseen in the back of a BMW which disappeared into the underground park at the rear.

No Alfa, though, therefore no stake-out called Angelo Pascale – the lawyer had passed him the name and address that morning. He left the street and went to the apartment.

Francesca was looking better, more confident. Even though she sat in her customary place on Umberto's left, it was she who opened the meeting, she who asked Haslam to lead them and who summed up their decisions when they reached them. They would place the advert tomorrow, to begin the day after and to run for three days; they would draw up the script and include in it a demand for proof that Paolo was still alive, and they would also decide the size of their new opening offer.

Interesting discussion, Hendricks thought. He was seated on one of the benches sixty metres up from the apartment, the ICOM R1 fitted neatly in his jacket pocket and the earpiece virtually unnoticeable. The change of orders from The Man had also been interesting, yet in a way no more than he had expected. No one employed someone like him just for a surveillance job.

The discussion in the apartment ended. He watched as all except Francesca left, then returned to the Romanov and focused on the new task.

Remove Paolo Benini, The Man had said. And with expediency.

To remove Benini, however, required access to him, and under the present circumstances such access would be available at three points: while Benini was being held by the kidnappers, at the moment of exchange, or when he was with his family after his release. But the way things were going there was no guarantee the family could buy Benini back from the kidnappers, and no guarantee he could access him if they did. Especially given the time frame required by The Man.

The first hint of a solution came to him at breakfast the following morning. At first he rejected it as ridiculous, then made himself consider it. By lunchtime he had decided it was a possibility. The family wouldn't buy Benini back. He would. The only question was how.

No stake-out, Haslam noted the next afternoon, but until the advert appeared there wouldn't be. No stake-out the afternoon after that despite the advert, no Alfa therefore no Pascale, and no Pascale no Mussolini. No contact, Francesca and Marco confirmed when they returned from the clean phone. Don't worry, he told them, everything was all right. Think back, he told them, remember how it went last time. The kidnappers would probably be in contact tomorrow, if not tomorrow then the day after.

One other thing, he told them, told Rossi in particular. Security has been good, but it could be better. Don't use the same car each day; arrange to leave in a different car each evening, vary the times you arrive so that the kidnappers don't have a pattern to recognize.

'You think we're being watched?' the banker asked.

'Of course,' Haslam told him.

Christ . . . Hendricks felt the shock. They were talking about him. And if they were that meant there'd be a tail sitting on him. He moved his position slightly so that he could look round without the movement being apparent, and tried to check.

How the hell did the consultant know? He was still checking, his mind racing, trying to work it out. Forget the theory, he told himself, just spot whoever was sitting on him. He left the street and began walking, not too fast but quickly enough not to rouse suspicion; slipped automatically into the old procedures, cut back on himself and back again, looked for the signs. If they had a team on him it would be difficult to spot, but why the hell should they have a team on him, why should they have anybody on him? He went into a café, chose a seat from which he could watch the street, and waited.

If the consultant knew about him, then why hadn't he done something about it other than just tell the family? Because the consultant didn't know about him, he began to think; he could be certain of that because he was still listening in to their discussions. And he could do that because the apartment was still bugged. If the consultant had suspected the family was under observation by someone like himself, the first thing he would have done was check the apartment for bugs. But he hadn't. So when the consultant talked about a tail he was talking about someone else.

The kidnappers, Hendricks realized.

The following morning he rented a car and drove north from the city to the point where he had concealed the cache containing the weapons and ammunition he had purchased in Germany. The morning was already hot, the sun glistening off the snow peaks to the north and the land baked hard. The cache was intact. He walked past it up the track. The honeysuckle which climbed over the ruins of the farmhouse scented the air and the cicadas hummed on the slopes behind. He checked he was not being observed, crossed what had been the courtyard, went inside, and made his way to the end over the cellar. The ring in the trap door was only slightly rusted. He pulled it open, checked the cellar below, then let it fall back into place, returned to the cache and removed the weapons.

By three he was in Via Ventura.

It was so obvious, he thought. So why hadn't he seen it before, worked it out for himself?

The fact that the consultant had spotted someone meant that the stake-out was in the street. Either in a vehicle or on foot, probably both even if it was one man or woman. If he or she was on foot they could be anywhere, but if they were using a car the possibilities were limited to the parking bays cut into the pavement.

He walked down the street to the apartment block, looked back and checked which of the parking positions gave the best visibility, then walked back up the street and confirmed the numbers – eight to thirteen, counting down the street. He took the details of the vehicles parked there, went to the café on the corner, and ordered iced coffee.

Giuseppi Vitali's first telephone call next morning was to the leader of the unit holding Paolo Benini, his second was to the negotiator Mussolini, and his third was to the stake-out Pascale. It was time to re-establish contact, he had decided overnight. Crucify them this evening, he told Mussolini, no matter whether it's the father or the wife. Check them out, he told Pascale, see if the banker is still involved.

The day was humid, the slightest hint of thunder evaporating just before midday. Pascale left his apartment at one and was in Via Ventura forty minutes later. By two o'clock he had parked the Alfa in one of the spaces from which he could see the apartment block, and disappeared into the crowd. At four he returned and checked the car.

Two of the original vehicles had already been driven away, so the odds were already falling. Hendricks watched from one of the pavement tables outside the café on the corner.

Pascale returned to the car at six. Thin build, black hair – Hendricks logged the details – dark grey suit, stylishly large. One of three suspects.

Umberto Benini arrived at six-ten, looking ill and bent over a walking-stick. Almost certainly genuine, Pascale decided. Marco arriving just after and looking tense. No banker yet.

The Alfa was in place, therefore the kidnappers had decided to move. Good luck, Haslam told Francesca and Marco as they left, tonight Mussolini will phone.

Still no banker, Pascale thought. It was seven-twenty. The BMW screeched into the area in front of the apartment and Francesca and Marco ran inside. So where was the banker?

'They made contact.' Marco was excited, partly from the adrenalin and partly from relief that the call had been made. 'Francesca was brilliant.'

They sat round the table and listened to the recording.

'Yes.' Francesca's voice.

'Hello, Francesca, this is Mussolini.'

'What have you done with him, you bastard. What have you done with my husband?' The voice was angry, screaming.

'Three miliardi if you want to see him again.'

Mussolini was trying to say something else, threatening her, telling her that this time she had better play ball. Francesca was drowning him, repeating and repeating the one thing on the script.

'Screw the demand, Musso. Just prove to me he's alive and well.'

'Three miliardi, or you don't even get what's left of him.'

'Just prove you haven't killed him. You hear me. Prove Paolo's alive and well.'

'Tomorrow, same time.'

Haslam leaned forward, rewound the tape, played it again, then looked at her.

'Marco's right. You were good.'

'I just said what was on the script.' For the first time that evening she was trembling.

'What do we do now?' It was Umberto's first contribution.

Haslam allowed Francesca to answer. 'We do as they say. Wait for them to phone tomorrow.'

The kidnappers had made contact, Hendricks told Brettlaw that night; the wife had asked for confirmation that her husband was alive and the kidnappers were phoning back tomorrow. In the meantime he himself needed a check on the ownership details of three vehicles, all Italian registered.

The next morning he breakfasted early, then left the hotel and spent thirty minutes purchasing a number of items from stores in the area: a quantity of food, mostly tinned, plates and cups, a water container, reinforced chain and padlocks. Then he left Milan, drove north, and secreted them in the cellar of the ruined farmhouse. For one moment on the return journey, and with the traffic slowed by road works, he thought he might miss the noon telephone contact; as he entered the city, therefore, he parked the hire car and took the metro. The call was on time and gave him the vehicle ownership details he had requested the previous evening. By the time he had collected the car and made his way to Via Ventura it was almost four.

Of the vehicles whose ownership details he had requested, only the Alfa was in place. Therefore that was almost certainly the stake-out vehicle. As long as the driver was in the area, and as long as the man with the charcoal grey suit hadn't simply parked there again because it was convenient for work or a date. He waited, lost in the crowd, picked up the suit first, then the man, and knew he was right.

Ninety minutes later Pascale watched as Francesca and Marco left the apartment – slightly early tonight, he thought, so perhaps the pressure was taking its toll. He cleared Via Ventura and drove to the Inter Café a block and a half from the clean phone.

Tonight there might be two calls, Haslam had told Francesca, and if there were the first would be routine. Even so the flat with the clean phone was cold, almost chilling, and she picked up the phone on the first ring.

'Give me Marco.'

She passed the phone across the table.

'Marco?'

'Yes.'

'Same place as the first drop. Be back here at eight.'

They took the BMW. The lights on the corner were red against them; Marco tapped the steering wheel, unaware of the fact, and accelerated across the oncoming traffic the moment the lights changed. The evening was warm and the tables outside the Inter Café were busy. Marco parked thirty yards down, engine running, then hurried up the street. Francesca shifted across, adjusted the driver's seat and put the clutch down, slipped into first, released the handbrake and held the car on the footbrake.

The café was crowded, most of the customers watching the sport on the television above the bar. Marco checked the time and crossed the room to the toilet. The basin was grimy and the paper towels were crumpled in the bin beneath it. He knelt down and shuffled through them.

Please not another package, Francesca prayed. Her legs were suddenly weak and her muscles were trembling. She slipped the car out of gear but kept her hand on the stick, took her left foot off the clutch but continued to hold the car on the footbrake. Saw Marco coming out of the café, saw the look on his face. She pulled on the handbrake and slipped back to the passenger seat.

'It's all right.' She hardly heard his words. 'He's okay. Look.'

He gave her the Polaroid. The photograph showed Paolo sitting on a stool; he was thinner and his hair was longer, and the newspaper he held in front of him was that day's *Herald Tribune*.

'He's got both his ears.' Francesca laughed, cried, was not sure which. 'He really is okay.'

Pascale had been back in position eight minutes when the BMW returned, the wife and brother running into the apartment and both of them looking relieved. The mobile telephone rang. How'd it go, Vitali asked him. Fine, he said.

Mobile telephone plus clip-on scrambler, Hendricks was close enough to see; the controller calling the stake-out rather than the stake-out reporting in, therefore the communication one-way, the stake-out not calling the controller because he didn't have his number. He stopped thinking about the kidnappers and concentrated on the conversation seventy metres away in the apartment.

The discussion was brief and to the point. Paolo was well and hadn't been mutilated. When the kidnappers phoned at eight it would be with a demand, probably the three miliardi they had already asked for. The only question was what Francesca should offer in return. A hundred and seventy-five million, they had almost agreed the night before, except that the figure seemed too much like a negotiating sum, Haslam now suggested. A hundred and eighty million, they decided, Francesca should also hint that she and Umberto had been abandoned by the bank without actually saying so. When she and Marco left it was with a script she and Haslam had prepared together.

The call was slightly early, as if to take her by surprise.

'Three milardi if you want him back, Francesca.'

'I can't, it's too much.'

'Not if you want him back. Or perhaps you don't, perhaps we should just dispose of him and forget it?'

She gave herself time; didn't reply; looked at the script. 'A hundred and eighty million,' she told him.

The laugh was abusive. 'Is the bank going broke?'

Remember what you and Dave worked out; remember what Dave said to say and what not to say. 'A hundred and eighty million,' she repeated.

'Chicken feed, Francesca. I'll phone tomorrow to see if you've changed your mind.'

Tomorrow the kidnappers would come down, the family's crisis management team agreed thirty minutes later, possibly by a miliardo. And tomorrow Francesca could go up by thirty million, perhaps thirty-five. The day after the kidnappers would come down and Francesca would go up again.

I'm holding on, Dave – Francesca looked at Haslam. I'm still in one piece, but only because I know you're here.

You're doing well, he willed her to understand; you're much stronger than you think. And you have to be, because you're the one who's going to bring Paolo home.

'You all right?' he asked her.

'I'm all right,' she told him.

He would check one more day, Hendricks decided; then he would move the day after. The next afternoon he was in Via Ventura by two.

The Alfa was in place. Haslam took an outside seat at the café on the corner, ordered iced coffee, and waited.

It was time for Pascale to reappear. Hendricks sat inconspicuously beneath the trees and waited. No Merc 190 or Escort XR3i, therefore Pascale definitely the stake-out.

Haslam asked for the bill and left the café. It was four-thirty, time slipping, suddenly five o'clock. Pascale was on the opposite side of the road, crossing to the Alfa. Standard routine: sit in the car for ten minutes then get out and walk to the boutiques. The pavement was busy, most of the shoppers young and well dressed.

Hendricks left the seat and edged closer to the car.

Ten minutes gone, time for Pascale to move again. Haslam was thirty yards away, carefully positioned.

Hendricks closed on the Alfa slightly, watched as Pascale flicked through a magazine.

Pascale tossed the magazine on to the passenger seat and opened the door to get out. Good-looking girl in see-through blouse and no bra, he couldn't help staring, somebody behind her also looking.

Jesus – Hendricks felt the shock: Pascale had seen him. He turned, away from the girl with the transparent blouse, away from Pascale.

Something wrong – it was as if Haslam was back in the Falls or the Shankill. Not Pascale or the girl Pascale was looking at. The man behind the girl. Turning away. Turning too quickly. Turning so that Pascale wouldn't see him, so that Pascale wouldn't realize he was looking at him.

Christ, the stake-out had a tail.

He turned left, slowly and casually, not drawing attention to himself. Pascale was looking round, the tail already disappeared. So was it a tail, or was it someone embarrassed at being caught looking at a girl's breasts? He strolled past the Alfa and left the street.

The management meeting began twenty minutes later. Francesca was nervous, he thought, but understandably so; therefore he wouldn't mention the subject of the tail on Pascale until she and Marco returned from the clean phone. If he mentioned it at all.

Forty minutes later they sat in silence and listened to the tape.

'Two miliardi.'

'Two hundred and fifteen millions.'

'You're not trying, Francesca. What about the bank?'

'Two hundred and fifteen millions.'

'You'll have to do better than that, Francesca. Seven o'clock tomorrow.'

It was going well, Haslam told the committee in general and Francesca in particular; Francesca was doing her job and the fact that Enrico Rossi no longer appeared to be involved was paying off. Tomorrow Mussolini would drop again, probably to one and a half miliardi, possibly even one, and Francesca might go up by twenty millions to two hundred and thirty-five.

And the day after that Mussolini would drop again, possibly to below a miliardo. And once that happened agreement would not be far off. Therefore he wouldn't tell them about the shadow sitting on Pascale. The pressure on Francesca was already unbearable, anything more and it might tip the balance. And she was too close to getting Paolo out to do that.

Tonight he would come down and the family would come up, Vitali knew, the same tomorrow. And the day after that they would agree. Both sides knowing where it would end and playing according to the rules to get there. He finished the coffee and spent the next hour on the handful of outstanding matters connected to his machinery business. Then he closed himself off from the world and began to plan his research on the list of businessmen from which he would select his next target.

Pascale left his apartment at twelve.

The Benini job would soon be over – Toni hadn't said so in as many words, but all the signs were there. There'd be a fat little bonus at the end of it, in addition to the standard daily fee. He had other sidelines, of course, but stake-out on kidnappings was a nice

229

earner. Perhaps he'd get a couple of new suits, perhaps he might trade the Alfa for a newer model. He felt in his trouser pocket for the car keys. The alleyway was quiet, a couple passing by and some women talking, nothing out of the ordinary. He opened the driver's door and slid in.

'Don't look round, Angelo.'

He wasn't sure where the man had come from, was only aware of the voice from the rear seat and the image of the gun in the rear view mirror.

'Adjust the mirror away from you.'

So that he couldn't see the face of the man, even his outline.

'Now drive.'

What's going on, who are you? Not carabinieri, the carabinieri would have come in with sirens blaring. Therefore Mafia. But Toni was Mafia, or ex-Mafia, so Toni would have sorted out his arrangement with them, agreed the commission they would get on his freelance operations. He started the car and pulled away.

'Head for Bergamo.'

'Who are you?' he tried to ask. 'What the hell do you want?' He braked to avoid slamming into the car in front. 'There's a mistake, I'm one of you. We're on the same side.'

'Shut up and just do as you're told.'

They had been driving fifty minutes, the city behind them and the mountains in front.

'Turn off at the next exit.'

They left the autostrada, along a main road, turned off the road on to a smaller road, then off that one on to a track. Off that track and on to another, the surface rutted and the track climbing, the sun suddenly hot and the knots twisting Pascale's stomach.

'Stop.'

The trees hung over them and the dust rose in swirls from the tyres. He pulled on the handbrake.

'Switch off the ignition.'

The hood went over his head, no eyeholes, just a tear to breathe through.

'Get out.'

Run, he told himself; while his hands were still free, before they were tied. The metal of the gun struck him on the side of his head and the blackness clouded over him.

He was coming round, his head aching and the blackness still there, even though the hood was no longer suffocating him. He tried to push himself up and realized he was in a cellar, his hands manacled behind his back and chained to a wall.

There was no Alfa Romeo, therefore no Pascale; no stake-out, therefore there would be no telephone call from the negotiator. So what the hell was the kidnapper playing at? At the committee meeting Haslam allowed the family to decide what price Francesca should offer that evening – up twenty millions to two hundred and thirty-five million lire – then cautioned them there was a chance that Mussolini might not telephone.

When Francesca and Marco returned from the clean phone her eyes were smiling. 'They came down to one miliardo. I told them our offer. They're phoning again tomorrow.' We're going to win – it was in her face, in her confidence. We're going to get Paolo back.

Perhaps the kidnappers thought they were so close to finalizing a deal that they no longer considered a stake-out necessary, Haslam thought, except that that was when they would normally insist on such a precaution. It's looking good, he told them, but they mustn't get too optimistic, mustn't take anything for granted.

Vitali's call to Mussolini was at eight. The family had offered two thirty-five, the negotiator reported to him. Tomorrow go down to five hundred million, he told Mussolini. Then the family would go up to around two-forty, and the night after both sides would settle at between two-fifty and two-seventy. It would be a good deal, especially for the second time round, but it was time to get out of this one, time to settle it and move on. He told Mussolini he had done well and called the stake-out.

'Angelo, this is Toni.'

'I know you're Toni, but this isn't Angelo.'

Wrong number, Vitali thought, and dialled again.

'Listen to me, Toni,' Hendricks told him. 'Don't hang up. You don't know who I am, but I don't know who you are, therefore we're both secure.'

Christ, what the hell was happening, Vitali thought. What the hell was going on? He forced himself not to speak.

'I want Paolo Benini,' Hendricks said.

Who's Paolo Benini? Vitali almost asked but didn't; he was still fighting to control himself, to bring some semblance of composure into his voice before he spoke. Who the hell are you and what the hell is happening?

'I know you have him and I want him,' Hendricks told him.

231

'I'm prepared to pay the two thirty-five the family offered tonight, whatever currency and denomination you want. Except that if you fuck with me like you fucked with the family last time, then I fuck with Angelo.'

How the hell did whoever it was get on the line, how did they know about Angelo? About how much the family had offered that night and about what had happened before?

'Let me speak to Angelo.'

'Ten o'clock tomorrow morning.'

Two bidders for the same commodity – Vitali made himself coffee and tried to think like the businessman he was. The sun was streaming through the window and he had been in his office since six. Two buyers for the same item, therefore why not play each against the other? Because this one was different. Because one of the bidders had Angelo Pascale. Because something was running and he wanted no part of it.

At nine he confirmed that Angelo Pascale was not at his apartment and that his car was not parked in its normal place; at ten he phoned Pascale's mobile number.

'Let me speak to Angelo.'

He heard the scuffle as the telephone changed hands, then heard Pascale's voice. Where are you, he asked, how are you, are you okay? He was in a cave or a cellar, Pascale told him; he was chained to the wall and the man holding him was wearing a hood. There was another scuffle, Pascale cut off midway through a sentence, and he heard the other voice. Two hundred and thirty-five million lire plus Angelo, he agreed.

'How do you want it?' Hendricks asked him.

'Dollars. But I'll need to confirm that Angelo is alive and that the money's genuine.'

'I'll need to confirm that the man I'm getting is Benini.'

'I'll phone the evening after tomorrow. We can finalize the switch then.'

'Agreed.'

Hendricks's details were already worked out: the flight to Frankfurt the next morning and the return by rail to avoid the metal detectors, then the day in the foothills to zero the sniper rifle, even the location to which he would direct the men delivering Benini. For the rest of the day he checked the routes he would order the kidnapper's men to take, plus the exact details of the killing zone, then returned to Milan. That evening he took a light supper and was at the Leonardo by five minutes to midnight. He'd made contact and agreed a fee, he told The Man: 235 million lire, plus Pascale in exchange for Benini. The kidnappers wanted dollars and were phoning again in two days.

Cali would want to know how he'd decided on the price, Brettlaw told him. Start the false trail, he had decided that morning: for Hendricks, for Myerscough, for anyone else.

Cali was the new cocaine centre of Columbia. Implicit in the apparent lapse of security, therefore, was the suggestion that the organization he represented was connected with drugs, and that Benini and BCI were therefore involved in drugs or money-laundering related to drugs. But don't make such an apparent security slip too often, Brettlaw understood. Once and Hendricks would pick it up and believe it: twice, or the second time in the wrong place and the wrong way, and Hendricks would suspect.

'Why two thirty-five?' he asked.

Because it had been necessary to match the family's offer, Hendricks told him; plus it was a way of telling the kidnappers he knew what was going on, therefore of putting more pressure on them.

Brettlaw took the details of where and how Hendricks wished the money delivered and said he would be in touch the following midnight. Make it the day after, Hendricks told him, he was away that day and might not be back.

Brettlaw ended the call, left his office, and went to the first of the evening meetings. At eight-forty he left Langley and was driven to the University Club. He checked in, dropped his overnight bag in his room, thought about a sauna, knew he didn't have the time, and left the Club by the rear door. With him he carried a mobile phone and encryptor.

The flat was fifteen minutes' walk away, on the top two floors of a terraced house tucked incongruously among the modern concrete blocks round Washington Circle. The street was narrow, the pavements were lined with trees and cars were parked on either side, so there was barely room for one-way traffic down the middle. Almost like approaching a dead drop, he half-joked to himself.

Perhaps that was it, perhaps that was why he liked someone like Bekki. Sure he savoured the power of the top floor, sure he got a buzz from it, but sometimes he needed more. The two sides of man, Jung had said: Brettlaw DDO and family man, pillar of the establishment: Brettlaw out on the edge and needing more. The

233

dark side and the light side. Except that perhaps the light needed the dark in order to survive.

The sun had dipped past the roofs but the evening was warm. He walked up the four steps to the front door and pressed the buzzer for flat two, the last sideways glances barely noticeable. The door clicked open, he pushed through into the hallway, made sure the door was closed behind him, and took the stairs to the next floor.

The door was slightly ajar, Bekki's face just visible through the opening. Her hair was tucked up and she was only wearing a kimono.

'Good to see you.'

'You too.'

She kissed him – soft, slightly moist – and handed him a glass of sake. He put the jacket and briefcase on a chair, sipped the sake, and climbed the spiral steps. The bathroom was through an archway, a kimono – silk, a gold dragon on black – hanging on the wall. He undressed and stepped into the shower.

Paolo Benini was about to be removed, but not the others. Not the banker Rossi who had sought to open the secret of the Nebulus account, nor Manzoni, the BCI manager in London, who had supplied him with the Nebulus details. It had been easy to trace the question back, especially when he had run it past Myerscough. Without Myerscough realizing of course, even though it had been Myerscough who had given him Manzoni's name.

When a chain was weak you didn't simply replace a link, though. You removed the chain. Therefore deal with Rossi and Manzoni as he was dealing with Benini. Then the boxes would be sealed again, then everything would be secure.

The music drifted up from below. He dried himself, put on the kimono, and went downstairs.

When his driver called at the Club at five-thirty Brettlaw was waiting in the foyer. By six the ritual of his morning visit to the canteen had been performed and the bagel and coffee were on his desk. He lifted the telephone and called Cranlow in Bonn.

'Update me.'

'We made contact last night.'

'How?'

'A honey trap. Contact confirmed for tonight to make sure the three overnight at the address regularly. The bait managed to get some fingerprints and we're running a cross-match on them now.'

In case whoever had informed Brettlaw was running a scam or the honey trap had eyeballed the wrong target.

'What with?'

'Prints found on bomb fragments, weapons, safe houses used by alleged members of the group.'

'Who else knows?'

'No one.'

'And you've got it tight?'

'Tighter than you could believe.'

'If we get confirmation?'

'We go tomorrow.'

'My final say-so.'

'Of course.'

Brettlaw ended the call and finished the coffee. So what about Benini? Benini was finished, Benini was about to be no more. But what about Rossi and Manzoni? He took a sheet of paper from the drawer on the right of his desk and placed it on the blotting pad. In the centre at the top he drew a box in black, the single word he wrote in it in capital letters and also in black.

NEBULUS.

He sat back, thought for a moment, then sat forward again and drew a diagonal line from the bottom left corner of the box. At the end of the line he drew a second box.

BENINI.

Below that box he drew two vertical lines connecting two more boxes to it.

ROSSI.

And below it MANZONI.

In the dispassionate cold of morning the decision he had made the night before was even more logical. Except that he shouldn't have delayed on it, should have made the decision as soon as he had known what they had done. Hendricks wouldn't do the jobs, of course, partly because he was occupied with the Benini affair but mainly because that would risk establishing a connection.

The details were already coming to him: who would do the jobs and how he would suggest they be done, how he would establish the smokescreen to detach the deaths from Benini's and how he would create the cut-outs so they couldn't be traced back to him or the Agency.

He lifted the telephone and began the arrangements.

*

There was no Alfa, but there hadn't been the night before and Mussolini had still phoned. Haslam waited in the apartment and hoped he was wrong.

No phone call – Francesca shook her head as she and Marco returned from the clean phone. His face was white and hers was streaked with tears. You told us, Dave, you warned us that everything might be going too smoothly, but Christ how I wish you'd been wrong.

'I'll take care of her.' Umberto got up and led her to the bathroom, his arm around her. 'Francesca will be fine in a moment,' he announced when he returned, then he went to the cocktail cabinet, offered Haslam, Rossi and Marco a drink, poured one for Francesca and one for himself.

So what was happening: Haslam sat at the table and tried to work it out. Of course the kidnappers might call on time tomorrow, might even say something had gone wrong tonight, then resume the negotiations as if nothing had happened. Except that it wasn't logical that they hadn't phoned today. Especially when a settlement seemed so close.

Vitali's call to Hendricks was at seven fifty-three.

'You have the money?'

'Yes.'

'And Angelo is still OK?'

'Yes. What about Benini?'

'He's fine.'

'Where and when?'

'Tomorrow. Take the Bergamo road north, then turn east at junction four. Five kilometres after the junction is a garage. Call me on the scrambler when you're there.'

Then he would tell them to take the next turning left, after half a kilometre, and to drive along it for exactly one kilometre. The two-way radio concealed in the cairn of stones on the right side of the track, because if they phoned him on Pascale's mobile at that point they would hear the ring and know where he was positioned.

'What time?' Vitali asked.

'Seven tomorrow evening.'

The call from Bonn came through at five-thirty, half an hour to midnight in Europe. Forensics had found a fingerprint match with a bomb fragment, Cranlow informed Brettlaw, the honey trap had made contact with the target again and they were waiting to hear from her. Keep in touch, Brettlaw told him, and called Milan.

'Update,' he asked Hendricks.

'It's ready for tomorrow.'

'Green Go.'

The sounds scraped along the floor of the cave and the light came round the corner. Paolo Benini crouched against the wall and tried to hide his fear. Four men, more than usual and wearing hoods, but they always did.

The first opened the lock of the cell door and two came in, the fourth remaining outside. The second bent down, another set of keys in his hand, and unlocked the manacles round Benini's ankles, then clamped a pair of handcuffs round his wrists. A hood was pulled over his head, a hole for his mouth and nose though none for his eyes, and he was led out of the cell and up the slope of the cave.

The air and sounds were suddenly different. I'm outside – he fought to contain his excitement – I'm being released. The bank's done it, Myerscough and whoever Myerscough works for have pulled it off.

He was helped into something – the back of a van – and man-handled into something else – a large wooden box, holes for ventilation. The lid was closed and locked and the van pulled away. An hour later he was transferred to the boot of a car.

It's all right, he told himself; everything's okay.

The day was hot and stifling. Twice they checked him, gave him water which he drank through a straw; now they stopped again, the engine of the car still running. Ten minutes later, probably less, the car pulled away then turned left almost immediately – he could tell by the way he was thrown about – off the road and on to a track, the surface pitted and bumpy. The car stopped again. He waited: one minute, perhaps two, certainly no more. The boot was opened and he was lifted out and made to stand, the handcuffs taken from his wrists and the hood from his head.

The sky was bluer than he had ever remembered and the country-side was a blaze of colours he told himself he would never forget. He stood rubbing his wrists, then his eyes. The men around him were hooded, the car was behind him, and the track on which he stood was broken and dusty. He breathed in the air and listened to the sounds, the birds and the cicadas. Heard someone talking in to what he assumed was a telephone. Start walking, he was told. Go to the end of the track and turn right, there's a garage there. Don't look back.

He turned, saw them running into the bushes to his right, and began walking. Was still walking when he heard the exclamations as if they had found something or someone, then the sound of the car pulling away, heading away from him, the noise of the engine fading then gone. He stopped and looked round. The track was empty behind him, the valley rising on either side of him and freedom all round him.

Thank God for BCI, he thought; thank God for Myerscough and whoever Myerscough works for.

He wiped the tear from his cheek and turned towards where the kidnappers had said there was a garage.

For the third night running there was no stake-out, and for the second night no telephone call.

Pascale disappears but the kidnappers' calls continue – Haslam ran through the details. Pascale still doesn't show and the calls stop. Pascale being tailed before he vanishes off the face of the earth. So why was there a tail on the stake-out the kidnappers were using and why had Angelo disappeared, why had the kidnappers pulled out when they were so close to a deal?

Because somebody else wanted Paolo Benini. He was not sure where the thought came from. Somebody else had known that Benini had been kidnapped and had come in with a counter-offer. But why hadn't the kidnappers used the new offer to force up the price to the Benini family again?

Because whoever had intervened had kidnapped Angelo as a hostage against Paolo.

Crazy, he told himself, totally out of line.

But to do that they would need to know the state of the negotiations – he made himself think through it. And they would not know that simply by tailing the stake-out. Therefore they had been monitoring the family, and the simplest way to do that was to bug the apartment where the family held its discussions.

He could check himself, could buy the gear and sweep the apartment. But Quincey Jordan in DC was an expert, Quince would look where he wouldn't even imagine. Therefore he would call Quince. Just in case Francesca didn't hear from the kidnappers tomorrow, just in case there wasn't a simple explanation like the negotiator Mussolini having an accident or the clean phone being temporarily

238

cut off. And he'd call Jordan from the pay cabins at Central Station, because if the Beninis' apartment was bugged then Christ knew where else was.

The second hand of the clock on the wall opposite the desk was moving slowly, the minute hand even more so. Brettlaw unlocked the drawer, took out the sheet of paper, and studied the diagram on it. NEBULUS top centre, BENINI diagonally left, ROSSI and MANZONI below.

He checked the time and telephoned Milan on the encryptor.

'Benini is no longer a problem,' Hendricks told him.

In his mind Brettlaw selected a red pen and drew a cross on the Benini box. Rossi and Manzoni soon to follow, the plans already well advanced.

He ended the call and stared again at the diagram. Weak links and weak chains, he remembered. Next time he wouldn't wait until the Agency might be compromised; next time he shouldn't delay until his status as DDO, or his future as DCI, was threatened. Next time he would take action as soon as the next box was at risk.

He poured himself a Jack Daniels, lit a Gauloise, and stared again at the diagram. NEBULUS, BENINI, ROSSI and MANZONI. The bourbon was hot and searing. He downed it in one, poured himself another, and chainlit the cigarettes. Then he sat back in the chair, the silence round him, and his eyes and mind focused on the diagram. Abruptly he leaned forward, picked up a pen, and drew another line – diagonal from the bottom corner of NEBULUS, but this time to the right, then put the pen down.

Myerscough had said it would be all right, and Myerscough was never wrong. Except that Myerscough was sufficiently worried to warn him.

He took the pen again and wrote in the name MITCHELL.

Just a consideration, of course, nothing more. Mitchell was trawling, Myerscough had said; Mitchell was so far off target that he wouldn't get even a sniff. The only way Mitchell would pose a threat was if he began to investigate Nebulus, and there was no way Mitchell could do that, no way Mitchell could even know about Nebulus.

Except that Mitchell had already begun to investigate First Commercial, which was the first link in the chain to BCI. And if Brettlaw had decided to eliminate the risks posed by the Benini kidnap, then he should also consider the same executive action to eliminate risks posed by the Mitchell enquiry.

Of course not, he told himself. He reached over to the side of the desk and shredded the papers.

13

Even at six in the morning the Washington heat was rising and the humidity was settling like a blanket. Mitchell sat on the sun deck for twenty minutes, drinking cold orange juice and talking with the couple on the next boat, then went below, showered and changed. Nothing happening in the world today – the thought was barely conscious – no more than the usual number of choppers beating up the Potomac. At seven he checked his electronic mail, left the marina, took the metro rail to Eastern Market and walked to Sherrills.

Sherrills wasn't on the tourist map. Its exterior was inconspicuous and its interior was leftover fifties, with waitresses to match, Mitchell sometimes thought.

Pearson was waiting in his favourite alcove, the waitress serving him scrambled eggs. 'How's life on the river?' He looked up as Mitchell joined him.

'Cooler than it is on the Hill.' Mitchell draped his coat on the bench and asked for coffee.

'How's it going?' Pearson was friendly but businesslike. The pleasantries were for some other time and some other place. Not today, though, not with the war council tonight. Not when they were already into August, Congress in recess, and the calendar counting down to Labour Day.

'I think we're almost there.'

'Tell me.'

'Small local US bank, hundreds like it in the country. Five years ago it runs into trouble and is secretly bought up by an overseas bank. After that it begins to prosper, opens more branches, locally and across the state.'

'So where's it going wrong?'

'It runs two sets of books. One official and the other hardly anyone knows about. Only the first is declared, the other is kept for its special accounts.'

'This is since the takeover?'

241

'Yes.'

'Specifics?' Pearson asked.

Since the takeover the bank had increasingly been used for the movement of money when the movers wished to keep their transactions secret, Mitchell told him. Overseas transfers over $10,000 were supposed to be registered, he reminded Pearson, even though the Fed didn't have time to run routine checks on anything below twenty-five million. So, via its special accounts, the local bank was being used as a conduit for illegal currency movements.

'What sort of figures are we talking here?' Pearson had stopped eating.

'More zeros on the end than you want to think about. Drug money, dirty money; you name it they're doing it.'

'And the illegal transfers tie in with the bank which owns it?'

'Yes.'

In his life on the Hill, Pearson had become accustomed to combining the ideals of youth with the pragmatism of experience. Good story, he therefore thought, great platform for Donaghue. Small country bank manipulated by the city slickers; hard-working honest-to-goodness small-town Americans being screwed by out-of-state money-grabbers. The right story for the right time in the primaries or the run-in to the presidency. Plus the international angle.

'How are you getting this?' he asked.

'Through an insider. He was Vice President of Management Information Systems, which means he ran the computers. We'll have to cover him later. He became suspicious when he saw that a lot of money was going through, but little was staying in the community. A long-time buddy of the bank's president, thinks the president was innocent though greedy, got in above his head and can't get out. My man left just under two years ago on the verge of a nervous breakdown.'

'Why's he helping you?'

'He thinks they've set it up so that if the shit hits the fan it will all come his way.'

'How's he getting you in?'

'Via the computer system.'

'Didn't they change the security codes when he left?'

'Of course.'

'So like I said, how's he getting you in?'

There were two ways into a computer system, Mitchell explained: the front and the back. When a specialist set up a system he always left a back door so that if anything went wrong he could access it without shutting everything down. Obviously there was a security code for this, just as was there for the ordinary user at the front door. When organizations wanted the front door security changed – when the Vice President, Management Information Systems left, for example – they'd call in the specialist who installed the system. He or she would change the front door, but often left the back door open on the assumption that no one else knew about it.

'So you've got enough for Jack to announce an investigation?'

'As long as it's general and he doesn't mention the names of either of the banks involved.'

'What are the names?'

'The First Commercial Bank of Santa Fe and the Banca del Commercio Internazionale, usually called BCI, of Milan.'

'Schedule?' Pearson pressed him.

Because they were already running out of time.

'There's one more lead to follow. I'll wrap it up, then I'm away for a few days, finish the résumé when I get back. You'll have it by the end of next week.'

The week before Labour Day.

'Where're you going?' Pearson waved for the bill.

'Same as usual, Walker's Cay.'

A dot off the Florida coast a mile long and a quarter-mile across at its widest point. Thin dust-strip of a runway, marina, hotel and a straggle of private dwellings. Reefs and blue holes for scuba diving; its size and position a hundred miles out meaning that few people visited it, and its location at the northernmost point of the Abacos chain guaranteeing unrivalled offshore fishing.

'Flying down?' Both were founder members of the Congressional Flying Club.

Mitchell nodded. 'How about you?'

'Out of town with Jack.' Raising money and shaking the right hands in the right places: it was how every senator and every congressman spent most of his or her vacation. 'Eva's going with Cath and the girls to the Vineyard, Jack and I might make a couple of days with them. Then back to DC the day before Arlington.'

And the week after that was Labour Day.

'When will Jack decide?' Whether or not he runs for the nomination, Mitchell meant.

'When he judges the time to be right.' In other words I don't know and I wish to hell I did.

243

They paid and left, then walked together to the Hill, Pearson to Russell Building and Mitchell to Dirksen. One of the secretaries was already in; Mitchell wished her good morning then went through to the corner desk under the window.

Nebulus, Haslam had said, probably London; plus Romulus and Excalibur. It was too early to call the contact, he'd try him midday, tell him he was flying out to see him again.

The telephone rang.

'Mitch?'

'Yeah.'

'It's Ed. I forgot to say thanks.'

Pearson's first meeting with Donaghue and his staff was at nine and his last was at six-thirty. The agenda for the first was routine: the senator's list of engagements for the day plus the aides who would accompany him; matters arising, then any other business.

The last meeting was the war council itself, the members seated as always in the senator's room, Donaghue throwing them each a beer then sitting apparently relaxed behind his desk, Pearson in the chair backing the wall to Donaghue's right, opposite the fireplace.

Jack was showing no signs of the wear and tear which normally crept up on politicians at this time of year, Pearson thought. But, then again, Jack hadn't declared; hadn't even announced his decision to the men and women who would advise him.

They discussed the latest opinion polls and newspaper editorials, the feelings of key politicians and key decision-makers in the party, and the reaction to Angel Fire. Which of the king-makers had pronounced on their favourite son and which of the money men were still holding back.

'What's Lavalle's position?' Donaghue asked.

'Still waiting,' one of the lawyers told him.

'How'd you know?'

'I had another lunch with his lawyer last week.'

'Who did the inviting?'

'They did.'

'What about the opposition?' Donaghue asked the other lawyer.

'Neck and neck.'

'But?'

'McKenzie's in trouble.'

McKenzie was a senior senator and one of the front runners since his declaration six months earlier.

244

'Why?'

'Problems with a blind trust.'

The financial affairs of members of Congress were normally handled by trusts independent of the member, thereby preventing members from influencing votes in which they had a financial interest, but also protecting them from accusations that they might be doing so.

'Why problems?'

'There's a story beginning that McKenzie's trust isn't blind.'

And if the story was even half true McKenzie was out, no matter which way his rivals played it: either by leaking it to the press or to the party chairman then persuading the chairman to pressure McKenzie to withdraw for the sake of the party.

'We stay clean on it,' Donaghue told them.

They could be in the White House and Donaghue would be the same, Pearson suddenly thought. Total concentration on the document or briefing paper in front of him. A calmness, even in the hour of maximum danger. Perhaps he wondered why he remembered the words from the Kennedy speech. 'Senator Donaghue's timetable over the vacation period.' He brought them to the next item on the agenda. 'Jack and I are in Boston, Diane with us, Mark holding the fort in DC. Usual run of meetings and engagements. We return for Arlington.'

Which was why he had thought of the quote.

'As always it's a private function, though given the speculation about Jack declaring there might be press attention this year. If so we don't discourage it.'

Others – millions of others – came to the Kennedy Memorial. Many took photographs. Many, even three decades on, were forced to turn away, grown men in uniform not ashamed to take the handkerchiefs from their pockets and dry their faces. Politicians came as well, of course, often out of respect though frequently with the television cameras close to them.

With Jack Donaghue, however, it was different. With Donaghue it was personal.

Jack was thinking about it, Pearson knew, Jack was already seeing it and doing it.

The Lincoln crossing the Memorial Bridge, coming slowly along Jefferson Drive then into the cemetery itself, the slopes rising gently to their right and the white crosses running in lines along its contours, the Custis-Lee Mansion standing guard above.

245

The senator, his family and closest friends getting out of the cars, Donaghue straightening his suit then taking the two red carnations from the car, the others standing back as he made the journey alone.

The polished granite terrace to the right and the drop of the land to the Potomac, DC glittering white on the far side. Eight granite steps in front of Donaghue as he began his walk – Pearson counted them each year. Then the sweep left, the sheen of the granite suddenly replaced by the white of the marble; the last steps, then the square of rough granite slabs. The plaques on the left and right small and the plaque in the centre larger:

John Fitzgerald Kennedy

1917–1963

Behind it the eternal flame.

For ten seconds, sometimes longer, Donaghue would stare up at the sky, then he would kneel and place the two single stem carnations at the edge of the central plaque.

The first to the leader shot dead in Dallas, and the second to the naval lieutenant killed in action in the Pacific campaign of the Second World War.

Then Donaghue would straighten and his family would join him; Cath at his left side and a daughter either side of them.

Even now, Pearson thought, he still remembered the time and the place and the day Jack had told him.

Something you ought to know, Jack said: just in case the opposition found out, just in case they ran it against him. Especially given the fact that he was a Catholic.

What ought I to know? Pearson had asked; what the hell is it that you've got to tell? Why the hell do you have to tell me?

Because if we're going to make it together you have to know, Jack had said. Then Jack had told him.

About the fact that his parents were close to the Kennedys, which everyone knew. About the fact that his father was a good man though not a politician, which Pearson had come to know. About the fact that his father was not his father, which had taken Pearson by surprise.

About the fact that his blood father and John Kennedy had served in PT boats in the Pacific War – which Pearson had checked. About the fact that three weeks after Kennedy had survived the sinking of PT109, Jack Donaghue's father had been lost in action in a similar incident. About the fact that at that time his mother was carrying him, though when he died his father had not known. About the fact that to save the family name, to give him a name, a friend had married his mother and stood by her.

So once a year, in the February cold of a Boston cemetery, Jack Donaghue bowed his head at the family grave of the man who had raised him as his own. And each year, in the stifling heat of Washington in August, he came to Arlington and remembered the other man, because he had been killed in action and therefore had no resting place on which his son could place a flower.

When Jack had first run for public office times had been straitlaced and conservative and hypocritical, so that if the details of his birth had become known the young Jack Donaghue would not have made it. And now, twenty-five years later, more than forty-five years after his father had given his life for his country, there were people who would not hesitate to dig up his ghost and use it to stop his son becoming president.

'What if someone asks?' It was the lawyer charged with protecting Donaghue from attacks by the other side.

'They haven't asked before.'

'But Jack wasn't running for the presidency before.'

They waited.

'If they ask we tell them.' Donaghue swung his feet off the desk, crossed to the fridge, and threw them each a beer. 'It's nothing I'm ashamed of. Hell, they've probably found out already.'

Thirty minutes later the meeting ended; as the others left Donaghue thanked them but remained seated, till only he and Pearson remained. Russell Building was quiet around them, no voices, not even footsteps on the marble.

'So how's it going, Ed?'

How's it *really* going? How do we *really* stand at the moment?

'Just waiting for the day.'

'What about Jon's meeting with Lavalle's man?'

'Lavalle's been approached by every other runner, plus a few nobody would expect, but he's holding off.'

'Which means?'

'If you want you've got him.'

So why are we here, Jack? What else do you want to ask me?

Donaghue was sitting sideways, looking out of the window, looking back at the fireplace.

'You ever think about dying, Ed? You ever look back at when

your old man went, the moment you realized that you were the next generation to go?'

'I guess we all do,' Pearson said softly.

'I don't mean passing away quietly with the grandchildren round you and the family dog by the side of the bed.'

The hour of maximum danger, Pearson thought. 'One that doesn't allow you to make peace with your Maker?' he suggested.

'Something like that.'

'But you're a Catholic, Jack, I wouldn't have thought that worried you. In any case I'd have thought you'd been through that in Vietnam.'

Donaghue turned and looked at him and laughed.

'So I went through it in 'Nam, Ed. So I made it. So I'm immortal.'

The night outside was dark, the thinnest sliver of moon passing by the window. They were coming at him as they always came at him when he allowed them. Cath lay beside him and apparently asleep. Eyes closed yet fully awake, afraid to stretch out her hand and ask what was troubling him.

He was in the water, struggling to keep afloat, the Japanese destroyer coming at him in the dark and the men beside him sinking.

He was heading back down the delta, the firefight round them but they were almost out of it. The voices coming over the radio net and the C130 telling the men upstream there was no way the choppers could get in to them, no way they could get them out.

He was in the car, the world in front of him and the gunman waiting for him.

He made himself stop shivering, told himself he would disturb Cath. Wake her, part of him argued, remember what Ed once told him. Not just that if he threw his hat into the presidential ring the one person he'd need was the person he could turn to when he was up and running and needed to be reminded of reality. But that the person he'd need more than any other was the one he could turn to when he was alone and scared and needed someone to share his fears.

He closed his eyes and tried to sleep.

Mitchell left National at seven in the morning and returned at eight in the evening. By the time he was on the boat it was eight-thirty.

Romulus, Excalibur and Nebulus, Haslam had suggested, Nebulus probably in London.

No trace of Excalibur, the First Commercial contact had said after

248

two hours hunched over his computer, but Romulus was one of the special accounts at First Commercial used to transfer money overseas and Nebulus was the BCI account in London to which such money was wired, so Excalibur might be one of the accounts on the other side of the London switch.

Tomorrow he'd begin the summary he'd promised Pearson; probably leave out the Romulus and Excalibur details until he'd firmed them up; probably not even put them on the computer. Just as he hadn't put the names of any of the contacts on the file.

Walker's Cay coming up, Christ how he needed it.

He tried to make it twice a year: once in winter when he welcomed its warmth and once in summer for its breeze and its fresh clean air and crystal water. Most times he went alone, simply as a release from the pressure cooker of DC. Walker's Cay was his getaway, his hideout; he'd made the trip so often he didn't even need to look at the flight charts.

Leave the field at Leesburg mid-afternoon, then the three and a half hour flight to Charleston. Refuel, check in at the airport's Holiday Inn, rent a cheap car and drive downtown to eat. St Lucie County the next morning, refuel again and check the Customs re-entry forms and weather. Confirm that his computerized flight plan had been cleared, then head east over the blue of the water.

The call from Bonn came at eighteen minutes past ten. Brettlaw took it in the Chevrolet as his driver drove him home.

'It's on.' Cranlow's voice was calm, no excitement in it.

'Tell me.'

In Europe it was the beginning of the new day.

'The bait has confirmed all three of them are there. We go tonight, depending on your say-so.'

The Chevrolet turned up the driveway to the house.

'Green Go,' Brettlaw told him. 'Good luck.'

A little under eight hours later the Chevrolet dropped him at Langley.

In Paris it would be midday.

He collected the coffee and bagel and went to his office, ran through the overnights, then filled in the time checking reports he had checked yesterday. At nine-thirty he went to his meeting with the DCI.

In Paris it was three-thirty in the afternoon, ticking away to four.

The day was drifting, everything dealt with efficiently yet only

Paris in focus. At eleven-thirty the lawyers briefed him on the evidence he would give to the Senate Select Committee on Intelligence that afternoon, shortly before two the armoured Chevrolet slid unnoticed into the carpark beneath Senate Hart.

In Paris it would be eight in the evening and the bait would be leaving the safe house.

He took his position in front of the committee members and settled for the questioning.

In Paris the get-away team would be standing by with the Yamaha and the boys who would do the job that night would be finalizing their arrangements.

The sub-committee broke at five. Brettlaw spent ten minutes talking with the chairman, then left.

In Paris it would be eleven in the evening. On the Rue St-Martin the bait and the first target would be leaving the café and walking to the apartment.

The Chevrolet turned into the complex at Langley. Brettlaw spent twenty minutes with the DCI, then returned to his office. Maggie was leaving, telling him she would see him in the morning. He settled at his desk and began the wait.

Zev Bartolski about to be avenged. The bankers Benini and Manzoni already dealt with and Rossi about to be. Boxes within boxes. Everything sealed again.

He crossed the room, poured himself a Jack Daniels, returned to his desk and lit another Gauloise. Most people in the Agency would kill for his job; most people in the Agency wouldn't be able to do his job. Wouldn't be able to take the pressure.

In Paris it would be two in the morning. In Paris the bait would have notified the boys whether or not they were on go – no words, just one press on the catch of her handbag for every target in the flat, the transmitter concealed in the lining.

He felt the adrenalin, just as he had felt in his first days on the streets, the days he had made his first contacts in Moscow. The terrible gnawing, but the electricity which came with it.

In Paris it would be three in the morning. In Paris it would be going down.

He poured himself another Jack Daniels and lit another Gauloise. After tonight there would be only another two visits to the canteen, perhaps three, then it would be over. He opened the security safe, selected a file, returned to his desk, and made himself concentrate on it.

The ring of the telephone was from the other side of the desk but might have been from the other side of the world. Brettlaw closed the file, locked it in the drawer of the desk, placed the Gauloise in the ashtray, and straightened the blotting pad. Only then did he lift the telephone and allow himself to hear Cranlow's voice.

'It's done,' the Bonn Chief of Station told him.

'How many?' Brettlaw asked.

'All three.'

'Problems?'

'None.'

'The teams got away okay?'

'Like they'd never been there.'

'And it's deniable?'

'Totally.'

'When will it break?'

'Possibly later today, certainly tomorrow.'

Brettlaw ended the call and wondered if Cranlow had remembered.

* * *

The family's management meeting was grim, almost silent: there was still no contact from the kidnappers and no suggestion where they should go from here. And no Rossi: it was the first time the banker had failed to attend such a meeting, and there had been no warning that he would not be there.

Probably the car broken down, Haslam made light of it: Rossi would be back tomorrow, and tomorrow something might happen. As they left he made a point of hanging back, so that when Umberto and Marco took the lift he and Francesca were still on the landing. Tomorrow morning he'd like access to the apartment, he told her: no one else there, neither her nor the housekeeper. Why, she asked, gave him the keys anyway. Because there's a chance the apartment's bugged, he told her.

Jordan's flight was due at seven-thirty the next morning. Haslam arrived at Malpensa at seven, bought the *Corriere della Sera* and the *Herald Tribune*, settled in the cafeteria and ordered coffee.

Italian banker killed in London. The item was on the front pages of both papers. Alessi Manzoni, the London manager of the Banca del Commercio Internazionale, had been found hanging beneath Waterloo Bridge. A post mortem suggested suicide but police had not ruled out a connection between the death and either the Vatican or the Italian masonic lodge P2.

It was seven-forty. He checked that the flight had landed and went to the arrivals lounge. Jordan emerged from customs looking fit though slightly tired, and walking like the Secret Service man he had once been. Haslam waited till Jordan had seen him, then left the terminal and walked to the carpark, Jordan following him and making sure there was no tail.

'Thanks for coming.' They shook hands and loaded the overnight bag in to the boot of the BMW. 'You're booked into a hotel in the city.' Jordan was on a red-eye: fly in this morning and fly back tonight. 'The room's charged to a company owned by the lawyer we use here. You want to check in and change first?'

'Wouldn't mind. Some breakfast as well.'

They left the airport.

'So tell me.'

Why you think somebody's bugging somewhere. Why you've brought me in from Washington and why you've concealed my presence here. Why you had your lawyer ship the equipment separately so it wasn't associated with either of us and why you've used a cover at the hotel.

'Kidnap job,' Haslam began. 'A couple of problems earlier but it should have been straightforward from here in. Then things began to go wrong.'

'What sort of things?'

'We're running the show from the family apartment, plus a clean phone for the negotiations somewhere else. Standard procedure. The kidnappers have been staking out the apartment. No problems about that. Except that somebody's been sitting on the stake-out. Then the stake-out disappears but the negotiations continue for a day or so. Everything going well and an agreement expected within two days, then the negotiations suddenly end. No warning and no attempt by the kidnappers to push up the price.'

'Police?' Jordan asked. Or the security services, he thought. Theirs or ours or somebody else's.

'Doesn't feel like it.'

They turned in to the hotel. Jordan checked in, showered, then joined Haslam for breakfast. An hour later they left and drove to the apartment, Haslam parking the BMW in the underground garage in case the block was still under surveillance.

'How pro do you think they are?' Jordan got out.

'Very.' Haslam opened the boot so that Jordan could get the case.
'What floor's the apartment on?'

'Top.'

'In that case we don't need the gear yet.'

They took the lift to the fifth floor, then the stairs to the roof.

'Ever come up here?'

'No.'

The morning was clear, the sun was hot, and the transmitter was taped inconspicuously on the wall surrounding the roof, the batteries in place, and the wire from it threaded along the bottom of the wall and disappearing into one of the flues peppering the roof.

'IR device,' Jordan explained. 'The mike will be in one of the air vents in the flat. Probably tucked up a bit so you'd have trouble finding it.' He crouched behind the transmitter, then pointed to the apartment block eighty metres away. 'Floor four or five. All you have to do is find out whether one's been rented recently.'

'What else will they have set up?'

'RF device, probably concealed in the upholstery. RF is easier and quicker to install, but it's limited by the number of batteries you can put in. When you go in you're never sure how long you've got, so you drop the RF first; that way you've got at least something in place. Then the IR.'

'What else?'

'Nothing in the target location. Receivers and cassette recorders in the rented flat, plus a pocket set with you all the time, probably an ICOM R1 and earpiece, so that as long as you're in range you can listen in without going to the flat.'

So you could listen in to the family's negotiations and stake out the stake-out at the same time.

'Time to do it.'

There was no point sweeping Francesca's flat before they checked whether the person monitoring the apartment was still in place, and every point in not doing so.

'Yeah, let's do it.'

They left the roof and collected the car. Two men arriving at a block of service flats on foot would look strange, two men arriving in a BMW with a wallet of money and the concierge would tell them what they needed.

Haslam parked and they went inside; the entrance was marble and the concierge was in uniform and standing near the lifts. They'd telephoned about an apartment, Haslam told him, and was directed to the manager's office, Jordan hanging behind.

Looking for an apartment for a month or so, Haslam told the woman; preferably high up, fourth or fifth floor.

Thought you were both interested in an apartment – the concierge didn't need to say. Nice place, Jordan looked round, anyone check in recently? American, like you? the concierge suggested. Christ, Jordan thought; possibly, he said. The first notes changed hands.

Not like you, though, the concierge told Jordan, he wasn't black. Strange guy, though, never sure when he was here and when he wasn't. Was? Jordan picked up the past tense. Si signore, he left two days ago. More notes changed hands; you get what you pay for, Jordan thought, and came back at the concierge. How'd you know he was leaving? Because he was carrying the case he arrived with. Silver aluminium case, 'bout so big? Jordan suggested. The concierge nodded: how'd you know. 'Cause I use the same myself, Jordan could have told him.

What flat did he have – Jordan gave him the last of the notes. Four-two, the concierge told him, but you didn't get it from me.

There was one flat available on the fourth floor, the manager told Haslam, and another on the fifth. Perhaps he could inspect them, Haslam asked. As they left the office Jordan joined them. A colleague, Haslam explained. Four-two Jordan mouthed as they entered the lift; already pulled out.

The lift arrived at the fourth floor. Four-one, the manager said, and opened the door for them. Not quite what we were looking for, Jordan smiled at the manager, what about four-two?

It was difficult, the woman began to say: technically it's still rented, but the man renting it left a couple of days ago. Oh God, she thought. One man renting an apartment, then two men looking for him. Not just two men. Two men who smiled at her and were impeccably polite, yet two men whose physical presence suddenly terrified her in a way she would not have thought possible. Four-two's actually empty, she said, but she couldn't actually rent it out at the moment because officially it was still rented to someone else, which was why she hadn't suggested it. Even though he's left, she added.

She unlocked the door and let them in. Right flat, right angle to the roof, they both saw; bookcase out of place under the window and tell-tale marks on it where the receiver had been taped in place. Thanks, they told the manager, no need to mention it to anyone. No way she was going to, they knew.

254

They left the block and returned to the apartment. Three hours later Jordan finished the sweep.

'As I said, RF in the sofa and IR down the vent. Nothing else.'

'So what does that tell me?'

'Not much that you don't know already. The equipment was installed by a specialist. The gear itself is top of the range; if he came through Frankfurt he'd have bought it at the airport terminal. Cash, no questions asked.'

'How'd you know that?' Haslam asked.

'Because that's where I pick up stuff when I come into Europe,' Jordan told him.

They left the apartment, swept Haslam's room at the Marino, joined the queue to see Leonardo's *Last Supper*, then returned to the hotel.

Jordan's flight was scheduled for seven. Ninety minutes before that Haslam was in position on Via Ventura. There was no Pascale sitting outside the apartment and no tail looking for Pascale. Francesca arrived, then Umberto and Marco. No Rossi, though, not even slipping in the back way. Haslam left the street and went to the flat.

He'd telephoned the bank that morning, Umberto said, had asked to speak to Rossi, but Rossi's PA had informed him that Signore Rossi was not available. Which might mean whatever they chose it to mean. At seven Francesca and Marco waited again at the clean phone; at eight they reported to Haslam and Umberto that no call had been made. They would meet again tomorrow, they decided; and if they didn't hear from the kidnappers they would consider running another series of newspaper advertisements.

Francesca escorted them to the door. Perhaps he could stay, she asked Haslam, there was something she wanted to ask him. Umberto nodded his agreement, thanked Haslam, then he and Marco left.

The apartment was quiet. 'You'd like some supper,' Francesca suggested. She made a salad, then brought cold meats and wine from the kitchen and laid the table. Haslam opened the bottle and poured them each a glass.

'What happened this morning?' Francesca looked at him across the table.

'The apartment was bugged. We found two devices and traced them to a service flat seventy metres away. The flat was empty, so whoever was doing the bugging has gone.'

'So what does that mean for Paolo?'

'What it means is that somebody else knew about the kidnapping and might have intervened in it. Which might explain why the kidnappers broke off the negotiations. Other than that I don't know.'

He felt empty and tired and wished he could tell her more. She was still staring at him, across the table, across the top of her glass.

'Thanks, Dave.'

'For what?'

'For being honest.' She was still looking at him, still staring at him. 'I'm tired, Dave, and each day I get more tired. I keep going because it's my responsibility to Paolo, my job to get him back. Sometimes I just want to give up, but I can't, because I'm the only one left and because I have to keep the others going.'

He pushed back his chair, crossed round the table, and stood behind her. 'You'll make it,' he told her. 'You're good and you're strong, better and stronger than you think.' He took the glass from her hand and lifted her up.

'Rule number one,' he told her. 'In my job you don't get involved.'

'Rule number two?' she asked him.

'Rules are made to be broken.'

For a minute, perhaps two, they stood, barely touching.

'Wrong time, Dave, wrong place.' She stroked the collar of his jacket, brushed a speck of dust from it.

'Yeah, wrong time, wrong place.' He laughed back and stroked her face.

By the time he returned to the Marino it was ten-thirty. He closed the curtains, sat at the desk, and telephoned the lawyer's home.

'Ricardo, it's Dave. Sorry for phoning so late.'

'No problem. You got the shipment from the US?'

'Yes. Thanks for arranging it. We've finished with it, so you can send it back.'

'So how else can I help?'

'A check on all unidentified corpses found in Italy in the past five days.'

The call from Bonn came at ten, four in the afternoon in Europe. Brettlaw was called to his office to take it.

'They've found the bodies.'

'Anything else?'

'Not yet.'

'Thanks for letting me know.'

256

Brettlaw swivelled in his chair. Strange that Cranlow hadn't said anything. Cranlow wouldn't have forgotten, Cranlow wasn't the type to forget, especially something like that. But Cranlow hadn't even mentioned it.

Haslam left the hotel at five and was in the Benini apartment by six-thirty. For the third night in succession there was no sign of Rossi, and no indication where he might be or why he had not been in contact. Francesca and Marco left ten minutes later. When they returned at eight Francesca had been crying.

They know, he sensed it, saw it. In Francesca's eyes, dark red and rimmed in black; in the haunted way Umberto looked round him, body bent and face thinning; even in Marco's expression.

He took them through it. The bugs in the apartment; the fact that the kidnappers had broken off all contact; the disappearance not only of the man the kidnappers used as a stake-out but also of the man tailing him. The possibility that someone else had intervened.

'But we still run the advertisement again?' It was Francesca.

Good girl, he thought: still fighting, even though she knew she'd lost. 'Of course, it's what we decided. Similar wording as before. We'll run it for a week.'

When the meeting ended he stayed behind.

'Is he dead?' The words blurted out before Francesca could control herself.

'We said from the beginning that there was a chance the kidnappers might kill Paolo. We have to admit there's still that chance. But we also have to say that there's a chance he's still alive.' The last words were even more carefully delivered than the first. 'We have to say that he might be dead, but we also have to say that there's no reason the kidnappers should kill him.'

'But what about the people who put the bugs in the flat?'

'We don't know.'

She made them supper – soup and hot bread.

'You're a good man, Dave Haslam.'

'You're a great lady, Francesca Benini.'

When he returned to his hotel it was shortly before eleven; he poured a drink, switched on the television and tuned in to the late night news. Great world, he thought. Rising unemployment in Europe, the world economy still in stagnation, three suspected terrorists found dead in a flat in Paris.

*

By the time Brettlaw left Langley for Washington it was eight in the evening. The roads were quiet and the river was to his left, Georgetown University tucked into the top of the far bank.

'Message to DDO.' It was on the secure phone. 'Courier just arrived. For DDO's eye only.'

Langley, he told the driver. Fast.

The courier was waiting in security. Brettlaw settled in his office and telephoned for the man to be escorted up.

'Where from?' Brettlaw looked across the desk.

'Bonn.'

The box was wood, nine inches high, six by six across, and sealed. Brettlaw thanked the man, waited till he had been escorted out, then sat at his desk, placed the box on the blotting pad, and opened it. Inside was a polystyrene container, the top also sealed. He opened it. Inside, and protected by the polystyrene, was a circular metal flask. Brettlaw unscrewed the top and saw the ice inside. He tipped the ice on to the blotting pad and saw the small polythene bags around which it had been packed, the object in each similar though not anatomically identical. He re-packed the flask and telephoned Bonn Station.

Haslam woke at six and breakfasted at seven. The killings in Paris were on the front page of the *Herald Tribune*, together with speculation over which of the various Middle East organizations the dead men had belonged to.

At ten he met Santori.

There were ten bodies in the general age category he had specified, the lawyer told him, excluding those already identified or whose deaths were already explained. Two in Rome, four in the South, one near Milan, one in Venice and two in Florence.

'Anything interesting about any of them?'

'The one near Milan was shot.'

'Any chance of photographs?'

'I'll try.'

'If there are problems, concentrate on the ones closest to Calabria.'

When Brettlaw's Chevrolet arrived at Langley that morning the number of cars in the parking lots had increased; when he collected his coffee and bagel from the canteen the tables were slightly fuller. The overnight dispatches from Europe, he assumed, the first stories in the corridors and the first whispers of what the DDO was supposed

258

to have told the new Bonn Chief of Station when he had appointed him the day Zev Bartolski had been blown up. He thanked the cashier, balanced the plate and mug on his briefcase, and took the lift upstairs.

At seven o'clock he switched on the bank of television monitors and flicked between the morning news shows. Three suspected terrorists shot dead in Paris – all the channels were leading on it – plus the first questions about a possible connection with the assassination of the two Americans in Germany.

His wife phoned at nine.

Cath Donaghue had been in touch, she told him. Cath and her girls were already on the Vineyard and Jack was scheduled for a flying visit. She and their girls were due to go to Boston that afternoon, so Cath had suggested they all join her and Jack for the weekend. Brettlaw asked her to wait and checked his diary on the computer. Saturday should be clear but isn't, he began to say, but the major problem's the late night meeting on the Friday. He should see Jack, though, have a couple of beers, have a talk. Cancel Saturday and shuffle the Friday meeting back into the day, he decided; fly up on the Friday night and return Saturday night or Sunday morning. Let's do it, he said.

At lunchtime the Paris killings were again the lead item on all the bulletins: the images of the entrance to the flat on Rue St-Martin, the police cars outside and the stretchers being brought out, the bodies covered by white sheets. Plus the confirmation that the dead men were members of a breakaway faction of the Middle East group known as the 3rd October.

It was fifteen minutes after the last lunchtime bulletin that CNN carried the first report, direct by satellite from its reporter in Rue St-Martin, that the bodies in the flat above had been mutilated, reportedly as punishment for breaking ranks with the main guerrilla body to which they had originally belonged.

Fifty minutes later Maggie Dubovski informed him that Myerscough had requested a meeting.

'Tell him the schedule's full, but I can make tomorrow.'

'You're sure?'

'Tell him he's got five minutes.'

Maggie was right, Brettlaw knew the moment she showed Myerscough in. The man was trying to cover it, but he was running scared. Brettlaw told him to sit down, and waited till Maggie had left the room and shut the door.

'The lawyer Mitchell. You remember I told you he was investigating First Commercial in Santa Fe?'

'Yes.'

'He's on to Nebulus.'

Next time he wouldn't wait until the Agency might be compromised, Brettlaw had thought after the Benini affair. Next time he wouldn't delay until his status as DDO, or his future as DCI, was threatened. Next time he would take executive action the moment it was necessary.

'How'd you mean?' he asked.

'One of the sources on the Hill included it in her latest report. She doesn't know its significance, of course, it was one of several items she passed on. Not even the collator knows.'

'What does her report say?'

Myerscough handed it to him.

The details were in one of the appendices. Brettlaw skimmed through them then closed the file.

'I wonder who else he's looking at.' It appeared to be little more than a thought. Just enough to lay the first notion in Myerscough's mind that should anything happen to Mitchell responsibility lay elsewhere.

Hendricks would be the man, Brettlaw knew. He had done a good job in Milan, and there was no connection between Benini and Mitchell as far as Hendricks was concerned. If Brettlaw decided it was necessary.

'Thanks for letting me know so quickly.'

He waited till Myerscough had left, swung in his chair, switched on the computer, and left the message on Zeus. Nothing definite, of course, nothing firmed up. Just a precaution.

When he telephoned for his driver that evening it was just gone eight. He took the polystyrene container from the freezer section of the minibar, placed it in the travel bag he had brought with him that day, and walked to the lift. The sun was setting, the carpark was almost empty, and expectation hung in the air like a mist – in the way his driver held the door of the Chevrolet for him, in the way the guards at the gate saluted.

By the time he reached the street off Washington Plaza the sky was a brilliant red. Brettlaw checked in front and behind him, and went inside. The door on the first floor was slightly ajar, Bekki's face just visible, the silk shirt she wore came to the top of her legs and the G-string was black lace and almost non-existent.

'Welcome.'

He was always on edge, that was what gave him part of his attraction, part of his power. But tonight was different, tonight he was almost frightening. She kissed him and handed him the sake.

The NEBULUS box was top centre of the paper, BENINI diagonally left, ROSSI and MANZONI vertically below BENINI, and MITCHELL diagonally right. Benini, Rossi and Manzoni taken care of, so what about Mitchell?

The jets of the shower were hot and piercing. He rubbed himself dry, knotted a towel round his waist, and went downstairs. Bekki was already seated on one of the lotus chairs, the seafood on the hot plates on the floor: steamed scallops in spiced sauce, mussels in black bean sauce, prawns, and marinated half-steamed oysters.

He *was* on edge tonight. Of course he had been every day and every night since the death of Zev Bartolski. Yet tonight was different, tonight he was so close to the edge that he was almost over it. She held the sake to his lips and tilted the glass so he could drink.

Mitchell was no threat, Myerscough had originally said. Mitchell's enquiry wasn't leading anywhere and therefore was no danger. But Myerscough hadn't been there when the snow was deep and the fear was running hard. A loose end but no threat, Myerscough had said. In Brettlaw's lexicon, however, this was not logical. Nobody could be a loose end and no threat. A loose end was a threat. And now Myerscough had confirmed it.

He held the shell to her lips and slid the oyster into her mouth. She picked up a prawn with the chopsticks and brushed it across his lips, then withdrew it, played it against his mouth again. The wantun was light and delicate, disintegrating like rice paper in their mouths, and the sake was strong. She slid off the lotus chair and sat against the cushions on the floor, laughed as he knelt over and held the cup to her lips again, began to move as the liquid trickled down her neck and he followed it with his tongue. He slipped the shirt and G-string off, poured the sake over her breasts and licked the light brown skin. Poured more over her stomach and drank from it. The towel had fallen from his waist. She rolled him over and trickled the ginger from the scallops down his body, followed it down with her tongue.

So what about Mitchell?

If Mitchell had to be removed he had to be removed quickly. It was for this reason that he had placed Hendricks on standby.

261

Nothing definite, he had said that afternoon. Just a precaution. Except that nothing was ever just planning; riders like that were part of the game people like himself played even when they had already made the decision.

So why was he still unsure about Mitchell, why was he still hesitating?

When he left the flat the first grey was already in the sky; when his driver collected him from the University Club an hour later the grey had turned light; when the Chevrolet turned off the highway and through the gates into Langley fifteen minutes after that the sun was rising and the carpark was full.

Brettlaw waited till the driver stopped in the underground area next to the executive lift, then he took the polystyrene box from the travel bag, took the flask from the box, rolled the sleeves of his shirt two turns up, took his briefcase from the seat, and folded his jacket across his arm.

Forty seconds later he entered the canteen.

Every table was full, those not able to get a seat standing. Night shift and day shift, men and women from every department. Nobody standing in the line, nobody queuing for coffee and bagels. Everyone waiting, eyes on the door for the moment he came in.

He stepped inside, not reacting, knowing they did not expect him to react, that they expected him to behave totally normally. The room was electric, eyes fixed. He walked as he always walked to the point where the queue normally began, placed the briefcase flat on the counter, and made his normal order.

They were still watching, still transfixed. The night shift glad they had stayed on, the day shift glad they had come in at first light, the staff from up-country glad they had come in from the training grounds. Two even in from Europe so that they could say they had been there the morning the DDO stood in line in the canteen, the morning he asked as he always asked for bagel and coffee, the morning he delivered as he had promised. The morning the DDO told them that, on behalf of all of them, he had avenged the killing of Zev Bartolski.

The attendant pushed the plastic plate and beaker across the Formica.

It was the last time the DDO would come to the canteen, the last time he would need to come.

They were still looking at the briefcase, flat in front of him. The way he had carried it the first day, the day after the bastards had

262

butchered Zev Bartolski on the streets of Bonn. Looking at what was on it.

Even now – especially now – they remembered. Not just the day Zev had died, but the words of the DDO to Cranlow the day he had made him Chief of Station in his place.

I want them, I want their balls.

Brettlaw placed the bagel and coffee on the top of the briefcase, beside the silver flask, then carried it as he always carried it to the cash till at the end.

Still no one moved.

'Dollar twenty, Mr Brettlaw.'

Brettlaw balanced the briefcase on the edge, holding it with his left hand as he always held it, felt in his pocket with the right, and handed over the money. Then he held the briefcase in front of him again and turned to leave.

'Thanks, Mr Brettlaw.'

Perhaps the cashier was merely saying what he always said, perhaps something else.

It was a woman who rose first; someone from the Russian section, one of the analysts, mid-forties and soberly dressed, one of the people no one even knew existed. She was seated inconspicuously somewhere on the far wall. Abruptly she pushed her chair back, rose to her feet, and began to clap.

Thanks, Mr Brettlaw.

The voice of the cashier was lost in the sudden storm. Everyone clapping, everyone looking at the silver flask which Brettlaw carried before him. Knowing what was in it.

'My pleasure, Mack.'

He left the till and walked between them to the door, the applause still growing, deafening, everyone standing.

Fuck the enemy. Fuck Mitchell. Fuck any one who threatened his men and women out there in the field. Fuck anybody who tried to fuck with him. When he reached his office the clapping was still echoing through his head and the decision was fixed immovably in his mind.

14

The sun was rising and the sea below them was a silver blue; Brettlaw unscrewed the flask and poured a coffee for the pilot then one for himself.

Cancel Saturday and re-schedule Friday so he could make the Vineyard on the Friday evening, he had originally thought when the Donaghues had invited them for the weekend. In the end, of course, Friday had dragged on like Fridays always seemed to, and he'd been forced to put his departure back ten hours, leaving the private strip outside DC just after five on the Saturday morning. At least they weren't tangled up with the end-of-week air traffic jamming the seaboard, the pilot had told him; at least they weren't being diverted because of commercial flights coming in.

When they landed it was just gone nine, the day was already hot, and Mary was waiting. Brettlaw and the pilot confirmed contact numbers, then Mary drove him to Oak Bluffs. She and the girls had cut Boston short, she had updated him the night before; they had arrived on Thursday and were planning to stay till Monday. Jack was supposed to have arrived Friday afternoon but had delayed till this morning.

She cut across the island, drove through Oak Bluffs, and turned up Narangassett Avenue. The house was on the left: it was smallish and wood shingle, painted an assortment of colours. Jack and Ed had just arrived, everyone loafing over breakfast on the porch. Brettlaw helped himself to fresh orange juice, coffee and pancakes and joined them.

The families from the other houses were drifting past, on their way to the beach two hundred yards away. Ball game at eleven, one of them reminded Cath; parents are outnumbered so make sure the guys turn up.

At ten they hauled the Hoby to the beach and rigged it, the sandwiches in the cool box and the beer in a net in the water. At eleven they began the football, a mix of parents and children on either side, Jack and a couple of other fathers in one line-up, and Ed and Tom Brettlaw in the other. The game was light-hearted, nobody keeping score. At twelve they wound up and began to think about a swim to cool off.

Last play, one of the Donaghue girls suggested. Last play, Cath backed her up: one more, just for the boys. The Donaghue and Brettlaw girls were laughing, changing the teams slightly and reorganizing the positions, so that Donaghue and Brettlaw were now on the same side, Brettlaw quarterback and Donaghue what might pass for wide receiver.

'What's this about?' one of the other mothers asked.

'Jack and Tom were at Harvard together,' Cath told her. 'Played for the squad.'

The girls were laughing and joking, telling Donaghue and Brettlaw what to do.

First and ten: a total of four plays to advance ten yards and keep possession. The ball came back; Brettlaw took it, swivelled right, and passed to Donaghue. Donaghue made two yards and allowed himself to be tackled.

Second and eight: Brettlaw fumbled and was sacked.

Third and eight: Brettlaw took the snap and threw to one of the girls for a three-yard gain.

All right, the girls were telling Brettlaw and Donaghue, fourth and five. Let's do it.

Brettlaw was suddenly different, the other woman noticed, was suddenly nervous, suddenly on edge. Donaghue as well. 'This one's for real, isn't it?' she asked, suddenly fascinated. 'They're all for real,' Cath told her, 'but this is one that matters.'

Brettlaw took the ball and back-pedalled, Donaghue running wide of the boy opposing him. Brettlaw stopped and checked, then threw. Donaghue was still going wide, almost into the water, and the girls were cheering. The ball was in the air, apparently going to no one. Donaghue cut back, inside and behind the defence, taking the ball and crossing the imaginary end zone.

'Touchdown . . .' the girls chanted like cheerleaders.

'So what was that really about?' the other woman asked.

'The big match of the season,' Cath explained, 'the only one that mattered. The Crimsons and the Elis at the Yale Bowl. Yale leading, last quarter and time almost gone. Tom quarterback for Harvard and Jack wide receiver. Have to let the boys re-live their moment of glory.'

265

The woman was beginning to understand.

'That was the day Tom and Jack went into history,' Cath said simply. 'That was the day Tom and Jack beat Yale with the last play.'

'You were there?' the woman asked.

'You bet I was there,' Cath Donaghue told her.

15

The target's death to appear an accident, The Man had said, and even then nothing obvious. The request to the enquiry agency in New York had therefore been straightforward: telephone records and financial checks on three persons, names and addresses supplied. The information to be delivered to an accommodation address in downtown Manhattan which Hendricks occasionally used – false name and cash up front – by ten the following morning. The agency fee covered by a money order paid for in cash.

Two of the names on the list were irrelevant and the third was Mitchell.

Washington agency does credit check on Washington lawyer called Mitchell, Washington lawyer called Mitchell dies, Washington agency might get suspicious. New York agency does check – the check hidden among several – Mitchell goes missing, New York agency doesn't even know.

Next morning Hendricks caught the shuttle from National, and was in Manhattan by fifteen minutes to ten. The documents were waiting for him. Large brown envelope, well sealed, but most things which came to places like accommodation addresses probably were.

If Mitchell's death was to look like an accident he would need to know Mitchell's routine. Mitchell's routine was accessible – in part at least – by his spending patterns. And everyone's spending patterns were available for scrutiny through one of the credit rating companies for a handful of dollars, a few more if you wanted a little extra.

He walked two blocks to a delicatessen, chose a seat away from the window, ordered coffee, lox and bagels, opened the envelope, ignored the two sets of cover documents, and checked those relating to Mitchell.

The telephone records might take time to analyse, therefore he concentrated on the details of the target's financial life. Bank and mortgage details, credit rating, list of credit and charge cards. Most

267

of the cards were standard, the ones everyone had. One, however, was not: the aviation fuel card issued by one of the major suppliers. Mitch Mitchell was a pilot. In the old days it would have been six months' stake-out before he would have been in a position to even begin planning. Now it was almost too easy.

He noted the aviation card number, put the Mitchell file away, then took out the other two and selected an item for further research from each. The pay phone was on the wall by the counter. He smiled at the waitress, told her he would like more coffee, then telephoned the enquiry agency, thanked them for the prompt service, and said he wished them to make three follow-up enquiries. Glad to be of service, the woman at the agency told him and reached for a pen. Hendricks read her the credit card details of the first person on his list, the charge card details of the second, and the aviation card details for Mitchell.

'Might take a few days. If we pushed it which do you want first?'

'Make it Mitchell,' he told her as if it didn't matter.

'Should have it by tomorrow.'

They agreed terms, the money order to be wired immediately.

Hendricks finished breakfast, caught the next shuttle back to National, picked up the car from the satellite, and drove back to the house overlooking Chesapeake Bay. It was early afternoon, a breeze up and the whites of the sails flecking the blue of the water.

He locked himself in what he called his study and began the process of breaking down Mitchell's telephone records: which numbers he called regularly; which were in town and which out of town; which might be associated with the target's flying.

The sun was drifting over the water. Pity he couldn't be out sailing, Hendricks thought.

The first list was complete. He made coffee, then fetched the Lusk cross-directories from the room he used as a library. Normal directories listed subscribers alphabetically, followed by their numbers. The cross-directory reversed the format, listing numbers then subscribers. He settled again and began the process of attaching a name and address, private or commercial, to the numbers he had collated.

Mitchell flying out of Leesburg, Virginia, west of Dulles, he had established an hour later. Mitchell making a lot of calls to the Fixed Base Operator – the company in charge of the airfield – there. Therefore Mitchell probably with a plane himself.

The following morning he telephoned the enquiry agency in New

York, confirmed that the first of the second batches of details he had requested had come through, then drove to National and took the next shuttle. By one in the afternoon he was in possession of the details of the charges made to Mitchell's aviation fuel card.

The details included the tail number of the plane refuelled. In Mitchell's case the tail number was always the same, therefore Mitchell either owned or had a share in a plane. And Mitchell was doing some interesting flying: a lot local and predictable, but some quite fun and long distance.

He was almost there, at least with the preliminaries; might even get them wrapped up that afternoon. Hendricks telephoned a second enquiry agency and requested a check with the Federal Aviation Administration record centre in Oklahoma City on aircraft tail number November 98487, arranging for a money order to be wired to the company immediately and requesting delivery of the material to the accommodation address by six that evening. When he left New York on the mid-evening shuttle the details of Piper Arrow N98487 were in his briefcase.

The information from Oklahoma City included technical data and details of modifications made to the aircraft, plus present owners and their licence numbers. There were four, each with an address in DC, and the third on the list was Mitchell.

The Piper was based at Leesburg and Mitchell was using it regularly, therefore the owners were probably alternating weekends. Which suggested that the plane was on a lease-back arrangement, whereby it could be rented by other flyers through the FBO – the Fixed Base Operator. The advantage of this for the owners was not simply that it brought in income, but that the aircraft could be used as a tax write-off. And the advantage to him was that because the plane was available for hire there would be a scheduling book, and the scheduling book would not just contain the times the craft was available for hire, plus the full details of who had hired, but also when the owners had booked to use it. Including Mitchell.

The following morning he checked the FBO in the AOPA directory – the Aircraft Owners and Pilots Association handbook – then called Leesburg.

'Need to get some flight time in and Mitch Mitchell said I should look at November 98487. How's she looking over the next couple of weeks?' He was deliberately informal.

Who's Mitch Mitchell, he knew the manager might ask, and had therefore worked out a suitable response.

'Not good this weekend.' The radio in the airfield office was playing Country and Western. 'Looks better Saturday morning the weekend after.'

Therefore the plane was available for hire, therefore the details of when it was booked out, as well as when the owners wanted it, were in the scheduling book.

'When's Mitch got her next?'

It was the sort of conversation the FBO had every hour of every day.

'Like I said.' Which he hadn't. 'Fifteen hundred Thursday to sixteen hundred Monday.'

'Sounds like he's going somewhere good.'

'Walker's Cay, I think he said.'

'Thanks. I'll get back to you.'

He checked the atlas for Walker's Cay, then the Bahamas Tourist Board for hotels there. There was only one, named after the island itself. Then he checked Mitchell's telephone records for the number. Mitchell made regular trips to Walker's Cay, he saw, going there every six months. It was almost too easy, he thought again. He placed the telephone records to the side and called the Walker's Cay Hotel.

'Good morning. Just confirming a room reservation this weekend.'

'Your name, man?' Her English was Bahamian, almost sing-song, so she pronounced you as yo' and man as mon.

'Mitchell.'

The receptionist asked him to wait. 'Yo' arrive de Friday an' yo' depart de Monday.'

'Thanks,' Hendricks told her. 'How's the fishing?'

'Like de fishin' alway is.'

He thanked her again and logged into Zeus.

Brettlaw's call was on time. 'The committee's given the green light,' he told Hendricks. 'Any idea how and when you can do it?'

The committee was always going to give the green light, Hendricks thought. 'As long as the technical support is there, this weekend.'

'Tell me.'

Mitchell had a private pilot's licence, Hendricks briefed him. Mitchell was flying to a place called Walker's Cay, off the Florida coast, on Thursday, returning Monday. Take him out over water and no one would ever know it wasn't an accident.

Details, Brettlaw asked.

Still working on them, Hendricks told him.

'Anything you want in the meantime?'

'Depends whether you want me to arrange the device.'

'Assume you don't.' Boxes within boxes, Hendricks not knowing the bomb maker, and the bomb maker not knowing the target.

He would use Gussmann, of course. Gussmann was the best, as good in his field as Hendricks was in his. Gussman had done his time in Vietnam, plus Laos and Cambodia. Then Central and South America when the Soviets were pouring everything into the area and what Washington feared above all else was a communist advance up through the cluster of banana republics which comprised Uncle Sam's back yard. Gussman, like Hendricks, had done his duty for his country, and when his country no longer needed that duty – or thought it no longer needed it – had faded like so many others into the shadowland.

'Any guidelines as to the device?' Brettlaw asked.

'Probably two-stage,' Hendricks told him. 'Timer activating a barometric switch.'

Brettlaw reached for a Gauloise. 'I'll arrange it. Contact every twelve hours.'

'If I'm out of town I'll put a time and number on Zeus.'

'I'll be in touch.'

Brettlaw lit the cigarette and checked the procedure for contacting the bomb maker. So why had he delayed over Mitchell, why had he hesitated?

By the time Hendricks was back at Chesapeake the shadows were slanting across the garden and the blue of the bay was turning a silver grey. He poured himself a Black Label and settled at the desk.

Walker's Cay was 111 nautical miles off the coast and 900 nautical miles south of DC. Given the fuel capacity and range of the Piper, therefore, Mitchell would have to do the trip in three hops. Leesburg to Charleston, in South Carolina; refuel at Charleston then fly to St Lucie County, just north of Fort Pierce on the Florida coast; refuel again at St Lucie County, then head east across the water to Walker's Cay. He could make the trip in one long haul, including the refuelling stops, or take it easy and make it in two, building in a break somewhere.

November 98487 was booked out from three on Thursday afternoon, but Mitchell wasn't booked into the hotel on Walker's Cay till Friday, which meant he was overnighting somewhere, therefore making the trip in two hauls.

Hendricks checked through the telephone records for the dates on which Mitchell had used the Walker's Cay Hotel, then cross-checked the dates against any numbers for Charleston or St Lucie County. The Holiday Inn at Charleston airport – it stood out a mile. Mitchell following the same routine and overnighting there each time he flew down.

On the return trip, on the other hand, Mitchell was booked in to the hotel till Monday morning, and November 98487 was scheduled back at Leesburg that afternoon, therefore Mitchell was making the return trip in one hop.

He focused on the next detail.

He could place the device either in the tail plane or the engine compartment. The advantage of the tail was that Mitchell wouldn't check, and it would be easier and quick to install the device there. The advantage of the engine space was also twofold: it was separated from the pilot only by a thin layer of aluminium, therefore the pilot would be killed or seriously injured immediately; and it was close to the radio, so that the radio would also be destroyed immediately, even if the pilot survived long enough to try and send a MayDay. But Mitchell would include the engine in the regular pre-flight checks, so the device would have to be below the engine itself, which might be difficult and take time.

He put the decision to one side and listed the four locations at which he could place the device.

Leesburg, before Mitchell took off; Charleston, where Mitchell would refuel and overnight; St Lucie County, where Mitchell would refuel again and where he would also check the customs requirements for re-entering the United States; and Walker's Cay itself.

At St Lucie County it would be daytime and access to the plane would be observable and restricted. A trip to Walker's Cay could be pleasant but might provide a link, however tenuous, between himself and the target. Therefore Leesburg or Charleston. Charleston, when the aircraft was parked up for the night, Hendricks decided, then concentrated on the details of the device he would request from the controller.

He had already requested a dual mechanism device: a timer to activate a barometric device which would trigger the explosive charge when the plane reached a specified altitude.

If he set the timer to activate the barometric device on the outward trip, and Mitchell delayed his departure from Charleston or was held up at St Lucie County, it might detonate when Mitchell was leaving

Charleston or when he was arriving at or leaving St Lucie County. And the investigators would find immediately that it had not been an accident. Therefore he would set the timer for the return trip.

He poured himself another Black Label.

If Mitchell was booked in at Walker's Cay until Monday morning, and if November 98487 was due back at Leesburg at four that afternoon, Mitchell would have to leave Walker's Cay at around six in the morning. Therefore the timer should be set to activate the barometric device at around 3 A.M. on Monday.

The only remaining question was the altitude at which the barometric switch would detonate the bomb.

Flights out of Walker's Cay fell under the auspices of two sets of air traffic controllers: Freeport, to the south, then Miami. Because of the curvature of the earth, it would be some ten to twelve miles after take-off, and at an altitude around 4,500 feet, before Mitchell could establish radio contact with Freeport. Freeport would then clear him from them and give him the frequency on which he should contact Miami. Again because of the earth's curvature, that contact would not be possible until he had climbed another 2,000 feet, to around 6,500 feet.

For the first ten minutes or so of his flight, therefore, Mitchell wouldn't be in contact with Freeport. And for seven to eight minutes after, Freeport would have forgotten him and Miami wouldn't know he existed. So the barometric switch should be set either for an altitude below 4,500, before Mitchell contacted Freeport, or between 5,000 and 6,500, after Mitchell had cleared Freeport but before he contacted Miami.

Hendricks swung in his chair and telephoned the hotel on Walker's Cay.

'Thinking of flying down for a couple of days but might need to leave early in the morning. I'll have to inform Freeport Flight Services of my flight plan, of course. I assume there are phones in the room for me to do this.'

'Sorry, man; no phone in the room. There's a phone in the hall you can use.'

'But?'

'It has to be connected by the office.'

'What time does the office open?'

There was a pause, almost a chuckle. 'Seven-thirty.'

Give or take, Hendricks thought. Therefore Mitchell would have to file his flight plan the night before, and if he didn't establish radio contact the next morning Freeport Services would assume he'd changed his mind and decided to stay on a few more days.

'What about Customs and Immigration?'

'No problem, man. You pay the departure fee the day before.'

The way he said it sounded different. 'No problem, mon. Yo' pay de departure fee de day befo'. If dey not open when yo' go, yo' jus' poosh de papuhs under de do'.'

'Thanks.'

Therefore the timer activating the switch at three on Monday morning, and the switch set for 4,000 feet. Freeport not knowing Mitchell had taken off. The hotel, plus Customs and Immigration on Walker's Cay, assuming he'd left because he was no longer there when they woke up, and the world fast asleep when he went bang. Nobody bothering until he failed to arrive back at Leesburg, and by then it would be too late. As long as he could access the plane.

At six the next morning he called the Fixed Base Operator at Charleston.

'Probably flying through you later this week. Just checking about parking.'

'No problems. We tow you behind the hangars.'

'Thanks.'

He locked the house and drove to Dulles International. The number he had left on The Man's e-mail was for a pay phone in the departure satellite and the call itself on time.

'Timer set for zero three hundred Monday, barometric switch for four thousand feet.' The conversation was functional. 'The device to be left at a dead drop in Charleston on Thursday. Location to follow. Contact details as usual.'

'Understood.'

Hendricks left Dulles, drove to National, and caught the nine o'clock flight to Charleston.

By the time Mitchell finished the first half of the draft it was mid-evening, Dirksen Building quiet. Great evening, he thought, great position to be in: the report on schedule and Donaghue almost ready to declare. This time next summer they'd be sweeping the floor at the party convention; two months after that and they'd be running for the White House itself. By seven-fifteen the next morning he was on the Hill. He logged in to DUATS – the Direct User Access Terminal System – checked the met report, then filed his flight plan with the FAA. The first secretary arrived at eight, everyone else around nine. At twelve-thirty she brought him sandwiches and coffee; he thanked her and continued the draft.

By the time he finished it was already two-forty; he backed up the material, left the Hill, and drove to Leesburg. The check list took him twenty minutes. Fifty minutes later than he'd planned he lifted off and climbed steadily to his permitted altitude. Three and a half hours later he dropped smoothly into Charleston, checked in, and watched as the Piper was refuelled and towed to the secondary parking area behind the hangars, then he hired a rental car and drove to the Holiday Inn, on the edge of the airfield. When the evening turned cooler he drove in to the old colonial quarter of Charleston; by the time he returned to the Holiday Inn it was just after eleven and the relaxation was beginning to seep in. He set the alarm call for seven and was asleep immediately.

Brettlaw's call to Hendricks was at midnight. It's in place, Hendricks told him. Any problems? Brettlaw asked. No, Hendricks said.

A small glitch, perhaps, but no problems.

He'd woken that morning at six. Mitchell hadn't filed a flight plan the evening before, and the hourly met reports didn't start on DUATS till seven, so he'd known that Mitchell wouldn't file until then. At five past he'd logged in and entered the number for the FAA flight centre information service. The screen had requested his private pilot's licence number and he'd tapped in Mitchell's. Flight plans were logged under the registration of the relevant aircraft, rather than the name or licence number of the pilot, so he'd entered the tail number of Mitchell's Piper and waited. No flight plan had so far been logged under November 98487, the computer had told him. It was not until just after nine, when he tried again, that he knew the planning had not been in vain.

The office was quiet, the ashtray full of cigarette stubs, smoke in a halo above the desk and the Jack Daniels in a glass to his right. So how the hell had Mitchell found out about Nebulus, Brettlaw wondered, what the hell had he found out about Romulus and Excalibur?

Once one thing broke there was a natural disorder which dictated that others followed, he remembered thinking. Which was why he'd moved to close down Benini once he had become a problem, why he'd removed Rossi and Manzoni so expeditiously.

So why had he hesitated over Mitchell?

Not because he'd been unsure. The logic which decreed he should deal with Mitchell had been as impeccable as that which had determined he should remove Rossi and Manzoni. He had hesitated because of where else that logic might lead him.

He finished the bourbon and phoned for his driver.

*　　*　　*

Haslam's meeting with Ricardo Santori was over breakfast; the lawyer was early, already seated at a table by the window overlooking the courtyard, and impeccably dressed as always, his briefcase by the side of his chair. They shook hands and ordered fresh orange juice, coffee and scrambled eggs.

'Nothing more on the client?'

Haslam shook his head, then sat back while the waitress poured them each a coffee.

'You asked for photos of all corpses found in the past eight days.' Santori unlocked the briefcase, took out the file, and handed it across the table.

Probably not the thing for the breakfast table, Haslam thought, and looked at the photographs anyway. Most of the corpses were in reasonable condition, and none was that of Paolo Benini.

'Any others?'

'Not in the right category. I'll check again today.'

'What about the one you said had been shot?'

'That was north of here, and you said to concentrate on those from Calabria.'

'I know, but it's probably worth a look.'

Because the others had led them nowhere. He handed the file back and wondered how much longer he should remain in Milan.

The meeting the following morning was scheduled for nine. The telephone call from the lawyer came the evening before.

'I've just received the photo of the Milan corpse.'

'And?'

'It's Paolo.'

Oh Christ, Haslam thought, what about Francesca. He moved to the desk against the wall of the hotel room in case he needed to take notes.

'Do the police know who he is?' Because when they did they would tell the press, and the press would descend on the family like vultures.

276

'No,' Santori told him. 'The photograph and details were supplied informally.'

'You've got the pathologist's report?'

'The report plus the forensics on the ammunition used.'

'When can I see the body?'

'Tomorrow morning at seven, before the morgue's officially open. I'll pick you up at six-thirty.'

The night was long, though not as long as the next would be for Francesca. When the lawyer arrived next morning Haslam was waiting in the street. It was the way he spent his life, he supposed, hanging round waiting for a death.

The morgue was at the side of the hospital. Santori parked in the staff area and they went inside. There was something about the smell and sound of a hospital, even at this time of the morning. They turned into an office. The attendant was waiting; he gave them each a white coat and surgical gloves, and they followed him through.

The mortuary was spotlessly clean, the refrigerated units along one wall. The attendant pulled out the second from the right, third row up, and the stretcher slid noiselessly out. The corpse inside was contained in a white nylon sack. The attendant unzipped the top and pulled the nylon back.

Paolo Benini, Haslam confirmed. The bullet hole in the forehead, slightly off centre. He turned the head slightly. Entry clean, exit a bloody mess; bone shattered and hair matted with Christ knows what.

Pro job, military training. One-round head shot – the old term came back too easily. Within the defined distance a trained sniper would automatically go for the head shot, would know once he eased the trigger that the target was down. Wouldn't even need to look. In some circumstances wouldn't have the time to look.

They left the mortuary, walked back to the office, and took off the coats and gloves.

'Thank you.' Haslam shook the attendant's hand and walked out of the room, Santori remaining. The *bustarella*, Haslam understood, the clean crisp notes in the clean crisp envelope. Twenty minutes later they sat in a bar off Central Station drinking coffee; black, heavy lacing of cognac.

'What are you going to do?' The lawyer waved for two more coffees, two more brandies.

'Tell the family. Let them notify the carabinieri and go through the usual procedures themselves. Keep you and me out of it if we can.'

'What happened?' Santori knew the question was out of bounds but asked anyway.

Somebody intervened, Haslam might have said. The Beninis screwed the first negotiations, then somebody jumped in, secured Paolo's release, probably paid good money plus an additional kidnapping. And all to kill him.

'Who knows?' he said instead. They finished the drinks and rose to leave.

'A good job, Ricardo. Thanks for doing it discreetly.'

'That's what I get paid for.'

'Thanks anyway.'

He returned to the hotel, went to his room, telephoned the family, and asked for a meeting with them all at one. There were two ways he could react: he could allow the anger to overtake him, which would get him nowhere, or he could shut off, which was the way he had been trained. He placed the pathology and forensic reports on the desk, and sealed himself from the world.

The Benini kidnapping, the tail on Pascale and the bugging of the apartment. The killing of the Americans in Bonn the same time as the kidnapping – the first connections began to form. Paolo's death the same time as the deaths in Paris of those responsible for the Bonn incident.

Probably a coincidence, he admitted. Why was he even bothering, he asked himself. The Benini affair was finished. So why didn't he just shut up shop and wave it goodbye? Why didn't he just tell Francesca to look after herself, then pack his bag and leave? The Benini kidnapping wasn't his concern any more. He'd done his best, but it had been the family and the bank who'd screwed it, and now they'd paid the price.

Some price, though, some way of paying it. But even that wasn't his concern.

He'd been here, seen it, done it. Gone in, done the job, got out. Coup, counter-coup, wet job like the one somebody had done on Paolo or stop a wet job on someone like Paolo. Then left it behind, physically and mentally. Okay, so he'd remembered, because you never forgot, though sometimes it would be no more than a sliver in your subconscious.

The Benini kidnapping, the tail on Pascale and the bugging of the apartment, the killing of the Americans in Bonn . . . the correlations ran through his head again.

In a way it was like a parachute drop or a long exercise. The first thing you did when you landed or when you and the others stopped for a break was take out your map and check where you were, even though you might not be leading. Not that you'd expect anyone to understand.

Or perhaps it was simpler than that. Perhaps it was because Paolo Benini was his case, his operation, and somebody else had won and he didn't like losing.

Or perhaps it was Francesca.

He passed on lunch and walked to Via Ventura.

She knows, he thought the moment Francesca opened the door, perhaps she had known anyway.

An unnerving experience, telling someone of a death. Sometimes you felt involved, sometimes you felt so detached it was as if you weren't there. Sometimes it was easier than others, sometimes the unexpected happened. He remembered once, a house in Newcastle, sitting with a mother and father and telling them about the death of their son, telling them they should be proud of him because he was regiment; of how, because the regiment was a family, he would never be forgotten by them, that his name would always be on the clock at Hereford; but that because he was regiment that fact could never be made public. And then he had realized: that the parents didn't know that their son was regiment, didn't know that their son was SAS.

'What is it, Dave?' Francesca's face muscles were clenched and she was fighting to control herself. Where were Umberto and Marco, he thought; they should have been here already. Perhaps he should have broken the news to them first so they would be in a position to give Francesca the support she needed.

'Let's sit down.'

He sat with her, knew he was stalling and what it was doing to her. There's bad news, he was going to say, something none of us expected. Of course there's bad news, of course none of us expected it.

'I'm sorry, Paolo's dead.'

She nodded, head and eyes turned slightly, teeth grinding but no tears yet. 'You're sure?'

'Yes.' How are you sure, he knew she would ask. Don't say the word *morgue*, he told himself, don't use the word *body*. 'I've seen him.'

She was nodding again. 'How?'

279

'He was shot.'

Paolo didn't know it was going to happen, he was telling her. He thought he'd been released and was coming home. And he wouldn't have known anything, wouldn't have felt a thing.

She was still nodding, perhaps hearing him, perhaps not. The door opened and Umberto and Marco came in, saw the two of them on the sofa, saw their faces.

'Paolo's dead.' Francesca's statement was simple and her voice was detached.

She rose and took Umberto in her arms, held his head as if he were a child, stroked his hair and patted his back.

Why Paolo, it was still in Haslam's mind; why kill him?

Francesca sat Umberto down, poured him a brandy, and asked Marco to telephone the family solicitor.

'I'll need to identify the body.' They sat round the table drinking coffee. Francesca's strength brittle, like an eggshell, but holding together. 'I'd like you to come with me, Dave.'

In time, Haslam thought. Because they hadn't reported the kidnapping and didn't officially know that Paolo was dead. So there were certain things they had to do before Francesca saw Paolo. But until she saw him she wouldn't believe one hundred per cent that he really was dead.

'Of course I'll come with you. Umberto and Marco as well.'

Because it was the only way Umberto might begin to recover. If he wasn't there, if he hadn't done his last duty, he would look back and know he should have done. Marco as well, though for different reasons. Marco had done everything Paolo had asked of him, had supported Francesca and taken the risk of collecting the ransom packages and making the drops, had run the danger of kidnap himself.

The solicitor arrived forty minutes later. He was in his early fifties, and from one of Milan's most influential firms. The family should have involved him before – the look to Umberto was obvious. Except that in not doing so they'd made it easier for him now.

By five that afternoon he had steered them through what might otherwise have been a jungle of bureaucratic and political tangles. Party connections, Haslam assumed, probably membership of the same masonic lodge. Not to mention a handful of *pizzi* and *bustarelle*. At seven-thirty they drove to the hospital. Same attendant, Haslam noted, but no indication from either of them that they had met in the same place and for the same reason a little over twelve hours before.

The stretcher was on a pedestal in the centre of the floor, the tiles white and the room smelling slightly of disinfectant, the contours of the body beneath the sheet. The solicitor had done a good job, Haslam thought, made sure that the formalities ran smoothly. More than that. Had made sure that everything was ready for them, that the sheet covering Paolo was pristine white, that the morgue had been cleaned and the attendant was wearing a fresh tunic. That Paolo had been patched up: make-up round the entry point at the front, and bandages round the head so that the family wouldn't see that nothing existed at the back.

Yet even the solicitor could not prepare the family. Haslam sensed the way they were hesitating, the way they did not know what to do. He took Francesca's and Umberto's arms, drew them together, and moved them into place at the side of the body, Umberto on Francesca's right and Marco on her left.

The attendant eased the cloth from the face and they stiffened. Don't turn away, Haslam willed them. Don't just do your formal duty; do now what you'll wish you had done if you don't. He said nothing, held them in place, would not let them turn. Nodded to the attendant and solicitor to leave. Still held Francesca and Umberto in place. They had been standing a minute, two minutes, almost three. Even though he could not see her face he knew the tears were rolling down her cheeks. He still held her arm, made sure she was all right. Then he let go and left the room, as if he had never been there.

The solicitor was in the office, the relevant forms already signed. 'Paolo goes home tonight; the hearse is waiting. There'll be no delay over funeral arrangements.' Because he had fixed it. He snapped his briefcase shut. The attendant was standing in the corner. Thank you: Haslam crossed to him and shook his hand, saw the way the man nodded. Some things you couldn't pay for, even in Milan.

The procession moved off an hour later, the hearse in front and the cars behind, the sky a deepening blue around them. Two hours later, the blue gone and the brilliant orange of sunset replaced by the velvet black of night, they came to the village where Paolo Benini had been born and where he would be laid to rest. Even so late at night the villagers stood by the roadside and watched as they passed, dark figures dressed in black, the men taking off their hats and the women kneeling and crossing themselves. At four, as the first dawn was coming up, Haslam left and returned to Milan.

The telephone rang at ten.

'Dave?'

'Yes.'

'It's Francesca.'

'You okay?' he asked.

'Probably. The family are here, the girls came up this morning.'

He allowed her the silence.

'Paolo's funeral is on Monday. It's for family only. If you were able to, however, I'd like you to come.'

'Of course I will.'

He let her put the phone down first, sat still for ten minutes, then left the hotel and began walking. Fast, shutting out the analysis for as long as he could, then allowing it to seep back in.

Bonn and Paris connected with terrorism, which meant that if there was a link with the events in Bonn and Paris, then Paolo's kidnapping and execution might also be associated with terrorism. Therefore possibly Paolo as well.

It had been known, of course. Banks and bankers had been used as conduits for the movement of terrorist money round the world, as a channel between terrorists and their paymasters. So perhaps Paolo was involved in this, perhaps Paolo had been setting up the systems by which the funds could be moved and the movements covered if anyone came looking. Or perhaps Paolo was being used by those trying to infiltrate the terrorists, those who opposed them.

Either way, who had taken him out?

Not terrorists. Terrorists were good, but not at this sort of thing. Paolo's death smacked of Tel Aviv or Washington or London. Moscow in the old days. Just as the Paris killings and mutilations smacked of the same, even though the media had accepted the suggestion that the deaths of the three men in Paris was an internal affair within 3rd October.

Therefore the intelligence services.

But that assumed a link between the events, a logical beginning leading to a logical end, and the killing of the Americans in Bonn had not been logical because it had been an accident, the wrong men in the wrong place at the wrong time.

By the time he returned to the hotel it was late evening. The next day, Sunday, he rented a car and drove to the location where the police report said Paolo's body had been found. No reason to do it, of course, the case was closed, finished. But no reason not to. He turned off the autostrada, then on to a secondary road. Garage on left, he checked the directions the lawyer had given him; first left after garage then down the track.

Paolo would have been held in Calabria, where the kidnappers had cover from the carabinieri and the army. Nobody except the politicos hid a kidnap victim so far north, and they did so only because they didn't have the connections in the South. So if Paolo wasn't being held here, why was his body found here?

He stopped the car and reversed back. The garage was self-service and modern, with a covered forecourt and a shop at the back. Paolo brought here for the switch, he began to see it; the terms and location set by whoever had intervened, and the kidnappers waiting for the instructions at a telephone in the garage or on a mobile. He left the garage and drove on.

The track was another thousand metres. He turned off the road, zeroed the clock and drove eight hundred metres. The sun was searing and the dust billowed from the wheels. He stopped the car, got out, and looked round. In front of him the track disappeared towards the blue haze at the foot of the hills at the end of the valley, the escarpments rising on either side, brush at first then growing thicker, the occasional tree. Good cover, he thought automatically, easy to get away. Especially to the west, his left as he stood looking down the track. Over the escarpment and down the other side, probably another track in the next valley, and a car waiting.

So this is where Paolo died. Hands and feet untied, blindfold and gag off. Thinking he was free.

The cairn of stones was fifty metres further on, on the right. Probably a cellnet or two-way radio concealed in it; whoever was holding the stake-out calling the people delivering Paolo, rather than allowing them to call him on Pascale's phone, because that way they would have heard the ring and known where the gunman was. The last orders: collect the money, release Paolo, pick up Pascale. Visual exchange – both sides checking that the other was delivering. Paolo walking back up the track and the sniper on the escarpment controlling everything.

The ground on the side of the track dropped to a shallow ditch. He sat on the edge, ignoring the dust and the heat. So what about the Bonn connection? The link was tenuous: too many inconsistencies in the logic. Except there was nothing else.

Rossi going missing, of course. Plus the death of the BCI manager in London. Therefore Benini, Rossi and Manzoni.

He left the track and pushed his way through the undergrowth and up the escarpment, reached the top and looked into the valley on the other side, dropped down and picked up the track.

The turning was to his left, the walls round the farm crumbling and the weeds growing through the cobbles of the yard. No one around – he stopped and listened – no one for miles. Don't follow the track, though; never follow the track. That's what they'll expect, that's where they'll be waiting for you. He cut back into the trees and followed the slope till he saw the turn tracks of the vehicle, then he sat silently for fifteen minutes, confirming he was alone, and cut uphill again.

The stable was on the right of the yard, other outbuildings on the left, and the house in front. Two-storey, the bedrooms tucked under the roof, except that at the southern end – his right as he looked at it – the builder had utilized the fall of the land to provide a cellar.

He waited another fifteen minutes, then skirted the yard and went inside. The cobwebs on the door had been broken and the dust on the floor had been disturbed. Something being dragged. Or someone. The trap door was at the far end, in the floor of what had once been a kitchen. He crossed the room and began to pull it open, heard the sound of a twig snapping.

He turned slowly and edged back across the floor to the doorway. No cars parked on the track when he'd come in, no sound of cars since, and he'd left no indication that he was there. So perhaps they hadn't seen him, perhaps they didn't know he was there. Therefore wait, perhaps go upstairs, see what he could see from the upper windows without actually opening one, see if there was another way out. As long as the stairs were strong enough for his weight; as long as a floor wouldn't give way and betray his presence.

He heard the squeal, and looked right. A wild pig crossed the yard and disappeared into the shade of the stable.

Getting edgy, Dave – he laughed at himself.

He went back inside, lifted the trap door to the cellar, and dropped down. The empty food cans and water container were on the floor, and the chain and manacles were by the wall. He left the farm and returned to the car.

So where was he going now, he asked himself. The family house a couple of hours away? Listen to himself telling Francesca about the guilt he felt because he'd let Paolo down, then let her tell him it wasn't his fault? Listen to Francesca telling him about the guilt she felt because the family hadn't taken his advice, then tell her she wasn't to blame, that no one was?

He started the car and drove straight on, away from the garage and the road, for no reason other than that was the way the car was facing.

*   *   *

Friday afternoon Mitchell had relaxed, gone scuba diving, gentle stuff. Saturday morning he'd done the blue holes with an instructor, afternoon he'd taken it easy till four, then gone swimming again. Sunday he'd been game fishing, the sun hot and the salt stinging.

The trip ended at five. He showered, then checked with hotel reception that they had arranged with the kitchen to leave him an early breakfast the next morning. If he woke at five and left at five-thirty, he'd make the trip comfortably, be in DC by mid-afternoon. Except at that hour of the morning nobody else would be awake. He left the hotel, walked down the steps, and crossed the top of the marina to the customs and immigration sheds at the side of the runway.

'I'm leaving tomorrow morning early and wondered about paperwork.'

'What time yo' leaving?' The woman was friendly.

'About six.'

She looked at him as if the hour didn't exist. 'No problem. Pay de fee now an' poosh de papuhs under de do' when yo' leave.'

Which was what he had assumed.

Monday morning seemed quiet, even the traffic outside subdued. Haslam adjusted the knot slightly – black tie, dark suit – and brushed his jacket. The car was waiting; he settled in the rear seat and the driver pulled away. One more night in Milan, he had decided, in case there was a last-minute problem, in case the family wanted him for anything.

Two hours later the car eased quietly through the village which was the family home of the Beninis, and stopped outside the house to which they had borne Paolo three nights before. Then it had been dark, now the sun was high. The same eyes of the same villagers watching him the same way, though.

The family was assembled, Francesca standing straight-backed, dark glasses covering her eyes, a daughter on either side. He stood in front of her and shook her hand, was introduced to her daughters and shook their hands, stood in front of her again and embraced her. She took off her glasses and he kissed her on the cheek, then passed to Umberto. Thank you for all you did – it was in the nod of the father's head, in his handshake. He passed to Marco. You did well, Haslam told him, again in the handshake; you did more than anyone could have asked.

Paolo, Rossi and Manzoni. All dead. Assuming Rossi wasn't just missing. So what was the connection other than the fact that they all worked for BCI? The kidnap, obviously, but what about the kidnap?

They left the house and walked behind the hearse to the church at the other end of the village, the men and women lining the streets and bowing as the coffin passed.

Nebulus, because Rossi had asked the question about it and Paolo had answered it; because Manzoni was Paolo's man in London and presumably dealing with it, and had supplied the question to Rossi. And because there was nothing else. Assuming that Nebulus, Romulus and Excalibur meant something.

The church was dark and cold, the candles flickering in the gloom. Haslam stood at the back and listened to the service. Looked at the shadows on the wall and looked at Francesca. Perhaps he should have come the day before, perhaps it was best that he hadn't.

But if Paolo, Rossi and Manzoni had been taken out because of Nebulus, then why not the others who knew? Why not Francesca and Umberto and Marco? Because even though they'd heard the names they didn't know what they meant. He knew as well, of course. But whoever was responsible didn't know that, because he'd been out of the action when the names had come up. And there the chain had ended, because nobody else knew.

The service ended and they moved to the family chamber outside, stood as Paolo was buried alongside his ancestors. The committal ended and they looked down for the last time, hesitated, then Marco turned away, Umberto and the others behind him, till only Francesca and her daughters remained, alone and suddenly isolated, and unsure what to do. Francesca standing by herself, the girls letting go her hand and standing to one side but still needing someone. Haslam stepped back to them and knelt between the girls, put an arm round each; waited till Francesca was finished then gave them back to her. The rest of the family was waiting. Francesca and the girls joined them, then they left the churchyard and walked back through the village to the house.

Somebody else did know about Nebulus, of course.

Working on BCI, Mitch had told him, ever heard of it? Any thoughts on it or any connections? No thoughts, no connections, he had said the first time. Try Nebulus, he had said the second, probably London-based, plus Romulus and Excalibur. But Mitch was like him: removed from the action when the names had come up, therefore out of the frame. Except that Mitch had another connection, because Mitch was investigating BCI. So perhaps he ought to let him know. Not warn him, that would be over the top, just tell him to go carefully. Crazy, he told himself, he had been jumping at shadows too long. Just in case, he decided, work it all out with Mitch when he was back in the US.

It was eleven in the morning, five in the morning in DC, therefore he could phone when he was back at the hotel. But by the time he returned to the hotel it would be mid-morning in DC and Mitch would have left the boat.

So if Mitch had left the boat he'd probably be at the office, he argued against himself.

Only probably, though, and he didn't have the office number.

Marco was on the opposite side of the room. Haslam crossed to him and asked if there was a phone he could use. Marco nodded, not asking why, and led him to a sitting-room, then left him alone and shut the door as he left. The room was dark, the curtains closed. Haslam ignored the lamp by the telephone and dialled DC. Mitchell's number rang four times before the answer phone cut in and invited him to leave a message.

So Mitch wasn't at home, and if he wasn't at home he was probably away for the weekend, therefore away from BCI. Except that with Mitch you never knew where he was or what he was doing. Play it safe, he decided, and called the second number.

Even though the telephone was by his bedside Jordan took thirty seconds to answer.

'Quince, this is Dave Haslam.'

'You know what time it is?'

'Almost lunchtime.'

'So you're calling from Milan.' It was partly question but mostly yawn. *So why are you waking me up?*

'It's probably nothing, but Mitch might have a problem. Something to do with the investigation he's doing for Donaghue.

287

I've tried to contact him but he's not at the boat.'

Jordan rolled off the bed. 'He's on a break. Place off the Florida coast. Due back this afternoon. You want me to get in touch?'

Mitch was away, therefore Mitch was okay; but by the time Mitch returned it would be mid-evening in Europe and he himself would be in Milan or London or somewhere between. 'Be easier.'

'What do I tell him?'

'To hold off on the thing I suggested he look at. I'll call him when I can.'

If Mitch was due back this afternoon he'd probably be up, Jordan thought. 'I'll try him now.'

'As I said, it's probably nothing.'

He left the room and returned to the family. Francesca was talking to Umberto. Haslam crossed to them and gave Francesca a business card on which he'd written his home number in Hereford and the apartment number in Washington. If ever she or the girls wanted to come to England, he told her, or if they were in America. Thank you, Umberto nodded. Francesca as well. He kissed her on the cheek and left.

Five-thirty in the morning in Walker's Cay and no way anyone would be awake; five-thirty and they might just be heading home from the night before. Jordan went downstairs, checked with enquiries, and dialled the number anyway. There was no reply. Probably nothing, Haslam had said. But Haslam had phoned him, told him to tell Mitch to keep his head down. He let the phone ring for two minutes, pressed the receiver, and tried again.

He'd make St Lucie County by seven, Mitchell calculated. Clear customs and immigration, refuel, perhaps have breakfast at Curly's. Leave by eight, possibly eight-thirty, and hit Charleston by eleven. Refuel, then DC by three-thirty; by five he could be at his desk on the Hill. There'd be no need to phone Pearson, Ed would be up the coast anyway, grabbing a couple of days with Eva, probably with Donaghue and his family on the Vineyard.

He helped himself to the fruit juice and bread which the chef had left, made himself a coffee, and sat at the top of the steps leading down to the marina. The morning was quiet and peaceful: a few sea birds, nothing else. No one awake, either in the hotel or on the boats moored against the jetties.

The ring of the telephone pierced the tranquillity. He rose to answer it, then realized it was the switchboard and remembered that the switchboard was in the office and that the office was locked. Probably a wrong number anyway; nobody phoned Walker's Cay at five-thirty in the morning.

The ringing stopped. He walked down the steps and sat on the marina. Enjoy the place, he told himself: last time till it was over. No February trip next year: next February they'd be building for the first primaries. No August trip either: August next year they'd be wrapping up the convention. Nor the beginning of the year after that: because in two Januarys' time Donaghue would be taking the oath of office on the Hill. Great day to have his family there, he thought, great day to have his daughter at his side.

He ran back up the steps and left the glass and plate in the kitchen. The switchboard was ringing again. He walked past the office, collected his bag, and left the hotel.

The morning was in that no man's land between the last cool of night and the first warmth of the new day. He slipped the envelope under the door of the immigration office, untied the Piper, put his bag in the rear seat and began the pre-flight checks. In the still of the morning the telephone rang again.

Jordan was at his office by seven-thirty. Each quarter-hour since Haslam had phoned he'd tried the number on Walker's Cay. At seven forty-five he telephoned again and was surprised at his relief when the call was answered.

''Morning, any chance of speaking to Mitch Mitchell?'

He's having breakfast, he assumed the receptionist was going to say, could the caller hold while someone fetched him?

'Sorry, mon; he already gone.' The accent was sing-song and relaxed; perhaps he could do with some time on Walker's Cay himself, Jordan thought. 'What time?' he asked.

'Not sure of de time. Befo' anybody wake, I guess.'

'You're certain?'

'Yo' want I should check?'

'If you wouldn't mind.'

He waited.

'Yeah, Mitch gone. Checkout slip's at de desk and his room's empty.'

Leave at six – Jordan did a mental calculation – approximately seven hours' flying time, plus a couple more for refuelling and other delays. Mitch would be back in DC by mid-afternoon.

'Thanks for the help.'

289

At one, in case Mitch had left earlier than anyone had supposed, Jordan phoned his boat and office, in that order. At two he phoned Leesburg, again at three. At four he contacted the airfield for the third time.

Seven hours' flying time plus two on the ground, he had calculated. If Mitch had left at six he should have touched down by now. Only just, though. It had been seven-thirty, seven forty-five, when he himself had finally got through to the hotel. Assume the man who'd answered had only just come on, and Mitch might not have left till gone seven, which would put him in the air somewhere between Charleston and DC, probably half an hour out and talking to Washington Centre then Dulles Approach.

At five he telephoned the airfield for the fourth time.

'Sorry, still no sign,' the FBO told him. 'He's probably decided to stay.'

'Probably.'

He checked the number and telephoned the hotel on Walker's Cay again.

'Hi, I'm calling about Mitch Mitchell.'

'Yo' phone dis morning.'

'Yeah. Look, I know you checked his room, but any chance of making sure his plane's gone?'

'Problems?'

'No, just that when we last spoke he wasn't sure what time he was taking off, and I need to confirm a business appointment for him this evening.'

'Ten minutes, mon; yo' phone back den.'

'You need his plane details?'

'No, mon; his de only Piper in at de moment.'

'Thanks.'

Down the steps and along the marina – Jordan had seen the photos – up the slope to the beginning of the runway, the customs and immigration sheds under the trees. Nine minutes later he phoned again.

'Yeah, mon; he gone. No plane, so must ha' been real early. He poosh de papuhs under de do'. I spoke to de lady.'

'Thanks again.'

So where are you, Mitch, what's keeping you?

Probably nothing, Haslam had said, just tell him to hold off. He checked with enquiries and telephoned the Flight Service Station in Freeport.

'Good evening; I'm trying to confirm what time Piper Arrow November 98487 cleared Walker's Cay this morning.'

'Approximately what time?' The voice was relaxed.

'Between zero five thirty and zero eight hundred.'

There was a thirty-second pause. 'Sorry. No record of November 98487 leaving Walker's Cay.'

'Thanks.' He checked again with enquiries, called Miami Centre, and asked for the supervisor. 'Good evening. This is Quincey Jordan from DC. I'm checking whether a Piper Arrow, tail number November 98487, cleared Walker's Cay via Freeport and entered the US under your control this morning.'

You know how many flights we get through every hour, the supervisor began to say. The call from DC, he thought, and the caller sounding official. Probably Fed, smell them a mile off.

'What tail number?' he asked.

'November 98487,' Jordan told him.

The supervisor checked on the computer.

'Yeah, the flight plan was filed last night.' His finger moved towards the button on the console. 'Approximately what time did he leave?'

'Between zero five thirty and zero eight hundred.'

'What did Freeport say?'

'They have no record.'

So if they don't have a record, he's probably still sitting in the sun. Except . . . He checked the computer again: flight file but no record of the pilot activating it that morning, he noted. 'You spoke to Walker's Cay?' His finger moved closer to the button.

'The hotel confirmed his plane was gone.'

'Who's the pilot?'

Jordan knew why he was asking. 'Name of Mitchell. Government employee on the staff of Senator Donaghue.'

Knew it, the supervisor thought. 'Putting you on hold.' His finger had already hit the button. 'Coastguards. This is Miami Centre. Looks like we got a down. Might be a Federal involvement. I'll confirm in two minutes.' We're checking ourselves, he told Jordan, rescue on standby. A lot of water between here and Walker's Cay, they both knew, a long time since the man took off.

'Give me a number where I can call you.'

Jordan told him. 'Direct line. I'll be waiting. Who'll be calling?'

'Ken Williams.'

'Thanks for the help, Ken. It's appreciated.' He poured a coffee and dialled Milan. 'Dave, it's Quince.'

In Italy it was midnight.

'Yes.'

'We might have a problem. According to his hotel, Mitch left Walker's Cay early this morning. He should have landed in DC three hours ago. So far there's no trace of him and neither of the flight centres involved have a record of him logging in. Coastguards are about to start a search.'

'We're sure he left?'

'The hotel confirmed it twice. They also checked that his plane was gone.'

'There's a United flight out at ten tomorrow morning.' There were earlier flights, but none of them direct, and the ten o'clock flight only landed twenty minutes later. 'I'll be with you at two-thirty tomorrow afternoon.'

So what else, Jordan wondered. Who else? He pressed the console for another line and phoned the office on the Hill.

'Ed Pearson, please.' Except that Ed would be away, grabbing a few days with Eva. 'If he's not on holiday, of course.'

'He is.' The secretary was polite. 'He's back tomorrow.'

'What time?'

'Early afternoon.'

'You know where he is?'

'Yes.'

'Could you phone him, tell him Quince Jordan needs to speak to him urgently.'

She remembered the name from somewhere, the fact that someone called Jordan was a friend of the AA's. 'Of course.'

*   *   *

Summer holiday on Martha's Vineyard was as much part of the Donaghues' calendar as Christmas Day or Thanksgiving. Every year, for as long as they could remember, they had driven down from Boston, caught the ferry from Woods Hole to Oak Bluffs, and rented the house on Narangassett Avenue. Of course there were smarter places on the island, of course they might have been expected to stay somewhere else, but nowhere else would it take half an hour to walk the two hundred yards to the beach at the top end of the avenue for the simple reason that the people swinging in their hammocks really did mean it when they asked how you were doing. Nowhere else was there the Tabernacle, the festival in August, or the secondhand bookshop on the Vineyard Haven road for a rainy day.

This year, however, and apart from the day Brettlaw had visited, Donaghue and Pearson had spent their time in Boston, had finally made it Friday evening for the last three days. On Tuesday it would be back to DC.

It was nine-thirty Sunday morning, the sun already warm, the others getting up and Ed cooking breakfast. Donaghue picked up the car keys, left the house, and drove along the eastern shore, the beach to his left.

So what are you doing, Jack, he asked himself, where are you going? You know where you're going, so why?

Eight miles from Oak Bluffs he entered Edgartown. The old whaling station was clean and crisp, and filled with shops, restaurants and boutiques. Edgartown was expensive, the sort of place people would expect the Donaghues to stay. Edgartown had a Republican feel about it, he always thought.

Most of the shops were not yet open. He followed the road through the town, then cut left at the bottom, behind the white shingle fronts of the boutiques and cafés. The neck of water was a hundred yards across and the ferry was waiting. He bumped on, pulled on the hand brake, stopped the engine, got out, and leaned against the side of the car. Hands in pockets, faded Levis and T-shirt, and worn sandals. Sometimes people recognized him, sometimes they didn't.

There were only two other cars. Ten minutes later the barrier closed, the ferry pulled away, and an attendant began collecting the fares.

'Good morning for it, Senator.'

''Morning.' Donaghue fished in his pocket for some change. 'How's the season been?'

'Can't complain.'

They stood talking: about the weather and the regatta, where he was staying and how long he was on the island for. The ferry bumped on to the slope on the other side. 'Good to talk to you.' Donaghue shook the man's hand, climbed back in, started the engine, and drove off.

The road from the ferry was tarmac and virtually straight, sand dunes on the left. A mile from the ferry it swung sharp right, the bend almost a right angle, but a dirt track continued in a straight line off the bend. Donaghue slowed, checked there was nothing coming from the right, then swung off the tarmac and on to the track. The track itself was sand and rutted, trees on either side and occasional houses. After half a mile it left the trees, rose slightly, and stopped.

In front was a narrow stretch of water, forty feet wide, with more sand dunes opposite, the bridge which had once connected the two sides was old and broken, the supports jutting from the water, the cross sections closest to him either falling off or removed, and a mesh fence across the end to prevent anyone climbing on.

So why, Jack? What are you telling yourself? What are you trying to prove?

Early on a Sunday morning there were no other cars or people there. The tourists came later, grabbed their snapshots, then drove away again because there was nothing to do and nothing else to see.

He parked the car and walked to the bridge. Each year he came here: sometimes with Cath, once with the girls – just to show them. Normally by himself.

The morning was quiet, not even the sound of traffic. So many echoes, he thought; so many ghosts sitting on the Kennedys' shoulders.

Joe, the firstborn son. Killed in action during the Second World War.

John, the president. Assassinated in Dallas.

Robert, attorney general and presidential candidate. Shot dead in Los Angeles.

He stood still, fingers through the mesh, and looked at the bridge, at the water below. Tried to imagine what the night must have been like.

Edward, then junior senator. Following the family tradition and in Edgartown for the annual regatta. Staying in the cottage up the road, past the bend at which Donaghue had turned off, and throwing a party with friends and colleagues. Leaving midnight or there-abouts: nothing, or practically nothing, on the road. Heading in the direction of the ferry and coming to the right-angle bend but turning right, down the dirt track, instead of left along the tarmac road to the ferry and Edgartown. The night dark and the tide running strong. The car going off the bridge, Kennedy making it clear, but the woman called Mary Jo Kopechne still inside. In the years to come the incident costing him the nomination and the presidency.

And the others: the deaths, the illnesses and the court cases.

So many ghosts, Donaghue thought again. In the wartime skies over Europe, in the street in Dallas, the hotel kitchen in Los Angeles and the sandy peninsula off Edgartown. In the room in Russell Building.

He turned away from the bridge at Chappaquiddick and drove back to Oak Bluffs.

The Monday morning was cool, a thin strand of cloud in the sky. Brettlaw was in his office by seven. No visit to the canteen this morning – no need to visit the canteen any more. He lit a Gauloise, settled at his desk, and checked the time. Mitchell would probably be in the air by now, Mitchell was about to meet his Maker.

Maggie Dubovski arrived at five minutes to eight.

'Coffee?'

'Thanks.'

He smiled at her as she placed the mug on his desk, and checked the time again. So why had he hesitated over the lawyer? He fetched the Jack Daniels from the bar, poured a double into the coffee and lit another Gauloise. He knew why he had hesitated, had known from the beginning. The logic to remove Mitchell had been as impeccable as the logic to remove Benini and, after Benini, Rossi and Manzoni. He had not hesitated because of the logic, but where he had known that logic would take him.

Why are you making me do this – perhaps the thought was buried so deep that he didn't recognize it; perhaps he recognized it but refused to acknowledge it. You and I are friends, and now you're fucking me.

He took the sheet of paper, placed it squarely in front of him and drew the box as he had drawn it before. NEBULUS. The diagonal line from the bottom left corner and the second box at the end. BENINI. The vertical lines and boxes below. ROSSI and MANZONI.

All dealt with.

He finished the coffee and drew a line from bottom right of Nebulus. MITCHELL. Also dealt with, as Benini had been dealt with. But just as he hadn't sealed the Benini danger by dealing simply with Benini, so he hadn't sealed the Mitchell danger by dealing simply with Mitchell. Mitchell wasn't working independently, Mitchell was working for someone. So just as he had dealt with the secondary stages of the Benini danger by dealing with Rossi and

295

Manzoni, so he should deal with the secondary stage of the Mitchell danger.

The logic was impeccable and the coldness was upon him. He lit another Gauloise and drew a vertical line from the MITCHELL box.
PEARSON.

That afternoon the Donaghues had done what they always did on their last afternoon on the Vineyard. Driven to the bridge a mile from Oak Bluffs on the Edgartown road, the tidal lagoon inside and the channel passing beneath the bridge to the ocean beyond. Jumped from what everyone called the Jaws Bridge, where Spielberg had filmed the sequence in which the children are playing in a rubber boat in the supposed safety of the lagoon and the man-eater comes up the channel for them.

That evening they ate what they always ate on their last day: lobsters at Menemsha, the restaurant perched on the jetty, the sand dunes opposite and the tables covered with paper. Tonight was the last time they would do this – the feeling hung in the air. Next summer they wouldn't come because they'd be at the party convention. And if they came the summer after it would be with Jack as president and the Secret Service would have the area so tied up it would never be the same again.

By the time they returned to the house on Narangassett Avenue it was ten. They crowded into the sitting-room and sat round drinking beer and talking.

The telephone was in the hallway. When it rang there was an argument about who should answer it. Calls in the daytime were official and answered immediately, those in the evening were probably friends. It was Cath who stood up, beer in hand, sauntered through the door, and lifted the phone.

'Yes.' She listened, then cupped her hand over the mouthpiece. 'Ed, it's for you.' She put the phone on the table and drifted back to her seat.

'Yes.' Pearson was still standing.

'Ed, sorry to trouble you.' The secretary had been phoning since six. 'Someone called Quince Jordan phoned. Said it was urgent. He's waiting for you to phone back.'

'Thanks.' He took the number and called immediately. 'Quince, this is Ed. Been out and only just got your message.'

The others looked across, hearing the grunts as he took the message. Uh huh, yeah, got that. How long? What's being done?

'One moment.'

He closed the door to the hallway. When he came in three minutes later his face was white.

'Mitch Mitchell is missing. He took off from Walker's Cay this morning and hasn't shown. Coastguards have been searching the area for the past three hours.'

We have to talk, the look to Donaghue said it. Alone. Just the two of us.

They went outside and sat on the veranda; left the house and walked up the street.

'What is it, Ed?'

'Quince couldn't say on the phone.'

'But?'

'I get the impression he doesn't think it was an accident.'

Something about Jack's face, he thought. Something he wished he hadn't seen.

When they returned to the house it was almost eleven-thirty. For the next hour the four of them – Jack and Cath, Ed and Eva – huddled in the sitting-room and went through the implications. When the others went to bed Donaghue was still sitting, his hands clenched and his eyes fixed. At one he went upstairs, kissed Cath, and told her he was going for a walk.

'You want me to come?'

'You stay in case the girls wake.'

'You all right, Jack?'

'Sure I'm all right.'

Pearson heard him as he left. Something about Jack's face when he'd told him that Mitch's death might not be an accident, he remembered. He realized what it was and wished he had not.

Brettlaw's car was due at nine, but the evening briefings had dragged on longer than he had anticipated, so that it was gone ten-thirty when he telephoned his driver and told him he would be ready in five minutes. He cleared his desk in his normal manner, straightened the remaining paperwork, and flicked the TV monitor on to the late night news bulletins.

Washington lawyer feared missing in plane crash off Florida coast . . . he caught the update. Coastguard search called off tonight but to resume in the morning.

It was interesting that the disappearance had been picked up so quickly; the device had been due to detonate before Mitchell had reached an altitude where he could contact either Freeport or Miami, and neither Gussmann nor Hendricks would have made a mistake. Therefore either the FBO at Leesburg or one of Mitchell's colleagues or friends had checked when Mitchell was overdue, he supposed. In a way it was better, more natural.

He ignored the fact that his driver was waiting, reached forward, took a sheet of paper and drew the box at the top.

NEBULUS.

So what's the problem, Tom, why the second thoughts? He'd decided this morning about Pearson, so why hadn't he worked out how to implement it?

He drew the familiar structure down the left:

BENINI, ROSSI, MANZONI.

Then the matching structure on the right:

MITCHELL, PEARSON.

When things began to move they moved at a pace you could not imagine, and once one thing broke there was a natural disorder which dictated that others followed. Once the Benini risk had broken – totally outside his control – he had moved to cover it and any risks which might follow from it, had dealt with Rossi and Manzoni. Similarly with Mitchell. And Mitchell was reporting to Pearson.

Correct decision, therefore, the Pearson one.

Except, of course, that it wasn't.

He shredded the paper and took the executive lift to the carpark. Fifty-three minutes later he rang the door bell of the apartment off Washington Circle. Three rings, pause, another one. The door clicked open and he went inside, up the stairs, the single shaft of light from the door at the top guiding him and the smell of incense drifting down at him.

Bekki was waiting just inside; the jumpsuit was unzipped in front and she was wearing nothing underneath it. His hands were already sliding inside the cloth and round her buttocks, pulling her to him. Tonight would be short, almost a hurricane. Blowing out of nowhere, hard and fierce, and probably violent.

Benini connected to Rossi connected to Manzoni connected to Benini; therefore they all had to go. Mitchell connected to Pearson; therefore they had to go as well. Everything logical. Except that he hadn't taken the game to its logical conclusion, hadn't squared the circle, so to speak. Mitchell connected to Pearson and both of them connected to someone else. The chain neither starting nor ending with them, the chain starting and ending with someone else.

Her body was oiled; he was already naked, spreadeagled on the bed. She was moving against him, oiling his torso with hers. The oil was smooth and scented. She poured more across his shoulders and down his chest, massaged it into him. Cupped her hands and poured more liquid into them. Reached down and took his shaft, massaged the oil into it. Stroked him with both her hands. Knelt in front of him and took him into her mouth, sucked on him hard, changed position slightly and drew even more of the shaft into her mouth and throat. Changed position again so she was head to toe on top of him, took the head of his penis in her mouth and massaged the shaft with her hands, gasped as he slid his tongue inside her and began nibbling at her, almost eating her.

The enemy's still there, he had told Donaghue in the sauna at the University Club. Even the enemy within. But why you, my friend? We go back too far, been brothers too long. Been drunk together too many times, made the great play – the great play – at the Yale Bowl. So why are you spoiling it now, my friend, why are you so intent on destroying me?

He turned her and laid her on her back, stretched her arms and legs. Reached for the vial of perfumed oil, poured it in to his right hand and trickled some into his left. Ran his hands between her legs and massaged the oil into her till she was big and wide and open. Stroked her with his fingers and his hand. Turned her on to her front, strapped the thongs round her wrists and ankles and tied her down.

But Donaghue was an old friend. Delay and matters might blow over, yet delay and they might not. Bite the bullet, make the decision and get it over with, and he might just pull it off.

He poured the oil over her back and down her buttocks, then held himself against her, moved against her, brushed the head against her and heard the way she cried out, withdrew it then pushed into her without warning, heard the way she cried out again. Rode her like a stallion, his movements long and hard.

Donaghue wasn't his only way to the DCI's job, after all. Okay, his friendship with Donaghue was known, but Donaghue wasn't his only ally. So even Donaghue was expendable. Ways of doing it, though, ways of expending even someone like Donaghue. Interesting how once you began thinking about the details you overlooked whether or not you had actually confirmed the decision. Not the old saying that the end justified the means. Rather that the means determined the end.

He was riding her harder, organ thrusting into her and his full weight upon her. Don't stop, she was telling him, just keep going. Her body was changing as it closed upon her. Don't stop, for God's sake don't stop. She was shouting, screaming. Fuck me, keep fucking me. Fuck me any way you want but just keep fucking me this way now.

He was back on the Moscow streets, the snow driving hard and the adrenalin pounding harder. Was back on the sweep of the hill the afternoon they had laid Zev Bartolski to rest, the sky blue and the words of the anthem echoing in the still. Was back in the cafeteria the morning he had told them that he kept his vow to them, that he had avenged Zev's death for them.

'Shoot me.' Her body was convulsing, screwing up at him. It was rising through him, surging like a tide. 'Oh Christ shoot me now.' He was bursting into her, the shaft deep in her and his hands beneath her shoulders, pulling her hard against him.

Don't stop, she was telling him, screaming at him, just keep going.

He was still erect. He tore off the thongs and turned her on to her back, pushed into her again. Don't stop, she told him. I'm coming again, still coming; don't know which, but for Christ's sake don't stop. I want to scratch you, she was telling him, want to run my fingers down your back and scar you, want to hurt you. Don't do anything that would leave a trace, he had always said, don't leave any marks. Fuck it, he was telling her, fuck everything. Fuck Benini and Rossi and Manzoni. Fuck Mitchell and Pearson. Her nails were tearing at him, digging deep into him. Coming, she told him, fuck me harder, she told him, fuck me with your cock and your hand and anything you want to fuck me with. Her nails were deeper into his flesh, clawing at him. Fuck the enemy, he was thinking, fuck them all. Fuck Benini and Rossi and Manzoni; fuck Mitchell and Pearson. Fuck anyone who stood in his way. His mind was cold and clear and calculating. Fuck Donaghue, Donaghue was dead, Donaghue was finished. He even knew how he would do it and when it would be done.

16

The night was warm, a sea mist low on the horizon as the light came up. For four hours after he left the house Donaghue walked – round the sweep of the harbour and along the promontory to Vineyard Haven, then back the same way and through the cluster of brightly coloured wood-shingle houses clustered round the Tabernacle. On Illumination Night the Chinese lanterns would hang from their verandas and the place would be full of colour and laughter, but tonight it was as cold and bleak as the grave. So many ghosts, the thought weighed on his shoulders, so many secrets.

Tomorrow morning – this morning – they would be back in Washington. He and Ed leaving early, private plane from the airstrip on the Edgartown–West Tisbury road; Cath and Eva and the girls sticking to the original schedule, driving back to Boston and flying down late afternoon.

And the morning after the service at Arlington.

He was on the Jaws Bridge, was not even aware that he'd passed through Oak Bluffs and was on the Edgartown road. It was gone five, almost five-thirty, the morning cold and streaked grey. A police car trundled past and slowed, the observer glancing across at him. Couldn't sleep, he explained with a shrug. Perhaps they believed him, perhaps not. Perhaps recognized him, probably not. Want a lift? No, thanks anyway. He waved at them and walked back to Oak Bluffs.

Ed, Cath and Eva were up, and the coffee was bubbling on the stove.

'You okay?' Cath slipped an arm round him.

'Sure.' He looked at Ed. 'Any news?'

'I phoned Quince half an hour ago. Still no sign of Mitch. The coastguards should have resumed their search by now.'

Donaghue went upstairs and showered; by the time he came down the breakfast was on the table. For the next twenty minutes they went through the schedule for the day, then Eva drove the two of

301

them to the airfield. By eleven they were on the Hill.

Jordan was waiting. Donaghue and Pearson confirmed there had been no developments that morning, spent twenty minutes dealing with the other issues which required their attention, then Pearson went to collect Jordan.

'Care for a coffee?' Jordan asked.

We need to talk, Pearson understood he meant. Alone and private and out of the office.

'Sure, let's get some.'

They went in to the corridor and paced along it.

'What's up, Quince?'

'Any serious discussions about Mitch shouldn't be in your office or Jack's. You'll obviously talk about Mitch and try to find out what happened. But nothing involving Haslam's call to me or my attempt to contact Mitch.'

'Why? What the hell are you going on about?'

They turned the corner, the corridor empty.

'Dave calls me with a message that Mitch should be careful. Mitch goes missing. Mitch is working on an enquiry for you.'

Jesus, Pearson thought. 'You're saying Mitch was killed and the offices might be bugged?' he said.

'I'm saying we have to be careful.'

'The Caucus Room in five minutes,' Pearson told him. 'I'll get Jack.'

The Caucus Room was tall and large, columns rising to the ceiling and the ceiling itself exquisitely decorated. The Caucus Room was one of the most impressive rooms on the Hill, Donaghue always thought. He sat at one end of the committee table – the table almost lost against one wall – Pearson on his right and Jordan on his left.

'Tell us from the beginning.'

Early yesterday morning he had received a telephone call from Dave Haslam in Italy, Jordan told them. Haslam had said there was probably nothing in it, but something had come up which led him to believe that Mitch should be careful. Haslam had phoned him because he hadn't been able to contact Mitch. As Jack and Ed knew, Mitch was spending a long weekend on Walker's Cay. He'd telephoned immediately, but when he eventually got through Mitch had already left. When Mitch didn't turn up he'd checked with Freeport Flight Services and Miami Centre. They had confirmed that Mitch had filed a flight plan the night before, but hadn't activated it that morning, even though the hotel confirmed that his plane was gone.

'So what happened?' Donaghue looked at him.

'What do I think happened?'

'Yes.'

'Two possibilities. Either it was an accident, Mitch took off and had engine failure. Or his plane was deliberately blown up.'

'Tell me the pros and cons for the first.'

'It's not possible, for a number of reasons. There was no MayDay. Mitch was an experienced pilot. The first sign of trouble, especially over water, and he would have hit the button.'

'But you said neither Freeport nor Miami had any record of him,' Donaghue came back at him. 'So how does that fit in with your statement that the first thing he would have done if there'd been an accident would have been to send out a MayDay?'

'Back track. No one in the area – boats, planes or amateur radio hams – reported picking up a MayDay.'

Donaghue nodded and Jordan continued.

'There's another reason. The first thing he'd have done after takeoff would have been to log in with Freeport. Because Freeport is some distance from Walker's Cay, and because of the earth's curvature, Mitch would have made contact at an altitude of around 4,500 feet.'

'How does that prove it wasn't an accident?'

'There's a rule of thumb with private flying. Every thousand feet of altitude gives you a mile glide. If his engine had failed before he made contact with Freeport, he could have almost made it back to Walker's Cay.'

Donaghue was nodding, thinking it through. Donaghue could be sitting in the Oval Office, Jordan suddenly thought. He himself had been there, seen it, watched The Old Man deal with a crisis.

'What about the second alternative?' Donaghue asked and moved slightly. How and why might it have been a bomb.

The why first, Jordan said.

One: the fact that Haslam had phoned to say Mitch might have a problem, then Mitch had disappeared. Two: the fact that Mitch hadn't sent a MayDay or other signal. Three: the fact that whatever happened did so before Mitch had reached 4,500 feet, therefore before he had been in a position to tell Freeport he was in trouble. Four: the fact that whatever happened had given Mitch no time before and no time after.

And the how? Donaghue asked.

Simple, Jordan told him. A bomb on the plane, in a place where Mitch wouldn't look, with a barometric switch to detonate the bomb at a certain altitude.

'Why didn't it go off on the way over?'

'Probably because there was a double mechanism: a timer for Sunday night/Monday morning, then the timer activating the barometric switch.'

What else had Haslam said when he phoned, Donaghue asked. Which was to say: what reason had Haslam given for warning Mitch that he might have a problem. Only that he should hold on enquiries about something Haslam had told him, Jordan replied.

'Why wasn't he specific?'

'Either because the line wasn't secure, or because at that stage he wasn't sure himself.'

'So we can't really continue the discussion until he gets here.'

'No.'

The 747 was an hour out of Dulles. In the millisecond before he was fully alert the faces flashed in front of him: Paolo and Mitch. Then the eyes: Francesca and the girl's mother in Lima. Francesca again.

'Mr Haslam?'

He blinked awake and saw the steward. 'Yes.'

'Sorry to wake you, sir, but we've just received a message informing us that you have special clearance when we land. You'll be first off and there'll be someone to meet you. Do you have any luggage other than hand baggage?'

'No.'

Jordan was waiting for him in Pearson's office.

'Any news of Mitch?' Haslam dumped his bag in the corner.

'Coastguards are still searching,' Jordan told him, then led him into the corridor. 'We have a meeting with Donaghue and Pearson in ten minutes. Just in case anybody's fucking with us it's not in any of the offices connected to Donaghue.' In case the rooms were bugged or in case there was a leak on Donaghue's staff, Haslam understood. 'Anything you want before we start?'

'Some coffee.'

They collected a mug each, went to the Caucus Room and sat at the committee table. Not at the head, that was for Donaghue; one either side.

They had waited two minutes when Donaghue and Pearson came in. 'Thanks for getting here so quickly.' Donaghue shook Haslam by the hand and sat down, Pearson and Haslam also shaking hands. Donaghue in charge, Haslam sensed; Donaghue running the show.

'There's one thing I should say before I start,' he began. 'As you know, one of my jobs is advising on kidnaps. Normally I can't talk about individual cases, especially not identities. I'm breaching those rules only because of the special circumstances.'

Understood and agreed – Donaghue's nod said it.

'The case I've been working on in Milan involved a banker, Paolo Benini. Benini was an official of BCI, the Banca del Commercio Internazionale. For a number of reasons the negotiations didn't go well.

'There was a suggestion that the police were aware of my presence in Milan, the bank decided it was better if I was no longer involved, and I was withdrawn from the consultancy. The kidnappers secured a ransom payment in excess of the going rate but didn't release the victim. I was then called in again.'

He paused briefly, organizing his account.

'The negotiation started again, but something else had happened in the meantime. Not only were the kidnappers observing us, but someone was observing them.' What did he mean, Donaghue asked, how did he know? The details later, Haslam told them. 'At a point when the second set of negotiations were about to be finalized, the kidnappers broke off contact. At that point we discovered that the apartment of the family involved was bugged. Not Italian police or security services, someone else, we don't know who.

'Paolo Benini's body was found shortly after. He had been shot in the head. The assumption which follows from this is that someone else had intervened in the kidnapping, secured his release, then killed him.'

Donaghue was entirely focused on him, not saying anything, hearing everything before he intervened or came to any conclusions.

'Two other things happened about this time. The BCI banker who had advised the family suddenly disappeared, presumed dead. He hasn't been seen since. And the BCI manager in London was found hanging, apparently having committed suicide. The Mitch connection – if there is one, and I believe there is – stems from these two events.'

'Why?' Donaghue asked.

'A routine procedure in dealing with kidnappers is to seek confirmation that the victim is still alive – usually through a photograph or by setting a question which only the victim is able to answer. If it's a question it's normally personal. In the Benini case this is what we did initially. After I'd left, however, and before they paid the first ransom, the family asked a second question. At the insistence of the BCI representative, it was to do with banking.'

'Specifically?'

'What came before and after the last Nebulus. The answer was Romulus and Excalibur. I assume that Nebulus was an account used for channelling funds, and that what came before and after were the accounts where those funds originated and where they ended up.'

'What specifically are you suggesting?' Donaghue sat back in his chair, only apparently relaxed.

'That the accounts in question were black accounts, illegals, being used to launder money or to disguise the origin and destination of various funds. That Rossi was killed because he asked about them, and Benini because he gave the answer.'

'The London banker, Manzoni?'

Donaghue hadn't taken any notes yet remembered the name, Haslam thought.

'The morning before he was kidnapped Benini visited London. Manzoni ran the London branch of BCI. If Nebulus is, or was, based in London, Manzoni may have been killed because he disclosed the details to Rossi.'

'How does that tie in with Mitch?' Pearson asked.

'As I said, there was a period when I dropped out of the kidnap negotiations. During that time I was back in Washington. One evening Mitch asked if I knew anything about BCI. I wasn't able to say anything because of client confidentiality. When I re-entered the negotiations I had to come back to DC to clear up something. On that visit I mentioned to Mitch that if he was looking at BCI, he might see if Nebulus, Romulus and Excalibur figured at all.'

And in doing so I set him up. If he looked for Nebulus and found it. If he made some sort of connection. If the other side found out. But whichever way, I'm still on the wire.

'So where do we go from here?' Donaghue sat forward, hands resting on the table.

'It depends what we are prepared to assume.' Jordan took over the answers from Haslam.

'What do you suggest?'

306

'That Mitch is dead and that his death is not an accident. That he was taken out because of something he was working on in connection with his report.'

'Agreed, so what do we do next?'

'Make sure nobody's bugging us, and trace the leak.'

'How?'

It was late afternoon, the building emptying.

'Wait until the staff are gone, then check all your offices. Yours first, Jack. Plus Mitch's boat and office.'

'And the leak?'

'There are two obvious sources: somebody in your office, or somebody in Mitch's. So tonight we bug both, plus taps on home phones of all concerned when we can get in.'

'Why not go to the authorities?' Donaghue asked. 'Why not make it official?' What Jordan was saying sounded ominously like how Watergate started, and the room they were sitting in was where the Watergate dirty linen was washed in public.

'Because we haven't got enough to give them,' Jordan suggested.

Because the Feds would trample all over it . . .

Because even then the Feds would get nowhere . . .

Because all the Feds would achieve would be to scare off whoever was responsible . . .

Because to get somewhere sometimes you had to break the rules . . .

And because it was Mitch they were talking about, therefore it was personal . . .

'Any problems?' Donaghue asked.

'Only one: getting the gear into Russell Building without security realizing.'

There were electronic screens at each door, as well as at the entrance to the Capitol in case they came in via the underground rail system connecting the buildings.

'How much gear?'

'One briefcase.'

'No problem.' Donaghue again. 'There's one place where bags aren't checked.'

Because it isn't public and only one sort of person is allowed to use it.

'Where?'

'The entrance from the Senators' carpark.'

*

307

Brettlaw's office was quiet. He sat back in his chair and savoured the moment. It had been tight, but everything had been taken care of. In sixteen hours Donaghue would leave his car and walk by himself up the granite path to the memorial at Arlington. And thirty seconds after that the last threat to the black accounts would have been removed.

The dead drop in the luggage lockers next to platform thirteen at Union Station, the locks digital so no problems about keys. One mule making the two drops, a second mule making the first pick-up and placing the package overnight, not even aware it was a bomb, though he would know after.

There would be security, of course, especially round the memorial itself, but it would be perfunctory. Someone with Special Forces training could be in and out before the guards had stirred their coffee or lit their cigarettes.

The metal, slightly ornate litter bins at the side of the steps to the resting place of the late president. No security checks before Donaghue's visit the next morning because there was no need. Different if he was president, even a presidential candidate, but now he wasn't going to be.

The button man making the second pick-up from Union Station – the remote control device. Donaghue's convoy arriving and the area round the Memorial cleared of other visitors. Donaghue making the walk alone and the button man lost in the crowd.

The button man the only one to know that Donaghue was the target, and then only just as Donaghue was arriving. But the button man from one of the Aryan groups who hung out in Northern Virginia: military training and wouldn't give a shit when he saw the target because Donaghue was a liberal.

Boxes within boxes, no two boxes connected. Plus the cut-outs, so that nothing was traceable to Brettlaw or the Agency.

He crossed the room and poured himself a bourbon.

Thanks, Mr Brettlaw.

My pleasure, Mack.

Perhaps it was because his body clock told him it was midnight, even though it was six in the evening, perhaps because his mind was still in Italy; either way he was missing something. Haslam left the Hill and walked the five hundred yards to Union Station. The concourse was busy and the food hall on the lower floor was packed. DC in the tourist season, he couldn't help thinking.

What is it, Dave? What are you thinking?

He walked through the crowds, hardly aware of the smells and the sounds. Left the food hall and went upstairs, looked at the shops and people round him, the commuters waiting and the left luggage lockers against the wall.

The logic:

Benini, Rossi, Manzoni, Mitch. All suspected by the other side of knowing about the Nebulus account. Except that Umberto, Marco and Francesca knew, but they weren't in a position to be aware of its significance. He was, though, and the other side knew that, because he was the connection between Benini and Mitch. So he was the next one.

He bought a root beer and sat at one of the benches near the platforms. The area was packed: the woman next to him reading a copy of *Newsweek*, children playing and their parents telling them to keep still. Someone collecting a package from the luggage lockers.

He wasn't the next one, Haslam suddenly thought.

He left Union Station and walked quickly back to Russell Building. The staff had left, Donaghue was at a reception, and Pearson was alone.

'Want a coffee?' Haslam asked him.

Pearson understood. 'Sure.'

They went into the corridor and began walking.

'What's your schedule for the next few days, Ed?'

Why mine – Pearson looked at him. Why not someone else's? The realization hit him and the colour drained from his face. Benini, then Rossi and Manzoni because they were linked to Benini. Mitch because of the report. Himself because he was in charge of Mitch. Assuming Mitch had made the connection and assuming the other side knew, but they did because Mitch was dead.

'I never thought of that.' He sniffed, deliberately matter of fact. 'Normal routine tomorrow. In at seven-thirty, usual meetings till nine-thirty. Arlington ten till eleven, then the usual office work till one. Fund-raising lunch one to two, might drag on a bit. Back here after. Probably till eight.'

He shrugged, then mentally turned to the next page of his diary.

'Why Arlington?' Haslam asked.

'Jack's annual visit.'

'You always go with him?' Because if you do there's a pattern, and if there's a pattern the opposition might know of it and seek to use it.

'Of course.'

'Who else?'

Pearson shrugged again. 'His wife and family.'

'What does he do there?'

'He visits the Kennedy Memorial.'

'What does he do when he visits the Kennedy Memorial?'

Because that would tell about the pattern, which might in turn tell me how and where the opposition might try to take you out.

'He lays a flower there.'

'Why?'

'Why what?' There was the first hint of evasion.

'Why does Jack Donaghue lay a flower at the Kennedy Memorial?'

'Most politicians do.' Jesus Christ – it was in Pearson's face. You never been there? You never seen the people standing and staring, some kneeling and crossing themselves.

Of course . . . it was in Haslam's smile. Sorry I asked.

Pearson nodded. 'Thursday's much the same. In here at seven-thirty, meeting with Jack at nine . . .'

'Why tomorrow?'

'What do you mean, why tomorrow?'

'You said it was his annual visit. So why is it tomorrow?'

Why not? The shrug again. 'It's the date he always goes.' He continued with the list of engagements. 'Democrat Party head-quarters at twelve, committee meeting at two . . .'

The corridor followed the line of the building round the central courtyard, so that they were almost back at Donaghue's offices.

'Why with his wife and family, why the same date every year?'

Level with me, Ed, tell me the truth.

What if someone asks? Pearson remembered the discussion about the Arlington visit at the last war council. *They haven't asked before. But Jack wasn't running for the presidency before.*

Why come out with it, Pearson asked himself; why tell Haslam? Perhaps because they were suddenly on the Death Watch. Perhaps because of Mitch. Perhaps because Haslam had told him he was next and therefore he needed to trust him like he'd only trusted Donaghue.

'You really want to know?' he asked.

'Yes, I really want to know,' Haslam told him.

'You'd better come with me.'

He led Haslam through the administrative area and into Donaghue's room. It was early evening, the light soft. The desk against the window, the paintings on the wall, and the photograph of the two men above the dark green marble fireplace.

Pearson had put on his jacket, Haslam noticed.

Without speaking Pearson took the photograph from the wall above the fireplace, left the office, went to the Caucus Room and laid the photograph on the table.

'If Jack Donaghue runs for the nomination he'll get it. If he gets it, he'll make the White House. On the way they'll throw everything they can at him, they always do. They'll dig up everything in his past. Might dig up what I'm about to tell you, might not. His wife knows, of course, perhaps the girls. Plus those of his personal staff who have been close to him over the years.'

He paused, as if confirming his decision to tell Haslam.

'When I said that Senator Donaghue lays a flower at the Kennedy Memorial, that's slightly incorrect. He actually lays two. Single stem carnations. One is for the late president and the other is for his father. He cannot lay the second at the grave of his father, because his father has no grave.'

It was as if they were still in Donaghue's room, as if Pearson was standing at the fireplace.

'You know of President Kennedy's war record?'

'Yes,' Haslam said.

1943, the naval war in the Pacific, Kennedy commanding PT109 based on Tulago, one of the Solomon Islands. One of fourteen patrol torpedo boats ordered to intercept a Japanese convoy passing through their area on the night of 1/2 August. The attack unsuccessful, PT109 sliced in two by the Japanese destroyer *Amigari* as it returned to base, and Kennedy a hero because of his actions in saving his men.

'One of the PT boats which made it that night was commanded by Senator Donaghue's father.' Pearson stared straight at Haslam. 'Three weeks later, on a similar mission, he was killed in action.'

Haslam picked up the photograph and looked at the two men in it, both young, both in naval uniforms. Looked at the names at the bottom of the print.

Lieutenant John F. Kennedy.

Lieutenant Michael C. Moynihan.

Pearson waited till Haslam was looking at him again.

'Senator Donaghue's parents weren't married at the time. It was only after his father had been posted to the Pacific that his mother discovered she was carrying his child. Jack Donaghue was a close personal friend of both of them. He married her to save her the disgrace, gave the boy his name and raised him as his own. Jack Donaghue was a great man.'

Pearson had taken the photograph from Haslam and was staring at it.

'Actually they made a great couple, I met them several times. Had two other children.'

'Where are they now?'

'They're both dead. They're even buried together.' He turned and left the room, Haslam behind him.

'So now you know why Jack Donaghue visits Arlington every August 27th.'

They were standing in the corridor.

'But surely that wouldn't make any difference if he ran. His father died a hero, probably died without even knowing. Everyone acted honourably. They can't hold that against Jack.'

'You don't know how dirty it gets, Dave. You have no idea at all what the opposition will do to beat Jack Donaghue.'

They heard the footsteps and turned, saw Donaghue carrying the briefcase and Jordan appearing as if from nowhere.

Two hours later the sweep of the suite of offices assigned to Senator Donaghue was completed. Nothing was found. In case one of Donaghue's staff was the source of the leak, selected phones were bugged by intercepting the talk wires in the false ceiling, then running the tap wires to cassette recording equipment concealed in Donaghue's office. An hour later similar taps had been carried out in Mitchell's former office, with transmission by low power RF in an attempt to avoid the counter-surveillance measures permanently in place on the Hill, plus an amendment to the software of Mitchell's computer to detect anyone accessing his files.

Only after the sweep had been completed did Pearson hold his last meeting of the day with Donaghue, then he left the Hill and walked to the Hawk 'n Dove.

Eva was waiting for him at the main bar, the clock hanging from the ceiling above her. The name of the businessman – Harris – was on the clock face, and beneath it the establishment from which he had practised his profession – mortuary. He'd never noticed it before, Pearson thought; of course he'd noticed, he told himself, it was just that before he'd merely considered it amusing and slightly bizarre.

Eva drew out a stool for him and ordered him a Rolling Rock. 'Any news on Mitch?'

312

He shook his head, downed the beer and passed the glass back for another. It was five minutes before they spoke. The bar was empty, the manager in the other room.

'What's wrong, Ed?'

What do I tell you, Eva? Do I tell you that I'm scared and do I tell you why? Do I tell you that Haslam thinks I'm the next target, or do I tell you what's really troubling me? Which in a way is what scares me the most.

'Tell me, Ed.' Eva slid her hand through his arm and made him look at her.

He told her. About what had happened that day, about Mitch and about how he himself might be next in line.

'What else is it, Ed?' Eva asked.

Because I know you; I know every pore of your body and every crevice of your soul. Therefore I know when you're hiding something.

He shook his head. Eva slid her arm through his again. 'He hasn't said so, but Jack's not going to run, is he?'

'No,' Pearson admitted. 'Jack's not going to run.'

'Why not?'

'You remember last night, the moment I told you all that Mitch was missing, the moment I said that Quince had hinted it might not be an accident?'

'Of course.'

'Did you see Jack's face?'

'No.' Not that very moment, she corrected herself, because at that moment she'd been looking at Ed.

'I did,' he told her. 'It was as if Jack had seen a ghost.'

'So . . .'

'It wasn't Mitch's ghost he was seeing. It was his own.'

Haslam arrived at the houseboat ten minutes after Jordan. The couple on the next boat were holding a barbecue on the sun deck. He sat in the lounge area and watched the sweep – fast and efficient – then waited till Jordan and the others left and went to the Gangplank for a beer. It was almost ten, the evening still warm and a boat passing on the river.

So what are you thinking, Dave. Why are you still thinking it?

Something about the logic. Something about the chain which started with Nebulus. Something about Benini and Rossi and Manzoni. Something about Mitch and himself.

His mind was slowing down. Four in the morning according to his body clock, he remembered. He went to the bar and bought another beer.

Not something about Mitch and himself. Something about Mitch and Pearson. Because the logic was all about connections and Pearson was the next one, the last one, with any influence.

So what should he do about Pearson, how could he protect Pearson? Because Pearson was the logical one. Benini and Rossi and Manzoni, therefore Mitch and Ed.

He was tired, felt himself falling asleep.

Not Pearson. It hit him. Oh Christ, not Pearson.

The telephone was upstairs.

'Quince, this is Dave. Wondered if you fancied a drink.' Because something's going down and we're behind on it.

'Where are you?'

'The Gangplank.'

'Fifteen minutes.'

Haslam was waiting in the parking lot when Jordan arrived.

'Where to?' Jordan asked.

'Your office.' Because it's secure and there are things to do.

Jordan spun left across Water Street and accelerated down Maine Avenue.

'The logic leading to Mitch's death.' Haslam clipped on the seat belt. 'Benini, Rossi and Manzoni because they knew what Nebulus was about.'

Jordan passed the Washington Monument. 'Correct.'

'Then Mitch because of what he might have uncovered for his report.'

Jordan passed the Kennedy Center and turned in to Rock Creek Park. 'Correct again.'

'So where after Mitch? Assuming that it doesn't end with Mitch.'

'You.'

'Possibly, but who else?'

'Pearson, because he's in charge of the project and Mitch reported to him.'

They were out of the park and turning for Bethesda.

'Except it doesn't end with Ed, does it? It goes one more stage.'

The lights in front of them were changing to red. 'Oh Christ.' Jordan changed down and accelerated through. The next lights were already coming up at them, Jordan held his hand on the horn and kept his foot on the accelerator. 'Explain.'

314

'They were able to take Mitch out so quickly because they knew where he'd be. They get the same chance with Donaghue tomorrow.'

'How?'

'Same as Mitch, a bomb. Probably remote control device.'

'I meant how do they get the same chance with Donaghue.'

'Because tomorrow he does something he does every August 27th.'

The lights and trees and dark were a blur, Jordan driving as if there was no tomorrow.

'When?'

'Ten o'clock.'

'Where?'

'The Kennedy Memorial at Arlington.'

17

The night was cloistered around him. He'd made it last time, the time Kennedy had almost been lost, so he should make it this. The PT boat was surging under him and the Japanese destroyers were bearing down on him. Suicide, he had known from the beginning; from the moment he'd opened his orders.

The delta was hot and clammy around him, the foliage on either side thick and green and crawling with NVA. C130 somewhere above providing a radio net. Recon unit upstream cut to pieces on a hot extraction – the radio traffic he was able to pick up was thin and crackling. Made it to the river bank and digging in for the end. The choppers would get them, he knew, the guys who flew them were the best; but two slicks were already down and the recon boys were hauling wounded. Not his responsibility, though; his job this time had been to infiltrate another unit without anybody knowing they'd been there. The drop had gone well, then they'd run into World War Three, almost not made it out. And the recon unit now screaming for help was the other side of what he'd just come through, so that even to get to them he'd have to go through it again, plus whatever the recon boys were facing, then run the firestorm a third time. The medic was shouting at him to keep still and he was shouting at the medic to look after the others. Final message from the recon unit, the radio operator was telling him: down to last rounds and wondering if anyone could contact the Pentagon and ask whether they should swim for it. Perhaps he could hear the sounds above the purr of the Swift boat engines, perhaps he couldn't. Turn round and he probably wouldn't come back; not turn round and the recon guys certainly wouldn't.

The sun was hot and the Cadillac was open-top. The crowd were lining the route and cheering, the governor at his side telling how much his visit had meant. He smiled at his wife and glanced up, saw the square shape of the book repository.

The graves lined the slopes around him and the sun beat on

his back. He left the Lincoln and began the walk to the grave of the murdered president, the wide sweep of the granite terrace overlooking the Potomac to his right and the hill rising to his left. He was kneeling at the grave, placing the three single stem carnations on the plaque in front. One for Kennedy, one for his father, and the third for himself.

Donaghue woke and realized he was shaking, realized that Cath was holding his hand.

The eternal flame shone in the black and a veil of cloud was drawn across the moon. Haslam lay motionless between the white headstones and watched the patrol pattern of the security guards. Just like going into South Armagh, he thought, just like going into a roof space in the Catholic Falls or the Protestant Shankill in Belfast. Just like creeping on to the Argentinian airfields during the Falklands War or closing on the Scud convoys in the Gulf.

The car moved up the slope from the visitors' centre at the bottom of the cemetery, its headlights picking out the gleam of the headstones as it swung towards the Custis-Lee Mansion at the top. At two points it stopped, the men getting out to begin their foot patrols and meeting the others coming down the brow of the hill.

There were three points which received special attention: the visitors' centre, the mansion, and the Kennedy Memorial. Probably the Tomb of the Unknown Warrior as well, but where he was positioned Haslam couldn't see.

The car rumbled off.

The charge would be somewhere between where Donaghue's car stopped and the point where he placed the flowers on Kennedy's grave. He had phoned Pearson while Jordan had been making the other arrangements. Not asked him directly about Donaghue, and tried not to make the enquiry sound too important. But at midnight Pearson must have guessed something was wrong.

The guards moved off on their patterns. Half-hour patrols, then they switched. Only one he had to worry about: the guard assigned to the Kennedy Memorial. Twenty-eight minutes at the Memorial, then begin drifting towards the car point a minute before the changeover, the incoming man taking a minute to be in position. Christ, it would be tight.

If he was correct and a charge had been placed that night.

There was no other time it could have been placed – he and Jordan had worked through it. Yesterday and the risk of it being found was too great, tomorrow and anyone placing it would be seen. Therefore tonight. If Donaghue was the target, if tomorrow morning – if this morning – was the time and Arlington was the location. If he was right about a charge. He swept the area and concentrated on the Memorial.

Donaghue would have to be by himself when they hit him, because otherwise he might be protected from the blast by his family and colleagues. Therefore the location was in the forty yards between where he stepped from his car, and the top of the last flight of steps when he stood at the Kennedy grave, his family waiting at the cars till he had placed the flowers. And whoever had placed the charge had faced the same problems as himself – minimum time on location. Maximum two minutes to go in, drop it, and get out. Which eliminated practically everything.

Zero three forty – twenty to four in the morning. The light soon coming up and time running out. He listened to the sounds of the night around him and concentrated on the details of the walk which Donaghue would make.

Out of car then up the eight steps which faced him, the flower-beds on either side.

No go because family and officials would probably be standing either side of the steps.

Turn left up the walkway, the grass on either side.

Possible, except the turf was neatly cut and would be seen to have been disturbed.

Two more steps, the wheelchair ramp on right side, then four more steps on to the penultimate stage. The wide sweeping terrace covered with polished slabs to the right, ending with the wall carrying the Kennedy inauguration quotes, and the three-foot-high granite-faced wall to the left, flower-beds on top.

Probably not, because the height and thickness of the wall would divert the blast upwards and away from Donaghue.

Turn left at the end, then up the last steps to the marble around the Kennedy grave.

Again no go, because placing anything there would cause too much disturbance and take too long.

He swung back and concentrated on Donaghue's line after the steps with the wheelchair ramp. Granite-fronted wall to the left, fourteen paces to the end, past the litter bin, and another four to the centre of the last steps. Turn left, three steps, then two more paces to the last steps, the point where the polished granite ended and the gleaming white marble began. Eight steps, then the three paces to the grave itself.

The litter bins, he thought.

Two at the foot of the granite wall, on either side of the last sets of steps up to the grave and two more on the wall itself, either side of the top step. Easy to identify for whoever placed the charge and obvious for the button man.

The charge wrapped in something, no external wires to say what it was. Double-sided tape, so all the person placing it had to do was bend down, press it firmly on the bottom of the bin, and pull out. Provided the bins were on legs. Either that or put the device in the bin itself, assuming there was an inner mesh which you could take out and which would conceal the package when you put the mesh back. But that would take time and the bin itself might be bombproof.

The guard moved away, the smell of the cigarette smoke and the tang of after-shave hanging in the night air. Haslam gave him ten seconds and slipped forward.

The granite and marble were ghostly round him, the eternal flame flickering at the top of the steps. The litter bins were ornately cast metal: three feet high and almost two feet in diameter, so a charge could be taped on the bottom and not seen.

He confirmed he was alone and closed on the first bin Donaghue would pass, the one at the foot of the wall. No legs on the bin, therefore the bottom of the bin resting on the ground. Wire mesh inner section removable for emptying, but nothing in it, the bin on the opposite side of the steps the same.

Waste time removing the inner mesh and looking under it, or move to the ones at the top, waste more time coming back if they were the same?

He moved to the bins at the top. Left first. Standing on the wall and in line with the last step.

The bin was on legs and the bottom was three inches off the ground. He checked round him again, knelt by the bin, and felt underneath.

Oh Christ.

The envelope was taped in position, and a little over an inch thick.

Hope to God it's clean, hope to God it's not boobytrapped.

He flicked open the knife and felt along the edge of the envelope, inserted the tip of the knife and began to cut, the knife in his right hand and his left holding the package.

Fifty seconds gone, probably nearer sixty. Why the hell was he here and not someone else?

One side of the envelope was open. He slit along the next, slid his fingertips inside, and felt the package. No booby traps, thank you God. So far. He eased the inner package out – very slowly, extremely carefully – and laid it on the ground, shut the knife and put it back in his pocket. Minute thirty, almost a minute forty. He placed the inner packet on the wall to the right of the bin, felt under the bin again, ripped off the outer paper and pushed it into his pocket.

The footsteps came up the marble of the steps behind him. He lifted the package and began to move away, the bomb held in front of him. Not that it mattered any more; if there was an anti-tilt device he would have triggered it by now.

The footsteps were closer, past the steps with the wheelchair ramp and closing on the wall. Not enough time to get out, he knew, not enough time to cross the steps and clear the area. He moved back, towards the shrubs along the top of the wall, towards the guard. Melted into the shrubs as the guard turned the corner.

The guard walked up the steps and checked the memorial, moved back down the steps and leaned against the wall. If the man had a cigarette he could light it for him almost without moving, Haslam thought. If he had a pee he was close enough to shake it for him. Except he couldn't because that would mean putting down the bomb.

The dark was no longer so black, the grey seeping in to it.

Fifteen minutes passed, twenty, twenty-five.

The guard turned right, back toward the road. Haslam waited till he heard the voices – the man talking to the next guard – then moved off. The headstones were around him – neat straight lines stretching along the rise and fall of the hillside – and the Kennedy Memorial was behind him. He cleared the brow of the hill and dropped down the other side. Ten minutes later he was at the pick-up point, two minutes after that Jordan's car turned the corner.

The mist was rising off the river and the grey was turning milky light, Theodore Roosevelt Island to their right. Four-thirty in the morning and the world still asleep. Jordan braked slowly, aware of the package on Haslam's lap, then opened the door and helped him out. The carpark was empty and the footbridge was in front of them, the trees covering the island and rising like ghosts on the slope behind them.

The notice on the bridge said CLOSED AT DUSK and the metal

gate behind it was padlocked. Jordan cut through the chain and pushed the gate open.

'Good luck.'

Haslam crossed the bridge. The figure was waiting in the trees. Male, mid-forties, jeans, windcheater and baseball cap, no protective clothing. If you're crazy enough to be here I guess you don't need it, Haslam thought.

'This is it?' the man asked. No handshakes, no introductions, no frills. 'Tell me anything about it?' He took the package from Haslam.

'The target was one man. It was stuck beneath a litter bin, the target would have passed within six to eight feet of it.' Therefore four sticks. One would be a surprise, two and he'd be injured, three and he'd probably be dead, but only probably. 'I assume a remote device. No tilt or other mechanisms.' Or I wouldn't be in one piece now. 'I obviously don't know about anything else.'

'When's it due to pop?'

'Ten o'clock.' The time Donaghue's car was due to stop at the foot of the Kennedy Memorial. 'Not before.' Because Donaghue's timing would be immaculate. 'Within two minutes after.' Depending on how long Donaghue delayed at the car and how long it took him to walk to the last steps.

The man in the windcheater turned the baseball cap back to front, placed the packet on the ground, and knelt in front of it.

It was suddenly cold.

'How long will you be?' Haslam asked.

'How long you got?'

'You want a coffee?'

A laugh. 'When I'm done.' But no need for you to stay. Because the one thing I don't want is somebody breathing down my neck and asking me how it's going.

'See you later.' Haslam crossed back over the bridge. No point in staying, no point in pretending to be a hero. The padlock and chain were draped in place. He went through the gate, hung them back, and went to the car.

'How's it going?' Jordan poured him a coffee from the flask.

'So far so good.' Which they both knew he had to say.

They sat in the front seat and looked at the new day coming up. First stick out by now, second coming up. Assuming there were four of the little bastards. Then the detonation part of the device. After that the third and fourth sticks would be no problem.

'Another coffee?'

321

'Better save some.'

Fifty minutes had passed, almost fifty-five. The figure loped towards them. Jordan opened the rear door and the man in the baseball cap slid in and placed the package on the seat beside him.

'Coffee?' Jordan asked.

'Two sugars.'

'Anything in it?'

'What you got?'

Jordan emptied the bourbon into the mug. 'How was it?'

'Nice. Pro job. Good casing. Nothing to say what it was, so whoever dropped it probably thought it was the white stuff. No safety device inside. Whoever did it was ballsy. Remote control, as you said.'

'You got the frequency?'

The man with the baseball cap wrapped his fingers round the mug and breathed in the Jack Daniels.

'Of course.'

The smell of cooking drifted from the kitchen.

'Coffee?'

Jordan's wife put the plates in front of them – steak, scrambled eggs, hash browns.

'Prefer tea.'

She made him a mug and left them alone.

'So what do we do?'

Only Donaghue, Pearson, Jordan and himself knew about the bugging of the various offices on the Hill. And only he and Jordan knew about the bomb at Arlington – the bomb disposal expert had been told only what he had needed to know.

'There are three alternatives.' Though in the end there was only one.

'We tell the authorities.' Which they would not.

'We tell Donaghue.' Which they would have to, the only question was when.

'And we go for those responsible.' Which they had already accepted.

If they were using Donaghue as a bait, didn't they have a responsibility to tell him and didn't he have a right to know – they ran through the arguments. Tell him beforehand, however, and he wouldn't act normally, and that might alert the button man, which meant they might not spot him. But there was no longer a bomb waiting for him at Arlington, therefore the risk to his life was not immediate, therefore they didn't have to tell Donaghue at this stage.

'What about the device?' Jordan asked.

Because when it didn't go off the opposition had two choices. Either they could seek to cover the attempt by retrieving it, which was a security risk, or they could leave it, which was also a risk.

But the other side wouldn't go back for it. When the Donaghue visit took place with no extra security, the opposition would assume that the device hadn't been found. And if it was found later – next day, next week, next month – there would be nothing connecting it to Donaghue. And when they did find it the authorities would assume it was a crackpot with a Kennedy grudge and close the whole thing down for fear of copycat attacks.

Therefore the opposition wouldn't seek to retrieve it.

Except . . .

Haslam would remember the moment . . . When he stood in the Library of Congress that afternoon . . . In the office of the Senate Historian . . . When he and Donaghue were alone in the sanctity of Donaghue's office that evening . . .

Except that if they had come for Donaghue once, they would come for him again.

'You know someone who can take a look at it?' he asked.

Not a bomb disposal man. Rather, a scientist who could tell them about whoever had made it. Probably not who he was, but something about him, about his background. Who could check it against other devices and see if there were any cross-matches.

'I'll arrange it.'

'So what about this morning?'

They began the arrangements.

The gates at Arlington opened at nine, the morning was bright and the slightest trace of wind lifted from the Potomac. By nine-fifteen the cars and coaches were pulling in; by nine-thirty the carpark was half full and the summer visitors were climbing the slopes of the hill.

The man called Congdon was average – height, looks and clothes. Nothing to distinguish him from the tourist group to which he had attached himself, and nothing to suggest it was he who carried the signal transmitter in his right-hand jacket pocket – plastic covering, three inches by two by a quarter of an inch deep and the button inset, so he couldn't detonate it accidentally, but a thick rubber band wound round the device, keeping pressure off the button anyway.

The target arriving at ten, the instructions had said. Leaving his car and whoever was accompanying him and walking alone to the grave.

Congdon had already walked it, seen what it felt like. Up the steps and along the path; the steps with the wheelchair ramp, two paces then four more steps; then along the side of the granite wall to the centre of the steps to the grave, and turn left. Three steps, two paces forward, then the last eight steps, the point where the granite changed to marble. The job to be done when the target stepped on the first marble of the last steps.

There were four places, therefore, where he could stand and from which he would have a line of vision to the target. He had stood where the target would stand and checked, stood at each of the points and checked again.

The first was on the edge of the memorial itself, to the right of the steps as he looked below, which would be where the guards would move the crowds and which would therefore give him cover.

The second was at the top of the slope above the memorial, at the front of the Custis-Lee Mansion, but from here he couldn't see the exact step.

The third was on the small terrace on the path leading down from the Mansion, to the right of the memorial as he looked up; where he couldn't see the exact step, but he would be able to see the movement of the target's body and therefore be able to count the target's paces.

And the fourth was further down the path, probably seventy yards from the target, but where he would have line of vision only if he stood at the precise point between the two lines of graves marked at the ends by the headstones of James Phelan, of Pennsylvania and the Signal Corps, and Roy McCormack, of New York and the US Army.

In the first he might be too close to the action. In the others he would be further away, therefore his exit might seem easier, but he would also be isolated. And in the first he would be concealed by the crowd and once the thing went down there would be so much panic that nobody would spot him anyway.

It was five minutes to ten. On the bridge over the Potomac the three cars appeared in convoy. In the cemetery the guards sealed off the Kennedy Memorial and closed the roadway looping to it, the crowd realizing something was happening – probably somebody famous paying their respects to Kennedy – and stopping to look, being ushered by the guards to the space to the right of the memorial.

Signalling transmitter with a range up to a hundred yards – Haslam and Jordan had been through it. The button man either male or female, might well be the latter. Four points where he or she could stand. As long as he or she could see the killing point.

The cars passed through Memorial Gate then swung left through Roosevelt Gate and into Arlington Cemetery, then swung right, up the hill, into the loop leading to the Kennedy Memorial, and stopped, the drivers opening the doors and the passengers stepping out. Donaghue, Cath and the girls. Pearson and Eva; Donaghue's key aides and the members of his war council. Donaghue bent down, picked up the two carnations from the rear seat of the front car, and straightened his shoulders, the others standing by the cars as he began his walk.

Haslam and Jordan scanned the faces, waited for the tell-tale moment.

Eight steps – Congdon began counting – turn to the left. The morning was clearer, warmer, and the sky a cloudless brilliant blue.

The steps with the wheelchair ramp, then another four. The glistening marble of the terrace to his right, and the green of the hill and the granite wall to his left.

Eighteen paces to the point where the target would turn left, Congdon knew, to the point where the target would walk up the last two sets of steps. He felt in his pocket and eased the rubber band off the button.

Six paces. A woman to Congdon's left recognizing Donaghue. Nine paces. A serviceman to the right telling of Donaghue's support for the families of the MIAs. Twelve. Read an article couple of weeks back – from behind. Said he should be running for president. Eighteen.

Donaghue turned left, on to the last of the polished granite steps.

First step. Not too close to the button, Congdon reminded himself; not so close he would activate the device prematurely.

Second. Almost there, Jordan thought.

Third. Another four seconds, Congdon thought, perhaps three. Two paces across the flat at the top of the granite steps and the target would reach the white marble, step on the first step of the white marble.

Wait for it, Jordan tensed slightly. Listen for it, Haslam told himself. Hear the sound and look for the panic on the face.

ICOM R1 detector in his pocket, Jordan's as well. Tuned to the frequency at which the device was due to be detonated. Listen for the whirr as the bastard pressed the button then look for the reaction when Donaghue didn't go to heaven. He and Jordan knowing what each would do, cars in the park below to tail the bastard, plus tracking devices if they could approach his car.

Donaghue looked up, at the Custis-Lee Mansion on the skyline above, and stepped on to the white of the first step. Congdon pressed the button, face muscles tightening slightly in expectation.

Got him, Jordan shifted balance slightly. Got him, Haslam's eyes drifted past the man but didn't dwell on him.

Donaghue reached the top of the steps and paused slightly.

What the hell had gone wrong – Congdon tried not to show the panic. Try again as the target came back, he thought, but then the target would be surrounded by people and protected from the blast. He realized his finger was still on the button and took it off.

Confirmed, Haslam and Jordan both thought, glanced at each other to check. Nothing else though, nothing to alert the button man.

Donaghue crossed the three paces from the top of the steps and stood in front of the grave. Now he would kneel and place the flowers in position, Haslam knew. Instead Donaghue paused and looked down.

The grave itself was paved with heavy unpolished granite, and the low metal chain normally cordoning it off had been removed. At the front of the granite were three grey slate plaques.

The plaque on the left small:

Patrick Bouvier Kennedy

August 7, 1963 – August 9, 1963

The plaque on the right also small, the child lost in miscarriage:

Daughter

August 23, 1956

The other plaque in the centre:

John Fitzgerald Kennedy

1917 – 1963

Behind it the eternal flame.

Donaghue was back in the Pacific, back in Dallas, back in Vietnam, back in Arlington. He was in Arlington, he told himself, brought himself face to face with the present.

What's this all about, Jack? Haslam knew Jordan was covering the button man and focused on Donaghue. What's going on inside your head? He tried to imagine Donaghue's face and see into his eyes, tried to burrow beyond his eyes into his brain. I know what Ed told me about your father, but what else is it? What is it that you haven't told Ed, probably not told anyone?

Donaghue knelt, on his right knee, and placed the flowers side by side, adjusted them so they lay as one. Then he rose and came to attention.

What is it, Jack – Haslam was still staring at him, focusing on him. What's going down? What are you playing at?

What was *he* playing at – for the briefest of moments he turned the question back on himself. Why the hell was he so concerned and what the hell made him so personally responsible?

Because they'd killed Benini and he'd killed Mitch. Because . . .

There was the slightest movement, and Donaghue's wife and daughters joined him. As Donaghue swivelled slightly to greet them Haslam saw his eyes.

You're frightened, he suddenly realized. Not for today, because you didn't know about today. But you live in a world in which you're permanently running scared. You're a war veteran, a hero; yet every time you step outside your door in the morning you're afraid you aren't coming back, and every time you return you offer up a private prayer of thanks. And now you're more afraid than ever because in seven days you'll announce your candidature for the presidency.

So what is it, Jack? What's this really all about?

Jordan was still covering the button man. Haslam was leaving, moving to the area near the visitors' centre and the carpark.

Donaghue turned, holding his wife's hand, and walked back down the steps, across the terrace to the quotations carved into the granite curve overlooking the hill below and the Lincoln Memorial on the far side of the river. Then he turned again, returned to his car, and the convoy drove away.

The crowd moved back across the terrace of the memorial, some staring at the carnations as the guards replaced the chain in front of the grave. The button man moving with them, going back down

327

the hill to the visitors' centre, Haslam waiting for him to pick up his motor. If that was the way he'd come.

Congdon turned left, out the gate, and walked the two hundred yards to the metro rail. Which they'd also allowed for. Haslam ahead – targets never looked for tails in front of them. Jordan apparently nowhere in sight.

Blue line to Addison Road leading back into DC, Van Dorn Street the other way. Congdon took the escalator to the Van Dorn line, got on the Van Dorn train. Jordan in front now and Haslam behind.

Pentagon, Pentagon City, Crystal City. National Airport.

The button man was getting off, the bastard was going for a plane. Not going direct to one of the departure gates, going for a coffee. Either to calm his nerves or because his flight wasn't due yet. So which flight where? Did he have his ticket yet? If so, how could they guarantee getting on the same flight?

Congdon left the cafeteria, went out of the terminal, crossed to the satellite area, picked up his car, and drove away.

No problem. They'd got his photo, got his car number, got his fingerprints on the cup he'd used. Got him. At least knew how to get him when they wanted.

'I'll get these developed, run a check on the plates.' Jordan snapped the roll out of the camera. 'Also get the bomb to the friends. How about you?'

'The Hill, work out what to say to Donaghue.'

They returned to Arlington and picked up the cars. 'Meeting with Donaghue at six unless you hear from me.' Haslam followed Jordan out of the parking area, Jordan heading for Bethesda and Haslam into DC.

So what is it, Dave?

He crossed the Memorial Bridge, approached the Lincoln Memorial, and indicated for the DC turning. At the last moment he changed his mind, circled the Memorial and drove back across the bridge to the cemetery.

What's wrong?

The visitors' centre was air-conditioned: cool but crowded. Haslam drifted, not sure what he was looking for, studying the faces and glancing at the prints on the walls, flicking through the albums in the bookshop.

The photographs of the death of John Kennedy in Dallas:

The book repository in which the alleged solo gunman was positioned. Lee Harvey Oswald, the alleged solo assassin.

328

The moment in the car, the president pitching forward.
The photographs of Kennedy's funeral:
The gun carriage.
The black horse, the boots reversed in the stirrups.
The US marine folding the Stars and Stripes which had draped the coffin.
Jacqueline Kennedy, the veil over her face.
Kennedy's son John, three years old and in short trousers. Standing to attention and saluting.

He left the centre and walked back up the hill to the Kennedy Memorial.

I know you – it was as if he was looking at the photographs – I've seen you before.

He went back down the hill to the centre and scanned the blow-up photographs on the walls, then the smaller versions in the souvenir books. The blow-ups again.

Third row back, somewhere in the middle. Good-looking lady. So why do I know you? Where have I seen you?

He went back up the hill and stared in silence at the Kennedy Memorial, returned to the visitors' centre and stared in silence at the photograph.

Someone at the woman's side, someone with the woman, but he couldn't see who.

He walked to the enquiry desk and waited in the queue.

Why Arlington, he had asked Pearson. Jack's annual visit, Pearson had said, Jack's homage at the Kennedy Memorial. Lays a flower there. Actually Donaghue lays two, Pearson had admitted when Haslam had pushed him and he had made his decision. Single stem carnations. One for the late president and the other for his father.

Kennedy and Donaghue's father close friends, he had explained.

The naval war in the Pacific, 1943, Donaghue's father killed in action three weeks after the loss of Kennedy's PT109. But Donaghue's parents hadn't been married; it had only been after his father had been posted that his mother discovered she was carrying his child. So when Jack had been born the Kennedys had looked after him as if he was one of their own, and another friend, the Senator's official father, had married his mother for the same reason.

Which was why Donaghue went to Arlington each year, Pearson had told him. Each year on the anniversary of his father's death. One carnation for the dead president and the second for his father. Because he couldn't lay the second at the grave of his father, because his father had no grave.

329

The queue at the enquiry desk shuffled forward. So what was he looking for, why was he bothering? Because someone killed Mitch, and he was responsible for that; because someone tried to kill Donaghue. Christ, he thought, the bloody queue's going to take for ever. So why was he waiting, why was he going to ask, why didn't he just leave now? He came to the head of the queue.

'Could you help me?' He wasn't quite sure how to phrase it, still wasn't sure why he was asking. 'Is it necessary for there to be a body to have someone buried here?' He corrected himself. 'To have someone remembered here?'

'You mean to have a headstone here?' the woman asked him. 'To have a grave here?'

'Yes, that's what I mean.'

'Normally, yes,' she told him.

But . . . he picked it up and asked what she meant.

'Not if that person was killed in action.'

'Even if there's no body?'

The woman nodded. Because sometimes there would be no body. If an airman went missing in a bombing raid, for example, or if a sailor was lost at sea.

'Correct,' she said. 'If a person was killed in action, and there is documentation to prove it, then that person can be honoured here at Arlington.'

'Thank you.'

So what's going on, Jack? What's this really all about?

It was twelve-thirty; he left Arlington and drove back to Capitol Hill.

The meeting with Donaghue and Pearson was in the Senator's office at one. Haslam took a seat, accepted a coffee, and glanced round the room.

'How was this morning?' he asked.

'Fine, thanks.' Donaghue was behind his desk. 'Any news of Mitch?'

'The coastguards have called off the search, but we knew they would anyway.'

'So where do we go from here?'

What do we do about the taps we have in place, what do we do about Mitch? When do we go to the authorities? Except that unless we have evidence that Mitch was killed there's no point.

'There's something you should know.' Haslam put the cup down.
'What?'

Time to tell it and only one way.

'Somebody tried to kill you this morning.'

The colour drained from Donaghue's face. To his right Pearson froze in disbelief.

'There was a bomb at the Kennedy Memorial. Remote device to explode as you passed.'

'How'd you know, why didn't it go off?' Donaghue's face was death white.

'I removed it last night.'

Donaghue breathed deeply, gave himself time. 'Perhaps you should give me the details.'

Perhaps you owe me an explanation.

Haslam told him. So what is it, Jack? Why aren't you reacting properly? You appear to be reacting as anyone would react, but you're not.

'So what should we do?' Donaghue was in control again – of the meeting, of himself.

'We can go to the authorities, in which case they'll ask why we didn't go to them earlier.'

'But if we don't go to them now, we can't go in the future.'

'Depends,' Haslam said.

'On what?' Donaghue asked.

'On how we decide to play it.'

What's up, Jack? Why the hell don't you ask me why I'm running in circles instead of going straight to the authorities?

'Explain.'

'We're having the device examined to see if it can tell us anything about who made it. Which in turn might tell us something about who organized it. We're also running checks on the man who was supposed to detonate the device. I suggest we wait till we have this information, then decide.'

Jesus Christ . . . he saw the expression on Pearson's face, the mirror image – yet not quite the mirror image – on Donaghue's.

'When will that be?' Donaghue asked.

'This evening.'

What the hell's running, Jack? Why aren't you stopping me now, telling me this conversation is crazy? Why aren't you lifting the phone and informing the Feds?

'Agreed,' Donaghue told him. 'What time?'

What the hell is it with you, Jack? You're about to run for the presidency. And I tell you someone tried to blow you up this

331

morning. But instead of going to the authorities you go along with
me and allow me to play the game as if I was in Belfast or the Gulf
or some other God-forsaken corner of the world.

'Six,' he said. 'Unless Jordan comes up with something.'

The morning meeting with the DCI and the other Deputy Directors
was lasting an eternity. Sorry, Jack, Brettlaw thought; sorry, old
friend.

It was ten o'clock. Donaghue's convoy would be arriving at
Arlington, Donaghue would be stepping out of his car and beginning
his walk. It was two minutes past, the DCI asking one of the others
about developments in China. Brettlaw made a show of interest and
checked his watch again. Five past ten. Any moment the DCI's
phone would ring and his secretary would inform him of the news.
Then the DCI would put the phone down, gather himself, and tell
the meeting of the assassination of Senator Jack Donaghue.

It was ten-fifteen. The meeting ended and he left immediately.
So what the hell had gone wrong, what the hell was happening?

He returned to his office, asked Maggie for fresh coffee, lit another
cigarette and flicked through the news channels. Nothing on them
and no way he could ask anyone. The contact with the mule who'd
made the drop was at one, and the contact with the button man at
two. He thanked Maggie for the coffee, sat back at his desk, and
wondered again what had gone wrong and how he could plan around
it.

When Haslam telephoned Bethesda, Jordan was still not back; he
thanked the secretary and called the mobile number.

'Quince, it's Dave. Confirming the meeting for this evening.'

The conversation appeared neutral, almost sterile. Mobiles were
notoriously insecure. Haslam himself was using a pay phone near
the lifts rather than one in the Donaghue suite of offices.

'I've got it scheduled. You've had a prelim?' You've seen
Donaghue and Pearson and told them about this morning?

'Yes.'

'How'd it go?'

'They were interested.'

He put the phone down and began to return to the offices, came
to the corridor along which they were situated.

The rooms were numbered from the corner – 398, 396, 394, 392.
All were occupied by Donaghue's staff, plus two rooms opposite.

He stepped back and looked at the doors.

Not at the reception area, not at the other offices where the aides and the lawyers worked. At the door to Donaghue's office. Room 394. Locked, of course, access through the main area. Potential security risks if they came at Donaghue here, he thought automatically.

So what was it about Donaghue? Ed Pearson had confided in him the night before, but Ed hadn't told him everything even though he might have thought he had. Forget it, he told himself again; because you're not sure what you're looking for or where to start looking. Because you don't even know why you're looking.

He left Russell Building and crossed to the Library of Congress, the entrance to the library itself via an inconspicuous door at the rear.

Forget the intangibles, he told himself; focus on what's really important. Work out the procedures for whatever Jordan comes up with.

He cleared the security check and walked up the stairs. So what was he doing, what was he looking for, why was he wasting time? The corridor was high-ceilinged, with a marble floor and the bottom of the walls also marble but a dark yellow above. He turned right into the section before the main reading-room – a large desk on either side, the one on the right empty but assistants at the left, the walls lined with books and the atmosphere hushed.

'Can I help you?' The man was mid-forties, balding slightly, and peering at him through bifocals.

So what was he doing, why was he in the Library of Congress? 'I'd like to check on some senators.'

'Congressional Directory for the year in question. Alcove two, on the right. Level One.'

'Thanks.'

He walked through into the main reading area. The room was circular, designed after the Reading Room at the British Library in London, he'd read somewhere. The roof was domed and the windows arched, galleries running round the room with statuettes along the wall of the upper gallery. The ground floor was dominated by the reference desk in its centre, the desks circled round it.

What is it, Dave? What game are you playing?

He found Alcove 2 and climbed the spiral staircase. The gallery was ten feet wide and curved gently; the shelves were along the

333

wall to his right, and in sections running up to the balcony over-looking the main room below, and the Congressional Directories were in the third section, fourth row down, behind a pillar. The floor in front overlooked another alcove below, an iron railing around it.

The directories themselves were a mix of colours; he pulled out the most recent, leaned back against the rail, and checked the contents page. The section giving the alphabetical list of senators, plus their addresses, offices and telephone numbers began on page 251. He turned to it, then flicked through till he came to Donaghue's.

Name, room number and key staff, including Pearson.

So what had he been expecting?

He checked the contents page again. The biographical details began on page one, and were listed by state. The entries for Massachusetts were on page 93, the state's two senators first, then the members of the House of Representatives.

He settled back against the railing and read the entry for Donaghue:

Harvard. Boston Law School. Served with US Navy, discharged with rank of lieutenant. Silver Star, two Bronze Stars with Combat V, two Purple Hearts. Attorney. Assistant District Attorney for Suffolk County. Elected to the US House of Representatives November 1978, reelected 1980. Elected to the US Senate November 1982 for the term beginning January 1983. Reelected November 1988.

Plus Donaghue's office number, Russell 394; the committee positions he held; and the names and telephone numbers of his staff.

So what did he think he'd been looking for?

He returned the directory, then went through each of those for the years when Donaghue had been in the Senate, and before that in the House of Representatives. In each the basic details were similar. So perhaps what he was looking for didn't lie with Donaghue, perhaps it lay somewhere else. Perhaps it lay in a part of Donaghue's past before he came to DC.

But what did it matter, what was that important? He began again – the House and Senate details since Donaghue was first elected. He'd been here before, he told himself, already knew the facts he was reading again. He was getting nowhere; and if he was getting nowhere then it was time to leave.

*

It was five minutes to the contact call with the mule who'd dropped the device at Arlington. So what should he do about the device, Brettlaw wondered. Assuming it had been in place, of course; assuming nothing had gone wrong the night before. What should he do about Donaghue?

He leaned forward and punched the number. The call was answered immediately.

'Just checking how it went last night.'

'Fine. No problems.'

'Good. I'll call again when I need you.' Strange location for a drop, he knew the mule was thinking; last place the police and DEA would look, therefore dope or something else illegal. No questions asked and no answers expected.

The device in place, though, so what the hell had happened?

At one-fifteen he attended a briefing with the Finance Director, at five minutes to two he returned to his office. At two he telephoned the second contact number. The button man was confused – he sensed it immediately – probably running scared. Not scared, the button man wasn't a virgin, had done that sort of job before. More like running on adrenalin.

'What happened?' he asked.

'You tell me,' the man called Congdon came back at him. 'I'm in place, I do the job, and nothing happens.'

Therefore something wrong with the bomb or the control mechanism.

'Fine.' Brettlaw was already thinking ahead. 'Cali won't be happy, but that's their problem.' He sowed the seeds of the cover again, as he had sown them with Myerscough and Hendricks.

Except that Congdon was different; except that Congdon knew who the target was. Didn't know who was running him, of course, but until Donaghue was dead Congdon knew too much anyway.

'There's another job,' Brettlaw told him. 'I'll contact you with the details at eight.' And by then he would have set up Congdon's demise. Covered his tracks and closed off another box.

So what about the device? He sat back and lit a Gauloise. Either he could cover the attempt on Donaghue's life by retrieving it, which was a security risk, or he could leave it, which was also a risk. But he couldn't retrieve it until tonight anyway, and if it hadn't been found by then it wouldn't be found for a while. And every day it wasn't found, and every dignitary who visited the Memorial until it was, distanced it from this morning.

Therefore he would leave it.

Which still left Donaghue.

Capitol Hill was hot and crowded with tourists. Haslam left the Library of Congress and walked in front of the Supreme Court and past Russell Building. In the distance, somewhere along Pennsylvania Avenue, he heard the sirens of a Secret Service escort. So what had he been looking for, why was he wasting his time? Why, each time he decided to drop it, did it come back at him? He was at Union Station. He went downstairs to the food hall, bought an iced beer, and sat at one of the bars, watching the sea of faces and trying to work out what it was.

Not Donaghue, he decided, then corrected himself. The starting point might not be Donaghue, but the endgame was. He bought another beer and drifted up the stairs to the departures area; sat on one of the seats and ran through the things he knew about Donaghue, where he might find the key.

Not Harvard or Vietnam, he decided.

Not the House of Representatives or the Senate, because he'd checked them in the Congressional Directory.

Something about today, two things about today.

The photograph of the woman at Arlington and the corridor outside Donaghue's set of offices in Russell, the rooms numbered from the corner : 398, 396, 394, 392. Donaghue's room number 394. Quiet and peaceful, high ceilings and dark green marble fireplace, window on to the courtyard round which Russell was built.

So what is it, Dave? What are you thinking?

He left Union Station and walked back to the Library of Congress, nodded at the guard as the man recognized him from thirty minutes before.

The reading-room was quiet and the alcove on the second floor was still empty. He took out the last directory, leaned against the railing as he had done before, and checked the Donaghue entry. Room 394. Then he went back through the directories for each of the preceding years to 1983, when Donaghue had first taken his seat in Senate. Donaghue in Room 394, which was what he had assumed.

A librarian shuffled past him, selected a Congressional Quarterly Almanac, and smiled at him. He smiled back and looked for the Congressional Directory for 1982, the year before Donaghue moved from the House of Representatives to the Senate. The year was

336

missing. He pulled out the directory for 1981, and checked the contents section.

Rooms and telephone numbers, Senators: page 208.

The names were listed alphabetically; he ran down the column giving the room numbers and felt a sense of confusion. The rooms seemed to be numbered differently, some three digits, others four, occasionally two. More to the point, 394 was not listed.

He checked for the nearest rooms below 394: Senator Dodd of Connecticut, Room 363, and Senator Quayle of Indiana, 363A. Plus the nearest above: Senator Pryor of Arkansas, Room 404.

So what had he expected to find, he wondered. He ran back through the next batch of directories, the numbers even more confusing, then went to one of the assistants at the desk in the centre of the floor.

'Doing some research and want to check on a particular room in one of the Senate buildings,' he told her.

'Sorry,' she said. 'No idea how you can check on a room.' Changed her answer. 'Why not try the Senate Historian?'

'Where or who is the Senate Historian?'

'No idea. Try the Congressional Directory.'

Which I've already been looking at, he thought. He returned to the alcove, and pulled out the latest directory.

The entry for the Staffs of the Offices of the United States Senate was on page 163 and the reference was halfway down: Senate Historian Office, Senate Hart 201, telephone number 224 6900. Worth checking, he thought, even though he still didn't know what he was looking for. He could phone or he could call in person. He left the library and walked the two hundred yards to the Senate office buildings.

Room 201 was on the second floor, round the corner from the lifts, glass double doors leading to a small reception area, a woman – early to mid-fifties and well dressed – seated at a desk on the right.

Why are you still bothering, Dave; what are you still looking for? Why are you wasting your time, why aren't you following up on the plans for tonight? Why didn't you just telephone?

'Good afternoon.' He was polite, almost deliberately English. 'I'm doing some research and I wondered if you could help me.'

'Of course.' She looked up at him. 'How?'

'That's the problem. I don't know.' He wasn't sure why he'd said it in that way.

Some people might have reacted aggressively. Come back when

you do know, when you're not wasting my time. Instead she waited, perhaps tilted her head slightly, and allowed for him to explain.

'I was looking at Russell 394.' So why hadn't he said he was looking at Donaghue, looking at Donaghue's past? Why had he given the room number?

'Yes?'

You know, he suddenly thought. Even though you don't know what I want, because I myself don't know. But you know what it is. More than that. You have a reason for knowing.

'Actually I was looking at the history of Room 394.'

'Wrong room,' the woman said.

'I'm sorry. I don't understand.'

She stood and faced him. 'Which year are you interested in?'

'As I said, I don't know.'

She straightened her skirt slightly.

'When I said you had the wrong room, what I should have said was that you had the right room but the wrong number.'

'I'm sorry. I still don't understand.'

'They changed the numbers.'

How do you know – she saw it in his face. How, after all these years, do you and you alone know? She was still smiling at him, eyes and mind going back, the smile slightly different.

'We were on the same floor. Every morning I used to go out of my way so I could go past his office, even though he hadn't announced. Vice President Nixon had the office opposite. Nixon's door was always shut, but his was always open.'

Who did you go out of your way to try and see each morning? Whose door was always open? Why even now do you remember?

'In 1960 I was secretary to Senator McGee, of Wyoming,' she told him. 'That July the senator was at the Democratic Party Convention in Los Angeles. The vote for the candidate was a close one. Usually everything is settled before the convention, of course.' Through the primaries, she began to explain, in case he didn't understand. 'In 1960, however, the Democrats went into the convention not knowing who the candidate was going to be.'

She was half-smiling, shaking her head a little.

'At convention the votes are taken alphabetically, state by state. Everything's televised, but nobody ever sees the Wyoming vote, because Wyoming is end of the alphabet, therefore doesn't get its vote till late, and by then it's all over, by then the big states have cast their votes and made the decision.'

She was still smiling, still remembering.

'Except in 1960. In 1960 the vote was so close that the bigger states were holding back to see which way it went. Every state wants to be the one which puts the man over the top, you see; every state wants to be the one which casts the deciding vote. So all the big states who might have voted earlier were on the side lines and still waiting.'

She paused, very briefly.

'I was watching the roll call with friends. And suddenly it was late at night and Wyoming's turn, and he needed three votes.'

She was no longer with him. Was back in the room, the friends around her; the television pictures in black and white but the images distinct and about to be engraved in history.

'Going into the convention Wyoming's vote was split, but we all suddenly realized . . . That if we all voted together we could do it . . . That we could be the ones.'

She was no longer talking about *they*. Was talking about *we*.

'And that's what we did. As we watched on television the Wyoming delegates caucused on the floor, then the chairman stood and announced the Wyoming vote. That night we were the ones who placed the casting vote, you see; that night we were the ones who put him over the top. That night we were the ones who sealed the nomination. And even now I still see it and hear it and remember it.'

The cold was coming upon him, the realization of what she meant.

'So which room do I want?'

'Three sixty-two. When McGovern had it he put a plaque on the fireplace, but I think they took it down when he left.'

George McGovern, the Democratic candidate in 1972.

'Thank you.'

He left Hart Building and returned to the Library of Congress. 1960, the woman had said. He took the Congressional Directory from the shelf.

The rooms and telephone numbers of senators began on page 387. The first entry on the page was Senator Aiken, room 358, telephone number 4242, and the last was Senator Javits. He turned over and noted the first entry only because it was there: Senator Johnson of Texas, room 5121, phone number 5141.

The frost was setting hard, the first ice of winter. He remembered the words on the clock at Hereford.

> We are the pilgrims, Master, we shall go
> Always a little further . . .

He ran down the column and came to the sixth entry on the page. Room 362, phone number 4543. Looked at the name of the senator against it.

Turned to the biographical section, the entries listed alphabetically by state. Turned to page 69. The first entry was that of the senior senator for the state: Senator Leverett Saltonstall, a Republican. He looked below, to the second.

The name and details of the junior senator for Massachusetts.

The six o'clock meeting with Donaghue and Pearson was functional: no news on Mitch, nothing from the phone taps and no information till later on the Arlington bomb or the button man they had tailed to National. They would meet in the morning, they agreed, then they would decide whether or not to inform the authorities.

Donaghue thanked Haslam and Jordan, and Pearson rose to show them out.

'If you wouldn't mind, I'd like to speak with Jack by myself.'

Why – it was in Pearson's and Jordan's faces, the way they hesitated. Fine, Donaghue's nod said it. We're finished for the day anyway. 'Thanks again; see you in the morning.' He waited till Pearson closed the door, then sat in one of the armchairs at the end of the room furthest from the window. What do you want to talk about that you don't want Ed and Quince present? What's on your mind that we have to be alone?

'This conversation didn't take place.' Haslam wondered how Donaghue would react.

'Agreed.' Though I can't imagine why not.

'I don't expect you to reply to anything I say. In some ways I would prefer it if you didn't.'

'If that's what you think.' Donaghue crossed to the seat behind his desk.

So how should he begin, Haslam wondered: what should he say and how should he say it? Was he right or was he so far off course he was out of line? Was he out of line even if he was right?

'I was wondering when you were going to declare. What I mean, Jack, is that I was wondering *if* you were going to declare.'

'How'd you mean?' Perhaps Donaghue's reaction was predictable. What makes you think I'm not going to declare?

Time to tell it, Haslam thought, time to lay it on the line. Christ only knew what would happen if he was wrong, though; Christ only knew what would happen if he was right.

'You're afraid, Jack. You've been afraid every day of your political life. You should be president, but you're not going to be because of that fear.'

What are you telling me – he saw the anger flare in Donaghue's face.

So why not get up now, Jack, why not ask me to leave?

'Interesting room, Jack. Bit small for someone of your seniority, though.' Haslam was looking at Donaghue, into Donaghue's eyes. Through Donaghue's eyes to the soul behind. 'I thought there was a plaque on the fireplace, but I guess they took it off when McGovern left.'

The ghost flickered across the iris.

'Boston born, war hero, exemplary Congressional record. Potential presidential candidate for the Democrats.'

Recognize anyone, Jack – he didn't need to say it. Know what I mean?

Boston born, okay, he knew Donaghue was thinking. Swift boat commander in 'Nam and a couple of decorations, but so what? Two terms in the House, two in the Senate. Yes. Thinking about running for the presidency. Me, my record. So what the hell are you going on about? Why the hell are you wasting my time?

'I wasn't talking about you, Jack.'

'So who the hell were you talking about? What the hell did you mean?'

Haslam had not moved. Was thinking about the woman in the office of the Senate Historian, thinking about the floor of the 1960 convention, the night closing round them and Wyoming's turn to vote approaching. The realization coming to them that they could change the world.

'PT boat commander in the Pacific, war hero. Three terms in the House, two in the Senate, then ran for the presidency.'

Know who I'm talking about, Jack – again there was no need to say it. Know what I'm talking about? He looked round the room.

'Same office even. Different number now, of course, so nobody else knows. There's a photograph of him at his desk in front of the fireplace.'

Stop me now, Jack; tell me firmly but politely to go.

He stood and looked at the prints, looked at the face of the woman on the print next to the fireplace.

341

'Fine-looking lady. Third row back at Arlington. Guess you were at her side, except that someone was in the way so you're not in the photograph.'

He looked at the other photo: the two men in naval uniform.

'I know what I'm supposed to know, what you'll tell the press if they ask. Father killed in action, your mother carrying you, marries a friend of your father's. So each year you go to Arlington to remember your real father, because there's nowhere else to remember him, because he was lost at sea therefore there was no body to bury.

'Except you don't need a body to remember someone at Arlington. Do you, Jack? Except that if someone is killed in action and there are documents to prove it, he or she can still have a headstone at Arlington.'

For family to come and remember. For nearest and dearest to come and pay their respects. For sons to come and pay homage.

So stop me now, Jack. Get up and leave the room if you wish.

'Must have been hard, growing up as you did. I don't know when you learned the truth, don't want to know. Can't even work out who else knew.'

Stop me now if you want to, Jack, because if I haven't made myself clear so far, I'm about to now.

'Your mother, of course, probably not the man you looked up to and loved as your father. Perhaps the old man, particularly after the first son was killed and all the dreams were transferred to the second. Nothing allowed to stand in his way, of course, not even the fact that he was a father. Perhaps that was why your mother did what she did, out of loyalty. Moynihan's death in the Pacific a useful cover. You must even have hated your mother for what she did, probably hated her for even telling you.'

If that's how you learned, which is none of my business. And if what I'm saying is correct.

'Must have been hard, Jack. As close to the Kennedys as you could get without being one, but being one all along.'

He was staring at Donaghue, Donaghue staring at him.

Christ – it hit him.

'She never told you until the day he was assassinated in Dallas, did she, Jack? And then she took you aside and made you swear that you'd never tell anyone. And ever since then you've followed in your father's footsteps.'

He was still staring at Donaghue.

'Took one hell of a man to do it, though. A man who would make a great president.'

Or perhaps I'm wrong. Perhaps it's just a coincidence, perhaps he was simply a role model as he was to so many. Perhaps you set out to follow him, almost to resurrect him, because you admired him as so many did. I'm speaking theoretically, of course, Jack. As we said at the beginning, this conversation never took place.

'Except, of course, that you inherited one thing. Kennedy's ghost.'

Not just the ghost, the Kennedy curse. The firstborn son, Joe, killed on a night flying mission a year before the Second World War ended. The second son, John, the president of the United States, killed by an assassin's bullet. The third, Robert, also gunned down. The fourth, Edward, haunted for ever by Chappaquiddick. Then the next generation: the illnesses and the deaths, the cancers and the drug overdoses and the court cases. And you, Jack, the ghosts waiting for you at Arlington this morning. The bastards even waiting for you at your father's grave.

'They'll keep coming at you, Jack. The ghosts. The people who put the bomb on Mitch's plane. The people who tried to take you out. Again and again, Jack. They won't let up.'

Without warning Donaghue rose, walked to the fridge, threw Haslam a beer, and took one for himself.

'Why, Dave? What are you doing here?'

No confirmation, Haslam thought, but no denial.

'What I mean, Dave, is what are *you* doing here, why are *you* saying this?' Why Haslam as opposed to anyone else?

Haslam shrugged. 'Who knows? The nature of the beast, I guess.'

Donaghue crossed the room and sat again behind his desk.

'So what do you suggest?' he asked.

'I suggest you consider one thing to start with. That this morning at Arlington you laid to rest the ghost that's been sitting on your shoulder since the day you knew. That this morning the ghost came at you and lost.'

He laughed.

'So there are a few other bastards after you, but no longer the ghost. And the others we can deal with.'

Still no confirmation, he thought, still no denial.

343

Donaghue snapped the top off the can.

'As I said, Dave, what do you suggest we do?'

The girls were with friends and Jack wasn't due back till late. Cath Donaghue was finishing the brief she'd been working on for the next day when the Lincoln pulled up the driveway and into the garage at the side of the house. You're early, she began to say as Donaghue came in.

'Care for a walk?' He dropped his jacket on a chair.

'Sure.' She was suddenly worried, suddenly frightened. Oh my God, she thought: 'What's wrong, Jack, what's happened?'

'Nothing to do with the girls' – he understood what she was thinking.

They left the house and walked through the garden at the rear into the woods beyond. The evening was warm, the dusk around them and the smell of the pines sweet in the air. They were side by side, Donaghue with his shoulders slightly hunched and his hands in his pockets.

'Ed Pearson's a good guy.'

Sometimes Donaghue was looking at the ground, sometimes at the sky through the trees.

'A few months back he and I were talking about whether I should run and who I would need if I did. The obvious people, of course, except that Ed came up with one more. He said that the person I really needed was the one I could say things to that I couldn't to anyone else. Who would rein me in when I was going too fast, or pick me up and tell me to keep going when I was down. Who would tell me the truth. You're the one, Cath.'

'Of course I'm the one,' she told him.

I'm your wife, more than your wife. So we've covered the pre-amble, Jack, now tell me what's on your mind, tell me what you really have to tell me.

'Somebody tried to kill me today. If I run they'll try again.'

She felt the panic and fought against it. Kept walking, kept him walking. Wanted to ask him who and how and why but allowed him to explain in his way and his order of priorities.

'There's something else.'

Must have been hard, Jack. He remembered Haslam's words. *As close to the Kennedys as you could get without being one but being one all along. And ever since then you've followed in your father's footsteps. Or perhaps he was wrong, Haslam had said, perhaps it was just a coincidence, perhaps John Kennedy had merely been a role model as he'd been to so many. Perhaps Donaghue had set out to follow him, almost to resurrect him, because he'd admired him as so many had.*

He was talking to her, sometimes looking at her but sometimes staring through the trees, almost distracted. Why are you telling this to me? Cath's arm was through his. Why are you telling me now? He was still talking. Someone called Haslam, he was telling her, saved his life that morning then sat in his office that evening and said the conversation they were about to have never took place.

'Who's Haslam?' she asked.

'Someone from London.'

'With you or against you?'

'With me.'

How far with you, she asked. All the way, he told her.

How did he get the information on which his conversation was based, she asked; what motivated him then and what motivated him now. When she met Haslam she would understand, Donaghue told her. They were deeper into the woods, the sounds and the smells settling on them.

'Why are you telling me now?' she asked again.

'Because if I'm going to run, you have to know the dangers.'

'You mean that if you run they'll come at you again?'

'Yes.'

'And if they come at you, who'll be looking after you?'

'Haslam.'

They followed the path through a dry stream-bed and up the other side. So what are you asking me, she almost asked. Whether I should run, he would have replied. What's your favourite line, she asked instead.

'Of what? Poetry, literature, a song?'

'Just your favourite line.' They walked round a fallen tree. 'Perhaps favourite's the wrong word. What words are closest to you, what words will you always remember?'

'You know what words.'

'Tell me anyway.'

He was back in so many places, back at Arlington, standing on the granite terrace looking toward DC, the quotations carved in the slope of the wall in front of him. Three to his right, three to his left, and one in the middle. The words from the inauguration speech of the thirty-fifth president.

345

She felt the chill, the frost hardening suddenly to ice. No longer heard the voice of her husband, heard instead the voice of the man shot dead in Dallas.

They paused, only the sounds of the birds around them. She turned and made him stand straight, brushed an imagined hair from the collar of his shirt.

'I want you to promise me one thing, Jack Donaghue.'

Just think about the girls, some might have assumed she was going to say; just make sure they'll be safe. Except that wasn't what she was going to say, Donaghue knew.

'When you announce you're running, when you take the oath of office the year after next, you include those words.'

They turned back to the house. 'What happened today?' she asked at last.

'There was a bomb at the Memorial,' he told her. 'Haslam found it.'

'The same people who killed Mitch?'

'Presumably so.'

They dipped back along the stream-bed and up the bank on the other side. The light was going now, the half-moon already rising above the trees.

'So what are you going to do?' she asked.

'I'm not sure.'

'You remember *Hill Street Blues*?' She slid her hand round his arm again.

The television police series in the seventies and early eighties: Daniel Trevanti as Frank Furillo and Veronica Hamel as Joyce Davenport.

'Of course.'

'You remember Esterhouse.'

The desk sergeant who led the morning briefing with which each episode started.

'Yes.'

'You remember what he said at the end of each briefing?'

Perhaps Donaghue smiled, perhaps even chuckled.

'What's funny?' Cath asked him.

'Haslam had his own version of what Esterhouse said.'

'What's that?'

'Actually, he had two names for two slightly different things. He called them the First and Last Commandments.'

*

Pearson had been at the Hawk 'n Dove for more than an hour, sitting with Eva at one of the tables towards the rear and picking at the food. What's happened, she wanted to ask. Instead she stayed silent, gave him time to work through the storm in his head.

I want to tell you, he thought, but what can I tell you and how much can I tell you? That somebody might be after me? That there was a bomb intended for Donaghue at Arlington this morning?

'Ed.' The manager held up the telephone.

Pearson shook his head slightly at Eva, as if to say he had no idea what it was, and went to the bar. She watched him and saw the instant he changed, his facial muscles tightening and his back straightening.

'Yeah. Got it. I'll set it up now.'

He checked he had enough change and went to the pay phone.

'Jonathan, this is Ed.' She could barely hear him. 'My place, eleven o'clock.' Tonight or tomorrow morning – she could imagine the question. 'Tonight.'

He made the next call. 'Barbara, this is Ed . . .' Repeated the conversation another four times then sat down and looked at her.

'You as well, special request from Jack. He and Cath are on their way.' He asked for the check and looked at his watch. A lot of calls to make before eleven, a lot of deals to be struck and a lot of commitments to be asked for.

'What's up, Ed?'

Eva would never forget the moment: the way he looked at her and the gleam in his eyes.

'War council. We're back in. Jack declares next week.'

18

The meeting took place in the sitting-room, the members of the inner sanctum in a circle, Eva and Cath bringing in sandwiches and beer, then taking their places.

'We're going for it.'

It was the first time Donaghue had stated that he was running for the nomination: before tonight the plans and preparations had been based only on the assumption that he would.

'Press conference on the Hill next Tuesday.'

The day after Labour Day, the first day of the new political season. Nothing else scheduled, excluding the news events which no one could predict, so nationwide publicity guaranteed. Plus the impact of making the announcement at the heart of the nation's system of government.

'I'm in Boston the night before, and will fly down mid-morning.'

What's happened, Jack, Pearson wanted to know. What took place between you and Haslam that changed your mind?

One of the lawyers raised a pencil. 'What about Mitch? What do we do about the proposed banking investigation now Mitch is dead?'

'We hold on that, see what happens in the next few days.' Depending on what Haslam and Jordan came up with. 'Then we go ahead with it. We make our tribute to Mitch public.'

He moved down the agenda:

Op eds, how are we placed? . . .

Opinion polls. Who'll run them for us over the weekend, make sure we get the right results? . . .

Profile pieces. Who's set up to take them? . . .

'Lavalle.' The big money. 'Have lunch with his lawyer tomorrow; he'll cancel anything to get there. Make sure Lavalle's free this weekend.'

'What time?'

'Noon Saturday through breakfast Sunday.'

Why overnight Saturday, the lawyer wondered, what did Donaghue have in mind? 'Anyone else?' he asked.

Pearson read the names of the three largest financial supporters. 'Jack and I already have that in hand.'

The press secretary raised her hand. 'What are you planning for them?'

'River trip after lunch on Saturday.' Because even at this stage those invited would prefer to remain anonymous, but nobody would suspect a trip down to Alexandria or up to Georgetown. And that way the wives could be invited, could share the moment. That way Cath and Eva would swing the wives just as Donaghue and Pearson would swing the money men.

'What about O'Grady?' The party chairman. She realized. 'Christ, Jack. You've already spoken to him, haven't you?'

'He's attending on Saturday.' To show the money men that the man who controlled the party organization was on side, and that when the moment came the organization would be totally behind Donaghue.

'What about Saturday evening?' The press secretary again.

'What about Harriman?' One of the lawyers.

Pamela Harriman, the king-maker of the Democrats.

'Jesus, Jack. That's why they're overnighting Saturday, isn't it? That's where you're taking them for dinner.'

'Correct.' Donaghue moved to the next section on the agenda. 'Sunday: war council all day at my place. Monday: Ed and I and part of the team fly to Boston.' To lay the last foundation stones at home.

'Tuesday.'

The announcement itself. Most candidates declared in their home town, at least in their home state.

'I fly back mid-morning and declare at midday.' Time to catch the lunch bulletins, time for the majors to put something special together for the main shows early evening. 'The declaration will be made in the Caucus Room of Russell Building. Jonathan, you're in charge. Ed has a preliminary list of those who will be present.'

At most declarations most of those present were young, obvious party supporters. As Pearson read the list, sometimes names but sometimes just titles, even the war council were taken aback.

'Barbara,' Donaghue addressed the press secretary again. 'You and Jonathan liaise over where you put the key people. Make sure the TV positions are right.'

349

She could see it now, knew the impact it would have. 'Anything else, Jack ?'

'Yeah.'

Most declarations were made with the candidate standing between the Stars and Stripes on one side and the state flag on the other, blow-ups of the candidate within camera range.

'Black and white photos of the declarations made in the Caucus Room for the '60 and '68 elections. Get TV and press packs together to hand out on the day. Stills and news footage.'

Jesus – she remembered the candidates, remembered who had declared in the Caucus Room. 'Blow-ups of those candidates as background?'

'Of course.'

'Sure thing, Jack.'

They moved to the next point.

'Personnel. From Tuesday some of your jobs will change.' Most of them were paid by Congress, therefore banned from assisting in any electoral or political activity. 'We need to be squeaky clean on this. The most important position is Ed's. From Tuesday he no longer plays a formal role.' That would be the role of the campaign manager, and Pearson was too valuable on the Hill. Because while Donaghue was campaigning – and except that he would not be able to vote for him on the floor – Pearson would be Donaghue as far as his position as senator was concerned. Pearson was not out of it, therefore, Pearson was more important than ever.

They heard the ring on the door and turned. Pearson rose, let in Haslam and Jordan, and took them through to the kitchen. When they came back to the sitting-room Pearson whispered something in Donaghue's ear.

Donaghue listened carefully, then turned to the war council.

'I'd like to introduce two new members to the team. Dave Haslam and Quincey Jordan. Some of you might have seen them round the office. From this moment on, anything they say goes. Anything they want they get. Anything they ask you tell them.'

So you're Haslam, Cath thought. You're the one who talked with him, you're the one who's going to make sure he gets through. Because you're the one who's pushed him over the edge.

'What does *anything* mean?' It was one of the lawyers.

'What it says.'

The discussions lasted two hours, almost three, so that it was the middle of the night when the others left. There was something they needed to discuss – Donaghue tried to make it tactful. He waited till Cath and Eva had gone upstairs, then poured four large Jack Daniels.

'What's moving?'

'We're making progress on Arlington.' Jordan took the black and white blow-up photographs from his briefcase and gave them each a set. 'The device was straightforward. There were no fingerprints, but none were to be expected. Both internally and externally, however, there were a number of giveaways. The main thing is that the device was totally self-contained, by which I mean that there were no wires or external indications that it was a bomb. The detonating system was in the centre, the explosives themselves packed round it. Then there was an outer casing, in this case rectangular in shape, but it could be any shape or appearance you wanted.'

'And that's the giveaway,' Donaghue suggested.

'Yes.'

'How?'

'Devices like this were used a lot in Vietnam, but not by all our people.'

'Who by?' It was Donaghue again.

'Mainly by teams like Special Operations Group working with the CIA.'

'And after Vietnam?'

'They've popped up again, different times and different places. But all the hallmarks are the same.'

Oh Jesus Christ, Haslam expected Donaghue to say. Instead Donaghue sat quietly for thirty seconds, thinking through his questions and the order in which he would ask them.

'You're saying there's an Agency connection with the Arlington device.'

With the attempt on his life. And if the attempt was linked to the Mitchell enquiry, then an Agency connection with Mitch's death as well.

'So it would seem.' Haslam was careful.

'Agency or people within the Agency?'

'Uncertain.'

Brettlaw checked in at the University Club at eleven. He went straight to his room, poured himself a Jack Daniels, and took the glass with him when he showered. Next time – assuming there had to be a next time – he would use Hendricks. He dressed, finished

351

the bourbon, and left by the rear door. Fifteen minutes later he was in the flat off Washington Circle. Four and a half hours later, slightly earlier than normal, he left.

The number he called was a pay phone at National.

'How'd it go?' he asked.

'No problems.'

The button man Congdon, the only man who knew Donaghue had been a target, accounted for, and the man who had done the accounting not knowing why. Everything sealed again. Everything watertight.

Which still left Donaghue.

By seven Brettlaw was in his office at Langley. At eight he called Donaghue's home number, and wasn't surprised when he got the answer machine. Donaghue already on the Hill and Cath taking the girls to Sidwell Friends, he assumed.

'This is Tom Brettlaw. I'll try Jack at the office.'

Myerscough's request for a meeting came at nine. Make it nine-twenty, Brettlaw told Maggie: that way he'd know what Myerscough wanted, but had the excuse of the nine-thirty briefing with the DCI if he needed it.

Perhaps it was automatic, perhaps it was what he was going to do anyway. He swivelled in his chair, switched on the computer, called up Zeus, and left the message for Hendricks.

Myerscough was five minutes early.

'Mitchell.' He settled uncomfortably.

'What about Mitchell?' Because the Mitchell affair is dead and buried, so to speak.

'I still think his death's connected to his enquiry.'

'How?'

'The more I think about it the more I think there's a connection between his death and the Colombian syndicates.'

'That's what the papers suggested,' Brettlaw agreed.

'Just to make sure that we're covered I've ordered a final check on the file Mitchell was putting together for the Banking Committee.'

It wasn't the way he would have played it, Brettlaw thought; he would have treated Mitchell as a leper, untouchable after his death. Except that was the way Myerscough operated, and if he ordered Myerscough to hang back Myerscough might wonder why.

'Keep me informed.'

He ended the meeting and went to the briefing with the DCI. When he returned an hour later Maggie told him that Senator

352

Donaghue had phoned. He telephoned Donaghue's office on the Hill, was informed that the senator was at a meeting, but would return his call as soon as possible. Donaghue phoned ten minutes later.

'Tom, this is Jack.'

'Thanks for coming back. I was phoning to say how upset I was about Mitch. Apologies for not getting in touch earlier.'

It was the sort of call Donaghue had made about the death of Zev Bartolski in Bonn, the sort of call a lot of people had already made about Mitchell.

'Thanks, it's appreciated.'

'If there's anything I can do,' Brettlaw said.

'Of course. I was going to phone anyway. I think you and I should meet.'

Because there's something you as my future DCI should know – Brettlaw picked it up. 'When?'

'Today's as good as any.' Because this evening Washington closes down for the weekend and next Monday's Labour Day.

'I'll check if there's a squash court. What time?'

'Say three.'

'Three unless you hear from me.'

He checked his diary, telephoned the University Club, and cancelled his engagements for a ninety-minute block between two forty-five and four-fifteen.

Haslam had gone to bed at four and woken at six then cat-napped till ten. He had just stepped from the shower when Jordan called on the intercom from the front door. He pulled on a track suit and was in the kitchen when Jordan came in.

'The leak was a secretary on the Finance Committee staff. They phoned her this morning.' Jordan opened the fridge and took out the orange juice. 'Coded, of course, but a deaf school could have picked it up. The drop's later today. Same time, same place, whenever and wherever that is. The boys are sitting on her now.'

The Club was quiet and the changing-rooms were empty except for the two of them and an attendant.

'As I said, sorry about Mitch.'

Donaghue and Brettlaw changed and went through to the court.

'Best of three.'

'Okay with me.'

They shut the door and warmed up.

353

So what was Jack going to say, Brettlaw wondered; what was today all about? They had been on court five minutes and were already beginning to sweat.

'I'm declaring next Tuesday,' Donaghue told him.

So by next Tuesday it would have to be done – Brettlaw's mind worked analytically, almost automatically. If he was going to do it, he thought. But he'd already tried it once, so why the question?

'Where?' he asked.

'The Caucus Room.'

'A hell of a place to do it.'

Donaghue's people would already be on to the press, setting them up and making sure the announcement would get the coverage they wanted. Therefore there was no need to ask for more details, no need to take risks.

'Great news, my friend.' Brettlaw dropped his racket, walked across the court, shook Donaghue's hand, then embraced him. 'Great day for this country.'

'Clean so far.'

It was five o'clock, the Senate buildings emptying. Haslam sat in Pearson's office and listened as Jordan updated him.

'She's by herself. Seems to be leaving her desk.'

The transmitter of the RF was on low power, just avoiding the surveillance detectors on the Hill.

'She's into Mitch's computer.'

The penetration detected by an amendment to the system operator access.

'She's back. Packing her bag. Leaving.'

Terrible news about Mitch, the contact had said that morning. Probably one of the cocaine cartels, it was the way they operated. One last check on the material Mitch had collated, though; see if they could work out who was responsible for his death.

She left Dirksen Building and crossed the Mall to the National Air and Space Museum. Most museums and libraries in the area closed at five but the Space Museum was open till seven-thirty.

'Going down.'

When she entered the building she was carrying a newspaper, when she left she was not.

'Running.'

The pick-up crossed to the metro rail station at Smithsonian, took the blue line to Van Dorn and changed at Metro Centre. Red line

354

for Shady Grove. The doors began to close. At the last moment he jumped off and looked to see if anyone had followed him.

Not a field man, the woman on the platform thought, not someone who'd done the dry cleaning course, not someone who'd been trained how to lose a tail. She slipped into the crowd and followed him up the escalator.

Orange line to Vienna; third seat from the front, left side; the *Washington Post* folded neatly, but still slightly thick.

'They've switched.'

Rosslyn.

'Still running. Picked up a car.'

The Oldsmobile turned on to Route 123 and headed west.

The meeting in Donaghue's office that evening began at nine, Jordan leading.

'The leak was a secretary on the Senate Finance Committee staff: a call from her controller was intercepted this morning, though we weren't trying to trace it. Her orders were to copy Mitch's latest material. She did this when the others left this evening. The material was left at a dead drop at the National Air and Space Museum. The pick-ups tried to operate a couple of switches, but were kept under observation. The last switch was to a car. The car was tailed to its destination.'

'And where was that?'

'Langley.'

Donaghue did not react.

'There have also been developments on Arlington.' Jordan consulted his notebook. 'The button man was called Congdon. In one of his previous incarnations Congdon was a bag man for the Agency.'

'Where is he now?'

'Congdon disappeared off the face of the earth twenty-four hours ago.'

'What do you mean?'

'What Quince means,' Haslam said quietly, 'is that Congdon was the only man who knew that you were the target. So whoever was running him had to remove him.'

'You said last night there was a connection between the Agency and whoever made the Arlington bomb?' Donaghue looked at Jordan again.

'What I said was that the bomb had been made by someone with experience of working with the Agency in Vietnam.'

'But you're now saying that the button man also has an Agency connection.'

'Yes.'

'How proven?'

'Copper-bottomed.'

'You're also saying that the leak of information from Mitch's report was organized by the Agency?'

'What I'm saying is that the last pick-up drove to Langley.'

'Therefore if Mitch's death wasn't an accident, it would also seem that the Agency was responsible.'

'There's no direct evidence. But circumstantially, yes.'

Donaghue rarely swore. 'Christ,' he said now. It was almost a hiss, not quite under his breath.

'Agency or people within the Agency?' He had asked the same question the night before.

'We can't say.'

'But there's a difference?'

'Yes.'

'Plus . . .' Donaghue assumed there would be more.

'None of those need be Agency people. Or, more precisely, current Agency people. Except that one of the pick-up cars was tailed back to Langley.'

'Does that tie in with the Milan job?'

'It would make sense.'

'Specifically?'

Two specifics, Jordan told him; the first was that the man running the surveillance on the Benini kidnap was American. How do we know that, Donaghue asked. Because the concierge at the block where he'd set up his surveillance told me, Jordan came back at him. What about the second, Donaghue asked. BCI and First Commercial of Santa Fe, Haslam told him: Nebulus and Romulus and Excalibur.

'But even if that was the case, why would the Agency, or someone in the Agency, feel that all this was necessary?'

'Any number of reasons.' Haslam thought it through. 'Perhaps BCI was involved in some form of terrorism, and the Agency was using the bank to access that terrorism. Perhaps it was being used to launder black money. Perhaps the person or persons in the Agency genuinely believed that what they were doing was right.'

How'd you mean – it was in the turn of Donaghue's head and the hint of surprise in the eyes.

'A lot of people would argue that the world's a more dangerous place than at any time since the outbreak of the Cold War. The same people might even argue that we've seen nothing yet. The job of a professional intelligence officer in this situation is not only to report on the present, but to prepare for the future. In doing this, however, he has a problem. He needs the approval of his political masters, but what might be necessary for the security of the country in twenty years' time might not be a vote-winner today.'

'For example.'

'You name it. The Middle East, Africa, Eastern Europe. We might be appalled by what's going on there, but someone has to be building for the future. Someone has to be in there, making the contacts and cementing the alliances which will protect us in the future.'

'Even though we disapprove of what those same people might be doing at the moment?'

'At the end of the Second World War we recruited Hitler's scientists and intelligence people. What's so different now?'

'Maybe you're right.' There was a weariness in Donaghue's words. He rose and stood looking out of the window on to the courtyard. 'Specifics again,' he said after thirty seconds. 'Explain to me how the system would work.'

'How'd you mean?' Haslam asked.

'Acquiring intelligence is one thing, assassination is another. After the Castro fiascos the Agency is prohibited by Presidential Directive from engaging in the latter.'

They could probably overlook Presidential Directives, he knew both Haslam and Jordan were going to tell him. Agreed – a wave of the hand. But what about his main point?

'The guideline is plausible deniability. One of the ways of achieving this is to break down a task so that each person only knows his or her role, and nothing else. Take the Arlington case. The bomb maker wouldn't know the target, wouldn't even have contact with whoever planted the bomb, and the person who planted it would have been a different person from the one who was supposed to activate it. The person who activated it wouldn't know the identity of the target in advance.'

Donaghue sat down again. 'But somewhere, at some point, it must all come together. Someone must be planning it, knowing how and why the pieces fit.'

'Yes.'

'Who?'

Because if what you're saying is correct then that person is the pivot, that person is the one who killed Paolo Benini then Mitch; who tried to kill me at Arlington, and might try to kill me again.

Haslam turned to Jordan. You tell him, because this is your patch and you've been there, therefore you know it better than anybody.

Jordan nodded. 'As you implied, it has to be the point at which everything comes together. In this case that includes finance and operations, including covert action. There's only one place at Langley where that happens.'

'And what's that?'

'The Deputy Director of Operations, the DDO. Nothing, but nothing, happens without his approval. After the DCI he's God.'

'What about the fact that some of the people involved might not be Agency? That they might have been associated in some way in the past, but are no longer on the payroll?'

'All the more reason for it to be the DDO.'

What's the problem Jack, Haslam thought. Why are you sitting back slightly, why are you working out what you're going to say? What's so important about what you're going to say?

'The DDO, you said?' Donaghue looked at them both in turn.

'Yes,' Jordan confirmed.

'I played squash with him this afternoon,' Donaghue told them.

'Say that again,' Haslam asked.

'I played squash with Tom Brettlaw this afternoon. We were together at Harvard. If I make the White House he's my Director of Central Intelligence.'

He rose, went to the fridge and threw them each a beer, then sat down again with his feet on his desk. 'Let's get this straight. You're saying that Brettlaw is behind this?'

Your call – Haslam turned to Jordan again.

'What we're saying is that certain things are pointing to a certain conclusion. What we're saying is that if that conclusion is correct it points to a certain position within the Agency. That position is the Deputy Director of Operations. And the DDO at the present time is Brettlaw.'

Donaghue snapped open the can. 'So where does that leave us?'

'Where we were before,' Haslam told him.

'And where was that?'

'Looking at your timetable between now and Tuesday.'

'Why?' No problems, but why?

'Because if they come for you again it'll be before you declare.'

'Why?'

'The assassination of a senator would be bad enough, but they could pull it off, shelter under the cover of one of the cocaine cartels and put out the story that you were killed because you were going ahead with Mitch's investigations into the laundering of drug money. After Tuesday, however, you're a candidate for the presidency.'

And that would be a different ball game. Even though somebody got the president in Dallas in '63.

Donaghue tilted back in the chair. 'So now's the time we turn it over to the authorities.'

'No,' Haslam told him.

The ice settled on them, cold and bleak and biting.

'Why not?' *Because I have what you might call a personal stake in this.*

'Because if we did the first thing they'd do would be to throw a security screen round you so massive that the other side wouldn't even try to get near you.'

'Wouldn't that be good?' *Because it sounds pretty good to me.*

'In the short term perhaps, except they'd wait.'

'But we agreed they'd try before I was a presidential candidate.'

'Correct, but that's in an ideal world. If they have to wait, they will.'

You want to live with that, Jack? You want to live with the waiting? To continue living with Kennedy's ghost? Or do you want to face it now, get the curse off your back once and for all?

This isn't some banana republic in the back of beyond, Donaghue thought. *This is America. Not just America, this is Washington DC.*

'So if we don't tell the authorities, what do we do?' he asked.

'We look after you ourselves.'

'Who's we?'

'Our people.' Haslam opened his beer. 'Carefully chosen, of course, because the sort of protection we want is the sort nobody sees.'

How do you know you can trust them, Donaghue almost asked.

Because I've been there with them, Haslam would have told him: *behind the lines in the Falklands, dug in and overlooking the airfields on the Argentina mainland. In the shadows of Belfast or the hedges of South Armagh. Taking out the Scuds in the Gulf. Not just Brits, US Delta people as well.*

'What if they don't come?' Donaghue asked instead.

359

'What if who don't come?'

'The opposition.'

'We make sure they do.'

Christ, Donaghue thought. 'Why?'

'Because that way we control it.'

'How?'

'How would we control it?'

'No. How would you make sure they came at me again?'

You understand what you're saying – Donaghue looked at Haslam. You understand what you're proposing. The light in the room had faded, but no one moved to switch on the lights.

'Easy. The link is BCI and your link to BCI is the Mitchell investigation. Therefore we tell them you're continuing the enquiry.' Donaghue began to ask another question but Haslam stopped him. 'More than that. The thing they're really worried about is the Nebulus connection. So we not only tell them that you know about Nebulus, we tell them that that's what you're going for.'

The details later, Donaghue accepted: when and if he'd agreed, and when Haslam had had time to work it out. 'Brettlaw.' He brought them back to the central issue. 'How do we play it?' Because despite what you say he's a friend.

'We assume it's him and hope that it isn't.'

Donaghue finished the beer and threw the can in the bin. Please not Brettlaw – it was as if there was a voice which was his but not his, as if the voice was speaking on his behalf.

'Assuming it is the DDO, what do we do?'

It was interesting the way Donaghue had coped, Haslam thought: interesting the way Donaghue had stopped referring to Brettlaw and now referred to the DDO.

'What we'd do anyway. Set it up but let the opposition think they're running the show.' But we plan it. Close you off, organize your schedule so that it appears open but we control the times and places they might come at you.

'Thanks,' Donaghue said.

'Agreed?' Haslam asked him.

'Agreed.'

It was almost midnight; Haslam excused himself and used Pearson's office to make the phone calls, even though in Britain it was not quite five in the morning. The first was to an ex-directory number in Hereford.

'Alastair, this is Dave.'

360

The second was to a number in London, again ex-directory.

'Hello, Cathy. Long time no see.'

Twenty minutes later, and despite the hour, he made the first of his American calls.

It would have to be before Tuesday. More specifically: it would have to be before twelve noon on Tuesday, assuming Donaghue stuck to his timetable. Before that and Donaghue was merely a senator; after, and he was a candidate for the White House.

Brettlaw made the call to Hendricks at eight.

'The big boys were pleased with the Milan job. There's another. Probably next week, almost certainly DC.'

DC *should* pose extra problems because it was the nation's capital, Hendricks thought. Except that it didn't. One job was as easy or as difficult as another, depending on the requirements.

'When can you give me the details?'

'Tomorrow.'

The briefing with Myerscough took place seventy minutes later.

'We're clean.' Myerscough was confident, almost assertive.

'Nothing in any of the papers?' Brettlaw asked.

'In anything,' Myerscough was adamant.

'And nothing else we should worry about?'

'Nothing at all.'

The gods on his side, Brettlaw thought: he was cleared on the Benini death, cleared on the Mitchell enquiry and the Mitchell death, cleared on the Arlington bomb.

Senator Donaghue on the line for him, Maggie Dubovski told him. Brettlaw thanked Myerscough and lifted the phone.

'Jack, how're you doing? Good game on the Vineyard. Good run around the other day. To what do I owe this pleasure?'

Because we both understand this call is about business.

'Had an idea last night, Tom. Wanted to run it past you.'

And today is the last day we can talk before Tuesday, and Tuesday I declare.

Priorities, Brettlaw thought, nothing that couldn't be postponed for a couple of hours or cancelled for another day. 'How about lunch?'

'Make it a sauna.'

Because that way we guarantee we can be alone.

'Two-thirty.'

When Brettlaw arrived the last members were leaving the

361

dining-room. He nodded at the porter and went to the fitness rooms. Donaghue was already in the cabin. Brettlaw collected a towel, stripped and showered, then joined him.

'Thanks for coming at such short notice.' Donaghue was on the middle bench, beads of sweat already forming on his forehead and across his chest and stomach. 'There's something I wanted to ask you.'

Brettlaw sat with his back to the wall and waited.

'As I said before, I'm declaring on Tuesday. I'm shut up with advisers all weekend.'

Therefore not accessible, not somewhere Hendricks could get at him. Brettlaw's brain was on autopilot.

'I'm in Boston on Monday. Private dinner with local supporters.' *Possible, Brettlaw thought, but no time to plan for it. Even so it was the sort of detail he needed, the sort he had feared he would have to ask for.* 'Back again on Tuesday. Late morning flight in and press conference immediately after.' *The last chance, perhaps the only one.*

'So what did you want from me?' Brettlaw asked.

Donaghue splashed some water on the coals. 'I wondered if you'd care to accompany me?'

Is it you, Tom? Everything points to you, but I still can't believe it. Don't want to believe it.

'Where and when exactly?' Brettlaw sat forward slightly.

'Wherever you think fit. The press conference might be a little obvious, I would have thought, but any place and time either side of that would be good.'

'Jesus, it's hot in here.' Brettlaw pulled the towel round him and went outside.

So how are you going to react, Tom? Donaghue watched as Brettlaw closed the door. *Even if you react the way Haslam said, it still doesn't mean anything. Even if you come up with the answer Haslam said you would, it still doesn't mean that you're the guilty party.*

The water in the plunge pool was ice cold. Brettlaw slid in and dipped below the surface.

You're weak, Jack. I thought you were strong, thought you were the right man for the presidency, but now I know you're not. Plus you're giving me my cover. Because no one could suspect me if I was sitting next to you when Hendricks did the job. And that way I'd know the exact timetable, the precise procedures. With the know-

ledge that your campaign staff will give the general details of it to
the press anyway, so I'm covered again.

He pulled himself out of the pool, wrapped the towel round his waist, and returned to the sauna cabin, the details coming together and locking into a plan.

'What time are you due in?' he asked.

'Eleven-thirty. The press conference is at twelve.'

'As you said, the press conference might be a little obvious. How about we meet at the airport, ride in together.'

Which is what Haslam said you'd suggest, Donaghue thought. *Because that way you'd know the inside details and be able to plan. And that way you'd be covered because you'd be there when it happened.*

'Sounds good. Your car or mine?'

Brettlaw appeared to think about it. 'Yours. Mine and it might be rather obvious again.'

Which is also what Haslam said you'd say. Because yours is nondescript and armoured but mine's easily identifiable and totally without protection. Still don't believe it's you, Tom, still can't believe it's you. Still can't believe you'd do this to me, no matter what your reasons.

When he returned to the Hill, Haslam and Pearson were waiting in his office. Donaghue closed the door and sat at his desk.

'It's Brettlaw,' he said simply. 'Let's get it done.'

He and Pearson left Russell and drove to the court house. No Haslam, because his presence might give the game away. The judge was waiting, and the affidavit had already been prepared.

For attention of Her Majesty's Custom and Excise; to be executed the moment the banks opened in the City of London on Monday morning.

Brettlaw's call to Hendricks that evening was to a telephone at the Kennedy Center, the irony escaping him.

'The target will be flying in to National airport. He'll then be driven by car to the Capitol Building.'

A politician, Hendricks thought; not that it concerned him. 'Code name?'

'Dove.'

'Scheduled or private flight?'

Which would tell him whether the target stepped out of the plane to a waiting car, and was therefore exposed on the runway, or moved from the plane straight into a covered air bridge.

'Not yet decided.'

Which limited the time he had to plan – Hendricks was already calculating, rejecting some options and developing others.

'What do we know about the drive from National?'

'Dove will be travelling in a Lincoln town car. Registration number, colour and other identifying features will be available. Dove will be in the rear seat. One other person will be in the seat with him. Only Dove is to be hit.'

It would be tight, Hendricks thought; not impossible though. 'How will I know which is which?'

'We're able to control which side Dove sits on. That can be decided after your planning.'

'Vehicle protection?'

'The car's private; it's not armoured. At present there are no plans for Dove to be protected.'

'Which route will he take?'

Because although there was an obvious route, there were variations.

'We can control the route.'

'The lanes Dove's car will be in?'

Because the execution would have to be precise.

'Those as well.'

'Time of day?'

Because that would govern the amount of other traffic on the road, which would in turn affect the minutes and seconds which would be vital to whatever plan Hendricks came up with.

'Late morning.'

'Which day?'

Because that would determine how many people would be around – on the pavements or in the parks. Which would affect how Hendricks got in and, more importantly, got out.

'Mid-week. Probably Tuesday.'

'Dove's Lincoln. Are the windows tinted?'

'I'm not sure. I'll have it checked.'

'What are the chances of getting them down?'

Even if it wasn't tinted the glass might present a problem, especially given the need for accuracy and the fact that he had to take Dove but leave the person travelling with Dove untouched.

'I imagine we could manage that.'

'Any other arrangements?' The ways we make sure Dove's in the right place at the right time, he meant: the traffic cones and road diversions which would direct the target along the correct route; the cars which would guide him into the correct lanes. Either that or the other ways to deliver Dove to the middle of the killing zone. 'You want me to set them up?'

If that's the way we play it.

Boxes in boxes, Brettlaw thought. No link between the support units and Hendricks, no link between the units themselves, and the cut-outs to separate the operation from the Agency and from Brettlaw.

'No. I will.'

The first of the Fort Bragg team arrived at eight-thirty that evening and was temporarily assigned to the Donaghue home. No fuss, not even the neighbours noticing his arrival. The first of the London team came in ninety minutes later.

At ten that Friday evening Haslam and Jordan locked themselves in Haslam's apartment, swept it for bugs, then went through Donaghue's timetable for the next eighty-six hours. Donaghue to carry the code name Hawk, they had decided. Eagle was too over the top.

'Tonight.' Haslam fetched them each a beer. 'At home; one man inside, one outside.

'Tomorrow: war council at his home in the morning. Hawk doesn't go outside. Leaves at eleven-thirty, marina at twelve. Picks up his guests at Alexandria at one. Back to his house by seven. Pamela Harriman's at eight.

'Danger points on the river trip.'

Saturday afternoon would always be a problem, but Donaghue couldn't change it, because the trip on Saturday afternoon was as vital to his election campaign as their protection was to his life.

'The marina itself, the pick-up at Alexandria and the time he's on the boat. We're covering him, but it's the one time he can't be under wraps.'

But nobody knew – which was all they had going for them.

'Saturday evening: close protection cover to and from the dinner engagement, guards in place that night.

'Sunday: he doesn't leave the house. His war council will be with him all day, so everything will appear normal.

'Which brings us to Monday.' And Monday the storm clouds would gather. Monday the other side would know. 'The Customs and Excise boys go in at ten, London time. Even if they don't find anything, which is highly probable, the secret will be out the moment they read the terms of the warrant.'

So by the time Washington came to life five hours later the opposition would know and be planning.

'Hawk's at home with Ed till two, then they leave for Boston. Car to the airport, take-off at three. Private flight up, at our request, and landing details kept vague. Private suite at his hotel. The carpark is under the hotel; we control the elevator from the park to the floor on which he's staying. All his meetings have been rearranged so that people come to him, rather than him to them. Checks on those visiting him. Discreet, of course, only those on the list get in, but by then everyone will know that he's declaring Tuesday, so they'll know his schedule is tight and will accept it.

'Nobody else gets near him, which includes hotel staff. Our people collect his food from the kitchen and clear it after. Overnight security tight but discreet.'

Three bedrooms in the suite and no one knowing which Donaghue would sleep in. Even then there would be two men in the bedroom with him, one awake and one resting, but the one resting would do so with his mattress across the foot of the door and the door opening inward.

'What about the press?'

One of the problems, possibly the biggest: Donaghue needing the press for the build-up to Tuesday, but the press itself a danger.

'Ed's drawn up the list, only those people he knows will be allowed in.'

'Fine for reporters but what about the crews?'

'You don't know Ed.'

'Why don't I know Ed?'

'He's a pro. Next Tuesday is what he and Jack have been building for since the day they met.'

So Ed and Jack didn't know just the reporters but knew the crews as well. Knew their first names, shared a joke with them, had a drink with them. Even when the news wasn't necessarily good, or when Donaghue was facing a delicate issue. Made a point of telling them they understood they were doing their job, and still asked about the family.

'Tuesday?'

'He's scheduled to leave the hotel at nine. We bring him out at eight.'

They came to the fact that Donaghue had insisted his return to Washington would be on a scheduled flight.

'Under wraps; nobody knows how he's flying till the moment he steps on the plane.'

'TV coverage.'

Because the one story every Massachusetts newspaper, news agency, and radio and TV station would want that morning – the one thing Donaghue would himself want – would be a Boston boy on his way to DC to announce he was going for the presidency.

'We're covering it with our own crew. Professionals but security cleared. All the shots anyone could want: early morning conference with his advisers, breakfast, last adjustments to his speech. In-car shots, then Jack getting on to the plane. Everything made available to all the stations. That way they'll be happy because they know no one's getting something they're not.'

So Boston was closed off and the only time the other side could move against Donaghue was when he was back in DC.

'What about vehicles?' Donaghue's own Lincoln, plus the cars he would use in Boston. 'What about a bomb under the chassis?'

'When he's not using it the Lincoln will either be in the garage or under observation. It will be checked before he goes anywhere near it. Same for the motors in Boston.'

Which left National airport in DC, the run-in to Washington, the moment he left the car to enter Russell Building, the walk to his office and the walk which would follow this to the Caucus Room where he would declare.

'We're covered at the airport and with the walk-in, because we can control both.'

Which left the run-in to the Hill.

The first light sneaked through the curtains. Perhaps Donaghue had slept a little, though if so it had been restlessly. He rolled off the bed, trying not to wake Cath but aware she had lain awake all night, and went downstairs. The shadow was in the kitchen. For one moment, he realized, he had forgotten about the man in the house. If he had looked out of the window he would not even have seen the other in the woods at the rear. Haslam would not have expected him to.

Saturday morning, seven o'clock – it was like an hourglass, the sand running away.

National was quiet. Haslam and Jordan parked in the short-term area and began the check.

There were no special VIP facilities, only a stop point where Congressmen were usually picked up. Therefore they would bring Donaghue straight through and fast, nobody knowing too far in advance, though the word would get out once he was in the air, and the Lincoln parked immediately outside the exit.

They returned to the car, and began the route in, Jordan driving and Haslam beside him, beginning at the point where the Lincoln would be waiting.

First set of lights and the sign for Route 395, the metro station above them on the left. No cover, therefore possible top shot, except the Lincoln wasn't a convertible.

Interim airport right. Join main carriageway, three-lane. George Washington Memorial straight ahead. Ease into right-hand lane for 14th Street Bridge.

On to bridge. Ignore N1 going left and take 395 right.

First exit: Maine Avenue. First sign: C Street SW towards Capitol and the House.

Road dipping down below ground level, twenty–thirty-foot walls on either side. Running into first underpass, two-lane, then out before you could blink.

Second underpass, much darker, four-lane. The underpass long and curving, then climbing slightly, main carriageway continuing straight.

Off at first exit marked D Street NW and US Capitol.

Single lane, climbing slightly more steeply. S Street NW straight on, light at end of tunnel in fifty yards.

Take sharp right marked Capitol. Single-lane, steeper and curving. Fifteen seconds then out of underpass.

Tall concrete buildings on either side. National Association of Letter Carriers to right and traffic lights at First Street ahead. Mail vans parked on right. Wide pavement. Road coming from right, just as they left the underpass, so that at the lights the road was two-lane.

The lights were at red; they stopped and checked around them.

Central reservation, what the Americans called a median, to the left: wire fence, trees and shrubs. Road on other side to underground carpark beneath US Department of Labour, which part of the underpass also went under. Federal Home Loan Bank on other side.

Haslam checked the name of the street: Indiana.

Christ it feels cold, he thought, almost like a valley. No way out if they came at you here: as long as they controlled things and as long as they guaranteed you had to stop at the lights. He could feel it, knew Jordan could feel it.

The lights changed and they pulled forward, were suddenly in the open, into the lawns and the green, the Hill to their right.

Fifty yards, then traffic lights at junction with Louisiana, another fifty and lights at junction with New Jersey. Fifty more, then another underpass, traffic light at the beginning and cars and service vehicles parked on either side. Possible location but too closed in, no get-out route for the hitman.

Into the sunlight and stop at the lights, the corner of Russell Building on the other side.

Straight over, running into Capitol police now. Along the side of Russell Building, right at the next corner and up First, then right into the Senators' carpark in the courtyard round which the building was designed. Barrier in place and only Senators allowed through.

So that's it, they both thought. They returned to National and drove the route again, considering the various options as they did so, then they returned to National and began again.

By the time they finished it was eleven o'clock. They checked with the men at Donaghue's house and drove to the marina.

The war council convened at nine, most of the next two hours taken up by the arrangements for the declaration the following Tuesday.

The list of those invited . . .

Travel and accommodation where necessary . . .

Who would stand in the front rows . . .

Who the television cameras would pick out . . .

Who would stand next to who . . .

The press, TV and radio kits . . .

The pre-set positions for the cameras . . .

The photographs of the two men in front of which Donaghue would declare . . .

At eleven-thirty Ed Pearson and Eva left for the marina; five minutes later Jack and Cath Donaghue followed them, sitting in the rear seat of the Lincoln. The riverboat was standing by, Jordan on deck and Haslam on the jetty. Thirty seconds after the Donaghues arrived the boat cast off and turned downstream.

Three of Donaghue's guests, plus their wives, had arrived in Washington the evening before, staying discreetly in the Hays Adams, a hundred yards from the White House across Lafayette

Park. The fourth had arrived by himself, apologizing that his wife was unable to come because of illness. At eight that Friday evening a large bouquet had been delivered to her house, an hour later Cath Donaghue had phoned the woman personally to wish her well. At eleven on the Saturday morning the woman had flown in to National and joined her husband.

At twelve-thirty they were collected by Cadillacs and driven separately to Alexandria. The afternoon was pleasantly warm, no trace of humidity, and the riverboat was waiting.

'Glad you could make it, thanks for coming.' Cath Donaghue kissed the woman who had flown in that morning.

'Try to stop me being here.' The smile was fixed against the pain and the fire gleamed in her eyes.

Only after the boat had cast off and was heading down river did they go on deck, the men to the lower of the sun decks, near the stern, and their wives to the forward sun deck above the lounge.

'Guess we have to give the men their time together.' Cath passed them each a vodka tonic, Donaghue doing the same behind.

'You met Jack at Harvard?' The questioning began, quiet but purposeful. 'When did he tell you he opposed the war? How did you feel when he fought in it? How do you feel now?' Vietnam was still an open wound.

Find out about Cath Donaghue, each of the husbands had said, find out how she'd be in the White House. Find out about Ed Pearson's partner; see if she's a stuck-up university type or someone you can trust.

'What issues should we run with in the campaign?' Cath and Eva turned the questioning. 'What about health care? How do women feel about the budget deficit?' Only once did she look back, at the men locked in discussion twenty feet away.

Jack: talking but also listening, picking up on points made by the others. Ed: thoughtful and attentive. Lavalle and the other money men. The party chairman. And that evening, dinner at the kingmaker's in Georgetown.

The river was quiet and peaceful, Cath glanced back and knew that it was not yet time, glanced again and knew the moment had come. 'I think it's time we joined the men, don't you?' she suggested. They walked down the flight of wooden stairs to the lower sun deck, their husbands rising to greet them, and Ed pouring the champagne.

The party chairman rose to his feet. 'May I ask you to join me in a toast.'

He raised his glass to Jack and Cath Donaghue. 'Ladies and gentlemen, the next President and First Lady of the United States of America.'

Hendricks was at National at two; at two-fifteen he turned right on to Route 395 and drove the course for the first time, repeating the run, and the route alternatives, until four-forty. Then he parked the car, took a cab to Union Station, caught the 5.35 to Philadelphia, collected the rental he had ordered from the Hertz desk, and checked in at the Ritz-Carlton.

Hire a Lincoln town car in DC and seventy-two hours later a VIP gets taken out in one, and someone might get suspicious. Hire a Lincoln in a city a hundred and fifty miles away, however . . .

The next morning, Sunday, he drove to DC.

The obvious preference was a sniper rifle at a distance, except that the Lincoln had a hard roof, which limited the range of options available with a top shot. Therefore it would almost certainly have to be done at street level.

He could take out Dove from another car, which would be difficult unless he did it when the Lincoln was stationary, perhaps at a set of traffic lights. But then he couldn't guarantee the exact position Dove's car would stop, or his own position relative to it. Plus the fact that there were a limited number of lights on the route Dove would take.

He could do the same, but use a motorbike; that way he removed some of the problems, but not all of them, and created others.

Or he could do the job on foot, up close and able to move, but only as long as he could control the exact position at which the Lincoln stopped and as long as he himself had a way out.

Pity the car wasn't an open-top, he thought; pity it couldn't be like Dallas when they took out Kennedy.

National was quiet. He parked away from the terminal, switched off the engine, and shifted to the back.

If Dove was seated on the side he himself stood, the line of fire would be too restricted, especially if Dove was towards the corner rather than the centre. He might just be able to see him as long as Dove was in the position he himself was in now, but if Dove moved even slightly towards the corner he would lose either all of him, or that part of the body which it would be necessary to hit in order to guarantee that the shot or shots were fatal.

If Dove was on the opposite side, however, the angle of fire would be much wider, especially if he moved into the corner, but still not bad if he moved towards the centre. But the automatic reaction would be to move away from the gunman and into the corner, and in doing so Dove would increase the scope of the killing zone.

Therefore he would take Dove from the opposite side. The only other decision was where. In a way, he had already made it. He switched to the front seat, spun the Lincoln out of the parking lot, and drove the course.

Out of the airport and on to Route 395, right lane towards 14th Street Bridge. Over bridge and keep right on 395. First underpass, second. First turning off: D Street NW and US Capitol. Second turning almost immediately: D Street straight on, Capitol right.

He came out of the underpass, the traffic lights in front, the National Association of Letter Carriers to the right and the Federal Home Loan Bank to the left, the lights in front of him red. He stopped where Dove's Lincoln would probably stop, glanced round, and tried to imagine it. The lights turned green, then red again almost immediately. It was Sunday morning, no traffic and hardly any pedestrians. He reversed slightly and pulled in to the kerb. Knew the precise point at which the Lincoln would have to stop, and how he would achieve it. Where he himself would stand. His own way in and, more importantly, his own way out. Where he would position the get-away bike and the route he would take once he made it.

It was just gone midday. He drove the 150 miles to Philly, returned the rental, and caught the 4.04 Amtrak back to DC.

Sunday morning was almost peaceful.

When Hughes collected the Lincoln it was not quite six-thirty and the roads were empty. Jordan and Haslam were waiting off the Beltway. Hughes picked them up, then headed north; three miles later they turned off, two miles after that they pulled in to an industrial site, the units closed and the site deserted.

Top shot out, therefore ground location – they stood round the car and examined the options. Restricted angle of fire – they noted the window sizes and the position of a rear passenger relative to the windows. Continued restricted angle of fire if the gunman was on the same side as the target – assuming the gunman was under instructions to pick out a specific passenger and not sweep the rear area with a sub-machine gun. Therefore the gunman firing through the rear window from the opposite side.

The only question was where. They left the industrial estate and headed for National.

A 737 was banking over the Potomac and following the river down. Hughes ignored it and stopped at the point where Donaghue would enter the car on Tuesday. Then for the next two hours, and with Jordan still in the front seat, he drove the route from National to Russell Building, Haslam sitting in the rear and checking the angles of fire as they passed key points, confirming their conclusion about the gunman operating from a ground location. On the first two runs Jordan issued directions, on the third he sat without speaking.

'So where?'

They all knew where. The traffic lights by the National Association of Letter Carriers, just after the Lincoln came out of the second underpass.

'How do they guarantee Hawk stops in the correct lane?' Jordan asked.

Because there were two lanes at the lights, and he could take either of them.

'Easy.'

There had been a morning in Northern Ireland, beautiful and still, not unlike this morning. An army truck taking a route it often took, but on that particular morning breaking down. Someone passing the word to the IO, the intelligence officer, of the local Provo unit, and the local Provo unit deciding it was too good a chance to miss. Except everything was staged, the men waiting in the ditch immediately opposite the truck and no way out of the ambush. There had been complaints in the press, of course, the normal sort of accusations, but it was South Armagh and they had been after this particular unit for two long years.

'How easy?' Jordan asked.

'The road there is two-lane.'

'Yes.'

'The gunman is waiting, his get-away already set up – probably a motorbike. He's decided which side of the Lincoln he's going to stand when he takes out Hawk and conveyed this to his controller. Couple of minutes, perhaps less, before Hawk's due, a truck breaks down at the lights, in the other lane. Which means that Hawk's Lincoln has to pass in the lane predetermined by the hitman.'

373

'You've got Hawk in the correct position, but you haven't slowed him down or stopped him.'

'In the run-in to the second underpass they put a slow-down car immediately in front of Hawk. They make sure it's clearly identifiable – make, model and colour. So the shooter knows the car behind it is the target. The front car comes out of the underpass, then stops at the lights. Something apparently innocent like the engine stalling. And Hawk is left sitting there; nowhere to go and no way he can get out. Unable to go forward because of the car, unable to go round the car because of the truck, and unable to go back because it's one-way and there'll already be cars coming up behind.'

'But how can you guarantee that the right car is in front of Hawk at the right time?'

'No problem.'

Brettlaw's telephone call to Hendricks was at seven.

'The killing zone is the traffic lights by the National Association of Letter Carriers after the Capitol exit from the second underpass,' Hendricks told him.

'Agreed.'

'Dove should be sitting in the right rear seat. At the killing point Dove's car should be in the right-hand lane. We'll need a system to ensure this. I suggest a breakdown in the left lane just before he gets there.'

Because that way he, Hendricks, could be on the median, so there would be no bystanders in his way; that way he could shelter behind the truck until the last moment as well as use it as cover for his escape; that way he would be on the opposite side of the car from the front seat bodyguard if Dove was carrying one.

'What else?' Brettlaw asked.

'The angle of fire into the rear seat is difficult. We'll therefore need a system to ensure Dove's car stops at the tail of the broken-down vehicle.'

'Car in front stalls. The stall car clearly and easily identifiable, so you know the one behind it is Dove's.' Brettlaw had already thought it through, the structure the same no matter where the hit took place.

'In that case we'll need a system to guarantee that it's our car in front of Dove's at the correct time.'

The Man had also thought it through, he knew.

'A series of other cars coming on the carriageway, in front and

374

behind Dove's car, so that we make sure he's in the right lane at the right speed. The stall car is one of them, probably comes in late. The others pull off, but at a time and in a way which guarantees that the stall car is in front at the crucial moment and Dove can't overtake it.'

'When can you arrange that?'

'It's already done.'

Hendricks assumed it would be. 'When will I know whether it's a go?'

'When I do.'

The briefing of the London and Fort Bragg teams began at eight, in the sitting-room of the safe house off Eastern Market. Mostly men, one woman, Haslam in charge. The procedure was standard and straightforward: the target, the threat, and the overall structure of the next forty-two hours; the assignment of tasks and the possibility of run-throughs. At the end of each section Haslam paused and invited questions and comments.

By the time he held his final meeting of the day with Donaghue it was one-thirty in the morning, Donaghue looking slightly strained and both of them drinking whisky, plenty of soda.

'I'm still worried about Brettlaw.'

They were alone, looking across the garden at the back of the house. Donaghue in a rocking chair his grandfather on his mother's side had made, the one he had sat and rocked the girls to sleep in when they had been babies. The bottle on the floor to his right, top off.

'What about Brettlaw?' Haslam was in another chair opposite.

'Whether or not he's the one.'

'You know what we've set up. If it's Brettlaw, then it's finished. If it's not, he has nothing to worry about.'

And if it wasn't Brettlaw, and the opposition still came for him, then Haslam and Jordan still had it covered, Donaghue thought. He reached down and passed Haslam the bottle; Haslam refilled his glass and passed the bottle back. Donaghue placed the bottle on the floor and stared out of the window, then looked back.

'The evening in my office. The conversation which never took place.'

'Yes.'

'This one didn't take place either.'

'Understood.'

375

Donaghue put his glass down.

'What I'm about to say is based on the assumption that if it is Brettlaw then he's acting independently of the Agency, or that the knowledge of it is confined to a small number within the Agency.'

Which makes what I'm about to say easier; he picked up the glass and refilled it.

'The Agency's had a bad run recently: Iran-Contra, the Gulf War. A lot of people think everyone there is bad, and that with the end of the Cold War we can do without it. My position is that ninety-nine point nine nine per cent of the men and women at the Agency are good honest people working their butt off for what they believe in.' Which was probably the way Tom Brettlaw started, he thought. 'I also believe that in the present state of the world we need the Agency as much as we ever did. Different role, perhaps, different war. But we need it and the people in it.'

So what are you saying, Jack?

'When I'm president I'll sort out what I disapprove of, get rid of the people I think are wrong. And then I'll give the rest my full support. Therefore I don't want the Agency to suffer in any way because of what might happen on Tuesday.'

'Specifically?'

'If it is Tom Brettlaw, I don't want anyone to know.'

And . . .

'No matter which way it goes down, Tom comes out a hero.'

Sunday had drifted into Monday; in London the first drizzle settling from the grey of the sky and the first sheen of wet sparkling on the grey of the pavements. By seven-thirty the first commuters were arriving at their offices, between eight and nine the trickle had become a flood; by nine-thirty it had quietened again.

The three cars stopped outside the office block on Old Broad Street at nine forty-five, the drivers remaining in them and the men who stepped out walking quickly and confidently in to the building, the security guard trying to stop them.

'Her Majesty's Customs and Excise.' One of the men held his identity card in front of the man and kept him occupied, the others already in the lift. Twenty seconds later they stepped out in to the marble corridor of the fifteenth floor, turned right, then left through the glass double doors of the Banca del Commercio Internazionale.

'Good morning.' The team leader smiled at the receptionist. 'Mr Lapucci's office.'

Fifteen seconds later he faced the manager's secretary. 'Good morning. Mr Lapucci, please.'

'He's not available. He's in a meeting.'

'Her Majesty's Customs and Excise.' He showed her his identity card. Customs and Excise with more powers than the police. One minute later he stood in the office which Manzoni had once occupied.

'Under the powers invested in me, I have here a search warrant authorizing me access to all files relating to the accounts of the companies known as Nebulus, Romulus and Excalibur.'

Myerscough's call came an hour after Brettlaw had arrived in his office. There was something about Myerscough's voice, about the slight increase in the speed with which he asked for a meeting, that prompted Brettlaw to tell him to come up immediately.

'The Mitchell enquiry,' Myerscough was uneasy, a flickering of the eyes and a chewing of the lip.

'What about the Mitchell enquiry?'

'British Customs have just raided the BCI offices in London.'

Slow down, Brettlaw wanted to tell him, start from the beginning, give me the details. 'How does that affect us?' he asked.

'Under the legislation under which the search was conducted, the warrant was required to specify the accounts or files in which the Customs were interested.'

'And what accounts did the warrant specify?'

Myerscough passed the fax across the table.

'Nebulus, Romulus and Excalibur.'

Brettlaw reached for the cigarettes. 'We're sure?'

'Positive.'

Brettlaw sat back and lit the Gauloise. 'How did British Customs become involved? Why did you refer to the Mitchell enquiry?'

'Because the British were acting after receipt of an affidavit from Washington, and that affidavit referred to the laundering of drug money and the Mitchell enquiry.'

'Thanks,' Brettlaw said. For briefing me, for keeping on top of the situation. Thank Christ he was covered, thank Christ he'd planned everything so that he was protected. 'Let me know if anything else comes up.'

'Of course.' Myerscough rose to leave.

'One other thing,' Brettlaw stopped him. 'You said the affidavit was from Washington.'

'Yes.'

'Who signed it?'

He knew who. Your decision, Jack, not mine; I didn't sign your death warrant, old friend. You did.

'Senator Donaghue.'

19

It was the sort of day you remembered. Where you were when you heard and what you were doing. Who you turned to and who you telephoned.

When Donaghue glanced at the clock it was two in the morning. He straightened the papers on the desk in front of him and concentrated on the speech, making sure it had the right pace and balance, the right quotes in the right places. Two quotes above all others.

The first on the small wooden plinth at the front of his desk in Russell Building, Room 394:

> Other men look at what is and say why;
> I dream of what might be and say why not.

The second on the granite of Arlington, and which Cath had asked him to include:

> In the long history of the world
> only a few generations have been granted
> the role of defending freedom
> in its hour of maximum danger.
> I do not shirk from this responsibility
> I welcome it.

Except that in his mind he had rewritten it slightly:

> In the long history of the world
> only a few generations have been granted
> the role of defending freedom.
>
> In the hour of maximum danger
> I do not shirk from this responsibility.
> I welcome it.

He realized that he was saying the words aloud, realized he was standing beneath the Stars and Stripes in the Caucus Room in Russell Building, the cameras on him and the world waiting. Realized that he had paused and looked up, perhaps hesitated for one moment.

'I therefore declare my candidature for the Democratic nomination for the Presidency of the United States of America.'

The room was quiet; he put down the pencil, crossed to the door and told the men outside that he was going to bed. They came back with him and closed the door. The first man settled in a chair and the second pulled a mattress across the bottom of the door and lay down.

It was two-thirty in the morning, eight-thirty in Europe. Haslam stared at the ceiling and thought of the other times he had felt like this: on selection, on a particular patrol, most often when he or the men he was leading were cut off and alone and looking as if they weren't going to make it.

> We are the pilgrims, Master – we shall go
> Always a little further. It may be
> Beyond that last blue mountain barred with snow . . .

When this one was over he'd go east, he decided, make the golden journey to Samarkand. Not the one in his head, which he'd made already, but the actual one. When this one was over he'd stand by himself at the beginning of that track and look up and wouldn't look down till he was there.

He lifted the telephone and called Milan, not sure why and not expecting anything other than a recorded message. Francesca answered on the third ring. She sounds different, he thought: at least she could answer the phone without the fear it would be Mussolini turning the screws on her.

It's Dave, he told her, just phoning to make sure everything was okay. Good to hear him, she said, good of him to phone. So how were things, he asked: how were the girls, how were Umberto and Marco, how's Francesca?

They laughed at how he'd referred to her in the third person. Things were fine, she told him; it hadn't been long since the funeral but the lawyers were good and she and the girls were beginning to adjust. And what about him, she asked, where was he phoning from and what was he doing?

They talked about Washington, about Milan, about nothing in particular; about how he really should visit next time he was in Italy and how she should visit when she and the girls were in Britain or the US. She had to go to work, he said; yes, she agreed, she had to go to work. Keep in touch, they told each other, good luck with everything. And thanks for everything.

Good of him to phone, Francesca thought, good of him to think of her. She spent five minutes with the housekeeper, checked the time, and telephoned the office that she would be a little late. It was gone eight-thirty, almost a quarter to nine. Washington was six hours ahead, so in Washington it would be the middle of the afternoon. Never been to Washington, she thought, perhaps she ought. She left the apartment and called the lift.

Washington wasn't six hours in front, she suddenly remembered, Washington was six hours behind. In Washington it was the middle of the night. The fear bit into her, the terrible awful chill. She turned and ran back into the apartment, tried to remember where she'd put the card with his number on and called Washington.

'Yes.'

She recognized his voice but was terrified at the hardness of it, as if he had been expecting someone else.

'Dave, it's Francesca.'

She realized she hadn't thought out what she would say. What's up, she wanted to ask; why were you phoning at this hour? 'Thought I'd phone back,' she said, and remembered the poem he'd quoted at her.

'Going for the last mountain?' she asked him.

'Something like that,' he replied.

'You know what you're doing?' she asked him.

'I hope so,' he laughed.

She remembered something else about the place he called Hereford.

'Dave.'

'Yes.'

'Tick tock, beat the clock.'

Donaghue woke at six, if he had slept at all. He showered and dressed, then asked the shadows to leave him, and telephoned Cath. Everything was going well, he told her: the local publicity the night before had been more than they could have hoped for; the reaction to the items which had appeared over the weekend had been overwhelmingly favourable; and the timetable that morning was tight but unchanged, no bad weather to delay the flight down and no last-minute hiccups.

'I'd like to meet you at the airport.' She didn't know why she suddenly thought of it. 'I know the plan is for me and the girls to be waiting for you on the Hill, but I'd like to see you arrive, like to make the drive with you.'

'I'm sorry. Any other day, any other time. But not today.'

She understood. 'Good luck.' It was all she could do to whisper, 'We'll be waiting.' She didn't want to put the phone down, didn't want to let him go.

'Jack.'

'Yes.'

'I love you.'

'I love you too.'

Haslam and Jordan spoke at five, again at six and at seven. Haslam in DC and Jordan in Boston with Donaghue. The security was watertight, Jordan was confident: there had been no problems, no suggestions of a threat so far. Everything on schedule and going to plan.

The team moved into the Caucus Room at seven-thirty: the platform had been constructed the evening before, now they raised the massive black and white blow-ups behind it and began checking the camera positions and sound systems.

The beggar was at Union Station shortly after eight. Not badly dressed. Dressed like the others. Jacket, Levis and trainers. Polystyrene coffee cup for whatever anyone would give him. Washington was full of men with polystyrene coffee cups, some drifting, some with their own pitches – the key points on key streets, the tops of escalators from metro rail stations. Each had his own style: some, though not many, mute, almost threatening; others witty and cheerful and telling you to have a good day.

By nine the beggar had moved a short way, across the green park separating Union Station from the Hill, the sun warm and the sky blue, though there weren't as many tourists now it was September. He held the beaker out as a couple of Texans passed him – wide-brimmed hats and distinctive boots. One more beggar, they thought. Early thirties, a little over six feet tall, thin build. Black. But most such men in DC were black. It wasn't prejudice, it was a fact of life.

The beggar drifted closer to the Hill and stuffed the cup in his pocket. The Capitol police didn't like beggars: beggars were bad for the image, bad for the tourists and the politicians. Everything quiet, he thought: still early, of course, nothing moving yet, but nothing would.

He drifted off the green of the Hill and into the shadow of the traffic lights on Indiana, the valley of death on the road from the underpass.

The woman passed him, not acknowledging him. Late twenties, tall, good-looking. Light jacket, Levis, trainers. Interesting that one of the people Haslam had brought in from London was a woman, but if Haslam had brought her in and put her in the prime position she wouldn't just be good, she'd be the best. Interesting tactic, too. If the hitman checked out the killing zone beforehand, a good-looking woman would be the last thing he would suspect.

He remembered a story – never proven, nothing more than a whisper. Something about an IRA operation in Central London, something about a woman being instrumental in countering it. Something about a woman disturbing three Provo gunmen placing a bomb under a surveillance car somewhere in England. Manchester, he thought it was. Something about the woman taking all three of them out.

He left the Hill and edged back towards Union Station.

Hendricks's first recce was at nine. Apparently casually, certainly unnoticed, the attention to detail precise and unflustered. No problems so far, no diversions or other distractions to worry about.

Dove leaving National – he ran again through the plan. Escort cars making sure he was in the correct position for the slow-down motor. Truck breaking down at the traffic lights, slow-down car stalling beside it and Dove in the trap. The get-away bike in position on D Street – across the central reservation, up the steps, diagonal right across the garden in front of the Labour Department, then down the steps on other side.

He left the Hill and disappeared along the Mall.

Hawk leaving city, Jordan told Haslam. On way to airport.

The first of the crowd assembled in the Caucus Room, reported to the organizers and were assigned their specific positions; the first of the camera crews arrived and began to set up, the first of the journalists.

Most such crowds were the same, the ABC reporter knew: young and preppy, hats and banners and cheers. Not this one, though; this

383

one was different. Young and old, different ages, creeds and colours. As if they stood for what the country had struggled for in the past, he suddenly thought, as if they represented the dream it still clung to for the future. Blue-collar, white-collar. Men and women. Civilian clothes and uniforms. Serving officers and veterans. Three men in the second row talking about a Swift boat op in 'Nam and laughing about the way The Old Man had bellowed into a bullhorn for the boats they knew didn't exist to follow him in. Jesus Christ, he realized. I need interviews with them now, he told the Donaghue PR.

The woman in front and along from them was young, the radiance of youth on her face, her blond hair falling on to her shoulders and her child in her arms. The man next to her was in the dress blues of the Marine Corps, the eagle, globe and anchor on the collar, the sergeant's chevrons on his sleeves, and the medal ribbons across his left breast. The top row the most important, and the ribbon on the wearer's right of the top row the most important of all. The Silver Star, the small star on the ribbon indicating that the award had been won a second time; Bronze Star, three stars and the 'V' indicating they had been won for heroism in battle. The service ribbons at the bottom, the Vietnam service ribbon in the middle. One ribbon to the right of the Silver Star.

'Mind if I take a close-up of the decorations?' one of the cameramen asked.

'No problem,' the marine told him.

'What was that all about?' the reporter asked as he and the cameraman moved on.

'You see what he was wearing?' The response was tight, almost angry that the reporter hadn't noticed. 'Top right, next to the Silver Star. The Congressional Medal of Honor.'

'Mommy,' the reporter heard the voice of the girl in the arms of the young woman next to the marine. 'Why has that man only got one arm?'

At airport, Jordan told Haslam. On plane. Taking off in two minutes. Arrival at National on schedule.

Switching to communications van, Haslam told him. He left Donaghue's office and walked to the dark blue Chevy transit – smoked windows, no radio antennae or other give-aways. Checked before he rapped on the back door to be let in.

It was ten-thirty, the morning suddenly speeding up. Donaghue in the air and heading south, an hour out of National.

'Blue One. Red stable.'

Blue One the code for the forward car which would check the route a minute ahead of Hawk, Red the code for the route Hawk would take and White for the car itself. Purple for the close protec tion team at National, Green for selected points on the route in and Black for the team at the killing zone.

'Green One. Market not moving.' The two men at the metro station overlooking the point where Dove would exit National.

'Green Two. No movement.' The point at which Dove's Lincoln would turn right off the Parkway and on to the 14th Street Bridge.

All the references able to be taken as financial terms, no indication of what they actually involved, in case they were intercepted either accidentally or deliberately. Haslam left the van and checked the traffic lights on Indiana.

The television lights were in place in the Caucus Room, the cameras in position and the monitors in the corner, the Donaghue supporters filling the floor.

Why the Kennedy photos as backdrop, the NBC reporter asked the press secretary; why John and Robert? Because they also declared in this room, she told him. Christ — she saw the way his face froze — he should have known, should have checked it out, should have got library material of their declarations. Great piece if only he'd known. Everything on here, she gave him the tape, just make sure it looks good.

The car to take her and the girls to the Hill was standing by. Cath Donaghue looked in the mirror and retouched her lipstick.

'What's wrong? Why is your hand shaking?'

She turned and saw her eldest daughter looking at her from the doorway of the bathroom.

'Nerves.' She tried to laugh it off. 'Getting excited.'

Brettlaw's armoured Chevrolet was waiting. He took the executive lift to the basement and left Langley.

Still nothing happening at the Hill, Hendricks checked; the climb up from the underpass was clear and the traffic was light. No prob lems, no more police than usual. He cleared the killing zone and walked towards Union Station.

The only problem would be his instinct, Hughes knew; plus the training which would tell him to get Hawk out the moment he saw the broken-down truck funnelling him into the killing zone, the moment the car in front stalled, the moment he saw the gunman. He turned the Lincoln into National, knew it was too early, and pulled away again.

'Blue. Stable.'

'Green. Nothing moving.'

'White.'

'Purple.'

'Black One.' The beggar. The irony of the code colour suddenly hit Haslam. Too late to change it, he told himself.

'Black Two.' Nolan, the only woman on the team, Irish accent.

Haslam himself Black Three when it went down.

The reception committee at National was moving into place, the airport manager and the airline representatives, Brettlaw arriving and shaking hands, and the close protection team inconspicuous. Hendricks checking the killing zone again. Nothing happening, all clear. The beggar and Nolan checking: nothing obvious, no one obvious, but there wouldn't be.

It was ten minutes to landing. Donaghue and Pearson checked the speech for the last time, Jordan opposite them.

The boy was ten years old, seated with his mother towards the rear.

'You think he'll mind?'

Of course he'll mind, the woman knew she should say. He's too busy, too many things on his mind. 'Ask him,' she said instead.

'Come with me.'

'Go by yourself.'

The boy gripped the Polaroid camera and made his way down the aisle, the nerves consuming him. Halfway along he hesitated and looked back, saw the way his mother nodded for him to go on.

'Excuse me.' He stopped by the two men seated on the left and realized he had forgotten to say sir. 'Would you mind if I took your photograph?'

Donaghue smiled and turned to Pearson. 'I think we can go better than that, don't you, Ed?'

'Sure we can.'

Fifteen rows back the woman watched as Pearson stood, took the camera from her son, sat him by Donaghue, and took a photograph of the two of them together. The boy watched as the print rolled out and the image rose on the slippery grey of the plastic.

'What's your name?' Donaghue asked him.

'Dan.'

'Dan who?'

'Dan Zupolski.'

The print was dry. Donaghue took a pen from his pocket and signed it.

To Dan Zupolski, from his friend, Senator Jack Donaghue.

It was eleven twenty-five.

The doors of the Caucus Room opened and the supporters turned, the cheers erupting and the television crews cursing slightly that they hadn't been warned. Cath Donaghue walked in and stood on the platform. 'Sorry to give you a heart attack, boys.' She knew what the crews had thought and smiled at them, acknowledged the way they laughed back.

He'd seen it all before, the NBC correspondent told himself. Except not like this, not like today. He wouldn't admit it, of course, but one hell of a day to be the front man, one hell of a thing to tell the grandkids.

One hell of a smile, the CBS man whispered. One hell of a First Lady.

Cath looked at the people in front of her, the room packed, the hats and the banners and the slogans.

'I thought you'd like to know. We've just heard from the airport. Jack's plane is five minutes out; he'll be landing on time at eleven-thirty, be here at twelve.'

There was a roar. She held up her hands to still it.

If this was the prelim, Christ knows what the main event is going to be like, the CNN reporter thought. Give me some crowd cut-aways now, he told his cameraman. Couple of veterans, couple of kids.

'How's it looking?' He heard the voice of his producer down the line.

'Looking good, looking great.'

Looking fantastic.

'What time's he due?'

'Twelve noon, everything on schedule. Why?'

'We're going live on it.' CNN network, CNN global. 'Coming to you at eleven fifty-five.'

The applause quietened, the supporters expectant. Cath Donaghue looked up and smiled again.

'Before Jack arrives, I just wanted to thank you all for coming today.' She looked round them. 'For taking the trouble of coming today.' As if the honour was hers and Jack's; as if, by being present at that place on that day, it was those in front of her who were doing the Donaghues a favour.

387

She looked round them again and smiled again. Take care of him, Dave, she prayed; make sure he gets here, please God don't let me down. 'It's a great place to be, a great day to be here. Thank you all.'

Even after she had left, even after she was back in Room 394, the applause was still echoing down the white marble of the corridors.

The 737 banked over the Potomac and began its run-in, the wing lights blinking against the silver and the silver brilliant against the blue of the morning sky. Jordan glanced at Donaghue and realized he was looking at the White House.

'Ready, Jack?'

What are you thinking? he meant.

I'm thinking about something Haslam said. I'm thinking about a conversation Haslam and I agreed never took place.

'As I'll ever be.'

The Boeing bumped gently on the runway then taxied to the terminal, a stewardess asking passengers to remain seated. The flight deck door opened and the pilot and co-pilot stepped out and stood with the cabin crew at the front of the plane. The fuselage door to the terminal opened; in the passenger bridge on the other side Jordan saw the line of officials.

'Okay, Jack. Let's do it.'

Donaghue stood and straightened his suit, Pearson slightly behind him and Jordan at his shoulder. The rest of the passengers were still seated. He passed along the line of crew members and shook hands with each of them, thanked each of them.

'Give it to 'em today, Jack.' The voice was from the back of the plane.

'Good luck, Mr President.' Another voice.

Abruptly the passengers rose and began to clap. Donaghue turned and waved his thanks at them. Left the plane and looked for Jordan, knew he was beside him.

'Purple One.' Donaghue in the jetway, everyone wanting to shake his hand this morning, everyone wanting to wish him good luck.

'Purple Two.' Through the terminal, shaking more hands.

'Purple Three.' At the Lincoln. The close protection team scanning the faces and looking for the first tell-tale movement. Brettlaw stepped forward and Donaghue shook hands with him, embraced him.

'Good to see you.'

'You too, old friend.'

The Lincoln was waiting, doors open. The close protection team still looking – not at Donaghue but at those around him. Jordan at Donaghue's side and watching Brettlaw, watching Brettlaw's face and eyes and wondering what he would do.

Brettlaw to be standing on the left side of the car – his instructions to the close protection team had been specific. Therefore Donaghue greeting him and shaking his hand on the left of the car. Therefore Donaghue would get in the left door.

Time to go – Pearson looked at his watch and whispered to Donaghue.

Donaghue turned to the left door. Brettlaw took his arm and steered him round the back of the car to the right, held the door open for him and watched as he settled in the right-hand rear seat.

Correct position for Donaghue, of course – Jordan's thoughts were calm and structured. Driver on left side in front and bodyguard on right; therefore the key man seated behind the bodyguard, so that the bodyguard had a natural arc of protection from the front of the car to the rear. Except that it should have been Jordan's job to tell Donaghue where to sit. So was Brettlaw the man or not? He closed the doors and took his place in the front right seat.

'White One. In play.'

'Blue go,' Haslam ordered. The forward car left National to check the run-in. Sixty seconds later Hughes followed it out, the car carrying Pearson and the other personal staff hanging back.

'White One.' Jordan again. 'Market opening. Am buying.'

Market opening, the code that Brettlaw appeared to be involved. Buying, the code that Hawk was positioned in the right seat. Selling and it would have been the left.

Eleven thirty-three – Hendricks checked his watch. Dove leaving National at eleven-thirty, fourteen minutes run-in, depending on the traffic. Not much today, so Dove due in eleven minutes.

Metro station above them on the left, interim terminal on right. Jordan checked off the danger points and slid the Heckler and Koch across his lap.

'Green One. Market stable.' No top shot.

Joining main carriageway, three-lane, George Washington Memorial in front. Slip road right to 14th Street Bridge.

'Green Two. Stable.' No problems, no attempt to pull Hawk off his route. So far so good, Jordan thought. They began to cross the bridge.

Haslam checked his watch. 'Bank to White and Black. Am going on to floor.' He left the communications van and walked the two hundred yards to the shadow of Indiana. The day was warm, only a few tourists. He pulled the light woollen hat out of his pocket, put it on, and made sure his earpiece and throat mike were working.

They were over 14th Street Bridge, N1 going left and Hughes keeping right on the 395. The traffic thin in front and behind them, and the clock steady at sixty miles an hour. First exit – Maine Avenue. First signs for C Street SW, Capitol and the House, first underpass coming up. Dark blue Chevrolet behind them for the past thirty seconds – Jordan checked the rearview mirror again, knew there was no need to confirm that Hughes had also seen it.

They were out of the first underpass, forty seconds from the second. Pale Chrysler sedan coming in front of them. Chevrolet behind them and in the outer lane so they couldn't overtake.

'White One.' Jordan used the Hawk code. 'Probably buying. Repeat. Probably buying.'

They were approaching the second underpass. Chrysler still in front and Chevrolet still in outer lane behind. Green Oldsmobile coming off the feeder and accelerating so it was in front of the Chrysler, then moving to the outside lane. Chevrolet exiting, Nissan taking its place, and Chrysler accelerating away.

'White One.' Jordan's hands were on the H and K. 'Still buying.' Both rear windows still shut, he noted. The shadow fell across the road and they entered the underpass.

Hendricks saw the truck emerge from behind the Letter Carriers building and begin pulling over to the left lane. There was little other traffic, two mail vans parked by the kerb. The truck belched smoke, shuddered, and ground to a stop at the lights.

A hundred yards in front of them Hughes and Jordan saw the bright yellow saloon. Driving slowly, allowing them to close as if they were being drawn in on a piece of string.

The cars which had been in front of them accelerated away, the yellow car still in front, still in the same lane, and the Oldsmobile level with them in the outer lane so they couldn't overtake.

Brettlaw was leaning forward slightly, Jordan noticed. Lowering the electric window.

The underpass was climbing.

First exit. D Street NW and US Capitol. Road still climbing, single-lane and curving, the Oldsmobile still with them. They closed on the yellow sedan.

Not a lot of time any more, and even that time running out.

390

Second exit. The light at the underpass exit and D Street ahead, Capitol right. Yellow sedan turning, Hughes following it, the Oldsmobile straight on. The underpass single-lane again, curving and climbing.

Time gone.

Jordan turned to the men in the back and gave the orders.

Twenty yards then into the sunlight. Control his instinct, Hughes told himself, let himself be caught in the trap. No evasive stuff until after they'd come at him. Christ, why the hell hadn't the wife said he was out when Haslam called.

They were out of the underpass and into the sunlight, into the valley between the buildings on the left and the right, the traffic lights fifty yards in front.

The truck was in the left lane, traffic cones behind it to indicate it had broken down.

The yellow Ford passed the first cone, was almost alongside the truck, the Lincoln unable to pull past it.

Eleven forty-four.

The valley of the shadow of death.

The Ford slowed and shuddered. Appeared to stall then stopped.

Two men in the front of the yellow car, Nolan saw. *Her two.*

Truck driver by front of cab, the beggar saw. *His.*

Dove in the trap, Hendricks saw. Get-away bike, engine running, a hundred yards away. The driver of the yellow Ford was starting the engine again. Hendricks cleared the back of the truck. Two paces, one pace, from the Lincoln. Window open.

First shot, second.

Dove trying to move away, trying to protect himself. Moving further into the corner, yet in doing so increasing Hendricks's angle of fire. Five shots, six. Most in the chest, two in the head.

He turned and began to run. Saw the man behind him. No face, balaclava over his head, only the eyes through the holes.

The Pascale tail, Haslam thought. The bastard who'd shot Paolo Benini.

Hendricks was still turning.

Haslam squeezed the trigger. Double tap. Double tap again. Four rounds in Hendricks's chest. Double tap, fourth double tap. He moved forward, changed mags and covered the gunman in case he was still alive. Kicked the gun away, bent slightly, and shot him in the head.

'Dave. Down.'

He turned and dropped.

The truck driver was moving forward, pump action shotgun coming up. Hearing the shout and turning. Seeing the beggar. No face, only the eyes through the balaclava, polystyrene coffee cup on ground. The beggar double-tapped the trigger. A second time then a third. The truck driver was falling, shotgun still in his hand. The beggar still firing, changing mags, kicking the shotgun away and shooting the driver in the head.

The engine of the yellow Ford was booming, thundering, the driver smashing his foot on the accelerator and the passenger bringing up the Uzi. The woman was in front of them. Tourist, appearing from nowhere. Light balaclava, no face, eyes through the holes and Browning Hi-Power already firing at them through the windscreen. Two shots on driver – Nolan swung left – two on passenger. Move position slightly. Two more on passenger – swing right – two more on driver. The Ford was still moving but out of control, front smashing into the side of the truck. Nolan was still moving, crouching. Used mag out, fresh in. Was by the door. Two rounds, one in the head of the passenger and second in the head of the driver.

Hughes eased his foot on the accelerator, bounced over the lip of the kerb, and screamed the Lincoln across the pavement and down First.

Eleven forty-five.

In the office in Russell Building, Cath Donaghue smiled at her daughters and made sure everyone had coffee. The room was full and the staff crowded together, the television monitors in the corner, opposite the coffee machine. CNN on one channel, NBC on the second, ABC on the third. Fourteen minutes to the press conference, one of the war council was saying, CNN covering it live, Jack should be here soon.

Eleven-fifty.

Cath Donaghue smiled at the girls, smiled at Jack's secretary.

Eleven fifty-five.

Jack should be here already. Great day, they were all thinking, one they'd all remember. Across the room Cath saw Eva and smiled at her. Next stop the White House, the return of the smile said.

The screen of the monitor showing ABC went blank – enough for some but not all to notice – then the words NEWS FLASH came up, the screen going to a studio presenter. The woman looked stunned, as if she could not believe what she was about to read.

'We are just getting reports that shots have been fired at the car of Senator Donaghue in Washington.'

Quiet, someone was shouting. Listen.

'I repeat. We are just getting reports that shots have been fired at the car carrying Senator Jack Donaghue from National airport to Capitol Hill.'

Just like Kennedy – one of the older staffers stiffened; just like the words of the first report from Dallas in '63.

Oh my God, Cath heard the first moan. Please God, no. She was staring at the set, hardly hearing the words. Was turning away and reaching for her daughters, putting an arm round their shoulders and bringing them to her. Comforting them.

The news flash ended. Please don't go back to the normal programme, part of her prayed. At least pay him that respect. Not Jack, she was still praying, please not Jack.

The screens in the Caucus Room were showing the faces of the men, women and children on the floor. Some singing and others laughing. All waiting. The CBS screen flickered and changed, went to a NEWS FLASH caption, then to a studio presenter.

'Reports are coming in that shots have been fired at the car carrying Senator Jack Donaghue from National Airport to Capitol Hill, where he was due to announce his candidacy for the presidency.'

Quiet, someone was shouting, trying to make himself heard. Listen.

A second screen flashed to a studio.

'We are just receiving reports that the car carrying Senator Jack Donaghue has been ambushed in the centre of Washington. A number of gunmen are believed to have been involved.'

The faces in the room stared at the monitors, silence descending. The shock then the realization. No one speaking, no one able to speak.

The announcer glanced at a sheet of paper he had been given then looked up. His voice was suddenly changed, the urgency replaced by a sombreness, almost a bleakness.

'We are now receiving reports that Senator Jack Donaghue has been assassinated.'

Going to you now, the CNN controller screamed at the cameramen and reporter in the room.

Head and shoulders of the girl in the front row, the cameraman knew instinctively, got there half a second before the reporter whispered the instruction in his ear.

'Mommy.' They all heard her. 'What's wrong?'

The first tear rolled down the woman's face.

'Mommy, why are you crying?'

Perhaps the words of the reply were incorrect, perhaps they summed up what they all felt.

'Because they just shot the president.'

They stood still, stood silent. Did not know what to do or what to say. The first screen was flashing again.

'To confirm. Senator Jack Donaghue has been assassinated.'

They were still unsure what to do or what to say.

The voice was deep and gravelly. The voice of the marine veteran at the girl's side. The sleeve of his right arm was pinned just above the elbow, for that reason it was his left which he now held across his chest.

> O say, can you see,
> by the dawn's early light,
> what so proudly we hailed
> at the twilight's last gleaming.

Another voice joined in, then another.

> Whose broad stripes and bright stars,
> through the perilous fight,
> O'er the ramparts we watched
> were so gallantly streaming.

For one moment the marine's voice faltered. For one moment he was in another place and another time. For one moment he was on a river bank in Vietnam the day he knew he was going to die. The child in the arms of the woman next to him was heavy, the mother suddenly unable to bear her. He turned, took the child, and held her in his one arm, the girl's arms tight round his neck.

> And the rocket's red glare,
> the bombs bursting in air
> Gave proof through the night
> that our flag was still there.

Another news flash came on the CBS screen.

'To confirm. Senator Jack Donaghue has been assassinated in

Washington. At this moment the senator's body is being flown by helicopter to the Naval Hospital at Bethesda.' The newscaster was fighting to control her emotion. 'When he was shot he was on his way to a press conference to announce his candidacy for the Democrat nomination for the presidency.'

The tears were running down her cheeks. She looked away from camera, did not know what to do. Keep going, the programme director told her down the earpiece. Tell it as it is, say what you have to.

She made herself look up and they knew what she was going to say.

'They got John Kennedy. They got Martin Luther King. They got Bobby Kennedy.'

She could not say the last line.

And now they've got Jack Donaghue.

She wiped her face and struggled to regain her composure.

'A personal reflection on the news from Washington this morning that Senator Jack Donaghue has been assassinated on his way to declare his candidacy for the Democratic nomination for the presidency.'

Some in the Caucus Room had locked arms, some were standing to attention. The words reached out from the Caucus Room, down the marble corridor, hung in the memories of Room 394.

> O say, does that Star Spangled Banner
> still wave
> O'er the land of the free
> and the home of the brave?

Cath Donaghue clung to the girls and remembered the evening she and Jack had walked in the woods. Remembered how she had asked him his favourite words, how she had made him promise he would include them in his speech that day, in his inaugural speech when he became president.

She turned to one of the lawyers.

'You have a copy of Jack's speech?'

'It was faxed down this morning.'

Cometh the hour, cometh the man. Eva remembered the quote. Cometh the hour, cometh the woman.

You're sure? she asked Cath; because if you are then I'm beside you.

'Yes.'

Get it, she told the aide.

Someone to her left was crying, someone else trying to hold the group together. Cath Donaghue took the speech, sat at the desk, and added two sentences at the beginning.

This is the speech Jack was going to make. Today I make it for him.

Turned to the last page.

In the hour of maximum danger I do not shirk from this responsibility, I welcome it.

Amended the line which followed.

Today, and in Jack's place, I therefore declare my candidacy for the Democrat nomination for the presidency of the United States of America.

'You're absolutely sure?' Eva asked Cath again. 'You know what it means, know the dangers you yourself are about to face?'

'Yes,' Cath Donaghue told her.

There was a movement at the door. She turned and saw Haslam. Bastard, she wanted to shout, no words coming out. You were supposed to be looking after him. You were the one who said you'd protect him. You were the one I trusted.

He knew where he had seen the eyes before. The mother of the girl in Lima; Francesca in Milan.

'The press conference is in five minutes.' Haslam was in front of her, looking at her. 'Jack's on his way up, you and the girls had better get ready.'

'Why?' she asked. 'What do you mean?' The words were sticking in her throat. 'What have you done?'

Remember *Hill Street Blues*, she had asked Jack, remember the desk sergeant and what he told his people. Haslam's got his own version, Jack had said. Actually Haslam has two names for two slightly different things. He calls them the First and Last Commandments.

Haslam was looking into her soul, into his own. Imagining the moment.

The Lincoln was clearing the first underpass and closing on the second, the shut-out cars all round them, directing them into the killing zone. The Lincoln leaving the sunlight and entering the black. First exit, second exit. The brightness at the mouth of the underpass rushing up at them and the light of the shadow of the valley of death beyond.

Jordan turning to the men in the back.

So why had Brettlaw done what Jordan told him?

Perhaps he'd known it was the end of the game and he was being given the way out . . .

That if he hadn't done as Jordan ordered, then Jordan would have made him . . .

Perhaps it had been automatic, perhaps he'd forgotten . . .

Perhaps . . .

Another time and another place for the theories, Haslam told himself.

Donaghue's desk was under the window in front of him, the photographs above the green marble fireplace to his right. He looked at them, looked again at Cath Donaghue. Imagined the turmoil and fear as Hughes left the secrecy of the second underpass and drove into the killing zone. He was still looking at Cath, still held by her eyes.

'Jack's fine,' he told her. 'Jack's okay.'

How? she was screaming silently at him. What have you done and how did you do it?

You know what you're doing? Francesca had asked him. Hope so, he'd told her.

Dave, she'd come back at him. Tick tock, beat the clock.

'Jack's fine,' he told Cath again. 'Jack's okay, Jack will be here in two minutes.'

How? she was still screaming at him. What happened? The television said there was a gun attack on his car and that he'd been assassinated. So why? What happened? How did he get out of it?

It had been close, Haslam thought, Christ it had been so close. But in the end they'd had no option, in the end they'd had to leave it that late to win.

The Last Commandment: Don't get caught.

And the First: Do it to them before they do it to you.

'Jack and Tom Brettlaw changed places five seconds before the end.'